The author of twenty-five books, **Erica Spindler** is best known for her spine-tingling thrillers. Her novels have been published all over the world, selling over six million copies, and critics have dubbed her stories "thrill-packed, page turners, white knuckle rides, and edge-of-your-seat whodunits."

Erica is a *New York Times* and *USA TODAY* bestselling author. In 2002, her novel *Bone Cold* won the prestigious Daphne du Maurier Award for excellence.

Also by *Erica Spindler*

SEE JANE DIE
IN SILENCE
COPYCAT
SHOCKING PINK
DEAD RUN

ERICA SPINDLER
ALL FALL DOWN

MIRA

First published in Great Britain in 2000. This edition 2006.
MIRA Books, Eton House, 18-24 Paradise Road,
Richmond, Surrey, TW9 1SR

© Erica Spindler 2000

ISBN-13: 978 0 7783 0062 5
ISBN-10: 0 7783 0062 5

58-1006

Printed in Great Britain
by Clays Ltd, St Ives plc

For Dianne Moggy, Editor and Friend.
Thanks for making the journey so much fun.

ACKNOWLEDGEMENTS

In our busy world time is the one thing we never seem to have enough of, yet the following people gave generously of theirs so that I could bring *All Fall Down* to life. They did so enthusiastically and openly, sharing their expertise and experiences; my heartfelt thanks to each.

Barton M Menser, Assistant District Attorney, State of North Carolina, 26th Prosecutorial District: for patiently explaining the workings of the district attorney's office.

Keith Bridges, Community Education Coordinator, Charlotte/Mecklenburg Police Department: for educating me about the CMPD, from the size of the force to interrogation procedures.

Elaine and Leon Schneider, friends: for not only sharing Charlotte with me, but their home, as well. Special thanks to Elaine for squiring me to all my appointments and greeting me with a smile even when those appointments ran long.

Tommy Patterson, Investigative Group, Inc: for bringing the technical side of surveillance alive for me.

Special Agent Joanne Morley, FBI, Charlotte Field Office: for answering my questions about FBI protocol and for describing the Charlotte Field Office.

Linda West (aka author Linda Lewis), attorney: again and always, for being my legal editor and expert.

David Shilman, pharmaceutical representative, Organon: for information about the professional life of a drug rep.

Bobby Russo, Bobby Russo's American Black Belt Academy: for information about the art of tae kwon do.

1

The closet was small, cramped. Too warm. Dark save for the sliver of dim light from the bedroom beyond. In it, Death waited. Patiently. Without movement or complaint.

Tonight was the night. Soon, the man would come. And like the others, he would pay.

For crimes unpunished. Against the weak. Against those the world had turned their backs on. Death had planned carefully, had left nothing to chance. The woman was away, the children with her. Far away, in the loving and protective arms of family.

From another part of the house came a sound— a thud, then an oath. A door slammed. Excited, Death pressed closer to the door, peering through the narrow space, taking in the scene beyond: the unmade bed, the dirty laundry strewn about, the trash that littered the floor.

The man stumbled into the room, toward the bed, obviously inebriated. Immediately, the small dark space filled with the smell of cigarettes and booze—booze he and his buddies had consumed that night. Laughing. Thumbing their noses at the gods. At justice.

He lost his balance and knocked into the bedside table. The lamp toppled and crashed to the floor. The man fell face first onto the bed, head turned to the side, foot and arm hanging off.

Minutes ticked past. The drunk's breathing became deep and thick. Soon, his guttural snores filled the room. The snores of a man in an alcohol-induced coma, of one who would not awake easily.

Until it was too late.

The time had come.

Death eased out of the closet and crossed to the bed, stopping beside it and gazing down in disgust. Smoking in bed was dangerous. It was foolhardy. One should never tempt fate that way. But then, this was a stupid man. One who had not learned from his mistakes. The kind of man the world would be better off without.

With the toe of a shoe, Death eased the bedside wastebasket to the spot under the drunk's dangling hand. The cigarette was the man's brand; the matches from the bar he had frequented that night. The match flared with the first strike of tip against the friction strip; the flame crackled as it kissed the tobacco, hissing as it caught.

With a small, satisfied smile, Death dropped the glowing cigarette into the filled wastebasket, then turned and walked away.

2

Officer Melanie May hovered just beyond the motel room's door, gaze riveted to the bed inside, to the murder victim bound by ankles and wrists to the bed frame.

The young woman was naked. She lay faceup, her eyes open, her mouth sealed with silver duct tape. The blood had flown from her face and the top of her body, downward toward her back, pooling there, giving those areas a ruddy, bluish cast. Rigor mortis appeared to be complete, which meant she had been dead at least eight hours.

Melanie took a shaky step forward. Chief Greer's call had interrupted her morning shower. A towel clutched to her chest, she'd had to ask him to repeat himself three times. Not only had there not been a homicide in Whistlestop since she joined the force three years ago, as she understood it, there had *never* been a homicide in the tiny community, located on the outskirts of Charlotte.

He had ordered her to the Sweet Dreams Motel, ASAP.

First order of business had been arranging care for her four-year-old son, Casey. That done, she had hurriedly donned her uniform, strapped on her gun belt and pulled her still-wet, shoulder-length blond hair back into a severe twist. She had speared in the last bobby pin just as the doorbell pealed, announcing that her neighbor had arrived to watch Casey.

Now, not quite twenty minutes later, she was staring in horror at her first murder victim and praying she didn't puke.

To steady herself, she shifted her gaze to the room's other occupants. From the number of them, it appeared she was the last to make the scene. Her partner, Bobby Taggerty—his rail-thin frame and shock of bright red hair making him look like a walking matchstick—was photographing the scene. Her chief stood in the corner of the room, engaged in a heated discussion with two men she recognized as homicide investigators with the Charlotte/Mecklenburg force. Outside, keeping the Whistlestop PD first officers company, were two Charlotte/Mecklenburg uniforms. A man she didn't recognize—but whom she assumed was also CMPD, probably on the forensics team—squatted beside the bed, examining the corpse.

What was the CMPD doing here already? Melanie wondered, frowning. And why in such great numbers? Sure, the WPD was a tiny force operating within the large area serviced by the CMPD—a department of fourteen hundred sworn officers and state-of-the-art facilities, including a crime lab. And sure, her force had an interagency aid agreement with the bigger department. But still, protocol demanded an initial WPD investigation followed by a Whistlestop request for aid.

This was no ordinary murder. Something big had gone down.

And she wasn't about to be muscled out. Even by muscles as impressive as the CMPD's.

Determined to assert that fact, Melanie strode across the threshold, stopping short as the stench of the room hit her. Not from decomposition, which had not yet begun, but with the evacuation of bladder and bowel that sometimes occurred with violent death.

Melanie brought a hand to her nose, stomach heaving. She squeezed her eyes shut and swallowed hard. She couldn't throw up, not in front of the CMPD guys. They already thought the Whistlestop force was rinky-dink, made up of wannabes and couldn't-hack-its. She wasn't about to prove them right—even if she agreed with their assessment.

"Hey, you? Sweetpants." Melanie opened her eyes. The man beside the bed motioned her forward, his expression disgusted. "You going to fall apart or get your ass in here and do a job? I could use a hand."

From the corners of her eyes she saw her chief and the investigators glance her way, and, annoyed, she crossed to the man. "The name's May. Officer May. Not 'Hey You' or 'Sweetpants.'"

"Whatever." He handed her a pair of latex gloves. "Put those on and come down here."

She snatched the gloves from his hand, pulled

them on, then knelt beside him. "You have a name?"

"Parks."

When he spoke, she caught a whiff of alcohol on his breath. From that and the looks of him, she decided this murder had dragged him away from one hell of a binge. "CMPD?"

"FBI." He made a sound of impatience. "Can we get started now? Chickie here's not getting any fresher."

Melanie didn't hide her surprise or her dislike of Parks, though he appeared to care less what she thought of him. "What do you need me to do?"

"See that? Under her ass?" He indicated the shiny tip of something peeking out from beneath the body. "I'm going to hoist her up. I need you to get it for me."

She nodded, understanding. Although the victim had not been a large woman, death would make her difficult to maneuver, even for a man built as strongly as Parks. With a grunt of exertion, he inched the victim's hindquarters off the mattress. Melanie grabbed the shiny scrap—a foil condom wrapper, open and empty.

Parks took the packet from her hands and examined it a moment, eyebrows drawn together in thought. Melanie watched him, wondering why he was at the scene. Why had this victim's murder rated not only the representation of two police forces but also the FBI?

He lifted his bloodshot gaze to hers. "You got any idea what happened here, May? Got a good guess?"

"Judging by the bluish tint to her skin and the lack of any visible wound, I suspect she was smothered. Probably with a bed pillow." She pointed to the one just to the left of the woman's head. "Beyond that, not yet."

"Read the scene. Everything we need to know is right here." He indicated the skimpy lingerie draped over the chair and the empty champagne bottle on the floor. "See those? They tell me she came to play. Nobody forced her into this room or onto this bed."

"And being tied up was part of the fun and games?"

"In my opinion, yes. Think about it. There are no visible bruises on her body. It would take a lot of strength to tie a struggling adult prone to a bed. Even a huge man couldn't do it without exerting extreme force on the victim. Also, check out her wrists and ankles. They're in almost perfect condition. They'd be torn up if she'd fought for long."

Melanie did as he suggested and saw that he was right. There were only slight burns from the ropes, ones indicative of a short struggle.

"This guy's in his late twenties to mid-thirties. Handsome. If he's not successful, he looks like he is. He's going to drive an expensive car, something foreign. Sporty. A BMW or Jag."

Melanie made a sound of disbelief. "There's no way you can know that."

"No? Take a look at the victim. This girl wasn't just any skank. She was a babe. Young, gorgeous, rich. The best family, the best—"

"Wait a minute," Melanie interrupted. "Who is she?"

"Joli Andersen. Cleve Andersen's youngest daughter."

"Son of a bitch," Melanie muttered. Now she understood. The Andersens were one of Charlotte's oldest and most influential families. They were big into banking, politics and on the boards of a number of Charlotte's most visible civic and charitable organizations. Melanie didn't doubt that Cleve Andersen had a direct line to both the mayor's and governor's office.

"That's why you're here," she said. "And the CMPD honchos. Because she's an Andersen."

"Bingo. With a vic like this one, word always travels fast. Housekeeper finds the body and, after screaming, runs for the motel manager. First thing he does is check chickie's ID. Then the scenario gets really interesting. He panics and calls the CMPD and tells the dispatcher not only what's gone down, but who's dead. Next thing I know, my butt's being hauled out of bed to lend aid and offer expertise."

Melanie absorbed his words. "So, the family already knows?"

"Hell, yes. Before you or your chief did, Sweet-pants." He returned his attention to his analysis of the scene. "The chain of events only underscores my theory. This girl was accustomed to the best of everything. No way she was going slumming with some gas-station attendant."

"What about drugs? Or rebellion from her parents?"

"There's no sign of drug use here. As for rebellion, look at the way she dressed, her Z3 parked outside, her history. It doesn't fit."

Melanie frowned, recalling the things she had read about the Andersens' youngest daughter, acknowledging that he was right. "So why'd she go to a motel room with some guy she didn't know?"

"Who said she didn't know him?"

Melanie shifted her gaze to Joli Andersen's once-beautiful face, now frozen in death, to her wide-open, terrified gaze, imagining the girl's last moments. "And then he killed her."

"Yes. But he didn't plan to. My bet is, she began to complain when the game turned unpleasant. Or maybe he couldn't get it up and she began to belittle him or laugh. This guy's the classic inadequate, her criticism would have sent him over the edge. He taped her mouth to shut her up, but then she began to struggle in earnest. That upset him more. She wasn't acting the way she was supposed to, the way he had imagined it in his head. So he presses a pillow over her face to get her to shut up and behave."

"If he didn't plan it, how come the tape?" Melanie shook her head. "In my book, that's coming prepared."

"I didn't say he hadn't acted out this scene before. He no doubt has, dozens of times, and some of those times with hookers. Understand, this is like a play he's written in his head, one he keeps adding to, fine-tuning. The beautiful girl. The rope. Her submission. The tape. And tonight, the murder. Ask around with the professional girls, somebody will turn up who knows this guy.''

Melanie gazed at him, half-awed, half-disbelieving. Though his analysis all made sense, it seemed to her that he would have to be psychic to know all he professed to. ''Don't you think what you're doing is a little bit dangerous? Basically, you're just guessing.''

''What do you think police work is? Educated guessing, following gut instincts. Luck. Besides, I'm a damn good guesser.'' He glanced over his shoulder, holding up the foil packet. ''Any of you come across a used rubber?''

No one had. One of the CMPD guys ambled over. He took the packet and held it up, squinting at the small print on the front. ''Lambskin.'' He shook his head, making a sound of disgust. ''You'd think these people would have gotten the message by now. Only latex protects.''

Parks frowned. ''I doubt he had sex with her. Not the kind of sex he'd need a condom for.''

''No? The packet's open, right? Rubber's missing.'' The CMPD honcho dropped the packet into an evidence bag, sealed and marked it. ''He probably took it with him. Or flushed it.''

Parks shook his head. ''She brought the condom, not him.''

The investigator arched his eyebrows. ''How do you figure?''

''The last thing on his mind was protection. Look at this place, he made no attempt to clean up. I can see fingerprints on the champagne bottle from here.''

"So?"

"So," Parks continued, "why would this disorganized inadequate flush a used condom but leave his fingerprints? My bet is, this place is swimming in biological and trace evidence."

While Parks repeated his theory to the investigator, Melanie examined the area around the bed, careful not to inadvertently disturb or destroy evidence. She had a hunch. If Joli had brought the condom and the killer hadn't used it, she would bet it was still on or around the bed, just as the packet had been.

Her hunch paid off, and Melanie held up the still-coiled condom. "This what you boys were looking for?" When the two men looked at her, she grinned. "The space between the mattress and the frame. You might check it out next time."

Parks smiled; the investigator looked irritated and snatched it from her. "He never even got around to fucking her. Sick bastard."

"He got around to it all right," Parks countered, standing and yanking off his gloves. "He just didn't do it with his penis. Check her body cavities. I wouldn't doubt he left something behind. Hairbrush. Comb. Car keys. If you're really lucky, they'll be his."

Melanie stared at him, mouth dry, the horror of his words sinking in. For the last minutes she had been able to focus on the job, not the crime. She had been able to forget that the victim they were talking so dispassionately about had been, only hours before, a living, breathing human being; a person who'd had hopes, fears and dreams, just like she did.

She couldn't pretend anymore.

Hand to her mouth, Melanie jumped to her feet and sprinted from the room. She made it as far as the first parked car, a white Ford Explorer. Hand on the vehicle's left front panel for support, she doubled over and puked.

Parks came up behind her. He held out a wad of toilet paper. "You okay?"

"Fine." She took the tissue and wiped her mouth, totally humiliated. "Thanks."

"Your first stiff?"

She managed a yes, not meeting his eyes.

"Tough luck, her getting whacked in Whistlestop. A couple blocks over and you would have avoided all this unpleasantness."

She looked at him then. "Are you always this awful?"

"Pretty much." A ghost of a smile touched his mouth, then disappeared. "It's nothing to be embarrassed about, you know. Some people just aren't cut out for this type of work."

"People like me, you mean? The kind of cop the Whistlestop force was made for?"

"I didn't say that."

"You didn't have to." She straightened, furious, sickness forgotten. "You don't know anything about me. You don't have a clue what's right for me or what I can or cannot handle."

"You're right, I don't. And let's keep it that way, shall we?"

Without another word, he climbed into the Explorer, started it and drove away.

3

By three that afternoon, Melanie was running on nerves and caffeine. After throwing up, she had retrieved a Coke from the motel vending machine, rinsed her mouth with it, then gotten back to work. The CMPD forensic team had arrived, and she and Bobby had worked alongside them, logging in and bagging evidence. The medical examiner had come, followed by the body-removal service the county contracted to transport bodies to the morgue. She and Bobby had then reported to WPD headquarters to officially start their day.

Melanie poured herself another cup of coffee, ignoring both her sour stomach and dull headache. She didn't have time for queasiness or fatigue—the shit had only just begun hitting the fan. And no wonder. With this case there was plenty of it to go around: the FBI was involved, the CMPD, Charlotte's most powerful citizen and of course, Whistlestop's little band of blue. The victim had been young, beautiful and rich; her death gruesome and kinky.

Front page, made to order.

"May!" Chief Greer bellowed from the doorway to his office. "Taggerty! Get in here. Now!"

Melanie looked at Bobby, who rolled his eyes.

Something had definitely sent their boss into orbit. And Chief Gary Greer in orbit was a sight to behold. Six-foot-four, built like a bull and with skin the color of fine dark chocolate, he commanded both respect and fear. But despite his overwhelming physical presence—or perhaps because of it—he rarely lost his temper. When he did, everybody hopped to attention.

In fact, Melanie had seen him this angry only once before: when he had discovered that one of the officers on night patrol had been letting hookers walk in exchange for blow jobs.

Melanie grabbed her notepad and jumped to her feet. Bobby followed her. When they reached the man's office, he ordered them to sit.

"I just got off the phone with Chief Lyons. Bastard politely suggested we bow out of this investigation. For the good of all involved, turn the entire thing over to the CMPD."

"What!" Melanie jumped to her feet. "You didn't agree—"

"Hell no! I told him to kiss my hairy, black butt." He laughed. "That put old Jack in his place."

Melanie smiled. Her chief had been a homicide investigator with the CMPD himself, and a highly decorated one at that. Four years ago he had been shot in the line of duty; the incident had nearly cost him his life. After he'd recovered, his wife gave him an ultimatum—the job or the marriage. Only forty-six and too young to be put out to pasture, he'd chosen the marriage and accepted this position. Although outwardly comfortable with his decision, Melanie suspected that he, like she, longed for real crimes to investigate.

"They're not going to push us out," he continued, yanking at his tie to loosen it. "The murder occurred in our community, and I have citizens to account to. Like it or not, they're stuck with us."

His mouth thinned. "This is a big one. All eyes are going to be on us. Pressure for a quick resolution is going to come from all quarters and it's going to be intense. The press is going nuts already, and Andersen's begun pulling in markers. Keep your heads and do your job. Don't let the heat get to you.

"The truth is," he continued, "the CMPD's more experienced. They have more manpower, better facilities, deeper pockets. Fine, we accept their help. But that's as far as we bend. Any questions?"

"Yeah," Melanie said. "The FBI guy, Parks. What's his story?"

"Wondered how long it'd take you to ask." Her chief smiled, his first of the afternoon. "A bit of an asshole, isn't he?"

Bobby laughed. "A bit? That guy was a walking, talking pucker."

"And no stranger to the bottle," Melanie added.

The chief frowned, looking from one to the other of them. "He'd been drinking?"

"Drinking?" she repeated. "No, that word implies restraint. Moderation. Parks looked and smelled like he'd been on a year-long binge."

Her chief seemed to digest that information, his expression tight. "Connor Parks is a profiler. Until a year ago he was a bigwig at Quantico, what was then called the Behavioral Science Unit. I don't know the details, but rumor has it he publicly embarrassed the Bureau. He was censured and demoted."

A profiler. No wonder. Melanie had attended an FBI-sponsored seminar on profiling a year or so ago. She had found the information presented fascinating. The way the agent had explained it, every killer unwittingly left a signature at the scene of his crime. It was the profiler's job to read that signature, to put himself or herself in the head of both predator and prey and re-create the how, why and most importantly, the who of the event.

Which was exactly what Parks had been attempting to do today.

"So what's he doing in Charlotte working on our puny case?" Bobby asked.

"Charlotte's his demotion." The chief looked from her to Bobby once more. "Make no mistake. The man's good at what he does, booze or not. Use him."

"With that personality, he'd better be good," she muttered, jotting a note to call him, then meeting her chief's gaze again. "What's next?"

"I want you to question the victim's friends, her family members and fellow students. Find out who she was seeing, where she hung out and what she was into. But first, get over to CMPD headquarters. Make sure they haven't already sent somebody out. If they have, find out who and track them down. We have to appear a united front. Andersen will flip if it looks like we're not. Next thing I know, the mayor'll be crawling up my ass."

That'd be a neat trick. To hide her smile, Melanie glanced down at her notes.

"Anything else?" Bobby asked.

"Yeah," he barked. "Get moving!"

They did, jumping to their feet and hurrying out of their boss's office. The first thing Melanie did was call her twin sister, Mia. The other woman picked up right away. "Mia, it's Mel."

"Melanie! My God, I was just watching channel six. That poor girl!" She lowered her voice. "Was it awful?"

"Worse," Melanie replied grimly. "That's why I'm calling. I need a favor."

"Shoot."

"It's crazy around here, and I don't expect it to let up in time for me to pick Casey up at preschool. Would you mind?" Melanie glanced at the picture of her four-year-old son on her desk, her lips lifting in an involuntary smile. "I'd ask Stan to do it but I don't have the time for one of his lectures about why I need to quit my job and how my being a cop is bad for Casey."

"He's full of crap. But, yes, I'd love to get Casey from school. And since I'll be in the neighborhood, I suppose you'd like me to head around the corner and pick up your uniforms at that dry cleaners?"

"You're a lifesaver. On both accounts."

From the corners of her eyes, she saw that Bobby was ready and waiting at the door. "Look, when you pick him up this time, don't pretend to be me. It really freaks his teachers out."

"Lightweights." Mia cackled, sounding absolutely wicked. "What's the good of being an identical twin if I can't have a little fun with it? Besides, Casey likes it. It's our little game.''

Melanie shook her head. Actually, she and Mia were both identical twins and triplets. When Melanie told people so, they always laughed, thinking she was making a joke. But it was true. She and Mia were identical twins but they also had a fraternal triplet sister, Ashley.

What made it even more fun was Ashley's striking resemblance to her sisters. When together, the three fair-haired, blue-eyed look-alikes drew the startled gazes of passersby. Even their friends had been known to do double takes.

''Remember how we used to trick our teachers?'' Mia murmured, her tone amused.

''I'm thirty-two, not ninety-two. Of course, I remember. You were always the instigator. And I was the one who always got blamed.''

''Try reversing that, sister dear.''

Bobby cleared his throat, tapped his watch and pointed at the chief's office. She nodded in acknowledgment. ''I would if I had the time, Mia. Right now I've got to go solve a murder.''

Her sister's wish of ''Go for it, Sherlock'' ringing in her ears, Melanie hung up the phone and hurried to meet her partner.

4

The Mecklenburg County District Attorney's office was located in Uptown Charlotte, in the old county courthouse building. Built in the days before the advent of the office high-rise—those unadorned rectangles filled with low-ceiling rooms jammed with vanilla cubicles, each no bigger or smaller than the other—the courthouse was now a part of Government Plaza, residing with modern-day, state-of-the-art wonders like the Law Enforcement Center.

Rabbit warrens, Assistant District Attorney Veronica Ford called such buildings. Monuments to the depersonalization of modern life. In contrast, the old courthouse possessed an aura of faded grandeur. To Veronica, it fit her image of a place where the wheels of justice turned slowly but surely, a place where, though sometimes mired in a flawed, old-fashioned system, justice had its way.

Just as it fit her image of Charlotte, a city of both the old South and the new, a city of blooming trees and skyscrapers, of southern gentility and frenzied commerce. A city she had felt at home in from the moment she'd arrived, nine months before.

Even though running late for a team meeting, Veronica eschewed the rickety but reliable elevator and took the wide, curving central staircase to the second floor, trailing her hand along its ornate wrought-iron handrail. Veronica loved the law. She loved her part in it, relished the fact that without her the world would not be quite as good a place to live. She believed that—perhaps naively, perhaps with conceit.

But if she didn't, what would be the point of working for the D.A.? She could make a helluva lot more money with a lot less stress practicing corporate law.

"Afternoon, Jen," she called to the receptionist as she stepped onto the top landing.

Pregnant with her first child, the young woman was positively glowing with happiness. She smiled at Veronica. "Morning to you, too."

"Any messages?"

"Several." The woman indicated a stack of pink message slips. "Nothing urgent."

Veronica crossed to the reception desk, set her Starbucks travel mug down and handed the other woman a take-out bag from the same establishment. She grinned. "I brought the baby a little something."

"One of the cranberry-nut scones? The baby loves those."

"The very ones."

The receptionist squealed with pleasure and dug into the bag. "You are a complete peach, Veronica Ford. The baby and I thank you."

Veronica laughed and flipped quickly through the messages, seeing nothing that couldn't wait until after her meeting. "How late am I? Rick here yet?"

Rick Zanders was the Person's Team supervisor. The lawyers on the Person's Team, of which Veronica was one, handled all violent crimes committed against a person—with the exception of homicide and crimes against children. Those included rape, assault, battery, sexual assault and kidnapping. The team met every Wednesday afternoon to discuss the status of ongoing cases, to be informed about what was new, to discuss strategy and offer assistance when needed.

"Only a couple minutes before you, and he had several calls to make before the meeting." She glanced at her watch, then over her shoulder. "I bet you still have ten minutes. Apparently, Rick knows the Andersen family personally." Jen lowered her voice. "You heard about the murder?"

"I heard." Veronica frowned. "What's everyone saying? Is there anything more than what's in the media? Any suspects?"

"Not that I've heard. But I bet Rick has some of the details." She shuddered. "It's so awful. She was a really nice girl. So pretty, too."

Veronica thought of the attractive blonde she had seen pictured on television that morning. She hadn't been in Charlotte long enough to have met any of the Andersens personally, but she had heard of them. As she understood it, Joli Andersen had had a bright future ahead of her.

"They said on TV that she was strangled," Jen continued, whispering.

"Suffocated," Veronica corrected.

"Do you think they'll catch the guy?" The receptionist laid a hand protectively over her swollen belly. "Knowing a person like that is walking the streets of Charlotte gives me the creeps. I mean, if someone like Joli Andersen can get killed, anybody can."

Veronica knew Jen wasn't alone in her fears, not today. No doubt those same words, or a variation of them, had been uttered in nearly every household in Charlotte over the past few hours. A murder like this one, a victim like Joli Andersen, drove home just how dangerous the world was. And just how fickle fate.

"I can assure you of one thing, Jen, this will probably be the most intensive manhunt Charlotte has ever seen." Veronica stuffed her messages into her pocket, then collected her coffee cup and briefcase. "And when they do catch him, we'll nail him."

The receptionist smiled, looking relieved. "Justice always wins out."

After agreeing, Veronica made her way to the conference room. There, the other lawyers— with the exception of Rick—were already assembled. And as she had known they would be, they were all talking about the same thing—Joli Andersen's murder. She called out a hello, dropped her things at a vacant spot at the table and ambled over to a group of her colleagues. They all began talking to her at once.

"Isn't it unbelievable?"

"I heard Rick dated Joli for a while. This is going to hit him really hard."

"Are you sure? He's quite a bit older than—"

"—heard that the FBI's been called in."

"A top profiler. Rumor has it that—"

"The crime involved some sort of kinky sex."

Veronica jumped on the last, the first bit of new information that interested her. "Where did you hear that? That wasn't on any of the news reports."

The other attorney looked at her. "A friend in homicide. He didn't give specifics, but indicated it was...unpleasant."

Rick entered the room, his face ashen. Immediately all conversation ceased, and the assembled ADAs took their seats. He cleared his throat. "Before any of you ask, I don't know much more than you do. The murder occurred in Whistlestop. At a motel. She was suffocated. They have no suspects as of yet, but the FBI is putting together a profile of the killer. Apparently there was biological evidence left at the scene, though I don't know of what nature. In deference to the Andersen family, the police have agreed to keep the most prurient aspects of the crime from the press."

He ran a hand across his forehead; Veronica saw that it shook. From the looks of him, Veronica suspected the rumor about him and the young Joli was true. She wondered if their past relationship might also make him a suspect. Probably, she decided. In this investigation, no stone would be left unturned.

"Why don't we get down to business?" Rick murmured. "What have we got? Anything new?"

Laurie Carter spoke up. "I've got a pretty good assault with a deadly weapon. Two neighboring housewives get into an argument over a cup of borrowed sugar. The argument turns ugly and neighbor one whacks neighbor two with a sauté pan."

Laughter rippled around the table. A lawyer named Ned House arched his eyebrows. "A sauté pan's your deadly weapon?"

"Hey," one of the other female prosecutors piped up, "you ever try to pick up one of those suckers? They're heavy."

"It did the trick," Laurie said dryly. "Landed our victim in the hospital. Concussion, stitches, broken nose. The whole bit."

Rick shook his head. "You're joking, right?"

"No way. And here's where the story really gets fun. Turns out neighbor two's been borrowing more than sugar from her neighbor. Seems she and Mrs. Sauté Pan's husband have been doing the suburban cha-cha-cha when they thought nobody was looking."

Ned made a clucking sound with his tongue. "And people think the 'burbs are safe."

"Plead it down," Veronica murmured. "Sure she did it, but the jury's going to sympathize with the scorned wife."

"Unless the jury's predominantly male," Ned countered.

Veronica shook her head. "Doesn't matter. This is a country founded by Puritans. In the back of their minds, the jurors, male or female, are going to figure the slut deserved it."

Rick agreed. "Simple assault's the best you're going to get out of it. Plead it down."

They moved on, discussing two other assaults and an attempted rape. Each time, the other lawyers looked to Veronica for her opinion. Although she had only been with the Charlotte D.A.'s office nine months, she had been with the Charleston District Attorney for three years before that. There, she had earned the reputation of being a careful prosecutor who went after each viable case with a vengeance.

The truth was, she hated bullies. Hated the cowardly scum that roamed the streets preying on those weaker than themselves. On women. Children. The elderly. She had dedicated her life to making the scum pay.

That dedication had translated into a ninety-seven percent conviction rate. It never failed to astound her how awed the other prosecutors were by that number. To her, it hadn't been hard to achieve. If she went forward with a case, she believed she could win it. And she never stopped until she had.

Rick turned to her. "Veronica, how's the Alvarez date-rape case coming?"

The other lawyers looked expectantly at her. When this case had first come in, Rick had recommended against it. It'd be tough to win, he'd said. Date rape was always iffy from a trial standpoint. And this case was more so because the girl involved had a reputation and the boy was a national merit scholar, the captain of his high-school football team and from a prominent family.

But Veronica had fought for the case. She had seen Angie Alvarez's bruises. She had listened to her story and seen the real terror in her eyes. This was America, Veronica had told Rick. Just because a boy could throw a football or his daddy had money didn't make him above the law. "No" meant "no" for everybody.

She had vowed to Rick—and herself—that she would make this case work. And now she had.

Veronica smiled, remembering how, during their first interview, the boy had smirked at her. *Cocky little prick. She had him now.*

"I have another girl," she said.

Rick straightened. "And she's willing to testify?"

"Willing and ready."

"What kept her quiet before?"

"Fear. Her mother warned her that if she sought justice, the opposite would happen, her reputation would be ruined and no nice boy would ever have anything to do with her. Her mother begged her to put it behind her and go on as if nothing had happened."

"What changed?"

"Simple. She hasn't been able to put it behind her." Veronica dropped her hands to her lap so the other prosecutors wouldn't see her flexing her fingers. She didn't want them to know how deeply this case had affected her. "Besides, there's safety in numbers. And believe me, this boy's been busy."

"There are more girls?" Laurie said, shaking her head, expression disgusted.

"Looks like there might be. My witnesses have heard rumors. I've got someone checking into a couple of them."

"Nail this creep to the wall," Laurie muttered.

"Done." Veronica smiled, determined. "At this point it's just a matter of how high and how many nails."

5

It was nearly seven that evening before Melanie was able to leave work to pick Casey up at her sister's. It had been an exhilarating, exhausting, eye-opening day. She had learned more in the past twelve hours than she had from all her classes at the academy combined or from the police manuals she pored over at every opportunity.

Homicide investigation, she had discovered, was a tedious process. It required patience, logic, intuition and tenacity, qualities that could be honed but not necessarily learned. Dealing with the victim's family and friends called for not only a sensitive and deft hand, but a thick skin and quick mind as well.

Those closest to Joli had painted the portrait of a happy, well-adjusted young woman, one who liked men and who liked to party. From those interviews, Melanie had assembled a list of the clubs Joli had frequented and of the men she had dated in the past year. The list of both had been extensive.

Everyone Melanie had spoken with had either been in shock or been grieving. Dealing with their pain had been the most difficult part of the day for the Whistlestop cops, perhaps even more upsetting than the crime scene itself. She'd been unable to remain detached—she had looked into their eyes and felt their loss keenly.

After a time, she had found herself avoiding their gazes.

Melanie pulled up in front of her sister's palatial, plantation-style home. Like Melanie's ex-husband, her sister had chosen to reside in southeast Charlotte, an area populated by the very affluent and dotted with one exclusive, gated community after another. Melanie had always found the area too grand, almost overwhelming in its obvious wealth.

She climbed out of the car. Casey was playing with action figures on the front porch; Mia was on the porch swing, watching him. Smiling, Melanie took a moment to drink in the picture they made. The breeze stirring Mia's fair hair and filmy cotton dress, the gentle rock of the swing, Casey's happy chatter. Nice. Domestic and warm. Like something out of an Andrew Wyeth painting.

Melanie cocked her head. Most of the time, when she looked at her twin, she simply saw her sister, Mia. But sometimes, like now, she experienced a strange sort of déjà vu. A sense that she was looking at herself. A different version of herself, from her previous lifetime, before her divorce.

Casey glanced up and caught sight of her and jumped to his feet. "Mom!" he shouted and tore down the steps to meet her.

She opened her arms; he launched himself into them, hugging her tightly. She squeezed her eyes shut and hugged him back, his sweetness chasing away the ugliness of the day.

She loved him so much it hurt. Before Casey she

hadn't believed such a thing possible. How could loving someone hurt?

Then her obstetrician had laid Casey in her arms and against her heart, and she had understood. Instantly. Irrevocably.

"Did you have fun?" she asked, loosening her grip on him and gazing into his eyes, eyes the same bright blue as hers and her sisters'.

He nodded excitedly. "Aunt Mia took me for ice cream. Then we went to the park an' she pushed me on the swing. I went down the big slide, Mom!"

"The big slide?" She widened her eyes to show that she was properly amazed and impressed. He had been wanting to go down that slide for weeks, but each time he had started up the ladder he had chickened out before he reached the top.

"I was really scared, but Aunt Mia followed me up. And she went down right behind me, just like she promised."

She kissed his cheek. "That's my big, brave boy. You must be really proud of yourself."

He bobbed his head, grinning from ear to ear. "But you hav'to be careful, 'cause you can fall like Aunt Mia did. She hurt her eye."

Melanie lifted her gaze to her sister, standing at the edge of the porch, facing them. Melanie made a sound of dismay. Her sister's right eye was black and blue, the right side of her face swollen. "You fell off the slide?"

"Of course not." She smiled at Casey. "Silly Mommy. Actually, I tripped on a shoe."

"One of Uncle Boyd's big, stupid boots," Casey chimed in.

"We don't say stupid," Melanie corrected, frowning at her son, then returning her attention to her sister. "It's not like you to be clumsy."

Mia ignored the comment. "Have time for a glass of wine? Boyd has a meeting tonight, so I'm fancy-free."

As when they'd spoken on the phone earlier, Melanie picked up on something in her sister's tone that troubled her. "After this day?" she said lightly. "I'll make time."

She ruffled her son's hair, an unruly mop of golden curls, then nudged him toward the porch. After collecting his toys, the three went inside. Melanie switched on the Cartoon Channel, then headed into the kitchen where she found Mia opening a bottle of Chardonnay.

Melanie sank onto one of the iron and wicker bar stools that lined the breakfast counter. "You want to talk about it?" she asked.

"Talk about what?" Mia poured a glass of the chilled wine, slid it across to Melanie, then poured another for herself.

"I don't know. Whatever it is I'm hearing in your voice. Something's bothering you."

Mia gazed at her a moment, then turned and crossed to the breakfront, slid open the middle drawer and came out with a pack of cigarettes. She shook one out and, hands shaking, lit it.

Melanie watched as her sister took a deep drag, holding the smoke in a moment as if it had medicinal powers before she released it. She said nothing, though she despised her sister's habit—one Mia resorted to only when troubled. "It must be bad,"

Melanie murmured. "I haven't seen you with a cigarette in months."

Mia took another drag. She looked at Melanie. "Boyd's cheating on me."

"Oh, Mia." Melanie reached across the counter and covered her sister's hand with one of her own. "Are you sure?"

"Pretty sure." She sucked in a trembling breath. "He's out at night, a lot. Sometimes until really late. He always has a plausible excuse for going out. A meeting with the hospital administrators. Or the hospital board. Or one of his medical societies." She made a sound of disgust. "It's always something."

"And you think he's lying?"

"I know he is. When he comes home…the way he looks…the way he…smells." She made a sound of shame, turned and crossed to the sink. She bowed her head. "Like cheap perfume and…sex."

Melanie dropped her hands to her lap, angry for her sister. She hadn't wanted Mia to marry Boyd Donaldson, had tried to talk her out of it. Despite his good looks and professional reputation, something about the man had always seemed off to her, like a picture slightly out of focus. She hadn't trusted him, had resented the prenuptial agreement he had forced Mia to sign.

Now she wished she hadn't been quite so vocal with her criticisms. If she hadn't been, maybe Mia would have felt free to come to her for help sooner.

"Have you checked up on him?" Melanie asked. "Hired someone to follow him or called the hospital when he's supposed to be there? Anything like that?''

''No.'' She flipped on the water, doused what was left of her cigarette, then dropped it in the trash. ''I've been afraid to. It's like a part of me…doesn't want to know for certain.''

Because faced with proof, she would be forced to act. Not exactly her twin's strong suit.

''Oh, Mia, I understand. I do. But you can't stick your head in the sand with this one. If he's cheating, you have to know for certain. From the standpoint of your health alone—''

''Don't start with me. Please, Melanie. I feel awful enough already, thank you.'' Mia passed a hand over her face. ''It's my life and my marriage and I'll muddle my way through somehow.''

''So butt out?'' Melanie said stiffly, feelings hurt. ''Fine. Just don't expect me to be your sounding board, because I can't sit back and do nothing. It's not my way.''

''But it's mine?''

''I didn't say that.''

''Maybe you didn't have to.''

The two women locked gazes; Mia backed down first. ''Actually, I took your advice already. I thought, okay, what would Melanie do? So I confronted him. And guess what?''

Melanie swallowed hard, her mouth dry. ''What?''

''He went berserk.'' Mia indicated her black eye. ''You see the result.''

Melanie stared at her sister a moment, not wanting to believe what she was hearing. "You don't mean...he hit you?"

"That's exactly what I mean."

"That son-of-a-bitch!" Melanie leaped to her feet. "That no-good, two-timing... I'll kill the bastard. I swear, I'll—"

Melanie bit back the words, struggling to get hold of her anger. She closed her eyes, took a deep breath and counted to ten. Growing up, she'd had a reputation for being a hothead. Her temper had gotten her into trouble time and again—once nearly landing her in reform school. If not for an understanding social worker, she would have ended up there.

As an adult she had learned to control her hair-trigger emotions. To think before she acted. To consider the consequences of her actions.

But old habits died hard. And when it came to her sisters, particularly Mia, she had always been ferociously, even blindly, protective.

"What are you going to do?" she managed to ask through gritted teeth.

Mia sighed, the sound too young and helpless for a thirty-two-year old woman. "What can I do?"

"What can you..." Melanie made a sound of disbelief. "Call the cops. Have his butt hauled in, then press charges. Leave him, for heaven's sake!"

"You make it sound so easy."

"It is. You just do it."

"The way you left Stan?"

"Yes." Melanie went around the counter to her sister. She caught her hands and looked her straight in the eyes. "Leaving Stan was the hardest thing I ever did. But it was the best. I knew that then. I know it now.''

Mia started to cry. "I'm not strong like you, Mellie. I'm not brave. I never have been.''

"You can be.'' She squeezed her sister's fingers. "I'll help you.''

Mia shook her head. "No, you can't. I'm just a sniveling, stupid excuse for a—''

"Stop it! That's our father talking. And Boyd. It's not true.'' She searched her sister's gaze. "You don't think I was scared when I left Stan? I was scared shitless. I'd never had to take care of myself, let alone a child, too. I didn't know how I would support us, if I could. And I was terrified he'd try to take Casey away from me.''

Melanie shuddered, remembering her terror, the way she had second-guessed her every decision. Her ex-husband was a prominent lawyer, a partner in one of Charlotte's top firms. He could have wrested custody away from her without even breaking a sweat—he still could. As it was, he had pulled strings and gotten her application to the CMPD academy denied.

She had left him anyway. For herself. And Casey. She hadn't been the person Stan needed or wanted, though for a long time she had tried to mold herself into that woman. One who needed a man to lean on, one who was satisfied to sit back and let her husband call the shots while she tended to house and home. She had failed miserably. And in the process had become a person she had neither known nor liked.

Their marriage had become a battleground. And a battleground had been no place to raise a child.

"You can do it," she said again, fiercely. "I know you can, Mia."

Mia shook her head, her expression defeated. "I wish I were like you. But I'm not."

Melanie drew her sister into her arms and held her tightly. "It's going to be all right. We'll get through this. *I'll* get you through this. I promise."

6

When Melanie and Casey arrived home an hour and a half later, after a quick stop for fast food, they found Ashley waiting for them. Melanie wasn't surprised to see her. A drug company rep, her territory the Carolinas, she often dropped by Melanie's on her way back into town.

"Look who's here, Casey," Melanie said, drawing to a stop in the driveway. "Aunt Ashley."

McDonald's Kid's Meal forgotten, the child bolted out of the car the moment Melanie got his safety buckle undone. "Aunt Ashley! Look what I got from Aunt Mia! A megaman!"

Melanie smiled as she watched her son launch himself into her sister's outstretched arms. Her sisters had always been the most important people in her life and their love for Casey warmed her heart.

Melanie collected her purse and the Kid's Meal, then crossed to the two. "Hey, sis, have a productive trip?"

Ashley lifted Casey, propping him on her hip, then turned to Melanie. She smiled. "You know pharmaceutical sales—drugs, the wave of the present."

Melanie laughed. Her sister was a paradox. Although extremely successful at what she did, she was a believer in natural and holistic healing. Whenever one of them got sick, she suggested herbs, roots and teas instead of one of the miracle drugs she made a living selling.

They climbed the front steps to the house. "You could have let yourself in. Less mosquitoes."

"I know." She hiked Casey higher on her hip. "But it was too pretty a night to wait inside."

Melanie unlocked the door and flipped on the foyer light. They made their way to the kitchen, turning on lights as they went. It was a small house, a cottage really, with two bedrooms, family room and kitchen. Though it would practically fit in the master-bedroom suite of her ex-husband's home, Melanie loved it. In her opinion, what it lacked in size, it made up for in charm. Located in one of Whistlestop's older neighborhoods, it had an abundance of windows, hardwood floors throughout and high ceilings.

And best of all, she had paid for it herself, no help from her ex or anybody else.

"Did you eat?" she asked her sister as she got Casey settled at the breakfast counter. "I was going to throw together a salad. I have enough for two."

"Thanks, but I'll pass." She shrugged out of her suit jacket and draped it over the back of a chair. "I had a late lunch with a doctor."

Melanie glanced at her sister and frowned, noticing how thin she looked. Slightly taller than her and Mia's medium height, Ashley had also been blessed with a more curvaceous build. Tonight, however, her tailored trousers seemed to hang on her. "Have you been ill?" she asked.

"No. Why?"

"You look thin."

Ashley cocked an eyebrow. "Compared to what? The way I usually look?"

"No, silly. *Too* thin."

"There's no such thing." She crossed to the refrigerator. "Have any cold beer?"

"Think so. Help yourself." Melanie unwrapped her son's cheeseburger, laid it and his bag of French fries on a plate and set it in front of him, snitching a fry as she did.

"Juice, Mom."

"Milk," she countered. "Then juice if you're still thirsty."

Casey only grumbled a bit—he knew it would be a losing battle—and dug into his burger. Melanie poured him the milk, then retrieved the salad fixings from the refrigerator. "You heard about Joli Andersen?"

"On the radio." Ashley poured a beer into a chilled mug, took a sip and made a sound of appreciation. "Nothing like an ice-cold beer at the end of a long, hard day."

Melanie grinned. "You sound like a commercial."

"I do, don't I? Maybe I missed my calling." She took another sip, then set the glass on the counter. "So, tell me about today."

Melanie tore off a hunk of iceberg lettuce, washed and patted it dry, and began ripping it into pieces over her bowl. "What do you want to know?"

"Just the basics. You know, was it really gruesome? Did you kick major CMPD butt? If you ruined your shoes when you threw up.'' The last she said with a laugh, but at Melanie's expression, brought a hand to her mouth. "Oh, Mel, I was just teasing. You didn't really—"

"Totally humiliate myself? Try again. I puked my guts out in front of everybody."

"Oh, sis, I'm so sorry."

"It's okay, I—" A lump formed in her throat, and she cleared it. "It was the worst thing I've ever seen, Ash. And to everyone else it was...no big deal. Business as usual, I guess."

She began peeling a cucumber, no longer because she wanted to eat but for something to do with her hands. "They talked about what happened to that poor girl so cavalierly. With so little, I don't know, care. That's what finally did it. Until then I was holding it together, focusing on the job."

Ashley gave her a quick hug. "Tossed cookies or not, I know you were great. My sister, Super Cop."

Melanie smiled and shook her head. More than anyone else, Ashley had supported her decision to become a police officer. She had always seemed to understand not just Melanie's want to do it, but her need to as well. "I'll tell you this, Ash, the work was fascinating. There was this guy at the scene, a profiler with the FBI. The way he worked was amaz—"

"Mom, what's the FBI?"

Melanie looked at her son, realizing not only that he had been listening, but that he was fascinated.

"It's a law enforcement agency, honey. A big, important one."

"That's what I thought." He stuffed a French fry into his mouth. "Are you talking about that lady?"

Melanie frowned. "What lady?"

"The one who was muttered."

Murdered. "What do you know about that?"

"I heard Aunt Mia talking with my teacher."

Ashley made a sound of disgust and Melanie glanced at her son's plate—it was clean save for the pickles he'd peeled off his burger and a hunk of the bun. "Honey, are you finished?"

He nodded, then yawned. "Can I watch TV now?"

She leaned across the counter and wiped his mouth with a napkin, feeling a pinch of guilt at having kept him up so late. "Sorry, sweetie, time to hit the sack. It's already thirty minutes past your bedtime."

"But Mom—" he dragged the words out, part plea, part whine "—I'm not tired."

"I'm sure you're not, but it's still your bedtime." She helped him off the tall stool and nudged him toward the door. "Tell your Aunt Ashley goodnight."

Casey did as she asked, managing to wheedle the promise of three bedtime stories from her before they cleared the kitchen.

Melanie glanced apologetically at her sister. "Be right back."

Ashley smiled. "No problem. I'll be here."

When Melanie returned to the kitchen fifteen minutes later, she found Ashley standing at the sink, staring out the window above it, her expression almost unbearably sad.

Melanie took a step toward her, concerned. "Ash? You okay?"

Her sister turned, expression lifting. "Sure. Our little tiger asleep?"

"Not yet. He was so revved up." She frowned. "I can't believe I was so indiscreet earlier, talking about my work that way. He was listening to everything we said. I have to be more careful what I say around him, he's not a baby anymore."

"Sounds as if our sister and his teacher have to be more careful as well." Ashley plucked a chunk of cucumber from Melanie's salad bowl. "Now, tell me more about this FBI guy?"

"The way he worked was fascinating, that's all. He looked at the crime scene, analyzed it, then drew a conclusion about what had happened. I found it nothing short of amazing."

Ashley grinned. "Goodbye dog-poop patrol, hello homicide."

Melanie thought of all the calls she had taken from citizens irate over a neighbor's dog pooping in their yard, or trampling their flowers, or chasing their cat up a tree; she thought of all the traffic tickets she had issued and of how she had longed to do real police work. Now, finally, she had her chance.

But at what cost?

She looked at her sister, feeling guilty. "Being so grateful for this murder makes me feel like an awful person. You know what I mean?"

"Don't be a dork." Ashley reached around her

and helped herself to a baby carrot. "You had nothing to do with Joli Andersen's murder."

"I know, I just—" She sighed and reached for the bell pepper. "One thing I already know, when this case is solved it's going to be difficult to return to business as usual around the WPD."

Ashley made a face. "You wouldn't be stuck in that rinky-dink department if not for that bastard you married. Someone needs to teach that prick a lesson."

"Ashley!" Melanie glanced over her shoulder toward the family room and bedrooms beyond. "First off, watch your language. Casey could hear. Second, remember, Stan is Casey's dad."

"And that's the only reason we let him live."

"Very funny." Melanie sprinkled grated cheese on her salad, then held the bag out to her sister.

Ashley helped herself to some of the cheddar-jack. "I can't help it, Mel. I hate him for keeping you out of the CMPD academy. That was your dream for as long as I can remember, and he stole it."

"The Whistlestop force isn't the CMPD, but I'm still doing police work." She crossed to the refrigerator for the salad dressing, choosing Italian. A smile tugged at the corners of her mouth. "Which is a constant thorn in Stan's side. He can't stand the idea of the great Stan May's ex-wife being a cop. The fact that I wear a uniform drives him nuts. I love when I'm wearing it and run into one of his colleagues' wives." She laughed. "They always look horrified."

The truth was, she disliked the uniform almost

as much as Stan did, and not because it was un-flattering and too masculine, but because it identi-fied her as a small-time, small-town cop. In the WPD, unlike the Charlotte/Mecklenburg force, there was no such thing as working "plainclothes." Her chief wanted his force to be immediately rec-ognizable to the community and for citizens to see his officers out and about, all the time.

She drizzled dressing over the salad. "Besides, who knows what the future might bring? If I dis-tinguish myself in the WPD, I don't think Stan's influence with the CMPD will be as likely to keep me out. That's why it's so important for me not only to be working this murder, but for me to help solve it. Just taking up space isn't going to cut it."

"It never does." Ashley's smile faded. "Sounds like you have it all figured out. Of course, you al-ways have."

At the quiver in her sister's voice, Melanie frowned. "So have you, Ash. You've always gone after what you wanted, what you believed in with heart and soul. It's only Mia..." Melanie let the thought trail off, thinking of her other sister, of the predicament she had gotten herself into.

Melanie sighed. "You haven't talked to Mia in a while, have you?"

"At least a week. Since our last coffee klatch." Ashley drew her eyebrows together. "Why? What's wrong?"

The salad that a moment ago had looked so ap-petizing suddenly lost its appeal. Melanie laid down her fork and shoved the bowl aside. "Boyd hit her,'' she said, then filled Ashley in on her and Mia's conversation.

Angry color sprang to Ashley's cheeks. ''That bastard! What did she do?''

''Take a guess.''

''Nothing, right? Because she's scared.''

''You got it.'' With a sound of distress, Melanie stood and crossed to the window. She stared out at the night for a moment, then turned back to her sister. ''What are we going to do?''

''What *can* we do?'' Ashley lifted a shoulder. ''It's her marriage, Mel.''

''But he's hitting her! We can't allow it.''

''She's the one who's allowing it. Not us.''

''How can you say that?'' Melanie shook her head, angered by her sister's attitude. ''You know how dangerous this is for her. It would be for any of us, because of our pasts. All three of us are susceptible to the victim mentality and to being sucked into a relationship of escalating abuse.''

''Speak for yourself.'' Ashley plucked another wedge of cucumber out of Melanie's salad and popped it into her mouth. ''Our father was a monster. But he's dead now and I'm over it.''

''Right. That's why you steer as far away from men and relationships as possible.''

Ashley narrowed her eyes. ''This isn't about me and my dating habits.''

''No, it's about helping our sister. Something *you* don't seem interested in doing.''

For a moment, Ashley was completely still. Then she rose to her feet. Melanie saw that she was shaking. "I love our sister as much as you do, Melanie, so don't you even think about going there."

"I wasn't suggesting—"

"Yeah, you were. In your way." Ashley looked her straight in the eyes. "You want the truth? You've made her too dependent. You're always taking care of her, rushing in to save the day. You've been doing it since we were kids. What does she expect you to do this time? End her marriage for her? Arrest him? Shoot to kill?"

"Very funny, Ash."

"I'm not laughing. You've got to let her grow up."

Melanie stiffened, fighting to keep her temper in check. "So, you think I should just stand back and let her be victimized. Very nice, Ash. Sisterly."

"Until she does something to help herself, yes, that's exactly what I think you should do. Be there for her, sure. Offer advice. But stop trying to save her."

"Maybe *you* can do that, but I can't."

Ashley sucked in a sharp breath. "Cut the sanctimonious act. The reason you're so protective of her is because you feel guilty."

"Guilty?" Melanie repeated, arching her eyebrows in exaggerated disbelief. "What do I have to feel guilty about?"

"Silly question, Mel. You feel guilty because Mia was Dad's whipping girl."

"That's nonsense. Why should I—"

"Because even though the two of you looked exactly alike, he picked her to hurt."

Feeling her sister's words like a blow, Melanie

took an involuntary step backward, then swung away from her sister. Legs shaking, she crossed to the door to the family room, listened for Casey, then carefully eased the door three-quarters of the way shut. "That wasn't my fault," she said finally, heavily. "It was Father's. I have no reason to feel guilty over it."

"Of course not. But you do. You're still trying to make up to her for you being the golden child."

"You don't understand. You've never understood."

Ashley's mouth thinned. "Because I was never a member of your little twin's club. Right? Not Ashley, the one who was different."

"Mia and I don't have a club and we've never excluded you, Ash."

"Oh, please." Her voice thickened. "I was the third sister. The third wheel. I still am."

Melanie made a sound of frustration. "You make me crazy when you're like this."

Ashley took a step toward her, then stopped. "Has it ever occurred to you that it's because I'm different that I see so clearly? You, Mia, Dad…everything?"

"Mia needs me. She's more sensitive than either of us. More vulnerable. That's why Dad singled her out, he knew she wouldn't fight back. And that's why I had to stop him."

Ashley opened her mouth to respond, but the phone rang, cutting her off. Melanie answered. "Oh, hello, Stan."

Ashley made a face and grabbed her purse. "I should go."

"Stan, could you hold a moment?" She put her hand over the mouthpiece. "Please stay."

Ashley shook her head, her expression—for one fleeting moment—lost. "I'll call."

Melanie held a hand out, regretting their argument. "Coffee on Friday?"

"I'll try. No promises."

"I love you."

Ashley smiled. "Ditto, kiddo." She started out the door, then stopped and looked back, her expression wicked. "Tell the prick I said hello and to burn in hell."

Melanie watched her go, then turned her attention back to the phone. "What can I do for you, Stan?"

"Which one of your sisters is there?" Stan asked, ignoring her question. "Wimpy or bitchy?"

Melanie dismissed his barb. "Ashley was. She just left. She asked me to tell you hello."

"I'll bet. More like, to burn in hell."

Melanie choked on a laugh. "What do you want, Stan?"

"That thing today, the murder, were you involved?"

"Involved?" she repeated, purposely playing dumb.

He made a sound of annoyance. "With the investigation. Are you involved?"

"The crime occurred in Whistlestop. Yes, I'm involved in the investigation." She smiled to herself, aware of his ire. "But as I'm sure you can understand, I'm not at liberty to discuss the details."

He swore. "I couldn't care less about the details. I don't want my wife having anything to do with—"

"Ex-wife," she corrected. "You're Shelley's problem now, thank God. You haven't forgotten about her, have you?"

"Cut the crap, Melanie. Of course I haven't forgotten about Shelley."

"And as your ex," she went on, "you have absolutely no say in my life. None. What I do is my business. Only mine. Got that?"

"Except when what you do is potentially harmful to my son."

"*Our* son is fine. Happy, healthy and loved. My involvement in a murder investigation is no more harmful to him than your legal wranglings are."

"That's where our opinions differ."

She laughed without humor. "Our opinions differ on everything, Stan. If there's nothing else, it's late and I'm hungry and tired."

"Oh, but there is. We need to talk about the future, Melanie. Casey's future." He paused for a moment, then went on. "He's starting real school next year."

She glanced at her watch, then longingly at her salad. "I'm aware of that, Stan."

"Then you're also aware that I live in the city's best school district?"

It took a second for his words to sink in. As they did, a flicker of fear burst to life inside her. She tamped it down. He couldn't mean what she thought he did—she was jumping to conclusions, overreacting. After all, they had been divorced three years, and in that time Stan had seemed more than satisfied to be an every-other-weekend father.

"The best?" she countered. "By whose standards? The schools in my district are highly rated. Not as fancy, maybe, but—"

"Come on, Melanie," he said softly and patiently, as if he were speaking to a willful child, "don't you think it's time for us to set our personal needs aside and ask ourselves what's best for Casey."

"You mean *who's* best for him, don't you?"

"Maybe I do."

She squeezed her eyes shut and counted to ten. She was living the nightmare that had dogged her the entire first year of her divorce—that Stan was going to try to take custody away from her.

She gripped the receiver so tightly her fingers went numb. "I already know who's best for him. Me. I'm his mother, Stan."

"And I'm his father. I can offer him a stable, two-parent home in one of Charlotte's finest communities. Which, by the way, is gated for security."

"Let's not forget a swimming pool, tennis lessons and lunches at the club," she said sarcastically. "And maybe while you're at it, you should sweeten the pot with a yearly trip to Europe?"

"Those things are important."

"What's more important than love, Stan? Than constancy? He's been with me since the beginning, a change now would confuse him. Besides, all his friends from preschool—"

"Kids adjust."

He said it so casually, so carelessly. This was

Casey's life they were talking about. His feelings. That the man could blow them off so easily made her blood boil. "You son-of-a-bitch," she whispered, voice shaking. "All you care about is yourself."

"That's your opinion."

"I won't let you do this."

"You can't stop me."

"Mom?"

She looked over to find Casey in the doorway, eyes wide with alarm. The phone must have awakened him—if he'd ever fallen asleep. She pulled herself together and smiled reassuringly at him. "I'll be off in just a second, honey. Crawl back into bed and I'll come snuggle with you. Okay?"

Casey hesitated a moment, then did as she asked. She returned her attention to her ex-husband. "It's inappropriate for us to have this conversation right now. I'll have to get back to you."

"This isn't going to go away, Melanie. I intend to sue you for custody of our son. And I intend to win."

7

The conference room in the Law Enforcement Center was too hot. The personalities around the long, oval table too strong. Each person accustomed to having their way. Melanie moved her gaze from one face to another. Charlotte's mayor, Ed Pinkston, and Chief Lyons of the CMPD, her own chief, the district attorney. Representatives from all their offices, as well as the SBI—the State Bureau of Investigation. Connor Parks. A man with him, also FBI, she guessed. Whistlestop's mayor was not in attendance, a fact Melanie found curious. Or ominous, she amended, shifting her gaze to her chief's set face.

They had been called together that morning because the daughter of Charlotte's most prominent citizen had been dead a week now and that citizen was demanding answers. So was the press.

And they were no closer to an answer than they had been the day after her murder.

There would be no glad-handing here today. No give-and-take, no backslapping and mutual support. Instead, a head or two might roll—Melanie's included. Even the CMPD guys looked apprehensive.

The Charlotte mayor stood to bring the meeting to order. Before he could, the conference-room door opened. Cleve Andersen and another man walked through. An uncomfortable hush fell over the room.

"Sorry I'm late," Andersen said briskly, moving to the head of the table, taking a place beside Mayor Pinkston.

The mayor cleared his throat. "Cleve, we didn't expect—"

"I thought it best," the man interrupted. "The decisions made here today affect me. My family." He smiled, the curving of his lips automatic, the consummate player doing his thing. "As you know, I'm not one to let others lead."

He indicated the man who had entered with him. "My attorney, Bob Braxton. Now—" he settled into his seat and turned his gaze to the room's other occupants "—shall we begin?"

Mayor Pinkston looked as helpless as a fish flopping on a dock, hook still embedded in its mouth. Clearly, the politician didn't have the guts to oppose the more powerful man.

Apparently, Connor Parks did. "Excuse me," he said, standing, facing the businessman. "With all due respect, Mr. Andersen, you don't belong here."

The room fell quiet. All eyes focused on Andersen. He stood stiffly, his chiseled features tight with restraint. Or dislike. "Young man, my daughter is the topic of this meeting."

"Exactly the reason you shouldn't be here. We don't have the time to tiptoe around your feelings. Go home to your grieving family, Mr. Andersen. That's where you belong. It's where you can do some good."

An ugly flush climbed up Cleve Andersen's pale

face. Melanie held her breath. Parks had verbalized what each person at the table had certainly been thinking. Although Melanie applauded his courage, she wondered at his sanity. He hadn't exactly soft-pedaled his opinion or couched it in deferential terms.

"I don't recognize you," Andersen said. "What's your name?"

"Agent Connor Parks, FBI."

"Well, then, Agent Parks, let me tell you something. I didn't get where I am today by sitting on the sidelines and waiting for others to make things happen. I take charge. I make things happen."

"Again, with all due respect, this isn't big business. This is law enforcement. Something you know nothing about. I'm afraid this time you're going to have to take that seat on the sidelines. Please, let us do our jobs."

"Cleve," the mayor said gently, laying a hand on the man's shoulder. "Agent Parks is right. No father should hear the things we must discuss in this room today. It would be better if you left."

The man swayed slightly on his feet. His mask of confidence and determination slipped, giving all a glimpse of the man underneath, one in great pain, one hanging on by an emotional thread.

Andersen looked at Ed Pinkston. "I've already endured the worst a father could," he said softly, the slightest quaver in his voice. "I was told my daughter was dead. That she had been murdered."

He moved his gaze around the table, from one face to the next, stopping, finally, on Connor Parks's. "I want her killer caught. I want justice.

And I'll have it, no matter the cost. Is that understood?''

Without waiting for an answer, he turned to his attorney. ''Bob, I'll trust you to handle this from here.''

Like the room's other occupants, Melanie watched the man stride toward the exit. She ached for him, for his pain. She understood his motive for coming today—sitting back and waiting would be hell on earth for a take-charge man like Andersen.

When the door clicked shut behind him, several moments of awkward silence ensued. Then the mayor cleared his throat and called the meeting back to order. After chastising Parks for the tone with which he had addressed the victim's father, he opened the floor to the two chiefs of police. They shared every step of the investigation so far—who had been interviewed, what had been gleaned from those interviews—and they assured the politicians no stone was being left unturned.

''I don't want to hear about turning over stones,'' Pinkston snapped. ''I want to hear about a suspect. I want to hear you tell me you're going to catch this sick bastard and I want you to tell me how you're going to do it.''

Chief Lyons of the CMPD turned to Pete Harrison, his lead investigator. ''Harrison?''

The man nodded. ''We have a suspect. Apparently, the night Joli was murdered she spent the early part of the evening in a club with friends. There was a guy there who was hitting on her most of the night. Really coming on strong. She wasn't interested and humiliated him in front of a group of people. Called him loser and told him to crawl back under whatever rock he'd emerged from.

"He blew his top. Told her he'd make her sorry and stormed off. A witness, one of the club's patrons, says she saw the guy in the parking lot later that night, around the time Joli left. Unfortunately, nobody knew who he was. He'd never been in that club before, paid with cash. And nobody's seen him since."

Andersen's attorney made a sound of disbelief. "You're saying you can't find this guy?"

"Haven't found him yet," Harrison corrected. "We will, trust me. We've got descriptions of him with every bartender in Mecklenburg County. He'll resurface."

"And when he does," Harrison's partner, Roger Stemmons, added, "we'll be there."

"I hate to rain on anyone's parade, but I don't think we should pin our hopes on this guy," Agent Parks offered. "He sounds like a disorganized inadequate, same as our UNSUB, but the—"

"Excuse me," Mayor Pinkston interrupted. "Our what?"

"Unknown subject. As I was saying, the other descriptions we have of him and of his behavior don't fit the profile."

For the second time that morning, all attention focused on Connor Parks. "Profile?" the mayor asked.

"Mumbo jumbo," Stemmons muttered, tossing his pencil onto the table.

"A psychological portrait of a killer," Connor told the mayor. "We create this portrait by comparing what we know about criminal behavior to the details of a particular crime scene. They're quite accurate.''

Connor looked at Stemmons, his expression bland. ''Actually, there's nothing metaphysical or mystical about profiling. Our conclusions are based on data collected from actual crimes and hundreds of hours of interviews with known serial killers and rapists.''

Stemmons scowled. The mayor settled more comfortably in his chair. ''So, tell us about this UNSUB, Agent Parks. What kind of man are we dealing with here?''

''He's a white male,'' Connor began. ''Twenty-five to thirty-five years of age. He's handsome and in good shape. He works out, most probably at a health club.

''He's a professional man, doctor, lawyer, accountant,'' he went on. ''If not successful, he has the trappings of success—the clothes, the car. A BMW is my guess. But one of the smaller ones, a 300 series, maybe. A few years old.''

One of the SBI guys inquired about Connor's reasoning; he responded with the same theory he'd presented to Melanie at the scene a week ago—Joli Andersen had been both beautiful and rich and since it appeared she had gone with this UNSUB willingly, he would have had to meet certain requirements.

Melanie spoke up. ''He's right about that. From interviews with her friends and co-workers, I learned that although Joli was an outrageous flirt, she was picky about who she dated. She had real high standards. He had to be good-looking. And he had to be well off.''

''Exactly,'' Connor murmured, then continued. ''His neighbors would describe him as nice. Quiet, maybe even shy. He lives or works near the crime scene, he picked the Sweet Dreams Motel for that reason.''

''How near?'' Chief Lyons asked.

''Three or four miles is my guess. But no more than ten.''

That caused a ripple of interest at the table, but Connor ignored it and moved on. ''As evidenced by the whore/madonna aspects of his ritual and the fact that he didn't penetrate the victim naturally, he had a strained but obsessive relationship with his mother. He has a history of broken relationships with women. If married, the union is an unhappy one.''

''What about priors?'' Bobby Taggerty asked.

''Good question. If there's anything, it's nothing serious. No convictions. He frequents prostitutes, you may find a charge for soliciting.'' Connor fell silent a moment. ''This UNSUB hasn't killed before, but he will again.''

A buzz moved around the conference table. Harrison spoke up first. ''You sure about that, Parks?''

''Positive. He's been nurturing his fantasy for a long time. With Joli the fantasy got out of control, because unlike the hookers he'd experimented with, Joli stopped behaving as he wanted her to. In an effort to control her, he killed her. Killing her provided him with a powerful sexual jolt. He's going to want that again. He's going to crave it.''

"We could check out the hospitals," Harrison murmured, "the doctors' and lawyers' offices in that area, start putting together a list of names of guys who fit this description."

"Do the same with the health clubs, cross-reference the lists, see how many matches we have," Stemmons added.

Connor nodded his agreement. "I also suggest questioning the area prostitutes. Like I said, our UNSUB's been working out the details of this fantasy for some time. He's practiced it on hookers. There are girls out there who know this guy by his ritual."

The man with Connor stood and introduced himself as Steve Rice, the Special Agent in Charge, or SAC, of the Charlotte field office of the FBI. "We should stake out the cemetery where Joli's buried," he said. "Set up video cameras. This kind of killer routinely visits his victim's grave as a way of reliving his fantasy. It's so stimulating for them, we often catch them masturbating."

"Jesus," Braxton muttered, looking as sickened as he sounded.

"If the stakeout yields nothing," Rice continued, "try flushing him out by engineering a big story about Joli in the *Charlotte Observer,* a human-interest piece. Get them to run a couple good pictures. Get him stirred up, excited. And keep those cameras trained on her grave. Trust me, it works."

For several minutes various other investigative avenues were discussed. When the discussion died down, Mayor Pinkston stepped in once more. "I'm encouraged by what we've done here today," he began, the consummate politician easing into his shtick.

While he pontificated, Melanie's thoughts drifted to her own problems. Problem, she corrected. Just one. Stan's intention to gain custody of Casey.

Melanie brought a hand to the back of her neck and massaged the knotted muscles. She had waited several days before calling Stan back. She had used the time to compose herself and prepare her case. She had been ready to calmly reason with him, to argue elegantly, to beg if forced to. Instead, she'd lost her temper and ended up shouting at him.

What was wrong with her? Why did she allow him to push her buttons that way? She swallowed a sigh. It had been the same during their marriage. She had been fire, he ice. She had argued with passion, he with coolheaded logic. Whenever they had argued, which had been often, the more passionate she had become, the more coolly rational he—in a never-ending, escalating cycle. By the end she'd realized that he had used his ability to disassociate from his emotions as a way to manipulate her. And as a way to constantly prove his superiority.

It had worked. After arguing, she'd always felt like a shrewish, raving lunatic.

She had promised herself she would never again allow him to get to her that way. She had fallen right into his trap anyway.

"—a few more administrative details we need to discuss. The first is the two-force involvement in this investigation."

At that, Melanie looked up. She glanced at

Bobby. She saw by his expression that he knew what was coming, too, and her stomach sank.

"We've decided to make a change. We feel strongly that by dividing the investigation between the two forces, we're watering it down. As of now, the CMPD is officially the force of record in the Andersen murder. They'll be aided, of course, by the FBI and SBI, but they'll bear the major responsibility for the investigation."

"That's bullshit!" Melanie said before she could stop herself. She got to her feet, face hot. "Pardon my outburst, Mr. Mayor, but the murder occurred in Whistlestop. We are prepared and eager to do whatever necessary to see that Joli Andersen's killer is brought to justice."

"I'm sure you are, Officer May. And believe me, your chief made a convincing argument in favor of awarding the WPD the case. However, we feel we must go with the experience on this one."

"But—"

"The decision's been made, Officer May," he said, working to look sympathetic but achieving an irritated expression instead. "But we have an important assignment for the WPD, one I'll let Mr. Braxton share with the group. Bob?"

The lawyer stood. "Mr. Andersen has decided to offer a reward for any information leading to the arrest of his daughter's killer. Chief Greer's team from Whistlestop will be overseeing the phone bank."

"What!"

This came from Melanie and Bobby, in unison. Melanie heard the CMPD guys snickering and the blood rushed to her head. An angry retort on the tip of her tongue, she swung toward Harrison and Stemmons, but Bobby had heard them, too, and anticipating her response, kicked her under the table.

Steve Rice stood. "With all due respect and sympathy to Mr. Andersen and his family, I have to warn you that these types of rewards rarely lead to anything but headaches for us and the PDs working the case. By tomorrow at noon, we'll be so busy following up on false leads, we won't have time to follow up on the real ones. I urge you to ask the Andersen family to reconsider."

"But couldn't it prompt a recalcitrant witness to come forward?" the attorney countered. "The promise of one hundred thousand dollars is a powerful motivator."

Melanie groaned. Chaos erupted at the table. That kind of reward would bring out not only every money-grubbing liar in the county, but every nutcase as well. It was a singularly bad idea. That she and Bobby had been assigned the phone banks was humiliating.

The rest of the meeting passed in an angry blur for Melanie. The only bright spot being that Andersen's attorney agreed to try to convince the businessman to lower the reward substantially.

The moment they adjourned, Melanie caught her chief in the hallway. "Why didn't you tell us?" she asked him, so furious her voice shook. "You let them sucker punch us. I feel like an idiot."

"I only just found out myself." Melanie heard the anger in his voice. "They cornered me minutes before the meeting."

"So, that's where was our illustrious mayor was this morning," Melanie said through gritted teeth. "Hiding under his slimy rock."

"Asshole politicians," Bobby muttered.

The chief sighed. "Don't be too hard on him, he couldn't win this one. The pressure came from high up."

"This is Andersen's doing, I'll bet," Bobby said, shoving his hands into his trouser pockets. "Who'd the man get to, the governor?"

Their chief didn't deny it. "Same old song and dance," Melanie said bitterly. "They're in and we're out."

"No," Bobby corrected, his normally placid features pinched with anger, "we're on the phone, taking down every reward-hungry nut's tip to nowhere." He stubbed his toe into the worn carpet. "Asshole politicians," he said again.

"I know you're disappointed. I am, too." The chief looked from one to the other of them. "But I did get us a couple consolations. First, though not actively participating in the investigation, we're still involved. Searches, lineups, interrogations—anything goes down, we're included. Second, I got us a handful of CMPD grunts to help with the phones." He smiled wickedly. "Poor bastards."

Bobby perked up slightly at that, but Melanie couldn't. This case had been her big chance, her way out of the WPD. Now it was gone.

Sometimes, she decided, life really sucked.

"Look on the bright side, Mel," Bobby said moments later as they crossed the parking lot to her

Jeep. "Now that we're out, we can't get blamed for tanking the investigation if this thing goes south."

"What 'if'? It's already gone south." Melanie made a sound of frustration. "The bright side was working the investigation. Damn."

"I know, partner. I'm pissed, too."

When she only looked at him, he laughed and bumped her with his shoulder. "Okay, maybe not as pissed as you. But hell, it's a matter of pride. The phone banks? Give me a break."

"Thanks for cheering me up," Melanie grumbled. "I feel so much better now. Positively giddy with delight."

8

Tuesdays were papering day for the Person's Team at the D.A.'s office. During that day a prosecutor from the team was available to advise on and review case merit for the police.

Although many of the prosecutors dreaded their papering-day rotation, Veronica Ford didn't. She enjoyed meeting with the police; she liked having the opportunity to hear and evaluate cases before anyone else touched them; she was always left feeling as if she had her finger on the pulse of the team.

Some days were slow, some—like today—hectic. Rape, assault and battery, it seemed, had become a sudden, favorite pastime in Mecklenburg County. Veronica decided it must either be a full moon or the beginning of an economic recession. Both played hell with law and order.

Jen rang her. "Veronica," she said, "an Officer Melanie May is here to see you."

"Melanie May," she repeated, recognizing the name, surprised at the coincidence. Especially since she had switched rotations with Rick so he could attend the Andersen case pow-wow that morning. The big news from that gathering was Cleve Andersen's one-hundred-thousand-dollar reward offer. The entire office was buzzing with it.

"She's with the Whistlestop force."

"I know who she's with. Send her back."

A moment later the police officer appeared at her door. Veronica smiled and waved her in. "Officer May, have a seat."

The woman returned Veronica's smile and sank into one of the two chairs facing the desk. "You look familiar," she said. "Where do I know you from?"

Veronica motioned to the line of Starbucks travel mugs on the credenza to her right. "We share an addiction to coffee."

"Of course. We frequent the same java joint." Melanie May laughed. "I'm a cappuccino girl. You?"

"Latte." Veronica settled back against her seat. "I confess, when the receptionist announced you, I knew exactly who you were. From the coffeehouse. Your uniform and name tag give you away."

"You're observant."

"I'm an ADA, knowing the police is part of my job. I'm aided by an excellent memory."

The policewoman motioned toward the travel mugs. "I have to ask, why six?"

Veronica glanced at them, then shook her head in self-directed amusement. "It started innocently enough. I forgot my travel mug one morning, so I bought another. I thought, why not? I could use a backup. I hate drinking out of paper."

"Then you forgot it again?"

"Exactly. It's evolved into this elaborate system of collecting, transporting, then washing." She shook her head, smiling at herself. "Of course, I don't call it obsessive-compulsive behavior, I tell myself I'm helping the environment by using plastic instead of paper. You know, saving trees. We can convince ourselves of anything, I suppose.''

''A lawyer with a conscience.'' Melanie grinned. ''How novel.''

Veronica laughed again. ''Uh-oh. Sounds like you have a problem with lawyers.''

''Not prosecutors. My ex-husband's an attorney. Corporate law.''

Veronica leaned toward her. ''High-priced hand-holders and nose-wipers.'' She made a face. ''No thanks. Give me a scumbag to put on ice any day.''

Melanie laughed. ''Well, here's your chance. I have a class-A creep for you.''

''Fill me in.''

''Name's Thomas Weiss,'' Melanie said, handing her the report. ''Batterer. Put his live-in girlfriend in the hospital. And not for the first time. However, this time it was bad enough, the girlfriend's ready to charge him.''

Veronica looked the case over. She jotted the victim's name, address and place of employment on her legal pad, then did the same for the accused.

She met the policewoman's eyes. ''It says here he owns a restaurant.''

''The Blue Bayou. In Dilworth.''

''I've been there. Nice place. Good food. Cajun.''

''That's the one.''

''And she's one of his bartenders.'' Veronica pursed her lips. ''He's done this to her before?''

''Yes.''

"But she's never pressed charges?"

"She has but dropped them. She won't this time."

"How do you know?"

"He threatened to kill her. She's really scared."

Veronica made a sound of regret and tossed the file back onto the table. "Sorry. No go."

"No go?" Melanie repeated, stunned. "But why? It's a good case."

"With what you've got, we can't win. And I'm not willing to start the clock ticking until I'm confident we can. Look at it this way, you've got nothing here but the girlfriend. One who's scared silly at that. Scared girlfriends with a history of taking a hike on a case do not make good witnesses."

Melanie leaned forward, her expression eager. "She won't change her mind this time. I'm sure of it. This time—"

Veronica held up a hand, stopping her. "If the victim waffles, if she shows the slightest bit of hesitation, the jury thinks 'So what?' This guy looks squeaky-clean on paper. He's the owner of a popular area restaurant. He's the picture of the successful, educated citizen."

"So he can get away with beating up his girlfriend?"

Veronica met the other woman's gaze evenly. "Yes."

Melanie made a sound of frustration, collected the report and stood. "This sucks."

"Tell me about it." Veronica followed her to her feet. "I'd love to nail this creep, Melanie. Trust me on that. Bring me more and I will. A witness to corroborate. A neighbor, kids. Another woman to stand up. If you can do that, I'll nail his ass to a stake. And that's a promise.''

9

Ashley let herself into Mia's house, using the key her sister had given her for emergencies. She closed the front door behind her, relocking it. She glanced at her watch and frowned. At nearly five o'clock on a Tuesday afternoon, she had been certain she would find Mia home.

She would be soon, Ashley decided, crossing the massive foyer, moving toward the kitchen. In the meantime, she might as well make herself comfortable. First stop, the refrigerator and one of Boyd's expensive, imported beers.

The click of her heels on the marble-parquet floor echoed, and Ashley paused, suddenly aware of how quiet the house was. No ticking clock or purring cat broke the silence. No drone of a TV inadvertently left on or muffled sound of children playing next door. She had always found Mia's home mausoleum-like. Had always thought it beautiful but cold. Unwelcoming. A kind of gilded cage.

Now, after what Melanie had told her about her sister's marriage, she realized just how on the mark her feelings had been.

Maybe she wasn't completely losing it, after all. Maybe she was hanging on by a thread, instead.

It had been exactly one week since she'd argued

with Melanie about Mia and her marriage and Ashley had been unable to put the confrontation behind her. She had been unable to forget the way the argument had made her feel—angry and resentful. Bitter.

She couldn't understand why Melanie refused to see the truth, why she refused to acknowledge that Ashley might be able to see the situation more clearly because she wasn't a part of her and Mia's little clique. Their little twin's club.

Three was a crowd.

Wannabe idiot. That's all she was. All she had ever been.

Her sisters and nephew were everything to her. They were the most important part of her life. The only part that meant anything.

But they had more in their lives. So much more that she sometimes thought they didn't need her at all. Thought that if she fell off the face of the planet, they would hardly notice she was gone.

Ashley sucked in a sharp breath, hating her thoughts, denying them. They weren't true. Melanie and Mia loved her. Her alienation was of her own creation. Her loneliness had nothing to do with other people—only herself. With her displaced anger.

Wasn't that what the shrink she had seen for a while had told her? That she would always be alone until she faced the truth about her past?

Ashley dropped her purse on the kitchen counter and crossed to the refrigerator, but didn't open it. On the appliance's shiny black front was a photo of her and her sisters, taken on their thirtieth birthday. Their arms were linked, they were smiling. Three women, strikingly attractive in identical flame-red dresses, near mirror images of one another.

Ashley settled on her own image and an ache of loneliness and longing settled in the pit of her gut. *Near mirror images. Not exact.*

Her part of the mirror contained a distortion. Subtle, true. But it set her apart. Ashley, the one who was different. Ashley, forever the outsider. The outcast.

Tears choked her and she cleared her throat, fighting them off. Wishing she could fight off the ache in the pit of her gut as easily, wishing she could find something to fill the empty, hurting place inside her.

Ashley passed a hand over her eyes. What was happening to her? It was as if she was becoming a person she didn't recognize. One filled with fear and rage. At times vengeful, others repentant. One who wanted to fit in but who always felt alienated, who longed for love but was afraid to allow anyone near her.

Why couldn't she let down her guard? With a man or anyone else? Why couldn't she let herself be loved?

Ashley blinked against the tears that blinded her. As she did, her vision cleared. Beside the photograph, also held by a refrigerator magnet, was a note from Boyd, informing Mia that he was going to be very late and that she shouldn't wait up.

The note's meaning registered and her equilibrium returned. Fall in love and end up like her sisters? One constantly fighting for her independence, the other too dependent even to try?

Making a face, Ashley opened the door and reached inside for a beer. As she did, she heard the sound of the garage door rumbling up. *Mia. No doubt trunk loaded with packages.* Her sister loved to shop and spent a good portion of her days enjoying Boyd's seemingly endless supply of money.

Ashley shook her head. Doctors. Overpaid, self-proclaimed kings of the universe. She played nicey-nice with them day in and day out—save for a few who were authentic healers, she could do without the lot of them. Her *esteemed* brother-in-law as well.

Ashley opened the bottle of imported brew, then fished around in the cabinet for a glass. The front door opened and closed; she heard the rustle and crackle of shopping bags and Mia humming under her breath. Ashley smiled. Her sister was nothing if not predictable.

Grabbing a handful of mixed nuts from the jar on the counter, she took her beer and headed toward the living room.

She found Mia there, back turned toward her as she bent over the coffee table, still humming under her breath.

"Sunny little tune," Ashley murmured from the doorway. "Where have you been all afternoon? Walt Disney World?"

Mia whirled around, one hand to her throat, the other pressed to her side. "Ashley! What are you doing here?"

"Getting a beer. Wiling away the time until my sister got home." Ashley sauntered into the room, munching on the nuts. "Do I need an invitation to pay a visit to my middle sister?"

"Of course not." Mia smiled weakly. "You scared me, that's all."

"My car's parked in front of the your house. Didn't you see it?"

"No. I must have been daydr—"

"Oh my God, Mia. Is that a gun?"

Mia looked down at the revolver she had clutched in her hand, her expression blank. A moment later, she returned her gaze to her sister's, cheeks pink. "Yes."

"What are you doing with it?"

"Nothing." Looking uncomfortable, Mia turned and stuck the weapon back into the decorative box in the center of the big glass and brass coffee table, then shut the lid with a snap.

"Nothing?" Ashley crossed the room, stopping to stand before her sister. She searched her gaze. It hurt to see her sister's bruises, the yellow and blue that no amount of makeup could hide. "Why do you need a gun, Mia? Planning on getting rid of your husband the old-fashioned way?"

"Don't be stupid."

"I don't think it's stupid." Ashley set her beer on the table, then reached around Mia. She opened the box. Inside rested a pearl-handled, snub-nosed revolver. Without even touching it she could tell it was the real thing, not a toy. "If the bastard were my husband, I'd be tempted. Though I doubt I'd shoot him. Too easy to get caught."

Mia made a sound of exasperation. "Stop it. The

last thing I would even think about is killing my husband.''

''That's where you and I differ, love. If my husband had done *that* to my face, he'd be history. And in short order.'' Ashley reached for the gun, then stopped. ''Is it loaded?''

''Of course not.''

She lifted the gun out of the box, weighing it in her hand. It wasn't nearly as heavy as she had thought it would be. Not nearly as cold. In fact, she rather liked the way it snuggled into her palm. She gripped it in both hands and held it out, police-style. ''Stop, motherfucker! Or I'll blow your brains out!''

Mia started to laugh, though her expression was horrified. ''Ash, you're too much.''

She laughed, too. ''I could get used to carrying one of these. What a rush.'' She handed the gun back to her sister and for the second time, Mia set the weapon back in its box. ''Do you think that's the way Melanie feels every morning when she straps that baby on? All macho and stuff?''

''Knowing Mel? Probably.''

Ashley reached for her beer and took a sip. It was already warmer than she liked. ''So, what's with the gun? Seems like a dangerous thing to have hanging around if you're not planning to whack somebody with it. Loaded or not.''

Mia's smile faded. ''Boyd's been…out a lot at night, and I just thought…for my own protection…''

Her words trailed off. Ashley sobered. ''You don't have to pretend with me. Melanie told me everything. About your suspicions. What Boyd did to you."

Mia brought a hand to her bruised face, wincing, though whether in pain or at the memory, Ashley wasn't sure. "It was awful, Ash. The way Boyd...I was afraid. I still am."

Ashley shook her head. "You don't need a gun, Mia. Just leave him."

"I can't." She shook her head. "I'm afraid of what he might do. He said if I ever tried, he'd...that he'd hurt me."

Ashley drew her eyebrows together, growing more concerned by the moment. More unsettled. Her brother-in-law had always seemed like an arrogant little prick to her, but he'd never seemed violent. But then, their father had been a pillar of the community.

"Being afraid all the time, you can't live that way, Mia."

"I know." She shifted her weight frcm one foot to the other. "When I met him I thought he was...everything. A real Prince Charming. Just for me."

"Almost a god."

"Yeah, almost." She sighed. "In my eyes he was perfect. My knight in shining armor. I thought the rumors circulating about him were based on jealousy, not fact. All that stuff about his wife's mysterious death, about his being questioned by the police, I ignored all that."

"So did I."

"Melanie didn't," Mia murmured, her tone bitter. "But then, Melanie always knows best."

Ashley looked away. It did sometimes seem that way. Melanie was always the smart one. The strong one. The one who made the right choices, good decisions. And even the rare times she did make a mistake—her marriage to Stan being the most notable—she corrected the mistake on her own, without help from anyone. Even her sisters.

Ashley's gaze landed on the pile of shopping bags by the front door. "Looks like you dropped major bucks today. Anything spectacular?"

A brilliant smile lit her sister's face. "A little black dress. I'd show it to you but Boyd—"

"Is going to be out late tonight. A meeting. He left a note on the refrigerator." At Mia's wounded expression, Ashley made a sound of regret. "Sorry, sis."

"It's not your fault."

"No, but I can still be sorry." Ashley touched Mia's arm, heart breaking for her sister. "You're too good for him. Dump his ass."

"I wish it were that easy." She looked at Ashley, her expression suddenly fierce. "And don't you dare say it is. Don't you...*dare*. I've already heard that from Melanie and I'm sick of it."

Turning, she strode to the shopping bags, snatched them up and started down the hall that led to the bedrooms.

Ashley stared after her, stunned. Her sister had always kept her emotions safely hidden—from others and herself. Ashley had decided long ago that Mia found it easier to deny her feelings than to deal with them. And a lot less frightening as well.

So, where had that very unMia-like outburst come from?

Ashley went after her. She found her in the master bedroom, unpacking her purchases, laying each lovingly out on the champagne-colored satin spread. She didn't acknowledge Ashley's presence with so much as a glance.

Ashley leaned against the door frame watching her for a moment before speaking. "Okay, so it's not easy. It's bloody complicated. Happy?"

"Don't be a bitch."

Ashley arched her eyebrows and folded her arms across her chest. "Seems to me I'm not the one who's hormonal here. Which is okay, I applaud you expressing your emotions. It's high time. But I'm not the one who hit you. So don't take it out on me."

Mia's movements faltered, but she didn't look up. "I know. I'm sorry. I guess I'm just mad at the world."

"I can dig that, Mia. I really can."

Her sister looked up, her expression defiant. "But?"

Ashley drew in a deep breath, choosing her words carefully. "The man hit you. He threatened you and frightened you. Maybe I'm simpleminded, but it doesn't seem like you're facing that tough a decision here."

"I know, but Boyd promised he wouldn't do it again and...and it was just that once."

Ashley made a sound of dismay. "My God, Mia. Wasn't once enough?"

Ignoring her, Mia returned her attention to her

purchases. Ashley watched her, silently tallying what her sister must have spent. It added up to hundreds of dollars, maybe more than a thousand. In one afternoon. Mia shopped several times a week.

Suddenly, she got it. Suddenly, she understood. "You know," she said softly, "buying things might make you feel better for a moment, but it can't substitute for love. Nor for tenderness. Or affection."

Mia stiffened. "Excuse me?"

Ashley motioned to the garments Mia had lovingly lined up on the bed. "It's the money, isn't it? That's why you won't leave him?"

Her sister's face flooded with color. "I made a vow in front of God, Ashley. I promised 'for better or for worse.' I have to give him another chance. That's what marriage is all about." She tilted up her chin. "But then, *you've* never been married, so you wouldn't understand."

Hurt took her breath. Anger followed on its heels. "That was a cheap shot, Mia."

"And accusing me of marrying my husband for money wasn't?"

"That's not what I said. I'm just trying to make sense of what makes no sense at all. Namely, why would you stay with a man who's not only unfaithful, but abusive as well?"

"What entitles you to question me, Ash? What do you know about love? Or about commitment? Nothing. And you never will because you close yourself off from everybody."

Ashley took a step backward. Her sister's words pierced to her core, to her every feeling of loneliness and alienation. She saw her future stretching endlessly before her, empty and loveless. She saw herself alone, always alone.

She struggled past the image. "I know what you and Melanie say about me. That I'm a coldhearted bitch who hates men. That I'd sooner kill one than open my heart to one."

"That's not true! We don't—"

"Well here's a good laugh for you, Mia. I long for love, too. Especially when I see one of those sappy TV commercials, the ones depicting two tanned and beautiful people walking hand in hand along some exotic beach. I see that, and I want it. Then I get a grip and remind myself that it's all bullshit."

"It's not, Ash." Mia reached for her hand. "In the end, love is all there is. It's—"

"A guy you trust punching you in the face, is that what you're about to say? Or one who holds you down and forces himself into—" She choked the words back. "I'm not the one with a problem, Mia. You are. Because you believe in fairy tales."

"No." Mia shook her head. "You have the problem. You're so afraid of being loved, you push everybody away. You refuse to see that there can be good—"

"What's the gun for?" she demanded, cutting her sister off, unable to bear hearing another word. "Hoping Melanie will swoop in like when we were kids and save the day? Hoping she'll put a bullet in your bastard husband's brain?"

"Stop it!" Mia cried, grabbing her arms and

shaking her. "Just stop! I hate when you get like this. What's wrong with you, Ashley?"

Tears flooded Ashley's eyes. She loved her sisters so much. So why couldn't they understand her? Why couldn't they make her feel better? Why couldn't anyone?

She fought the tears back, focusing on her pain and rage—the twin demons she relied on so often. Her friends. Her only friends. She would show Mia. And Melanie. Someday they would know what she had done for them. And they would be grateful. And sorry. So very sorry.

"Screw you!" Ashley wrenched free of her sister's grasp. "There's nothing wrong with me. You'll see. And when you do, you'll beg me to forgive you, Mia. You'll *beg*."

10

The tequila burned as it slid down Connor Parks's throat. He drained the glass anyway, refilled it, then tossed back another. Then another. He knew from experience that three shots, tossed back in quick succession, would catapult him to the edge of inebriation. From there he could sip and savor his way clear over.

In the past five years, he had become an expert on the numbing effects of alcohol.

Connor poured another finger of the liquor, then set the glass on the coffee table, on top of a folder stamped *Photos—Do Not Bend.* That folder was not alone, other folders, papers and files covered every available inch of the table, the floor around it and even the seat of an easy chair. The photos and files, the documents they contained, represented the past five years of his life. They represented his quest to find a killer and bring him to justice.

Not just any killer—the man who had taken his sister from him. His sweet Suzi. His only family.

Connor picked up one of the files, but didn't open it. He knew its contents by heart, could recite the words contained within by rote, the way he could the Declaration of Independence as a kid.

His sister's killer's profile.

He had spent every available moment of the last
five years studying it and the corresponding crime-
scene evidence. Without authorization, he had used
the Bureau's resources to search for and investigate
similar crime scenes and similar signatures. In the
process, he had thrown away a marriage, a career,
his reputation.

Even so, he was no closer to catching Suzi's
killer now than he had been the day he'd been no-
tified of her disappearance.

Connor passed a hand over his eyes, his head
heavy from too much booze and too little sleep. A
part of him wanted to give up, if only for the night.
He forced himself to go on, to focus on the facts,
such as they were. Though Suzi's body had never
been found, that she had been murdered had been
obvious from the scene.

*The scene. Her pretty patio home in Charleston.
The one he had helped her buy.*

With his mind's eye, Connor hurtled back five
years to that house, to that awful day. The day the
Charleston police had called him at Quantico and
informed him that it appeared Suzi had been missing for four days, that foul play was suspected.

*Connor stood in Suzi's foyer, orchestrated pan-
demonium reigning around him, his stomach in his
throat. As a professional courtesy, the CPD had
promised Connor and a fellow profiler immediate
access to the as yet unprocessed scene—if they
could be there ASAP. He had caught the first flight
home.*

*He surveyed his surroundings, the hairs on his
forearms and the back of his neck prickling. Violent*

death left an indelible mark on a place. It possessed an aura. Palpable. Resonant. Even when a scene appeared normal at first glance, as this one did, death made its presence felt.

Connor moved forward, deeper into the house. Some scenes shouted, some whimpered. He had seen it all. Scenes painted red by blood and gore; others as clean as a hospital room. He had seen murder victims who'd been brutalized beyond recognition and others who appeared more asleep than dead. And everything in between.

Or so he'd thought. Until today.

Suzi. It couldn't be.

Despair assailed him again. He fought it off and focused on the job before him. The UNSUB had taken great pains—and a good bit of time—to clean up after himself. That level of comfort told Connor much: that the UNSUB hadn't feared being disturbed or discovered, that he had been familiar with the neighborhood, maybe even the house.

Connor crossed to the bloodstains that marred the carpet in front of the fireplace and squatted in front of them. The UNSUB had attempted to scrub them away. Connor snapped on a pair of latex gloves, then inspected the largest stain. It was still damp. He brought his fingers to his nose. They smelled of pine cleaner.

He shifted his gaze, moving it over the room. Judging by the impressions in the thick pile, the carpet appeared to have been recently vacuumed. His gaze landed on the hearth, stopping on the set of iron fireplace tools. Broom. Shovel. Log iron. The fourth hook stood empty.

Connor made a mental note to ask the detectives about both observations, then moved on. The kitchen was clean save for the two bloody bath towels shoved into the garbage pail under the sink. They reeked of pine cleaner and had been used, he deduced, to scrub at the stains in the family room. He removed them from the trash can, carefully examined them, then searched the rest of the can's contents.

"Find anything?"

He looked up to find Ben Miller, the Charleston satellite office SAC, standing in the kitchen doorway, watching him, his expression sympathetic.

"An empty bottle of pine cleaner," Connor answered. "A Diet Coke can. Banana peel."

"We did as you requested, everything's as it was the first time the police came through. The CPD forensic guys are collecting evidence behind you."

"I appreciate it, Ben."

"You understand, of course, that officially you're not involved. That officially the Bureau's not involved."

"I understand." A lump formed in his throat, Connor looked quickly away. "Make sure they collect the vacuum bag. I suspect the UNSUB vacuumed the scene."

"I'll do that."

"And, Ben?" The man looked back at him. "One of the fire irons is missing. The poker. Anybody run across it?"

"Not that I know of. I'll check it out and get back to you."

Connor nodded and moved on to the hallway that

led to the two bedrooms. The hall storage closet was open, several suitcases spilling out. The way they would if Suzi had rifled through them, frantic to pack and leave for a trip.

He placed his hands on his hips and stared at the cases. Two cases, not three. One was missing; he knew because he had bought her that set for her high-school graduation.

What, he wondered, was this UNSUB telling them?

He stepped into the bedroom. Suzi's bed was unmade, the louvered closet doors open. Clothes hung askew; several wire hangers were scattered on the floor in front of the open door. Frowning, he crossed to the closet, staring at the contents, sorting through the facts in his mind.

After their parents' death, Suzi had become obsessively neat. Disorder had brought her to tears. The shrink he had taken her to had explained that losing her parents had thrown Suzi's life into chaos. Her eleven-year-old world, which had been safe and predictable, was suddenly, frighteningly out of control. She found comfort in orderliness, the doctor had contended, because orderliness represented a way for her to control her environment.

She had never outgrown it.

She would never have left her things this way, Connor acknowledged. No matter how big a rush she had been in.

Connor turned away from the closet and crossed to the dresser. The lingerie drawer was open. On the right side of the drawer, the sexy stuff was folded neatly—lacy panties, sheer nighties and filmy gowns. Apparently undisturbed. On the left side, in a jumble, were the cotton panties and bras, the slips and panty hose. The serviceable stuff a woman might wear every day, for herself, not a lover.

From outside came the sharp blare of a horn. Connor jumped, the sudden sound catapulting him back to the present. He blinked, momentarily disoriented, then passed a hand over his face, equilibrium returning.

He reached for his tequila, but set it back down without drinking, thoughts returning to Suzi's death. He ticked off what the scene had told him, reviewing facts he knew by heart. Judging by the attempted cleanup and staging, Suzi's killer was a highly organized individual. Intelligent. Educated.

Additionally, there had been no signs of a forced entry. Her bed had been unmade, the nightstand light on, her reading glasses neatly folded on top of an open book on the bed. That had led him to believe that the attack had occurred at night and that Suzi had known her killer.

He narrowed his eyes, working to fit the pieces together, looking for the one that was missing, the one that would bring the complete picture into focus. Suzi and the UNSUB had progressed from the foyer to the family room where, judging by the bloodstains, the attack had occurred. The UNSUB had disabled her with the missing fireplace poker, probably with one or several blows to the back of the head.

Connor picked up the shot glass. His hand shook so badly some of the alcohol sloshed over the glass's rim. He tossed the remainder back, returning to his mental survey. Judging by the clumsiness and indecision he'd found at the scene, the UNSUB wasn't a seasoned criminal. Nor did Connor believe Suzi's murder had been planned. Her attacker had seen the opportunity and taken it. After the fact, he had not only tried to clean up the scene, he had tried to hide the crime by taking the body and staging it to look as if Suzi had packed a bag and run off.

Connor swore, the brutally uttered word a shock to the silence. But with everything he knew, he was missing something. Some scrap of evidence, an obvious link. It didn't make sense.

Connor brought a hand to his eyes, struggling to see past his own emotions, to keep focus on this UNSUB's signature. Instead, he recalled his and Suzi's last conversation, a hurried phone call she had made to him at Quantico. One in which she had revealed that she was frightened. One in which she had begged him to come home.

"Con, it's me. I need your help."

Not again. Not now. "Suz, can this wait?" Connor glanced at his watch, impatient, overwhelmed by a caseload that seemed to grow with each second that ticked past. "I'm leaving for the airport in twenty minutes and I have about a hundred details to tie up before I go."

"No! It can't wait, Con. This time it's really serious, it's... I'm seeing this guy and...he, I..." She sucked in a broken-sounding breath. "I found out he's married."

His sweet, flighty sister always seemed to attract one kind of loser or another. He bit back a sound of disappointment, glancing at his watch again. "Oh, Suzi, we've been through this already."

"I know, I know. I'm an idiot. All the signs were there. But I...ignored them. Because I didn't want to believe it." Her voice took on a familiar, hysterical edge. "But then I couldn't ignore it any longer and I...I tried to break it off."

"Tried?"

"He threatened me, Con! He told me if I left him, I'd never see another man. Never! I'm really scared. You have to come home, you have to!"

He loved his sister. Twelve years her senior, he had raised her after their parents were killed. He was as much daddy to her as brother. But she was grown now and he had a job to do. A life to lead. In his three years with the Behavioral Science Unit, his sister had called with a dozen different crises. And each time he had dropped everything and raced home.

Not this time. The time had come for her to learn to stand on her own two feet. He told her so.

She began to cry, and he gentled his voice. "I love you, Suzi. But me running home every couple of months to fix your life isn't helping either of us. You have to grow up, baby. The time's come."

"But, you don't understand! This time—"

He cut her off, though it was the hardest thing he had ever done. "I've got to go now. I'll call you when I get back."

He never spoke to her again.

Connor swore, hatred burning in the pit of his gut—hatred of himself, his mistakes, the bastard she had been seeing. For he was certain Suzi's married lover was also her murderer.

But the man, whoever he was, had covered his tracks well. A familiar fury built up inside him, one born of guilt, frustration at his limitations and disbelieving horror.

Connor breathed deeply. The taste in his mouth turned, becoming foul, like piss and day-old beer. He knew the type of man who seduced, battered, then in a possessive, jealous rage, killed a bright, beautiful young woman like his sister—he knew the type because he had seen their handiwork all too often.

Connor brought his glass to his lips, hoping to wash away both the taste in his mouth and the images in his head, of Suzi and the countless other victims, of the unimaginable and unthinkable that through his work had become the everyday. Of Joli Andersen and the terror he had seen in her lifeless eyes.

No amount of drink would rid him of the images—he had tried before. The best he could hope for was oblivion.

It would have to do.

His doorbell rang, impeding his progress to that end. Muttering an oath, he stood and made his way to the front door, ready to chew out whatever unfortunate had happened onto his porch.

He flung open the door. Steve Rice stood on the other side.

Connor glared at him. "What?"

"Nice welcome." The man smiled, obviously

undaunted. "Should I consider that an invitation in?"

"Suit yourself." Connor swung the door wider and stepped aside so the other man could enter. Without waiting for him, Connor returned to the couch and his drink.

Steve closed the door, then picked his way around the stacks of paperwork, stopping directly across from Connor. "Mind if I sit?"

"Knock yourself out. Clear a space."

The other man carefully collected the papers that were spread over the seat of the easy chair, arranging them in a neat stack. He laid them on the floor, then sat, his gaze settling on Connor.

"Thirsty?" Connor asked.

"No, thanks. Unlike you, I've grown rather attached to my liver. I think I'd like to keep it."

"Amusing." Connor held his glass up in a mock toast, then drained it. "You here tonight as a friend or a boss?"

When he didn't respond, Connor followed his gaze and saw that the agent was staring at a framed photo on the lamp table. It was a picture of his ex-wife's son, snapped on one of the fishing trips they had taken together. The boy wore an ear-to-ear smile as he proudly displayed the bass he had caught.

Connor reached across and laid the frame flat against the table.

The man turned back to Connor. "Talked to Trish or her boy recently?"

"Not since she left me."

"That was a long time ago, Con. What, a couple years?"

Connor shrugged.

"I remember you being pretty fond of her boy. What was his name?"

Jamey. Connor fisted his fingers. "You going someplace with this, Rice?"

"Just curious."

"Well, fuck off."

The SAC looked at his hands, loosely clasped in his lap. "You have the TV on at all tonight?"

Connor looked up sharply. "Should I have?"

"Cleve Andersen's reward offer was the top story. After all, a hundred-thousand-dollar give-away is headline news. They also ran an accompanying clip of you criticizing the move. I believe you called it bone-headed."

"Which station?"

"All of them. Both the six and ten o'clock broadcasts."

"Shit."

"Yeah, shit." He looked Connor dead in the eyes. "Cleve Andersen's the victim's father. He's an important man in this town. He has connections that don't stop at the state line. Powerful connections. Are you hearing me?"

"I'm hearing you," he said and stood. "But you're not saying anything. Spit it out, Steve."

"First you challenge Andersen in front of a roomful of people, then you talk to the press. Andersen's on the warpath."

"And he's after my scalp."

"He did a little checking up on you this afternoon. Found out that you hit the bottle pretty heavy. Found out about your being censured. About your demotion.''

Connor stiffened. "I still do my job. Better than anybody. And you know it."

"I knew it once." He looked away, then back at Connor, his expression troubled. "You need to stop this, Connor." He motioned to the room, the papers, the bottle. "It's killing you."

Connor laughed, the sound hard and tight. "It'll take more than a little tequila to kill me."

"It's not the tequila I'm referring to. Let Suzi go, Connor. Let her go."

The words hit him with the force of a wrecking ball. "Let her go," Connor repeated, his voice thick. He met the other man's eyes, his burning. "And how the hell do I do that?"

"You just do it."

Emotion choked him. "You don't know shit. You can't imagine what I…what I've—"

A sound passed his lips, drawn from deep inside him, part fury, part pain. "It's my fault, you asshole! She asked me for help, begged me to come home. Instead, I lectured her about standing on her own two feet. I told her the time had come for her to grow—"

He struggled to get a grip on his runaway emotions. "Don't you get it? If I had listened to her, when she asked for help, if I had only—"

He bit the words back and swung away, shaking with impotent rage. With grief and regret.

"I'm sorry, Con." His friend stood and crossed to him. He laid a hand on his shoulder. "I'm recommending you for a leave of absence. Effective immediately.''

Connor turned. ''Because I offended Charlotte's leading citizen? Or because I'm tarnishing the Bureau's sterling image?''

''Look at yourself, you're a wreck. Embarrassing the Bureau is the least of my worries concerning you. I let you keep working like this, you're going to get yourself or another agent killed.''

''Don't do this, Steve.'' He said it evenly, without inflection. It was as close as he would come to begging. ''Without the Bureau, I'll never catch this guy. He'll get away with it, with taking Suzi.''

''Don't you see? He's already gotten away with it. You have to let this go. You have to move on.''

Connor shook his head. ''I've missed something, that's all. With the Bureau's resources—''

''Is that all this job's become for you? A way to fuel your obsession?''

''You don't understand.''

''No, I guess I don't.'' He held out a hand. ''I'll need your badge and weapon. I'm sorry, Connor. You've left me no choice.''

11

The phone awakened Melanie out of a deep sleep. Instantly alert, she grabbed for it, nearly knocking over the remnants of a glass of wine—a rare indulgence for her. "May here," she said, her voice thick.

The caller whispered something Melanie couldn't understand. She frowned. "Officer Melanie May. Who's calling, please?"

"M…Melanie. It…it's m…me."

"Mia?" She glanced at the clock, noting that it was nearly 2:00 a.m. Her heart leaped to her throat. "What's wrong? What's happened?"

Her sister began to sob, the sound deep and broken, as if wrenched from the very center of her being.

Alarmed, Melanie sat up. "Calm down, Mia. Tell me what's wrong. I can't help if you don't."

"It's…Boyd," she managed, the words choked. "He…he—"

Her sister dissolved into tears again, and Melanie climbed out of bed and crossed to her closet, portable phone still clutched to her ear. She opened the closet and pulled out a pair of jeans and a light sweater.

"Honey," Melanie said, fighting to keep panic

out of her own voice, "you have to calm yourself. You have to tell me what happened. What about Boyd?"

For several moments, Mia was quiet save for her very audible struggle for control. Then she spoke, her voice a tinny whisper. "He flew into a rage. He said...he—" Her voice rose. "I'm afraid, Mellie. You've got to help me. You've got to!"

Melanie glanced at her watch, calculating. "Where are you?"

"Home. I...I locked myself in the bathroom, I thought...I thought he was going to break down the door!"

Propping the phone to her ear with her shoulder, Melanie shimmied into her jeans. "Is he there now?"

"No...at least I...I don't think so."

"Good." Melanie got the jeans fastened, then tore off her nightgown and went in search of her bra. "I want you to stay put," she ordered, finding the undergarment and fitting it on. "Do not leave the bathroom. Do you understand?"

Mia murmured that she did, and Melanie nodded. "I'm coming right over."

"But Ca...Casey, you can't—"

"It's spring break, Stan took him to Walt Disney World yesterday." Melanie hooked the bra and yanked the sweater over her head. "I'm leaving now. Promise me you won't leave the bathroom."

When Mia had, Melanie hung up the phone, slipped into shoes and raced for the door. She stopped halfway there and went back for her gun. She wasn't about to take any chances, she thought, and strapped on the weapon. If Boyd was as out of control as Mia said, he could be capable of anything.

Twenty minutes later, Melanie wheeled her car to a stop in her sister's driveway. Jumping out, she ran for the front door. She tried it and found it unlocked. Heart hammering, she eased it open and stepped inside the dark house, unsheathing her weapon as she did.

"Boyd?" she called. "Mia? It's me, Melanie."

No one answered. She flipped on a light and gasped. It looked as if her brother-in-law had gone on a rampage. Chairs were overturned, lamps and knickknacks had been swept to the floor and broken.

"Mia!" she called again, this time sounding as panicked as she felt. Forgetting caution, she raced toward the back of the house and Mia and Boyd's bedroom. She reached the bedroom, then the master bath. She tried the knob; the door was locked. She pounded. "Mia! It's me! Open up!"

From inside she heard a cry, then something clatter to the floor. A moment later the bathroom door flew open and Mia fell into her arms.

"Melanie!" she cried. "Thank God! I was so scared!"

Melanie held her sister tightly, frightened by the way she trembled, by how small and fragile she felt in her arms. "It's okay, I'm here now. I'm not going to let Boyd or anybody else hurt you. I promise."

As the words slipped past her lips, Melanie realized she had uttered nearly the same ones when they were children, too many times to count. Her head filled with memories she would rather forget, of moments spent holding and comforting Mia, just as she was now. Of the times she had raced to her sister's rescue. Of the first time, only hours after their mother's funeral.

She squeezed her eyes shut against the ugly memories, against the way they hurt. That day Mia had become their father's favorite target, though Melanie had never understood why. Like an animal in the wild that turns on one of its own litter, he had done his best to destroy Mia. He would have, if not for Melanie. And Ashley. As often as they could, they had closed ranks, thus diverting his rage onto themselves.

And at thirteen, when his verbal and physical abuse of Mia had become sexual, Melanie had threatened his life. He had awakened from a deep sleep to find his arms and legs restrained by ropes and his firstborn twin holding one of his hunting knives to his throat. If he touched Mia like that again, Melanie had promised, she would kill him.

Melanie had meant what she said—he must have believed she did, too, because the sexual abuse had stopped.

Melanie tightened her arms around her sister, aching for her. Why Mia? she wondered. The most defenseless, most sensitive of the three of them? And now, why this? Why couldn't her sister have the love she deserved?

Why couldn't any of them?

Melanie drew away from her twin, holding her

at arm's length, meeting her gaze evenly. "Did he touch you?"

Mia shook her head, struggling, Melanie saw, to find her voice. "I didn't give him the chance. He went crazy and I grabbed the portable phone and ran. I locked myself in here...he tried to kick in the door...I thought he would. Then he just... stopped."

She drew in a shuddering breath. "I imagined him hiding out there, trying to trick me into coming out. I imagined him getting his gun—"

"He has a gun?"

Mia blanched. "He...I...I don't know...I meant, I imagined him getting *a* gun. I was so afraid, Mellie!"

Melanie glanced at the bathroom door. The white paint was marred by ugly, black heel marks. She turned back to her sister. "Have you called the police?"

"What?"

"The police. Have you called them?"

"No, I—"

"That's okay. We can do it now. I'll get the phone." She retrieved it from the bathroom floor and brought it to Mia. She held it out.

Mia shrank back and Melanie frowned. "You have to do this, Mia. You have to protect yourself. You have to stop him."

"I can't."

"Mia—"

"I couldn't bear for everyone to know!" She covered her face with her hands. "I'm so ashamed."

Melanie put the phone aside and took her sister's hands away from her face. They were cold, trembling. "Look at me, Mia. *You* have nothing to be ashamed of. He's the one who'll be embarrassed by this. He's the one who—"

"He'll get off. You know he will. He'll deny the whole thing, and everyone will believe him. I'll be labeled the pathetic, attention-starved wife."

"You have proof. Look at this place, the heel marks, the—" Even as she said the words, she knew that her sister had little beside bruises that were nearly two weeks old. Not even a 911 call.

"You see that I'm right, don't you?" Mia shook her head, tears slipping down her cheeks. "It'll be my word against his. Who do you think everyone will believe?"

Melanie had faced a similar prejudice when she left Stan, though he had never physically abused her. It had infuriated her then, it did now. She was sick and tired of a system that allowed the rich and powerful to run roughshod over those more vulnerable. They should be held accountable. Someone should make them pay.

Mia hung her head. "It's my fault. I questioned him about where he was going. I should have known better. I should have left well enough alone."

"Don't do that, Mia. That's a victim talking. It's bullshit." Melanie caught Mia's shoulders and shook her lightly. "He's your husband. You had every reason, every right, to question him."

"But I—"

"No! You will not become a victim. I will not

allow it, do you hear me? You've come too far.''
She shook her again, forcing her to meet her eyes.
''You have to leave him, Mia. You *have* to. It's the
only way.''

Mia started to cry again, nodding her head.
''You're right, Mellie. But I don't want to. I want
my marriage. The one I thought I had. The one I
dreamed of.''

Melanie's eyes filled with tears of sympathy. And
of understanding. She drew her sister back into her
arms. ''I know, sweetie. I want the same thing. I
want what I thought I had. But it's not going to
happen. You have to leave him before he really
hurts you.''

12

Melanie stayed with her sister until dawn. After straightening up the house, they curled up together on the king-size bed, sipping Irish creams and remembering the good times from their childhood, recalling friends they had known and fun places they had lived. Before long, Mia had nodded off.

Even after her sister had been soundly asleep, Melanie had agonized over leaving her. But she'd been forced to. It had been obvious Boyd wasn't going to return and she had hoped to get in an hour of shut-eye before having to get ready for work. Instead, she had lain awake, staring at the ceiling and worrying about her sister.

Though reassured by Mia's promise to leave her husband, Melanie wasn't optimistic she would keep her word. It wasn't uncommon for women caught in abusive relationships to marshal their personal reserves during a crisis, only to crumble as soon as the crisis passed. Or the man apologized and promised to do better.

Boyd had to be held accountable, Melanie had decided as she stood under the shower's stinging spray. He had to know his behavior was being monitored and that it wouldn't be tolerated. She wanted him to know that *she* wouldn't tolerate it.

She had a plan.

"Morning, Bobby," she called to her partner as she arrived at headquarters later that morning.

"Morning, Mel." Her eternally youthful partner looked up from the sports section of the *Charlotte Observer,* and his eyebrows shot up. "Looking good today, Mel-babe. Up all night with a sick kid?"

"In a way." She dropped her purse beside her desk and headed for the coffeepot.

He unfolded his lanky frame, grabbed his empty cup and followed her. He held out the cup, then frowned. "Wait a minute, I thought Casey was in Orlando with his dad."

"He is. Different kid." She filled him in on how she had spent the previous evening, though she didn't elaborate on her sister's troubles. "I thought we might pay the good doctor an unofficial official call."

Bobby grinned. "And shake him up a bit."

"You got it."

"I'm in."

Melanie added powdered creamer to her coffee and sipped. "Anything big happen overnight?"

"Not unless you call the high school being rolled big." He grinned. "Oh, and old Mrs. Grady reported a masked bandit in her trash again."

Melanie rolled her eyes. Her brush with real detective work had made WPD business-as-usual seem more pointless than it had before. "Raccoon?"

"Irritating little bastards, aren't they? She demanded immediate action."

"Poor Will." Melanie imagined pudgy, baby-faced Will Pepperman, the officer in charge of the night shift, dispatching a cruiser to the scene of the crime. No doubt he had gotten an earful from the lucky patrolman who had answered that call. Better him, though, than Mrs. Grady. Shrill would be a kind way to describe her voice.

They crossed to Bobby's desk and she perched on the corner. "How about the phone banks? Anything come in?"

"Anything promising? No. Anything at all? Yes." He handed her a printout. Melanie skimmed her gaze down the pages, a ball of frustration forming in the pit of her gut. "There must be a hundred calls here."

"A hundred and twelve. But who's counting?"

She made a sound of resignation. "Top or bottom?" she asked, referring to which half of the list he wanted.

"Sorry to ruin your day, but what you're holding *is* the top half of the list." She groaned and he made a sound of sympathy. "It does suck, doesn't it?"

"Royally." She met his eyes, wondering not for the first time how her partner remained so upbeat about the job. She decided to ask him. "You've been with the WPD ten years, how do you not let all this inconsequential...*busywork* get to you?"

He was quiet for a moment. When he answered, his tone was measured, for once, one hundred percent serious. "I'm thirty-eight years old, Melanie. I have four kids and a wife to support and only a two-year degree from a junior college. I make as much here as a CMPD guy at the same rank, get to carry a gun and look like a hotshot hero to my kids, but at the end of the day I know old Mrs. Grady's masked bandit isn't going to make my wife a widow and my kids fatherless. And that counts for a lot with me.''

Melanie looked at her partner with newfound respect. And also with a modicum of guilt—she should feel the same way because of Casey. But she didn't. Ambition, longing for real police work, burned in the pit of her gut. Some days it felt as if the blaze was going to consume her whole.

She forced a smile and held up her half of the list. ''Okay, Mr. Sunshine, paint this a happy shade of rose for me. Quick, while I still remember how to smile.''

''My pleasure.'' He tapped the printout. ''The fact is, about a third of this list can be eliminated as outright fabrications.''

She arched her eyebrows. ''That's supposed to make me smile?''

''Give me a minute. Another third,'' he continued, ''can be eliminated simply—a phone call, a computer check, stuff like that.''

''But the rest we'll have to follow through in a big way.'' She dropped her head into her hands. ''We'll be chasing down dead ends all day!''

''Not all day.'' Bobby grinned and leaned toward her. He lowered his voice. ''After handling those irritating, go-nowhere leads, we can pay a visit to your fist-happy brother-in-law. And dish him some serious shit.''

She lifted her face. ''The day's starting to look up at last.''

His expression became positively devilish. "I live to please, babe."

Several hours later Melanie and Bobby entered the lobby of Queen's City Medical Center. Located only five minutes from the Whistlestop PD, they had saved this stop for last—a kind of reward for the previous hours of grunt work.

They crossed to the information desk. "Hello," Melanie said to the woman staffing the desk. She held up her shield. "I'm Officer May. This is Officer Taggerty. We need to speak with Dr. Donaldson. Is he in?"

The woman's eyebrows shot up. "You can't mean Dr. Boyd Donaldson?"

Not drop-dead-gorgeous, ever-so-charming, top-of-his-class Donaldson? Melanie smiled sweetly. "Why, yes. That's exactly who I mean. Is he in?"

The woman hesitated, then nodded. "I'll ring his office." She did, then after a moment turned back to Melanie. "He doesn't answer. Would you like me to page him?"

Melanie said she would and in a matter of minutes he answered his page. The receptionist turned her back to them and spoke softly into the phone, no doubt informing the great Dr. Donaldson—as respectfully as possible—that the police were here to see him.

The woman hung up the phone and turned to them. "He'll be right down."

"Thank you." With a wink at Bobby, Melanie turned her back to the bank of elevators, pretending interest in the people coming and going through the hospital's front doors. She didn't want Boyd to see her right away. She knew that her brother-in-law liked to be in control of every situation from the git-go. This was her way of making certain that this time he wasn't.

They didn't have long to wait. He fell right into her ploy, assuming Bobby was the officer here to see him. "Afternoon, Officer," Boyd said, tone genial. "Dr. Boyd Donaldson. How can I help you?"

Melanie turned and smiled sweetly. "You're pretty good at sucking up to the cops. Where'd you get the practice?"

For a split second he looked baffled. Then a dull red flush spread over his handsome features. "Is this some kind of joke?"

"A joke? I don't know what you mean."

"You told Nancy this was an official call."

"Not at all." She turned apologetically toward the receptionist. "I'm sorry if we gave you that impression."

The woman looked upset and Boyd smiled re-assuringly at her. "Nancy, this is my sister-in-law. She's quite the little comedian." He turned to Melanie. "I really don't have time for a family visit right now. Call my secretary and make an appointment."

His attitude didn't surprise Melanie. Their relationship had always been adversarial. She had set the tone right off the bat by begging her sister not to marry him. He had followed her lead by doing his best to keep her and Mia apart after they were married, going so far as to tell his new bride that her twin was not welcome in his home.

He started to turn away. She stopped him with a hand to his arm. "Make time. Now."

He glanced pointedly at her hand. "Excuse me?"

"It's about Mia."

He hesitated, glanced at his watch, then made a sound of annoyance. "Fine." He motioned toward a quiet corner of the lobby. "But you'll have to make it quick. I'm due in surgery in forty minutes."

Melanie held on to her temper only until the three of them were in place. Then she let it rip. "Your concern for my sister's health is touching, Boyd. Truly awe-inspiring."

"I see nothing to be concerned about. I saw her this morning, she was fine. If she'd been in an accident or was ill, you would have told me up front. Am I wrong?"

He arched his eyebrows, the picture of arrogance, and Melanie's blood boiled. "You son-of-a-bitch." She took a step toward him. "I know about you, Dr. Donaldson. I know what you're doing and it had better stop."

His expression didn't change, though Melanie thought she saw a flicker of panic in his eyes.

She took another step closer. "If you hit my sister again," she said, not bothering to keep her voice low, "I won't be responsible for my actions."

Several people glanced their way and Boyd flushed. "If you're talking about that ridiculous black eye, Mia has no one to blame but herself. The woman has two left feet. In fact, because of her clumsiness, I was forced to attend the hospital's annual patrons' party alone. I didn't appreciate that.''

As if sensing that she was about to blow, Bobby laid a hand on her arm in silent warning. She heeded the warning, taking a moment to calm herself before speaking. ''That story,'' she began softly, ''might work for your golf mates and scalpel buddies, but not for me. I know about you and I promise if you touch my sister again—''

One of the hospital's security guards rushed over. ''Everything okay, Dr. Donaldson?''

''Fine.'' Boyd smiled easily. ''My sister-in-law's a bit confused about something. But she was just leaving. Weren't you, Melanie?''

She ignored the out. Leaning toward him, she lowered her voice. ''If you hurt my sister again, I won't be held accountable for my actions. Do you understand?''

A small, smug smile tipped the corners of her brother-in-law's mouth. ''That sounded like a threat.'' He looked at the security guard, then at Bobby. ''You both heard her, you're my witnesses.'' He returned his gaze to hers. ''I'd advise you to learn to control that temper of yours, sister dear. I have the feeling it's going to get you into trouble one day.''

13

Boyd watched Melanie walk away, his lips curved into a small, amused smile. He thanked the security guard, apologized for his sister-in-law's behavior, then excused himself—the very image of calm, control and self-confidence.

Save for the telltale twitch above his right eye.

He cursed the twitch and breathed deeply through his nose. Damn his sister-in-law. Sanctimonious, nosy bitch. How dare she confront him? How dare she come to his hospital and challenge him? Here, he was God. He called the shots—others bent to his will, deferred to his opinion.

She knew nothing about him. *Nothing.*

On his way past the information desk, he glanced over and found the receptionist studying him, her gaze speculative. The twitch became a spasm. That was how it started. A speculative gaze. A murmured question. A whisper, a rumor, an accusation.

He sent the woman a curt smile, and she ducked her head, obviously embarrassed at having been caught staring at one of the most important people at Queen's City Medical Center. She should be, he thought. He could have her fired. Today. One call and she would be out.

For a moment, he considered doing just that, then

discarded the notion. That would have the opposite effect he desired—singling out the woman in any way would draw attention to him and set tongues wagging. No, his smartest move would be to pretend the woman didn't exist and today's episode had never happened.

He made his way to his office, nodding to colleagues he passed, enjoying the way they looked at him. The way they looked *up* to him.

He intended to keep it that way.

Boyd unlocked his office door and stepped inside, closing it behind him. Melanie had accused him of striking his wife. Big deal. Nobody ever went to jail for that. If Melanie May even suspected the truth about him, he wouldn't be standing here now, let alone be the chief of thoracic surgery at one of the most respected medical centers in the Southeast.

No, Boyd decided. She was just blowing hot air, up in arms over his and Mia's disintegrating marriage.

Leave it to Mia to run crying to her sister. Spoiled, sniveling little twit.

He shook his head. When he'd married Mia, he thought her the perfect choice. As a nurse, she had been familiar with hospital politics and had possessed the social skills necessary to further his position within the hospital hierarchy. She'd looked good on his arm and most importantly, been docile, easily intimidated and absolutely enamored with him and the life-style that marriage to him would afford her.

He hadn't factored into his decision that her hellcat twin sister was a cop.

A cop. A sensation akin to panic settled in the pit of his gut. He had been so careful—about the women he chose, where he found them.

Not about all the women he chose. He had made mistakes.

He crossed to his desk and sank into his chair, only then allowing his guard to slip. Cops had a way of sniffing things out. What if his sister-in-law started snooping around asking questions of his previous colleagues and employer? Charleston was a lot smaller than Charlotte, people talked. What might she be able to dig up? *Who* might she be able to dig up?

Boyd fought the panic off. Melanie May was a two-bit cop from a municipality the size of the average shopping mall. How much harm could she do?

He snorted with disgust. None. Melanie May was no more dangerous to him than a mall cop.

14

Fate was a fickle creature. Sometimes it smiled on those least worthy, protected those deserving punishment, while turning its back on the good and the meek.

Not so Death. Death was just. Evenhanded. Death relied not on whimsy or chance but on forethought and planning. On righteousness.

The time had come. For this man, like the others, to pay. For crimes unpunished. For sins against the weak. Against those for whom justice was an empty promise.

Death emerged from the shadow cast by the restaurant and crossed the parking lot, heading toward the row of fruit trees that lined the lot's back edge. The trees were in full bloom, the blossoms a delicate white, fragrant. There, parked under a canopy created by their branches, the man's car waited.

Death reached the automobile and paused to breathe in the heavenly scent. To enjoy. The scent, yes. But the moment as well. The moment of victory over evil, goodness over might.

The time had come.

As was the man's habit, he had left the car's windows partially lowered. A dangerous habit when parked so near such sweet flowers. Foolhardy. Especially if one had an allergy to bee venom. Especially if a single, unexpected sting at an inopportune time might cause the throat to close, the blood pressure to drop, the heart to eventually stop.

Death carried a small, white bag—the kind used to bring home take-out food or bakery items. One printed with the name and logo of the restaurant behind him. From inside the bag came an angry hum. Death's messengers demanding release. Retribution.

"Soon," Death murmured, unfolding the bag's top and quickly tossing it through the car's rear, driver-side window. It hit the edge of the seat, then tumbled to the floor. The bag opened fully and Death's small but potent messengers came forth.

15

Melanie swung into the strip-mall parking lot, took the first available spot she came upon, hurriedly collected her purse and duffel bag, then climbed out of the car. The night air was slightly balmy, an indication that spring had more than arrived.

She slammed the door shut, locked it and started forward. She was running late for her tae kwon do class. In the couple of days since Cleve Andersen first announced his reward offer, the calls had poured in. One at the last minute had kept her well past shift change. But if she rushed, she could be on the mat in time to begin with the class. Her instructor did not appreciate tardiness, especially from his black belts. He thought it showed a lack of both discipline and respect.

"Officer May?"

Melanie stopped, looked over her shoulder at the blond woman hurrying to catch up with her. "ADA Ford, this is a surprise."

Veronica Ford walked up to her. She indicated Melanie's duffel. She had a similar one hooked over her own shoulder. "Seems we have more in common than wanting to nail the bad guys."

"It would seem so." They fell into step together. "You're a black belt?"

"Third-degree. You?"

"First." Melanie opened the dojang door, allowing Veronica to enter before her. They headed toward the dressing room. "When did you start here?"

"Two weeks ago. I was going to another dojang across town, but the fit was wrong."

Melanie understood. Each dojang had its own atmosphere; each instructor his own philosophy on training and martial-arts etiquette. She had tried several schools before settling on this one.

The two women quickly dressed-out, exchanging street clothes for the traditional white gis and pulling their long hair back with clips, then headed out to the training room. Black belts could use the dojang anytime it was open or attend any of the half-dozen one-hour slots the instructor had set aside for black belts only.

Melanie preferred the black-belts-only sessions for several reasons, the biggest being the ability to find a sparring partner who outclassed her. She had decided up front she wasn't going to pursue this discipline halfheartedly. If it was worth her time, and she believed it was, she was going to push herself as far as her physical abilities would take her. It hadn't been easy. A born cupcake, she had suffered through bruises and torn muscles, wounded pride and tears of frustration.

The day she earned her black belt had been one of the proudest of her life.

Melanie and Veronica warmed up. Tae kwon do

relied heavily on kicking techniques, employing a wide range of spins, leaps and kicks that were dazzling to watch but difficult to perform. They required the martial artist to be in good physical condition and incredibly limber.

Melanie had been at the discipline for five years and practiced a minimum of three times a week, but she still stretched for at least ten minutes before each session. Veronica, she saw, did the same.

Melanie eyed the other woman—she sat on the mat, legs spread into a wide vee. As she watched, the woman bent slowly forward until her chest touched the floor. Veronica Ford, Melanie thought, had not been born a cupcake.

She braced her foot on the waist-high practice bar and bent forward until she touched her forehead to her knee. Her hamstring complained. Loudly.

"Do you hate this part as much as I do?" Melanie asked, grimacing.

"More," Veronica answered. She gritted her teeth, bending forward once more and holding the stretch. "But it's a necessary evil. Like salads for lunch and panty hose."

Melanie laughed and switched to her other leg. "You do have a way with words, Counselor."

They finished stretching in silence, then moved on to their Poomse, a prearranged routine of blocks, strikes, punches, kicks and stances, similar in concept to a gymnast's floor-exercise routine.

"Want to partner for sparring?" Veronica asked, momentarily breaking concentration.

Melanie noted the other woman's moves. They

were beautiful—sharp, precise and strong. "If you promise not to totally humiliate me, sure."

"It's a deal. Freestyle?" Veronica asked, referring to a type of sparring where either opponent was allowed to attack at will, without notice of when, where or how the attack would come. It was the most advanced of the sparring techniques and the most challenging.

Melanie, finished with her Poomse, shook her head. "Are you kidding? I'm feeling outclassed here. Why don't we do a little one-step attack and defense and once I have a better idea of what I'm up against, move on to semi-free."

Veronica finished her Poomse and shrugged. "Fine with me. But you're way off base with the outclassed thing. We're pretty evenly matched."

"Said the spider to the fly."

They took their positions, facing each other, attacker and defender, each in the ready position. Melanie took the attack, calling it first.

She threw a direct punch, aiming at Veronica's head. "Kiai!"

The other woman blocked it easily, then returned with a left punch to Melanie's chest, stopping just short of actually touching her.

They bowed, then repeated the procedure, varying between kicks and punches, taking turns attacking and defending.

The remainder of the session passed in what seemed like the blink of an eye. Melanie was winded but exhilarated. It was the best workout she'd had in some time. So good, in fact, she suspected she would be sporting sore muscles tomorrow.

She told Veronica so as they made their way back to the dressing room. The attorney smiled. "Thank *you* for the opportunity to hone my skills."

"Right. You didn't even break a sweat. You're good."

Obviously pleased with the compliment, she smiled. "I love it, actually. It's the only time in my life that I actually *like* to sweat."

Melanie laughed. "Sorry we never got around to semi-free."

"That's okay. Next time."

They entered the dressing room and chatted about nothing of consequence while they changed into their street clothes. They headed out of the building and into the parking lot.

"You want to grab a cup of coffee?" Veronica asked.

Melanie didn't hesitate. Casey was still in Orlando with his dad, it was Friday night and she was free as a bird.

They chose a coffeehouse not far from the dojang, got their drinks and took a seat outside. The night air was mild; the sky dusted with stars. "I love this time of year," Melanie murmured, adding a sprinkle of sugar to her coffee. "Spring in the Carolinas, no place else measures up."

"I wouldn't know about anywhere else," Veronica said. "I've never lived anywhere but the Carolinas."

"You grew up in Charleston?"

"Mmm. My family was in the furniture business. Markham Industries."

It was a name Melanie recognized, a name anyone who had lived in the Carolinas for long would know. The Markhams were major players in the furniture industry and several Markhams had been in national politics.

"How about you?" the lawyer asked. "Lived here all your life?"

"No way. I was an army brat. Until I was fifteen we lived everywhere."

"The 'we' must include the look-alikes I've seen you with at Starbucks?"

Melanie smiled. "Mmm. Mia and Ashley. My twin and triplet sisters."

After she had explained, Veronica shook her head, her expression amused. "There's nothing ordinary about you, is there?"

"I don't know about that. A divorced working mom, you can't get much more run-of-the-mill than that."

"I must say, together the three of you make quite an impression."

"Yeah, we do." Melanie cocked her head, studying her companion, realizing that Veronica Ford, with her fine-boned features, fair hair and wide-set deep blue eyes, could be mistaken for their fourth sister. Melanie told her so.

"You think?" Veronica smiled. "That'd be nice, I think. I'm an only child."

"Lonely, huh?"

"Very. Though being an only, I was spoiled beyond belief.'' Veronica took a sip of her latte. ''After you were fifteen, what happened then?''

''My dad retired his commission and opened up a coffee shop here in Charlotte. And I do mean coffee shop. No lattes, mochas or cappuccinos. Just old-fashioned pot-brewed, and homemade pies.'' She lifted her froth-topped mug. ''Hence my addiction to the stuff.''

''Does he still have the shop?''

''He died four years ago.''

''And your mom?''

''She died when we were young. Breast cancer.''

''I'm sorry.''

Melanie lifted her shoulders. ''It was a long time ago. So, what about you? Aside from being an incredibly indulged, lonely only child, that is.''

Veronica laughed. ''Me? It's almost a cliché, isn't it? The poor little rich girl. Cared for by nannies and housekeepers while her dad grew his empire.''

''Doesn't sound so bad to me.'' A smile tugged at her mouth. ''Beats scrubbing a coffee-shop galley every night. What about your mom?''

Veronica's smile faded. ''Actually, that's another thing we have in common. My mom died when I was young. Thirteen to be exact.''

''We were eleven. What happened?''

''She shot herself. I found her.''

The words landed heavily between them. Melanie made a sound of regret. ''I'm so sorry. I shouldn't have asked. When it comes to mothers, I'm too nosy. Having lost mine, I—''

''Forget it.'' Veronica made a dismissive gesture

with her right hand. "I'm over it, as much as a girl can be over something like that."

Melanie understood those words completely. In a way, neither she nor her sisters were completely over their mother's death. They still grieved; still dealt with feelings of abandonment and betrayal. She imagined, because of the circumstances, those feelings were even more complicated for Veronica, the loss more acute.

The attorney cleared her throat and forced a smile. "I don't know about you, but I think a change of subject is in order. As a topic, dead mothers is a little too intense for a Friday night."

"Thank you." Melanie laughed lightly, enjoying the other woman's sense of humor. "You have a suggestion?"

"Tae kwon do seems neutral enough." She rested her chin on her fist and grinned. "So tell me, Melanie, why tae kwon do?"

She shrugged. "Obvious reasons. I'm a cop. It's an asset."

"Why do I have the feeling that answer's just a little too pat?"

"Because you're a lawyer."

"True." She flashed Melanie a wicked grin. "In that vein, let's consider the facts. First, we've already established that there's nothing ordinary about you."

When Melanie began to protest, Veronica held a hand up to stop her. "Second, the police academy requires all recruits to take a number of hours in self-defense tactics. Most are satisfied with that minimal training. You weren't. Why?"

"Easy. First off, the majority of recruits aren't women facing the possibility of having to take down a perp twice their size and strength. Second, I feel strongly that a woman, any woman, should be able to protect herself."

"Ah-ha."

Melanie looked at Veronica over the top of her cup, eyebrows arched. "Ah-ha what?"

"The real reason."

Melanie shook her head, both amused and annoyed at the woman's insight. Veronica was right. Because of her past, she had felt the need to be able to protect herself long before she had ever become a cop. While still married, she had attended a tae kwon do exhibition tournament and been amazed to see women defending themselves against men double their size. She had made the decision then and there that the martial arts were for her. The very next day she had enrolled in a program.

"Touché," she murmured. "I bet you keep those defense attorneys on their toes. You're good."

"Which is a very nice way of telling me I'm grilling you like a witness on the stand." Her eyes crinkled at the corners. "Sorry, I do that sometimes. Your turn, skewer and grill away."

"Okay. What about you? Why tae kwon do?"

"Same as you, I suppose. I see some pretty gruesome stuff in my line of work. I face the very real existence of violence against women every day. I vowed to myself that I'd never be a victim. Tae kwon do is a way to keep that vow."

They fell into comfortable conversation after

that, discussing everything and nothing, draining their coffees and going back for seconds.

As the minutes passed, they discovered they were alike in many ways—from being fans of police procedurals and true-crime novels, to loving triple-hanky movies and full-fat, double-fudge ice cream. Both had similar, clear-cut views on right and wrong. A moral gray area didn't exist for either of them. Both were fiercely loyal to the ones they loved and to their professions. Both had entered those professions hoping to make a difference in the world.

And both were survivors of troubled marriages, though Veronica was a widow, not a divorcée.

"He had a day meeting in Chicago," Veronica said in response to Melanie's question about how her husband died. "I took him to the airport that morning, the way I always did. Walked him to the gate and kissed him goodbye. That was the last time I ever saw him."

Melanie leaned forward. "What happened?"

"The plane exploded midflight."

"My God." Melanie searched her memory, seeming to recall the accident. "Was that about five years ago?"

"Yeah, it was." Veronica rested her chin on her fist, gaze fixed on a point somewhere in the distance. Or the past, Melanie thought.

"I was devastated at first," she continued. "Of course. Frightened. Confused." She blinked and returned her gaze to Melanie's. "The truth is, in retrospect, that explosion saved my life."

Pink tinged Veronica's cheeks and she shook her

head as if uncomfortable with her own admission. "When I got over the shock, when I was done grieving, I saw the truth. About myself and my life. About the man I had been married to."

"And?"

"He was a bastard. Cruel. Controlling. Critical. But that wasn't the worst part." She met Melanie's eyes. "The worst was, he hadn't taken my independence and self-esteem, I'd given them to him. I'd allowed him that control over my life."

"And you vowed, never again."

"Exactly." She tucked her hair behind her ear. "I'd dropped out of law school halfway through because he'd wanted me to. He needed a real wife, he'd said, not one who was so busy studying she didn't have time to attend to home and husband."

Veronica folded her hands around her mug. "After I got my feet on the ground, the first thing I did was go back and finish my degree."

"I'm impressed."

Veronica shrugged. "It was huge on my part, I see that now. But then...it was like I had been infused with an almost supernatural power. Like the light that had gone off in my head had turned on the power. I felt unstoppable."

"That's where we're different. When I left Stan, I was scared to death every step of the way."

"But you had a child to worry about. I'm sure you were concerned your husband might try to take him away from you."

I still am. It's happening. "It does change things." She glanced at her watch, amazed to see it was nearly 11:00 p.m. "I should go."

Veronica glanced at her own watch. "My goodness, it's so late."

She drained the last of her latte and stood. Melanie collected her purse and followed Veronica to her feet. Together they moved through the café and out to the parking lot.

"By the way," Veronica said as they approached their cars, parked side-by-side, "I stopped by the Blue Bayou for dinner Wednesday night. For that great blackened red fish salad they do and to get a look at your batterer and his girlfriend. He was just the way you—"

"He's dead."

She stopped and turned to Melanie. "Dead? You're kidding, right? I mean, I was just there and—"

"It happened last night. An automobile accident." Melanie jiggled her car keys while she spoke. "But there's a twist to the story. Turns out, Thomas Weiss was highly allergic to bees. He'd parked his vehicle behind his restaurant, near some fruit trees in full bloom. One or more of the bees must have flown into his car because he was stung while driving, several times. Witnesses reported his car weaving all over the road. They also reported seeing him flapping and flailing his arms, as if trying to shoo an insect away. He swerved across two lanes of oncoming traffic and crashed into a concrete embankment."

"Was anyone else hurt?"

"No, thank God. It could have been much worse." Melanie pursed her lips, thinking of what the medical examiner had said. "Although the crash killed him, the bee stings alone would have. He was already in anaphylactic shock when he died.''

Veronica shuddered and rubbed her arms. ''Fate's a strange thing, isn't it?''

''That's for sure. But for me, what was stranger was the girlfriend's reaction.''

''She was all broken up, I bet. Hysterical with grief.''

''All but wailing.''

''I all but wailed when my husband died, too. I'm sure she'll see the light.''

''That's generous of you. I have to say, I wasn't quite so understanding. I can't believe I thought she'd testify against him in court. You were right on the money about that.''

''I've been through it more times than I like to remember.'' Veronica retrieved her car keys from her purse. ''I had a good time tonight.''

''Me, too. Let's do it again.''

''Let's.'' Veronica smiled. ''How about next week, after class?''

''Sounds good.''

Lifting her hand in a final goodbye, Melanie went to her Jeep, unlocked the door and climbed in. She smiled to herself and started the engine. She had enjoyed the evening. How long had it been since she'd been out with a girlfriend? Sure, she saw her sisters, but that was different. They were family and they fit themselves into each other's everyday life.

Tonight had been purely social. And since her divorce, between her responsibility to Casey and her job, she'd had little time left for a social life.

She missed it, she realized. Going out with friends. Howling at the moon every once in a while. Dating.

Beside her, Veronica started her Volvo sedan. On impulse, Melanie lowered her window. "Veronica?" she called.

The woman looked over, then lowered her own window.

"How about lunch next Saturday? I'll see if Mia or Ashley can join us."

"Sure. Sounds fun. I'll call this week and we can decide on a place and time."

"Great. Talk to you then." With a final wave, Melanie backed out of the parking spot, then headed out of the lot. Funny how things happened, she thought, turning onto the wide, tree-lined boulevards Charlotte was known for. Funny how one day a person can be a stranger, the next a friend. How it can happen, just like that.

She smiled again, this time at her own thoughts. However it happened, she was glad Veronica Ford had come into her life.

16

The blood pounded in Boyd's head, the beat primal, intoxicating. It mixed weirdly with the throbbing music pouring forth from the club's sound system—together, the two created a strange, heady brew.

Boyd snaked his way through the crowded room, cruising, scanning faces, at once searching and discarding. He didn't fear being recognized; he wouldn't see any of his business associates here, nor others from his social circle. This establishment catered to swingers. People on the sexual fringe. The hunters. And the hunted.

People like him.

Boyd continued through the club, catching the occasional whiff of perfume as he did. The need for sexual release tightened in his gut, like a fist curling around his internal organs, alternately squeezing and stroking. Punishing and arousing.

He drew in a deep, steadying breath. He had to be careful. He couldn't allow his appetite to drive him. Impatience caused missteps. Each woman was a risk. He had to be smart. Cautious. He was Dr. Boyd Donaldson, he had everything to lose.

His gaze landed on a blonde, older than he usually liked, but potent-looking despite her age. She met his gaze boldly. They stared at one another for long moments, then her painted mouth tipped up in a knowing smile. A tingle raced up his spine, a bellwether of delights to come.

Returning her smile, he started toward her.

17

Melanie disliked lawyers' offices. Intensely disliked them. The hushed atmosphere, the plush carpeting and leather furniture, the smell of lemon wax and dusty law books. Because of Stan. And because nothing good had ever come out of her visiting one.

She hoped to change history today.

Melanie let out a pent-up breath, one she hadn't realized she'd been holding. It was Stan's fault that she was sitting here on this beautiful Friday afternoon, palms damp, heart fast. He had followed through on his threat to suc for full custody of Casey. His lawyer had contacted her this past Monday, almost three weeks after her and Stan's original conversation on the subject.

During that time, she had allowed herself to hope her ex-husband had changed his mind. She, eternal optimist, had allowed herself to believe he had reconsidered. She had hoped that during their time at Disney he had realized Casey should be with his mother.

"Mrs. May?"

Melanie cringed at the title. "Yes?"

"Mr. Peoples will see you now."

"Thank you." Melanie stood and followed the secretary down a corridor lined with bookshelves, filled with law books. One of Casey's preschool teachers had recommended this attorney. She'd had a friend who'd used him when battling her husband for custody of their two children—and she had won.

As far as Melanie was concerned, she couldn't have asked for a better recommendation; she had called Mr. Peoples that very day.

They'd spoken on the phone; he had seemed knowledgeable and pleasant enough. After filling him in on the situation, she'd given him Stan's attorney's name and number.

"Here you are," the receptionist said, stopping outside an office Melanie presumed was Mr. Peoples's. "Sure I can't get you a cup of coffee?"

"I'm sure. Thank you."

The woman rapped on the door, then opened it. The man behind the desk stood and held out a hand. He was the size of a mountain. "Mrs. May, John Peoples."

She crossed and took his hand. "Nice to meet you."

He indicated one of the two leather wingback chairs in front of his desk. "Have a seat."

She did, clasping her hands in front of her.

"Let's get right to it, shall we?"

She nodded. "Did you have a chance to talk to my ex-husband's lawyer?"

"I did." He folded his hands on the desktop in front of him. Melanie noticed that they were fish-belly white and pudgy. So pudgy that the flesh bulged out around his wedding ring.

"He has a very good lawyer," the man said. "One of the best, actually. Very smooth."

"I expected that, Stan being with one of the top firms in Charlotte."

"I'll get to the point. Your ex-husband's going to be hard to beat."

"Excuse me?" He repeated himself, and she shook her head, struggling for composure. It took her a moment to find the breath to speak. "You can't mean that?"

"I'm sorry, Mrs. May. I know that's not what you were hoping to hear. But I have to speak from my evaluation of the facts."

He cleared his throat. She noticed how the collar of his shirt squeezed uncomfortably at his thick neck. How, she wondered, did he breathe?

"Let's look at those facts, shall we?" the lawyer said. "Your ex-husband can provide a more stable home environment for your son, one that includes a father and a mother. Nor does he have a job that could call him away at odd hours without warning. A job, I might add, that puts you in danger's way."

Melanie stared at him. He sounded more like Stan's lawyer than hers, like he had bought Stan's shtick, hook, line and sinker.

She stiffened her spine. "I'm with the Whistle-stop PD, Mr. Peoples. Do you have any idea how I spend my day? How uniquely undangerous it is? How routine? I coax cats out of trees and bust teen-age shoplifters. I listen to complaints from citizens irate over their neighbors' pets or parking habits. Give me a break."

"What about the Andersen case?"

"That was a once-in-a-lifetime occurrence. In

addition, I'm no longer actively participating in that investigation.''

''Be that as it may, it's out there. And your ex-husband's lawyer is going to use it.''

She couldn't believe that the big case she had longed for might contribute to her losing Casey. Tears of frustration and despair stung the back of her eyes and she fought them off. She was a police officer and a single mother, she absolutely could not cry. She would not.

''Your ex lives in one of Charlotte's most prestigious neighborhoods, in a lavish home with a swimming pool. The schools in that district are ranked the best in the state.''

''But—''

He held up a hand to stop her. ''Since your son starts kindergarten next year and you and your ex-husband live on opposite sides of Charlotte, a joint custody arrangement would be impossible. He refuses to relocate. I asked. And your job requires you to make your permanent residence Whistlestop, and unless you're willing to give up your job—''

''Give up my job?'' She fisted her fingers, feeling cornered, helpless. ''And do what? I'm a cop. I love what I do. It's what I studied and trained for. I'm not giving it up.''

Red crept up his fleshy neck. ''It was only a suggestion.''

''Well, it was a bad one. Stan can move. A particular zip code isn't a prerequisite of his job.''

''As I said, he refuses.''

''And so do I.''

''Then a joint custody arrangement is impossible.

If you lose this suit, you will be relegated to weekend visits with your son. Or perhaps, as your husband now enjoys, every other weekend.''

She began to tremble. ''That won't do.''

''I'm sorry.''

''Are you?'' She tipped up her chin, disliking this man with every fiber of her being. ''Do I have to remind you that I'm Casey's mother? That I love him? That I'm an excellent, attentive and loving parent? Doesn't that count for anything?''

''Of course it does.'' He attempted a reassuring smile, but it came off as condescending. ''But your ex-husband's Casey's father. And, according to his lawyer, a good parent. Would you agree with that assessment?''

''Depends on your definition of a good parent,'' she said, hating the bitter edge in her voice.

''Let me rephrase that. Do you believe your ex-husband loves your son? And that he believes he has Casey's best interests at heart?''

''Yes,'' she whispered, a part of her wishing she could claim otherwise, ''I do.''

The attorney cleared his throat again. ''Perhaps you should ask yourself, considering that you're a single parent in a demanding and dangerous profession, if having your son only on weekends would be that much of a hardship?''

She met his cool blue eyes, not believing what she was hearing. ''I'm sorry, what?''

''Perhaps you should ask yourself what's best for your son.''

As his words sank in, Melanie got slowly to her feet, shaking with the force of her anger. ''I know what's best for my son. Being with me, his mother. How dare you suggest otherwise? How dare you suggest I simply give up?''

The lawyer's face mottled and he began to sputter some lame legalese. This time it was she who held up a hand, stopping him. ''Did my ex-husband's *great* lawyer happen to mention how late Stan works at night? Or how often he's out of town on business? That even though he only sees Casey every other weekend now, he still plays a four-hour round of golf every Saturday?''

She paused to breathe. ''It might not have occurred to you, but if he wins custody, he won't be raising Casey, his new wife will. *I'm* Casey's mother, Mr. Peoples. And I intend to raise him.''

''I'm sorry, I just—''

''You are sorry. A sorry excuse for a lawyer.'' She took several steps backward. ''Consider this attorney/client relationship terminated. I'm going to find a lawyer who not only believes I can win, but one who believes I should.''

By Sunday afternoon, Melanie was a wreck. She had left John Peoples's office the Friday before and drove home filled with righteous indignation. Spoiling for a fight, ready to take on Stan and an army of his high-priced lawyers.

However, as the hours had ticked past, her indignation had become self-doubt, then outright terror. Casey had been with his dad again this weekend, and her empty house had mocked her, a reminder of what her day-to-day life would be like should Stan win custody of Casey.

She didn't think she would be able to bear it.

She had immersed herself in the things she usually did on the weekends Casey was with his father—puttering in her small garden, seeing a movie she had been eagerly awaiting, catching up on the chores that had piled up during the workweek. None of those had taken her mind off the custody suit. She had called her sisters, but Ashley was out of town on business and Mia was down with the flu. Veronica had also proved unavailable, preparing for a trial set to begin the next week.

So, Melanie had paced. And raged. And cried. It had been the longest weekend of her life.

Now, it was over. Or, should be. Melanie glanced at her watch and frowned. *Four twenty-two.* Where was Stan? He usually had Casey home before this. She wanted him home before this. It took the child time to get settled back into their routine, for them to catch up. Then came dinner, bath and bedtime— he had preschool the next morning.

Melanie drew in a deep breath, growing angry. But Stan didn't concern himself with things as mundane as baths or a bedtime routine. He never had. Not before their divorce, not since.

She began to pace. What did he know about a four-year-old's schedule? About making sure he got enough sleep or ate a well-balanced meal? What did he know about sniffles and fevers and trips to the pediatrician's office? Nothing.

She flexed her fingers. Damn him for even contemplating taking Casey away from her. Arrogant asshole. He knew nothing about her place in their son's life and heart. And damn that idiot lawyer she'd seen for making her doubt herself. For making her so afraid.

From outside came the sound of a car door slamming shut. Melanie raced to the front door and threw it open.

"Casey!" she cried, acknowledging that she had never been so happy to see anyone or anything as she was to see her son's smiling face at that moment.

"Mom!" He barreled toward her and threw himself into her arms.

She enclosed him in hers, hugging him so tightly and for so long that he wriggled against her grasp.

Even so, she hugged him to her a moment more, breathing in his little-boy scent, letting it momentarily chase away her fears. Finally, she loosened her grasp. "I missed you."

He beamed at her. "I missed you, too." He glanced over his shoulder at his dad, then back at her, all but hopping with excitement. "Guess what, Mom?"

She pushed the curls back from his forehead. "What, hon?"

"Dad got me a puppy."

A sensation like ice water spilled over her. "A puppy?"

"Uh-huh." Casey bobbed his head vigorously. "I named him Spot. Dad says he's a golden retriever."

Under different circumstances she would have been amused and charmed by her son's choice of Spot for a golden retriever—not today, however. Melanie shifted her gaze to Stan, standing beside his silver Mercedes sedan. Tall, dark-haired, movie-star handsome. Once upon a time just looking at him had taken her breath away.

A lifetime ago. Now when she looked at him, all she felt was anger.

"We played all weekend," the child continued. "He likes to chase sticks and balls. And guess what? Dad even let him sleep with me!"

He paused as if expecting a response from her, and she forced a stiff smile. "That's great, sweet-heart. I'm glad you're so happy. You're going to take very good care of Spot, I know you will."

He puffed up with pride. "I fed him an' took him outside. And when he's a little older, I'll teach him tricks." His smile faded. "Spot cried when I left. I wanted to bring him with me, but Dad said Spot's my special daddy's house friend."

Melanie struggled to hold on to her temper. "I bought you a little something. It's in on the kitchen counter. Why don't you run and see what it is?"

After calling "Bye!" to his father, he raced into the house.

Melanie watched him go, then started toward her ex-husband, stopping directly before him. She saw herself reflected in his aviator-style sunglasses. "How could you, Stan?" she asked, tone measured.

He arched an eyebrow. "How could I what? Buy a gift for my son?"

"We talked about a puppy, we'd decided he was too young. We agreed that decisions as big as whether Casey was ready for a pet would be made together."

He lifted his shoulders, unapologetic. "One of

the partners' retrievers had a litter, he had one pup left. I saw the opportunity and took it.''

''You saw the opportunity and took it?'' she repeated, so furious her voice shook. ''We're not talking about some legal loophole here, we're talking about parenting our child.''

''You're overreacting, as usual. The dog's from championship stock, for heaven's sake. I couldn't pass him up.''

She stuffed her hands into her pockets to hide the way they shook. ''I don't care if he's the Westminster Kennel Club champion, you should have called me.''

''I didn't. I'm sorry.''

Melanie would have been mollified by the apology if she thought he meant it. If he didn't look so damn smug. And if she didn't know him so well.

''Why don't you admit the real reason you bought the dog? Because you knew I couldn't compete. Because you wanted an ace in the hole with Casey, a reason he would want to live with you over me if the judge asked him.''

An emotion flickered across his expression, one akin to regret. ''That's bullshit, Melanie.''

''Is it?'' She made a sound of frustration. ''I don't know why I expected you to play fair, but I did. For Casey's sake, I didn't think you would lower yourself to this kind of...of emotional blackmail. A puppy? Please, Stan...how low can you go?''

''Much lower, no doubt.'' Stan laughed, the sound tight and bitter. ''You always thought the worst of me. Because of your old man.''

"My father? *He* has nothing to do with this."

"No? You don't think that maybe, deep down, you believe that because he was a monster, all men are?"

"Diverting focus? Great courtroom technique, Counselor, but it's not going to work with me. We were married, remember?"

He released his breath in a long sigh. "I bought Casey the dog because I wanted to make him happy, okay? Because I'm his father and I like doing nice things for him."

This time it was Melanie who laughed bitterly. "Stan May never does anything 'just to be nice,' not even for his son. Stan May always works the angles, is always one step ahead, manipulating events to his own best advantage. Always."

He made a sound of disgust and turned away from her. "I refuse to talk to you when you're this way. You're not making sense." He climbed into his car and started it. "If you have a problem, call my lawyer. Better yet—" he yanked at his safety belt, then snapped the clip into the buckle "—have your lawyer call mine."

Melanie caught the car door before he closed it. "Casey's happy here. He's happy with me. Don't shake up his life this way. Think of him."

"I am," he said curtly, two spots of bright color dotting his cheeks. "I can give him so much more than you can."

"Only things." She bent to look him in the eyes. "Casey belongs with me, Stan. You know he does."

"I know no such thing." Stan slipped the gearshift into Reverse. "Besides, from this point on, that's up to the judge to decide."

18

The woman sitting across from Melanie wasn't pretty, though she might have once been. Her painted face bore the ravages of a street whore's life, one filled with abuses against both self and soul.

In the hopes of reviving the stone-cold trail in the Andersen investigation, the CMPD investigators had decided to follow up on Connor Parks's suggestion to question local hookers in the hopes one would recognize the killer from his sexual ritual and Parks's profile. They had ordered a street sweep the night before.

In Melanie's opinion they should have taken this action three weeks before, but since the Whistlestop force had been relegated to an *advisory* status only her opinion meant squat. The only reason she and Bobby had even been actively included in the interrogations was that the sweep had rounded up nearly three dozen working girls, way more than Harrison and Stemmons could comfortably handle without violating their charge-or-release-in-twenty-four-hours right.

Melanie fought back a yawn and glanced at her watch. She'd been here since just after midnight; it was now 8:00 a.m. She thought about another cup of coffee, then decided against it. Her stomach already felt like she'd dumped a quart of battery acid into it.

Melanie glanced at the form on the table in front of her. This hooker's name was Sugar. Of the eight working girls she had already interviewed none recognized—or admitted recognizing—the man from Parks's profile. Some had been cooperative, but most had been uncommunicative and angry. Judging by Sugar's expression, she was definitely going to fall into the latter category.

"Hello, Sugar," she said.

"I've got a call comin'. I want to make a call."

"We'll get to that in a moment. Cigarette?" Melanie slid the pack across the table to the woman.

The hooker said nothing, but helped herself to one of the smokes. Melanie lit it for her, then slipped the lighter into her pocket. She waited until the woman had taken a couple of deep drags before speaking. "I need to ask you a few questions, Sugar. We're looking for a john."

"Aren't we all?"

"A particular john. He's into some unusual stuff. Likes to tie girls up. Likes to insert things into their—"

The whore laughed, the sound gravelly from years of smoking. "They all like that, sweetheart. It's called fucking."

"Their body cavities," she finished. "Unusual things. Unnatural. Ringing any bells yet?"

"Fuck off."

"He's a professional guy. Looks like he has

money. Good-looking. Drives a nice car. Real smooth guy, at least at first.''

Something, some emotion, flickered behind the woman's eyes then was gone. She glared at Melanie. ''Tell me why the fuck I should help you? Pigs never did nothin' to help me even when I wasn't on the street.''

Melanie didn't blink at either her words or the venom behind them. ''Because a girl is dead,'' she said simply. ''And because another might die.''

Sugar took another and final drag on the smoke, then crushed it in the tin ashtray on the table in front of her. ''You're talking about that rich girl, aren't you? The one everybody's making such a stink over?''

''Joli Andersen. Yes.''

For a moment the hooker said nothing, her expression screwed up with bitterness. ''You think I give a shit about some spoiled little rich bitch?''

''Do you think she deserved to die because her daddy has a lot of money? Is that what you're telling me?''

The question, Melanie saw, had surprised the woman. She shook her head and reached for the cigarettes. ''I didn't mean that.''

Melanie leaned toward the other woman. ''A killer is out there. We believe he frequents, or has frequented, working girls. There's nothing to say that he won't strike one of your own next.''

''You cops don't give a shit about us working girls, so don't come on like it's any different. A guy kicks around a girl like me, you stand back and don't do nothing.''

"*You* could be next, Sugar. You know that, don't you?"

The hooker shook one of the cigarettes out of the pack. Melanie slid her the lighter. She lit the cigarette, hand shaking.

"You worried about something, Sugar?"

She inhaled deeply. "Yeah, I've got to take a pee."

"You know this john, don't you? And you're afraid of him."

She blew a long stream of smoke in Melanie's face, then smiled. "Fuck you."

"I can help you. You help me, I'll help you."

"I want my call."

"Did he almost kill you, Sugar? Did he tell you he was going to and you struggled but couldn't get away?"

"Shut up."

"Did he put the pillow over your face?" Melanie lowered her voice. "Could you tell he was getting off, knowing you were dying? Seeing you struggle to breathe?"

"I said, shut the fuck up!"

"What happened, Sugar? What stopped him?" Melanie reached across the table and caught the woman's hand with one of her own, gripping tightly. "He get scared off? You think you're going to be so lucky the next time?"

The hooker yanked her hand away and jumped to her feet, her face white. The cigarette dropped from her fingers and hit the edge of the table, then rolled to the floor.

"Nothin' happened! Okay? Don't know that john, don't want to know that john!"

She was lying. Melanie didn't know why she was so certain of that, but she was. She told her so. "You know it and I know it. The only way you're going to be safe is to finger him. Help me get this animal off the street."

Sugar went to the door and pounded on it. "I want my call! You hear me, I want my call."

Melanie stood and crossed to the woman, looking her dead in the eyes. "Tell me what happened, Sugar. Tell me about him, and I'll help you. That guy, the one who's kicking you around...you tell me about the man I'm looking for, and I'll take care of him for you."

"You're too late. Bastard's dead and buried. Thanks to fate and Mother Nature, not you cops. Now, do I get my call or do I walk?"

Melanie decided to let her walk, though she knew she might catch hell for it. Charging her wouldn't serve any purpose—she would be back on the street in a matter of hours. And it seemed to Melanie that Sugar had been dished plenty of shit in her life. She didn't need Melanie to be heaping on more.

She handed the woman a card, printed with both her office and beeper number. "Call me if you remember something. Or if you need anything. Anytime."

The woman took the card, her expression disbelieving. "You're just going to let me go?"

She opened the door. "Yeah, but don't tell the world. Okay?"

Sugar stared at her a moment, something akin to

gratitude in her expression, then nodded and ducked out the door. As she disappeared around the corner, Melanie turned to find Pete Harrison heading down the hall toward her.

"Get anything?" he asked when he got close enough.

"Nothing concrete." She glanced over her shoulder in the direction Sugar had gone, then turned back to the investigator. "Though I have a feeling the last girl was hiding something. She definitely seemed—"

He cut her off. "They're all hiding something, May. That's the nature of the profession."

"I understand that, but I got the definite impression that she'd run across our guy. When I pressed her, she lost it. It wasn't a matter of being secretive, Pete. She was scared."

"Write it up. I'll look over your report and decide if we need to follow up." He checked his watch. "She was the last. Turn in your notes on the way out."

"Excuse me?"

"We're finished. Thank you."

He was blowing her off. The jerk. Well, she would not be dismissed like some delivery boy. "Your guys get anything of consequence?"

"A few leads. If they pan out, you'll hear about it."

In the newspaper, same as everybody else. The bastard.

A tart reply flew to her tongue, but before she could utter it, Bobby emerged from the interrogation room behind the investigator. He had obviously heard their exchange because he made a face and mimed jerking off with his right hand.

Seeing the direction of her gaze and her obvious amusement, Pete swung around. Bobby smiled at the man, his hands now innocently in his pockets. "I take it we're finished?"

"We are," she answered, moving around the investigator and joining her partner. "What do you say we check in with headquarters, then grab some breakfast? I'm starved."

Bobby was, too, and they stopped at a diner located between CMPD headquarters and the Whistlestop PD. Bobby grabbed a newspaper on the way in before they made their way to a booth at the back of the restaurant.

The waitress arrived with fresh coffee and menus; they ordered right away—a waffle for her and bacon and eggs for him.

As the woman left with their orders, Melanie wagged a finger at her partner. Though incredibly thin, Bobby's cholesterol was borderline high. His wife, Helen, took that number very seriously—saturated fats had disappeared from the Taggerty household. "I bet bacon and eggs aren't on your diet. What would Helen say?"

He made a face. "Are you kidding? All I get anymore is rabbit food, fish or skinless chicken breasts. A real man can't live on that stuff. A real man needs things like bacon. Besides, my cholesterol number isn't high, it's *borderline,* there's a difference."

When Melanie only arched an eyebrow, he muttered something about all women being in cahoots and told her to stick it in her ear.

She laughed and took a sip of water. "Learn anything tonight?"

"Sure did." He added milk and sugar to his coffee and in his best Willie Nelson imitation sang, "Mama, don't let your babies grow up to be hookers."

"Funny."

He sobered. "Actually, not funny at all. Really sad." He was silent a moment, then went on. "Not one of the working girls I interviewed admitted having had business transactions with a guy that fit Parks's profile."

"Mine either." She looked away, then back. "But as one of the women I interviewed said, why should they help us?"

"A sense of civic responsibility?"

"Get real." She lifted her coffee cup to her lips, then set it back down. "Where was Parks, by the way? I'm surprised he wasn't there."

"You didn't hear? Suspended."

She hadn't heard, but she wasn't surprised. "For stepping on the wrong toes. Powerful toes. Am I correct?"

"You are, indeed."

"First us, then Parks." She made a sound of irritation. "He might not have been my favorite person, but he seemed to know what he was doing. A lot more than those jokers over at the CMPD."

"They're good guys. And good cops. You're just pissed 'cause you're not one of them."

He said the last as the waitress arrived with their

food. Melanie waited until she had walked away, then leaned toward him. "What's that supposed to mean?"

"It's not a secret, Mel. You long for the big leagues. I don't, but I understand. It's got to be frustrating sitting back and watching others do what you want to be doing. And then, when a big case does come along, to get pushed out... I suppose I'd have a chip on my shoulder, too."

"I don't have a chip on my shoulder."

"Yeah right." He salted his eggs, then took a big bite. "You mind if I read the paper while we eat?"

"Go ahead. But people will start to talk. It'll look like we're married."

With a laugh, Bobby snapped open his newspaper. Melanie dug into her waffle, thoughts on Bobby's comment. Did she have a chip on her shoulder? Did she unfairly judge the CMPD investigators because she was jealous?

She frowned, not liking the way that sounded. Not liking the way it made her feel.

She opened her mouth to question Bobby, then blinked, suddenly aware that she was staring across the table at a headline on the front page of the *Charlotte Observer.*

Man Acquitted of Sexual Assault Found Dead.

She leaned forward and quickly scanned the article. "Oh my God," she murmured. "Did you see this, Bobby? About Jim McMillian?"

"Who?"

"Jim McMillian. The rape case. Remember? Seven or eight months back, highly publicized."

Bobby nodded. "Rich guy? Hired a team of expensive lawyers from New York? They got him off, though the jury of public opinion found him guilty?"

"As hell. Pass it over, I want to take a closer look."

He did. The article reported that Jim McMillian had died of a heart attack, one caused by digitalis poisoning.

Melanie reread the last, not believing her eyes. "This can't be."

"What?" Bobby craned his neck in an attempt to see what had caught her attention.

"That's how my father died."

"A heart attack?"

"One caused by an elevated level of digitalis in the blood."

Bobby frowned. "The cardiac drug?"

"The very one. Like my dad, Jim McMillian was taking prescription digitalis."

"He overdosed on his heart medicine?"

"Essentially." Melanie explained. "The thing is, at only three to four times the dose used to regulate heart rhythm, digitalis becomes lethal. That's not all that much. And here's where it gets tricky. Sudden shifts in body chemistry can cause blood levels of digitalis to rise and bring on a heart attack. It's why patients on the drug are closely monitored by their doctor. Ashley explained it all to me."

"This can really happen?" He frowned. "My dad's on that medicine."

"A lot of people are. As I understood it, my

dad's death was a freakish occurrence. Rare. That's what's so weird about this.''

Bobby consumed his last bite of eggs and crumb of bacon, wiped his mouth and tossed his paper napkin on the plate. ''Considering McMillian's heart condition, I'm surprised the medical examiner did more than a cursory check before pronouncing him dead of a heart attack. A chemical analysis is rarely done in heart patients.''

Melanie pursed her lips ''I know. In my dad's case, he'd been to the doctor a couple days before and everything had looked great.''

''Weird coincidence.''

''Very weird.'' She frowned. ''How common do you think this cause of death is?''

Bobby leaned back in his seat and scratched his head. ''Not very would be my guess.''

''I've got a funny feeling about this.''

''So what else is new? You look for the big case behind every nuisance call we get.''

''Kiss off.''

He laughed, then sobered. ''Why don't you make a couple calls when we get back? Maybe this type of thing isn't as rare as you think?''

''You're right.'' She smiled. ''Levelheaded Bobby, always keeping me grounded.''

''Somebody's got to. Besides—'' his lips lifted in a devilish grin ''—a guy's gotta be good at something besides getting his wife knocked up.''

19

After arriving back at headquarters and filling their chief in on their evening's work, Melanie made the calls. It took some doing, but she finally connected with the head of the Heart Center at Mecklenburg County General. After speaking with him, she dialed the medical examiner's office. Fifteen minutes later, she hung up the phone and turned to Bobby. "Odd. I find this whole thing very odd."

"What did they say?" he asked.

"They both confirmed my suspicion that heart attacks brought on by elevated levels of digitalis are rare."

"But?" he prompted.

"But both felt that two such occurrences in the same state, four years apart weren't impossible."

"In other words, don't send out the cavalry."

"Exactly."

"But you're not satisfied?"

"I didn't say that."

"You didn't have to. You've got that look on your face. The one that tells me you're not willing to accept that this guy and your dad died by the same freakish twist of fate. The one that tells me you're going to chew at this thing until either something tastier comes along or you drop from exhaustion. It's your M.O., partner.''

"It is not."

He arched his eyebrows in exaggerated disbelief, then grabbed for the phone as it rang. "Whistlestop PD. Taggerty." He paused, listening, then grinned. "Hey, Veronica. She's right here, stirring up trouble, as usual. Hold on."

He pushed the hold button, then motioned to Melanie. She nodded and reached for the phone. In the weeks since their first meeting, she and Veronica had become fast friends. Not only had they made their sparring session followed by coffee a weekly ritual, they managed to speak by phone every few days and had even gotten together for a lunch with Mia.

Melanie had never had a friend she'd gotten so close to so fast.

Of course, it seemed that Veronica had that effect on a lot of people—they just liked her, right off. Mia had, Bobby, Casey. It seemed the only person in Melanie's life Veronica had yet to meet was Ashley, and they were remedying that this weekend.

Melanie brought the receiver to her ear. "Hey, girlfriend. What's up?"

"Seems that's what I should be asking you. What's this about stirring up trouble?"

Melanie laughed. "Don't mind Bobby—" she glanced at him and grinned "—he wouldn't recognize a crime if it took a chunk out of his backside."

Bobby flipped her off good-naturedly, then returned to the previous night's phone log. Melanie refocused on her friend. "Did you read the paper this morning?"

"No time. What's up?"

"Jim McMillian's dead."

"I know. Sam was talking about it yesterday." Sam Hale was the attorney who had presented the state's case against McMillian. "A friend of his at the CMPD called him the minute he heard. So, what does that have to do with you being a trouble-maker?"

Melanie explained about seeing the article, the coincidence of her father having died in the same way as Jim McMillian and about the calls she had made to the Heart Center at Mecklenburg General and the medical examiner's office.

Veronica was silent a moment—Melanie could almost hear her thinking, evaluating what Melanie had just told her. "It does sound kind of bizarre. What are you going to do?"

"What can I do? Keep my eyes and ears open, maybe nose around a bit, though I don't know how much."

Veronica made a sound of agreement, then changed the subject. "Sorry I haven't called until now, this trial's been a bear. Kid's dad hired an army of high-priced lawyers. They've had us scrambling."

"How's it going?"

"Jury's deliberating now. But I think we've got the little weasel. It was the second girl coming forward that did it." Melanie heard Veronica's smile. "This time the cocky little jock has gotten himself into something his daddy's money can't buy him out of.''

"Good for you."

"No," Veronica corrected quietly. "Good for all the girls he's hurt. And for the ones he won't be able to hurt in the future. Hold on." Melanie heard someone speaking to the other woman, then her muffled response. "Look, I don't have a lot of time, but I wanted to find out how your meeting with the lawyer went."

"Don't ask."

"That bad, huh?"

"Worse. I spent the entire weekend alternating between total despair and being royally pissed."

After Melanie filled her in, Veronica muttered an oath. "Son of a bitch gives us lawyers a bad name."

"You've got that right." Melanie tried to muster anger or righteous indignation, but felt nothing but weariness. "I'm not sure what I'm going to do now. I can't afford a lawyer the caliber of Stan's."

"Yes, you can."

"Pardon?"

"I know a dynamite female attorney in Columbia. She's top-notch. Specializes in family law, and she's definitely one of the good guys. Let me give her a call, see what her schedule's like. If at all possible, she'll fit you in as a favor to me."

"That'd be a miracle, though I don't know how I'd pay her. I'm a cop, remember?"

"You worry about keeping custody of your son, I'll take care of the rest."

"But, Veronica—"

"No buts," her friend said crisply. "Trust me. I'm going to hang up and call her now."

A lump of gratitude formed in Melanie's throat. "Thank you, Veronica. This is...too much. I don't know how to repay you."

"Repay me?" She laughed. "Don't be a dork, I like helping the people I care about. Call it my mission in life."

20

Melanie sat bolt upright in bed, instantly alert. She glanced at the bedside clock—3:40 a.m. She frowned and cocked her head, listening for what might have awakened her. The house was so quiet she could hear the bubbler in the fish tank in Casey's room.

Still not satisfied, she retrieved her gun from the top drawer of the tall bureau beside the bed and did a search of the house. She peeked in on Casey first—he hadn't moved since she tucked him in hours before—then went from room to room, checking all the doors and windows. She found nothing amiss.

So, what had awakened her?

And now that she was wide awake, heart pounding, every nerve in her body playing reveille, what was she supposed to do?

Since sleep wasn't an option, a pot of coffee and a leisurely look at the newspaper seemed her best bet. With that in mind, Melanie returned her gun to the bureau drawer, then went to the front door and peeked out the sidelight, looking for the newspaper. Seeing that it had been delivered, she darted out to get it, then went to the kitchen to start the coffee.

While she waited for it to brew, she slid onto one

of the stools at the breakfast bar and snapped open the paper. She scanned the day's major headlines, hopping from one news story to another, mind wandering. Suddenly she stopped, yesterday's big story popping into her head.

Jim McMillian, accused batterer, suddenly dead.

Thomas Weiss, the batterer she had been unable to charge, suddenly dead.

Melanie drew her eyebrows together as bits and snatches of conversations flooded her mind. What had Bobby called the two deaths? *Freakish twists of fate.* When she'd told Veronica that Thomas Weiss was dead, what had the woman said? *Fate was a strange thing.*

Melanie straightened and brought a hand to her mouth. That was what had awakened her, what had been plucking at the back of her brain, begging acknowledgment. Not the coincidence of Jim McMillian's and her father's deaths, ones separated by years, but the coincidence of the recent deaths of three alleged batterers.

Three? Melanie rubbed the bridge of her nose. Now why had she thought three?

Then she knew. She remembered. The hooker she had interviewed at CMPD headquarters. What had she said? That the man who'd hurt her was dead, that fate and Mother Nature had taken care of him for her.

Fate. And Mother Nature. Again.

Melanie got to her feet and crossed to the coffeepot, mind whirling. She got a mug from the cabinet, filled it but didn't drink. What was she thinking? That the three deaths were related? An older, wealthy entrepreneur, an up-and-coming restaurateur and a coke-head?

How could they be? What could link three such different men?

They were all alleged batterers.

And now they were all dead.

"Mommy?"

Startled, Melanie swung toward the kitchen doorway. Casey stood there, rubbing his eyes with one hand and clutching his stuffed bunny to his chest with the other.

She slid off the stool and crossed to him. "What are you doing up, sweetie? It's still dark out."

"I had a bad dream. Someone took you away, an' I couldn't find you."

His voice quivered, and she scooped him up. He wrapped his arms around her neck and pressed his face into her shoulder.

"That's not going to happen," she murmured, her tone fierce. But even as the words passed her lips, she thought of Stan and the custody suit. She tightened her arms around the boy. "Come on, baby, let's go back to bed. Momma will snuggle with you."

Melanie didn't have another moment to contemplate her theory that the deaths of Jim McMillian and Thomas Weiss were related, not then or even hours later, after she had arrived at headquarters. There she faced a dozen irritating, inconsequential chores, including the two pages of "leads" gleaned overnight from the Andersen hot line.

Not one of them had amounted to anything but wastes of her time.

Melanie supposed she should be thankful there hadn't been more tips to follow up this morning. When Cleve Andersen had first offered the hundred-thousand-dollar reward, the phones had rung off the hook. Now, after three weeks, the calls had slowed to a sporadic stream. But she wasn't thankful—she was frustrated. Chomping at the bit to prove her theory viable.

Finally, her desk cleared, she put in a call to the medical examiner. "Hi, Frank. Melanie May, Whistlestop PD. We spoke yesterday about Jim Mc-Millian's death."

"Sure, Officer May. What can I do for you?"

"I have just one question, could Jim McMillian have been murdered?"

He was quiet a long moment. "I classified McMillian's manner of death natural causes. Do you know something I don't, Officer May?"

"Not at all," she said quickly. The last thing she needed was for him to call the CMPD and inform them that she was snooping around one of their cases. "I phrased that badly. Could someone commit a murder in this way?"

"It's possible, but I see no evidence of that here. Digitalis comes from the foxglove plant. If Mr. McMillian had been poisoned, I would have found foxglove residue in the man's stomach, which I did not."

"But if the victim was already taking prescription digitalis, couldn't he be overdosed with the drug? The elevated digitalis in the blood brings on the heart attack and leaves nothing for the medical examiner to uncover, the victim having been poisoned by the very drug he took to stabilize his condition?''

The man cleared his throat sharply. ''Do you have any reason to suspect Mr. McMillian was poisoned? Except, of course, that his death mirrored the rather rare circumstances of your father's? Had McMillian been threatened? Had his wife recently taken out a large life insurance policy? Did he have enemies who would go to such lengths to be rid of him?''

''No...I mean, I don't know. But the coincidence of—''

He cut her off. ''You watch too many movies, Officer May. Death brings with it many inexplicable circumstances. The human body is not a machine, we can't always pinpoint exactly why it stops. So, unless you have some concrete reason why I should reopen Jim McMillian's file, I'll say goodbye.''

Melanie didn't, and a moment later she hung up the phone to find Bobby staring at her. ''What?'' she asked, hiking her chin up a notch. ''I'm checking out a hunch.''

''Have you lost your mind? Do you have any idea how dangerous what you're doing is? All it would take is one call from Frank Connell, M.E., and your butt would be in some very deep shit.''

''I know. Cover for me, okay?'' She thumbed through her notes from the day before, found what she was looking for and stood. ''If the chief asks, tell him I've gone hunting for a hooker.''

* * *

Melanie expected the address Sugar had given the police to be a dummy. Especially when she realized the location of that address—a decent apartment building on one of the nicer sides of Charlotte, far from the corner where the prostitute had been picked up. In fact, not all that far from Ashley's condo.

Melanie rang the bell. A woman answered. For a split second, Melanie thought she had been right. The woman on the other side of the door, with her freshly scrubbed looks, certainly didn't resemble the hardened streetwalker she had interviewed the other night.

Her eyes, the recognition in them, gave her away. "Sugar?" Melanie said.

The woman glanced over her shoulder. Only then did Melanie become aware of the sounds of cartoons coming from the TV.

"Kathy," she corrected. "Kathy Cook. What're you doing here?"

"I need to ask you a couple questions."

"I told you, I don't know that guy."

She started to shut the door, but Melanie stopped her. "The questions aren't about him. They're about the man you told me about, the one who beat you up."

She looked surprised. "Samson? Why do you want to know about him?"

"What did you mean when you said fate and Mother Nature took care of him?"

She darted a glance over her shoulder. "Look, my kid's here. I don't need no cop making trouble—"

"I don't want to make trouble for you. Please, tell me how he died. It's important."

"He ODed. Okay? Now, will you leave?"

"Overdosed," Melanie repeated, disappointed. It fit with this woman; pimps and other street people ODed all the time. Hardly the work of some master criminal.

"But before you climb all over my frame, I gotta work to support me and my kid, but I don't touch that shit. Not even to get me through."

Melanie had heard that before, many times. Some of those times uttered by people so stoned they couldn't stand erect. This time she believed it. She saw a ferocity in the woman's eyes, a determination she hadn't seen under the fluorescent lights of the interrogation room.

"He was an addict?" Melanie asked. "Someone you knew from the street?"

She shook her head. "I was off the street then, working a real job. Pay was okay. They had a center for my boy, benefits. Met him there. He worked across the street. He was a professional guy." She made a sound of derision. "When I met Samson Gold, I thought my luck had changed for good."

"When did he start beating you up?"

"Not at first. He seemed...different from the other guys I knew. Different than the—" She lowered her voice. "The johns. He moved in with me. That's when he changed. Started snorting coke pretty heavy. Turned crazy. And mean.

"He lost his job, then I lost mine because of him calling all the time. Threatening the people I worked with." Her expression tightened. "I went to the cops. They didn't do jack. One of 'em recognized me from the street and it was all over." She made a sound of bitterness. "Us working girls deserve whatever we get, you know. We're just whores."

From inside came childish giggles. Melanie thought of Casey and her heart hurt. "What happened then?"

"Fate intervened. Or my angel of mercy. He got ahold of some dynamite...you know, coke mixed with heroin. But strange shit. Not just any horse, pure stuff. A hotshot."

The woman drew her eyebrows together. "I could never figure out how he got ahold of that shit. No dealer's gonna make that mistake, you know? Pure stuff's impossible to get on the street, worth way more than an ordinary 8-ball. And if my man had known what it was, no way would he have snorted it. He was fucked up, but he wasn't stupid."

Melanie could barely contain her excitement. That made three. Three men dead from freakish circumstances.

"Mommy? Who's there?"

Kathy looked over her shoulder. "Just a friend, sweetheart. Go back to the cartoons, I'll be right there." She turned to Melanie. "I've got to go."

"I know. Thanks." Melanie touched her arm lightly. "It's not true. You don't deserve that kind of treatment. If you ever need help again, come to me. I'll do whatever I can."

She nodded, her eyes suddenly, suspiciously bright. Melanie suspected that Sugar...Kathy, hadn't known much kindness in her life.

"You don't have to worry about me," she said. "I'm getting out. Got me a line on a day job, one with good child care. Would've been out sooner, but I live here 'cause I want my boy to go to a good school. I want him to know nice kids, from good families. I don't want him to become like—" She bit the words back as if suddenly remembering she was speaking to the enemy. "I gotta go."

"One more question, how long ago did he die?"

She thought a moment, as if counting back. "Four months ago. Yeah, that's right, 'cause it was right before Thanksgiving. And I can promise you this, I'm still givin' thanks."

21

Melanie maneuvered her Jeep into one of the parallel-parking spots in front of Whistlestop headquarters. Mind racing with what Sugar had told her, she shifted into Park and cut off the engine.

She had three dead men. All batterers. All men who had slipped through the fingers of justice. All dead by different but bizarre twists of fate. All victims, in a strange way, of their own weaknesses.

She reviewed the facts in her head. A cokehead overdoses on a drug he had no business having, let alone snorting. A heart patient becomes the victim of the very substance he takes to protect him. A man deathly allergic to bees gets killed trying to avoid being stung while driving.

Was there a connection between the three deaths? Or were they nothing more than a weird coincidence? Or divine retribution?

Melanie rested her head against the seat back. She closed her eyes, sorting through her thoughts and feelings, acknowledging that she believed the deaths were not accidental. She believed these men were murdered. All by the same hand.

All by the same hand. If she was right, that would mean a serial killer was operating in the Charlotte area, targeting abusive men.

Melanie shook her head, also admitting how far-fetched others would find her theory. How hard to swallow. There had to be something that linked the three men to the killer. She had to find it.

She flung open the car door just as Bobby emerged from the building. "Bobby," she called, excited. "We have to talk."

He strode toward her. "Fire that wagon up. They've got a suspect in the Andersen case. Chief wants us there when they question him."

"Let's go." She slammed her door and restarted the Jeep's engine, pulling away from the curb the moment Bobby was inside. "Who've they got?"

"Name's Jenkins. The guy who threatened Joli the night she was murdered. He resurfaced a couple nights ago. The bartender recognized him and called the CMPD."

"Resurfaced at the same club?" She shook her head. "Either this guy's innocent or he's a complete moron."

"They ran a check on him through the computer, found he has priors. Robbery, aggravated assault. No convictions. Mr. Jenkins, it turns out, has a problem controlling his temper. Last brush with the law came when he broke a pool cue over somebody's head. Apparently, the guy questioned his sexuality."

Melanie frowned, thinking of the profile Connor Parks had created. The description of this man had never fit for her. Now that they had him in custody, he fit even less. He sounded like the antithesis of the handsome, smooth talker Parks had described. "And they think he's her killer?"

At the doubt in her voice, Bobby lifted a shoulder. "He seems like a natural to me. He had motive. He was there that night. He threatened her."

"We'll see," she murmured, unconvinced. "I'll be interested to hear what he has to say for himself."

They rode in silence for awhile, Melanie navigating the sometimes-tricky late-afternoon traffic. Even though they were heading through the heart of Charlotte, the landscape had the feel of a much more rural community than it was. Expansive rather than congested. Perhaps because the city, with its gently rolling hills, was so green, perhaps because it was a clean city, one beloved and cared for by its citizens in an old-fashioned way.

Melanie turned onto South Davidson, the Law Enforcement Center in sight now. Located in Government Plaza—which housed all the city-county buildings—the LEC was a fancy name for police headquarters.

"I covered for you, by the way," Bobby said. "Told the chief you were checking a tip that came in on the Andersen hot line, and that you'd gone out on a call and would meet me at CMPD headquarters. Lucky for us both you showed up."

She sent him a grateful smile. "Thanks, partner. I owe you."

"You want to tell me what's going on?"

"Remember the story in the paper yesterday about Jim McMillian's death?"

"Sure."

"I realized last night that what was bothering me wasn't that both his and my father's deaths were similar, but that three accused batterers were recently dead, all the victims of freakish accidents."

"Now you've lost me. What other batterers?"

She explained, beginning with the case that had come her way and finishing with her conversation with Sugar that morning. Melanie swung into the LEC parking area, chose a spot and cut off the engine. She looked at her partner. "That's three, Bobby. Three batterers, all dead of freakish twists of fate."

He drew his eyebrows together. "What are you saying? That those three deaths are related?"

"Hell, yes, that's what I'm saying." She glanced away, then back at him. "Don't you see it, Bobby? Don't you see how natural, how logical a conclusion I'm drawing?"

"I don't know, Mel. Truthfully?" She nodded; he rubbed a hand along his jaw. "I think you're stretching. How are these men related?"

"They're all batterers who've gone unpunished for one reason or another. And they all died under rather bizarre circumstances."

"Yeah, but they were all from different walks of life, they lived and worked on different sides of town, their ages, educational backgrounds, socioeconomic groups were all differ—"

"I get it," Melanie said, cutting him off, frustrated. "My theory has more holes in it than a block of Swiss cheese."

"Hey—" he held up his hands in a mock surrender "—don't kill the messenger. If you think I'm a tough jury, just picture the chief's response."

She opened the vehicle's door and stepped out.

Bobby did the same, and they started toward the building, an impressive one-hundred-forty-thousand-square-foot concrete-and-glass structure. "Saving my butt again, are you?"

"Somebody's got to." He grinned as she held open the door for him. "Besides, I've gotten kind of used to having you around. Life's never dull."

"Thanks. I think." They stepped into the LEC lobby, the cool of the air-conditioning enveloping them. They moved toward the elevators, passing the colorful fresco by world-renowned artist Ben Long. Melanie glanced at the work. She enjoyed his bold style, one that combined both classical and modern elements.

"Besides," Bobby continued, as they moved into one of the cars. "I'm not saying you're wrong, just that you haven't sold me yet. Do a little more digging, see if you put anything else together, then present it to the chief."

"Hold the elevator!"

Melanie caught the doors, forcing them to spring back open. Connor Parks stepped on. He had a champagne bottle tucked under his right arm. He smiled. "Hello, Sweetpants. Taggerty."

Bobby choked on a laugh. Melanie narrowed her eyes, irritated. "What are you doing here, Parks? I'd heard that Cleve Andersen had your butt booted off the case."

A smile tipped the corners of his mouth. "Funny, I'd heard the same about you. I guess we're both getting thrown a bone today."

Melanie acknowledged a twinge of admiration mixed in with her dislike for him—the man was one cool customer. Melanie cocked an eyebrow and indicated the bottle of wine. "Celebrating the bone or a conclusion to the case? Or do you simply prefer not to drink alone?"

The last was low—she had meant it to be. It hit its mark. His jaw tightened. The elevator stopped and the doors slid open. The three stepped out and into the hallway. Down to the right, several people milled about, including Steve Rice, Parks's superior. He motioned for Connor to hurry.

Parks met her eyes. In his she saw that whatever discomfort she had caused him had given way to amusement. "It's a prop, doll. Watch the big boys work. You just might learn something."

As he started to walk away she stopped him, irritated but unable to quell her curiosity. "That's the same brand of champagne we found at the Andersen scene."

His eyes crinkled at the corners. "See? You're learning already."

22

"**Y**ou're late," Rice said as Connor approached.

Connor glanced at his watch. "Considering you called and invited me to this shindig less than twenty-five minutes ago, I'd expected a different greeting. Something along the lines of 'Thanks for risking your life to get here so fast, Con.'"

"You sober?"

"Fuck you."

The SAC narrowed his eyes. "Are you?"

"Yes, goddammit. I'm sober. Twenty-two miserable days' worth. And counting."

"Good. I'm sitting in on the interrogation, just to add a little heat. You'll observe. I want you to note every breath this guy takes. They think he's the one."

"Sure you're comfortable with this, Steve? Not afraid I'll jeopardize anyone's life or career?"

"You want in on this or not?"

"Hell, yes, I want in on it." He handed him the bottle. As Melanie May had noted, it was identical to the one found at the Andersen murder scene. "You've got the other props?"

"Got 'em."

As if cued, Pete Harrison and Roger Stemmons strolled over. "Hello, boys," Rice said. "Why don't we see if we can get Mr. Jenkins's ass to pucker.''

Minutes later, Connor strode into the room where the suspect's interrogation was being viewed via video. He saw that May and Taggerty were in place at the table. With them, also facing the monitor, sat a representative from the district attorney's office and a handful of other cops.

He took the seat next to Melanie. In the other room, Jenkins waited. Connor's first look at the suspect confirmed what he had already known from verbal descriptions—Ted Jenkins wasn't their man. He didn't fit the profile. Although not physically unattractive, he had ''loser'' stamped all over him—from his unshorn, wavy brown hair to his sleeveless muscle shirt and the cigarette tucked behind his ear. He looked like a laborer or a dropout, a far cry from the yuppie executive Joli would have been drawn to.

Rice and the two investigators took their places. Pete Harrison set the champagne bottle on the table along with a stack of manila file folders. Jenkins looked sick with nerves, even though he hadn't been asked one question yet.

Connor bent and spoke close to Melanie's ear. ''Notice where Harrison put the bottle, just at the corner of Jenkins's vision? If he's guilty, he's not going to be able to ignore it. He'll keep turning his head to look at it. He'll start to sweat, his respiration will increase.''

''What's with the file folders?''

''Dummies. Labeled with Jenkins's name but filled with blank paper. To give the illusion that we've amassed a great amount of information on him.''

She looked unimpressed. ''And these are your big-boy, FBI tricks?''

''As a matter of fact. Developed by Special Agent John Douglas, of the Investigative Support Unit at Quantico.''

She had obviously heard of Douglas, considered by many to be the nation's foremost authority on crime-scene analysis and criminal profiling, and her expression changed subtly. ''Maybe I will learn something, after all.''

Past the initial introductions, the proceedings began in earnest, and Connor turned his full attention to them.

''What's with the bubbly?'' Jenkins asked, motioning with his head to the bottle.

''Why don't I ask the questions, Ted,'' Pete Harrison said, taking the lead. ''Where've you been the past four weeks?''

''Nowhere.'' He rubbed his hands along his thighs. ''Just hanging out.''

''Nowhere?'' the investigator repeated. ''Just hanging out?''

''Yeah,'' he said defensively, looking at Stemmons, then Rice. ''What's wrong with that?''

''What you mean to say is, you've been lying low.''

''No.'' He swung his gaze back to Harrison.

''Why haven't you been in to see us?'' This from Stemmons.

''Wh-why should I have been?''

The police exchanged glances. ''Oh, I don't

know. Maybe because a woman you were hitting on, one who rebuffed you—''

''—rather brutally—''

''—was murdered. That very night.''

''That had nothing to do with me!''

''That night in the bar, you threatened her. Didn't you, Ted?''

''N-no.''

''We have witnesses. You told her 'she'd be sorry.' Isn't that what you said?''

''Yes, but I...I didn't mean anything by it.'' He swung his gaze pleadingly between the three men. He looked like a rabbit who'd been cornered by two wolves.

Connor frowned. *But after his initial interest in the wine bottle, he seemed unaffected by it.*

''Maybe I should have a lawyer.''

''That's your right,'' Harrison said. ''If you think you need one?''

The man hesitated, then shook his head. ''I don't have anything to hide.''

''I'm glad to hear that, Ted.'' Harrison smiled reassuringly. ''Let's get back to the night Joli Andersen was killed, to your argument with her. You told her 'she'd be sorry.' If you didn't want to hurt her, why'd you say it, Ted?''

''I was mad.''

''Mad? Our witnesses said you were furious. So furious your face turned red and you began to stutter.''

''Yeah, okay...I was pissed off...she made fun of me. In front of everybody. But I didn't...I wouldn't actually...hurt her.''

The investigators exchanged meaningful glances. Stemmons leaned toward Jenkins. "I understand, man," he said, keeping his voice low and reassuring. "She was a foxy babe, you just wanted to get close to her. She had no call for what she did. Calling you a loser like that."

He lowered his voice even more. "I would have been so pissed, I'd have just wanted to shut her up. Any way I could. Is that the way you felt, Ted? So furious that you could put a pillow over her face, just to shut her—"

"No! I was angry! It was just talk. Saving face, you know?" He wetted his lips. "Yeah, I wanted her to shut up. But I...I just said that thing about...about making her sorry and left."

"But you came back later?"

"No."

"You came up to her in the parking lot."

"No! I never saw her again. I swear."

"We have a witness who says differently. We have a witness who says they saw you approach her in the parking lot."

"That's not true!"

"They said you followed her to her car."

He shook his head wildly, looking halfway to tears. "I didn't."

"You were the last person to see her alive, Mr. Jenkins. The very last person."

"No!" He jumped to his feet, visibly shaking. But not with rage, Connor saw, with terror. "I want a lawyer. I didn't see her again after I left the bar, and I'm not going to say another thing until you get me a lawyer!"

Several minutes later, Harrison, Stemmons and Rice entered the room. "Well?" Harrison asked. "What do you think?"

Connor turned away from the monitor. "He's not the guy."

"What makes you so sure?" the assistant district attorney asked.

"Because he's a loser, just like Joli called him that night. Look at the way he's dressed. His haircut. What kind of car does he drive? A piece-of-shit Ford or a Chevy truck? She wouldn't have had a thing to do with him."

The attorney stiffened. "I hardly think a victim chooses her murderer."

"You'd be surprised how many times a victim unknowingly does just that. But what I'm referring to is that we established that Joli Andersen went willingly with her murderer to that motel room. She wanted to be there, with that man. And that man was not Ted Jenkins."

"The whole thing in the bar," Bobby Taggerty piped up, "it could've been an act. A ruse to throw people off. They rendezvoused in the parking lot later."

"But why?" Steve Rice asked. "Neither was married. They didn't work together. As far as we know so far, Jenkins and Andersen had never met before that night. Why play a game like that?"

"He's not the guy," Connor said again. "After the initial question about the champagne bottle, he seemed to forget it was there. If he'd used that bottle in the manner it was used on Joli Andersen, he wouldn't have been able to take his eyes off it. Hell, he probably would have gotten a hard-on.''

The ADA released her breath in a huff. ''That's disgusting.''

''Yeah, it's disgusting. We're talking about a man who brutally murdered, then defiled another human being and got off on it. What did you expect? A sonnet?''

''I've got to agree with Parks,'' Rice said. ''Jenkins was right-handed. Studies show that when right-handed suspects look to their left when replying, they're generally recalling the truth. When they look to their right, they're fabricating. Jenkins is right-handed, yet throughout the interrogation he looked left when replying.''

''He didn't kill Joli Andersen,'' Connor said flatly. ''Keep looking.''

Harrison made a sound of frustration. ''I like this guy. He had motive, he's got a history of violence, he acted guilty as hell.''

''Go ahead, then,'' Connor muttered sarcastically. ''Play this out. It's only the taxpayers' money and that poor schmuck's life you're dicking with.''

''Parks,'' Rice murmured, his tone low, warning.

Connor ignored him. ''Go ahead, guys. Pretend this is a viable lead. It'll make you look like your heads aren't so far up your asses your eyes'll be brown forever.''

''You might be wrong,'' Melanie said softly. ''Your profile might be wrong.''

He looked at her. ''I'm never *that* wrong, Officer May. Never. Excuse me.''

He stepped out of the room and waited, knowing that his boss would be right behind him. He was.

"You just can't play it smart, can you?"

Connor shrugged. "What can I say? I'm flawed."

Rice shook his head. "You're worse than flawed. You're a pain in the ass. But you're a talented pain in the ass. Too good at what you do to be sitting home watching daytime TV."

"It's more stimulating than you'd think."

The SAC lowered his voice. "How have you been?"

"All right." Connor didn't look at him, he found suddenly that he couldn't. Because it was a lie. The last month had been a nightmare—he'd been alone with himself and his own thoughts, without even booze to dull the pain.

"I want you back. I need you back. The Bureau needs you back."

"But?"

"But it's not enough that you're sober, I need you to be performing at a hundred percent."

"Don't want much, do you?"

Steve smiled without humor. "Greedy bastard, aren't I? Call me when you're there."

Connor watched as the other man disappeared into the viewing room, then turned and started down the hall. He wouldn't be calling; Rice had set up an impossible scenario for him. Until he discovered what had happened to his sister, he would never be one hundred percent again.

23

"Hey, Ash." Melanie greeted her sister with a hug. "You're the first. Come on in."

"What a surprise." Ashley smiled wryly and stepped inside. "Considering Mia's never been on time in her life."

Melanie laughed, in high spirits. She had been looking forward to this get-together all week. "True. But Veronica's even worse. You'd think a lawyer would understand the importance of being punctual."

"So, I'm finally going to meet the great and mysterious Veronica."

"Not so mysterious. Besides, you could have met her before now, you've been busy."

"But she *is* great, right? The best thing to come along since cappuccinos on every corner?"

Melanie looked at her, confused by the edge in her sister's voice. "I don't follow."

Ashley shook her head. "Never mind, bad joke. So, where's my little tiger tonight?"

"Casey? He's with his dad. It's Stan's weekend." Melanie motioned toward the kitchen. "I was just whipping up a pitcher of frozen margaritas. Give me a hand."

Ashley followed her to the other room. Melanie

had prepared a vegetable tray; a hot bean dip and tortilla roll-ups. Ashley surveyed the platter and arched her eyebrows. "Awfully nice spread just for us girls."

"I was feeling festive."

"Hmm." Her sister plucked a carrot stick from the tray and dunked it into the dip. "Why?"

"I need a reason?" She dumped a can of frozen limeade in the blender, then followed it with tequila, triple sec and ice. She flipped the switch and the room filled with the sound of ice being pulverized.

When the concoction looked the right consistency, she turned off the appliance. "Hand me a couple of those glasses," she said. "Let's give these babies a try."

She poured and handed a glass to her sister. Ashley sipped, then murmured her approval. "Hits the spot."

"What have you been doing to keep you so busy?" Melanie asked, bringing the glass to her lips. "I haven't seen you in at least two weeks."

She shrugged. "Same as always, work's kept me on the road. Besides, I don't think it's me who's been busy."

Once again, Melanie was confused by her sister's tone. It was as if she was angry about something, some slight or exclusion. But before she could ask what, Ashley changed the subject. "I hear Mia and Veronica have been spending a good bit of time together."

"I don't know about that. They've gone shopping and to lunch a couple of times."

"Interesting."

This time Melanie didn't let the comment pass. She made a sound of exasperation. Ashley, it seemed, was in one of her moods. "And what's *that* supposed to mean?"

"Think about it. Mia's marriage is in shambles and what's she doing? *Lunching* and *shopping* with her new best buddy."

"Would you rather she sit home and cry twenty-four hours a day? Besides, I've been monitoring that situation. Boyd's been on very good behavior." *Ever since she and Bobby had paid him that little visit.* "As for your sister, her moods seem to swing between despair and gaiety. It's disconcerting, but considering the circumstances, to be expected. Don't you think?"

"I suppose. Personally, I think she should leave the prick. But she doesn't seem interested in my opinion." Ashley plucked a tortilla roll-up from the platter. "Tell me again how you met Veronica."

Grateful to be off the subject of her twin's troubled marriage, Melanie did, starting with their initial encounter on papering day and how they had recognized each other from the coffeehouse, and ending with running into each other at the dojang.

"Odd," Ashley murmured, "that you and she frequent the same coffeehouse and dojang. Charlotte's a big city."

"Not that big. The Starbucks is centrally located, which is exactly why we picked it and Mr. Browne is the only nationally ranked tae kwon do master in the Charlotte area."

At her sister's suspicious expression, Melanie

laughed. Ashley was like this—always seeing shadows, always looking on the dark side. Melanie gave her a hug. "You're going to like her, I know you are. She and Mia got along famously, right off."

"Famously," Ashley repeated, a sudden smile tugging at the corners of her mouth. "Now *that* I have to see."

She got her chance moments later when Mia and Veronica arrived simultaneously. Melanie found them chatting on the front porch. She greeted them, sending her twin a concerned glance. Mia's cheeks were flushed, her smile bright. Too bright, Melanie thought. *Tonight, it seemed, gaiety was to be the mood du jour.*

Melanie greeted them, made the introductions and within minutes had herded everyone out to the patio, drinks in hands.

"Where've you been hiding, Ash?" Mia asked, sinking onto one of the sling-back chairs. "I've missed you."

"Have you?" Ashley looked at Veronica, then back at Mia. "My number's in the book."

"You kill me, Ash." Mia shook her head and brought her drink to her lips. "I bet that sexy cop you're dating's been keeping you on your back."

Ashley flushed. "I haven't seen him in some time. You know that."

"I know no such thing. Besides, the way you disappear for days at a time—"

Veronica stepped in. "I, for one, am happy to finally meet the third twin." She smiled warmly. "Though I feel I know you already, Melanie and Mia have talked so much about you."

"I wondered why my ears have been burning. Now I know."

"I just love margaritas." Mia took another sip of her drink and made a sound of pleasure. "We should drink them all the time."

"I propose a toast then," Veronica said, lifting her glass. "To good friends and frozen drinks. May they always go together."

Echoing the sentiment, the others lifted their glasses. From that point on, any awkwardness between the four women melted away. They drank and laughed, snacked and talked—about everything but nothing of consequence: the weather, spring fashions, movies and the merits of Hollywood's latest hunk of the moment.

When their conversation fell into a lull, Veronica leaned forward, excited. "I can't believe I almost forgot to tell you, Melanie. I have good news. I talked to my friend, the attorney I told you about. She can take you on."

"She can?" Melanie brought a hand to her chest. "Thank God. I was really starting to stress over this. Stan's lawyer called me this week, inquiring as to who I had decided on."

Veronica dug a business card out of her purse and handed it to Melanie. "Not only that, she told me to tell you not to worry about her fees. She'll work out something you can live with."

"You're a lifesaver, Veronica. I can't thank you enough."

"What's this all about?" Ashley looked from one to the other, eyebrows drawn together in concern and confusion. "You in some sort of trouble, Mel?"

"Just the usual. Man trouble, with a capital 'S.'"

"Bastard husbands." Mia sighed and leaned her head against the chair back and gazed up at the star-sprinkled sky. "You can divorce 'em, but you can't escape 'em." She giggled. "Unless they die, of course."

Ashley sent her an aggravated glance, then looked back at Melanie. "Why's this the first I heard about it?"

"It's not." Melanie plucked a tortilla chip from the bowl and snapped it in half. "I told you about the lawyer I met with. About what a total ass he was. When I mentioned the episode to Veronica, she recommended a family-law attorney who also happens to be her friend. She also, graciously, offered to call and smooth the way." Melanie looked at Veronica and smiled. "Which I appreciate more than she can know."

Ashley sent Veronica an angry glance. "I could have given you a couple recommendations, Mel."

Veronica looked from Melanie to Ashley. "I'm sorry. Have I done something wrong?"

"Of course not," Melanie said quickly. "You did me a big favor, a huge one." She turned back to her sister. "This isn't a competition, Ash."

"That's right, Ash," Mia added, seemingly unaware of the tension at the table. "In fact, I vote we officially make her one of the Lane triplets."

"Triplets are three," Ashley snapped. "Not four."

"Quads then. How fun!" Mia stood, though none too steadily. "Barkeep, another pitcher!"

Melanie followed her sister to her feet. Although she thought Mia had consumed enough tequila for one night, she was grateful for the interruption. Sometimes she didn't understand her third sister at all. It was obvious that she had taken an instant dislike to Veronica, though Melanie couldn't fathom why. Veronica was one of those people *everybody* liked.

And Ashley was not. Maybe that was the problem.

"Refills coming up," she said.

"I'll help," Veronica said. She picked up the chip basket. "Got any more tortilla chips?"

"You bet. Ash, I've got some truly sinful frosted brownies in a box on the back seat of my car. Can you get them for me?"

Ash said she could, Mia announced that she had to pee and Veronica followed her to the kitchen.

"I'm really sorry about the way Ash is behaving," Melanie said. "I don't know what's gotten into her."

Veronica opened a bag of chips and dumped some into the basket. "It's pretty obvious she feels threatened by me, though I can't imagine why."

Melanie could. Ashley, for all her cynicism and bravado, was deeply insecure and highly sensitive. Far too often she wore her heart on her sleeve, though the casual observer would never know it. Veronica, on the other hand, was self-confident, bright and successful—if she'd had any demons in her personal closet, she seemed to have conquered them.

But understanding wasn't the same as condoning, and Melanie refused to pander to Ashley's moods. "I'm glad we have a moment alone," she murmured. "There's something I wanted to talk to you about."

"Oh? What's up?"

"Remember when I spoke to you about Jim McMillian's death?"

"Sure."

"Well, I've uncovered something…I mean, I think I've uncovered something and I wanted to get your opinion on it."

Veronica's gaze sharpened. "Shoot."

"I did a little digging, and—"

"This a private party? Or can anyone join in?"

Her third sister stood in the doorway to the garage, bakery box balanced on the palm of her right hand. Melanie motioned Ashley inside. She supposed it didn't matter if she shared her theory with her sisters. After all, at this point that's *all* it was. Besides, if she turned out to be correct, it would all end up on the front page anyway.

"Not a private party," she answered her sister. "A theory. In fact, I'd like your opinion. Pull up a stool."

"What's going on?" Mia emerged from the bathroom, cheeks flushed from having drunk too much.

"Big sister has a theory she's going to run by us." Ashley glanced at Melanie, all earlier tension erased from her features. She wiggled her eyebrows. "Something sinister, I hope?"

Melanie laughed. This was the Ashley she knew and loved being around—funny, slightly off center, acerbic. "Definitely."

"Hot dog." Ashley rubbed her hands together. "Right up my alley."

Mia plopped onto a stool. "Can we drink while we listen?"

"Lush."

"Sour sack."

"Ladies." Melanie tapped a spoon against the tile counter, interrupting her sisters. "Before I begin, I'm warning you, this theory of mine's a doozy. Try to keep an open mind." Melanie took a deep breath. "I believe a serial killer is operating in the Charlotte/Mecklenburg area. He, or she, is targeting and exterminating batterers and abusers who have either wriggled through cracks in the legal system or otherwise avoided justice."

Veronica nearly choked on her drink, Mia dropped a can of limeade and Ashley whistled and murmured, "Holy smokes, Batgirl."

Then the group fell silent. Melanie moved her gaze between the three women. "Now that I have your attention, let me tell you how I came to that conclusion.

"First," she said, "three men are dead. All accused batterers." She ticked them off on her fingers. "Jim McMillian. Accused of rape and sexual battery. Goes to trial, his lawyers get him off, though everyone knows he's guilty as sin. Eight months later, a freakish twist of fate finds him dead.''

She held up a second finger. "Thomas Weiss. I first become acquainted with this charming fellow when he puts his girlfriend in the hospital. We don't have enough to charge him, and he walks. Days later, he's dead—"

"The victim of a freakish twist of fate," Veronica supplied, then looked at the other two, sharing the story of the car accident and how it occurred.

"And number three?" Mia asked, eyes alight with interest. "Who's he?"

"Samson Gold. A cokehead who beat up on his girlfriend. Police did nothing, but fate did. He got ahold of a cocaine and pure heroin mixture that killed him.''

Ashley frowned. "Where'd you dig him up?"

"Pardon?"

"How did you hear about him? McMillian was a highly publicized case and Weiss you learned about through your work. Where did you hear about Gold? The obits?"

Melanie shook her head. "That doesn't matter. What's important here is, that's three dead batters. One too many, in my opinion, to be a coincidence.''

"This is so cool," Mia said, sliding off her stool, going for the box of brownies. "Like the plot of a movie or TV show." She slit the Scotch tape with her fingernail and lifted the box lid. "What are you going to do next?"

"I don't know." She looked at Veronica. "Any ideas?"

The attorney pursed her lips. "It's an interesting theory and if there's anything to it, very juicy. Do you have something that actually links these men or their deaths?"

"I've confirmed the details of all their deaths with the coroner's office and checked police records, but so far," she admitted, "no, I don't. But I know I'm right about this, I feel it in my gut."

"If I were you," Veronica murmured, "I'd tread carefully. Very carefully. I've seen too many good cases, and good cops for that matter, shot down for lack of evidence. You're not with the CMPD, which is a strike against you. You know as well as I, Melanie, that it's going to be hard to get anyone to take you seriously."

She *was* right, as frustrating as it was to admit. "You think I should let it go?"

"Can you?"

"And sleep nights?" She thought about it a moment. "I don't think so."

"Why not?" Mia chimed up. She lifted her glass. "I say, good riddance, A-holes!"

Melanie looked at her sister, shocked. "You don't mean that."

"Sure she does," Ashley said, wandering over to the box of brownies and helping herself to one. "Why wouldn't she?"

"That's right. Why wouldn't I?" Mia's words slurred. "Proceed slowly, sister-dear. If you give this guy enough time, maybe he'll zero in on Boyd and Stan."

Melanie frowned. "You're drunk, Mia."

She swayed on her feet, then grabbed the edge

of the counter for support. "Do I have to be drunk to wish my husband dead? He's a bastard and I hate him."

"Mia," Melanie said softly, patiently, "I understand the way you feel. I do. You're going through a tough time. But murder's always wrong. I don't even want you to joke about it."

"Who's joking?" Ashley asked. "Because I don't think Mia is."

"Don't you hate Stan?" Mia asked. "He's trying to steal your son. He's screwed you at every turn. Don't you hate him?"

"Some days? Sure. Do I ever wish he would just go away? Just disappear off the face of the planet? Yeah, sometimes I do. But I can handle Stan. I *will* handle him. Not rely on some wacko to bump him off for me."

"But I can't take care of myself, right?" Mia drew back, her expression hurt. "Because I'm not strong like you."

"I didn't mean that. I only meant—"

"Oh, come on." Ashley tossed the remainder of her brownie into the trash. "Be honest, Melanie. Criminals fall through the cracks all the time. Especially ones who do things like hurt women and children. Hardly a crime at all, for all the protection they get. Like that Jim McMillian, guilty as hell but some *lawyer* got him off. I'm with Mia on this, good riddance to bad rubbish."

Veronica weighed in then. "I'm a lawyer and there are times the injustice of the system gets to me. So I understand where you're both coming from." Her voice grew husky and she cleared her throat. "But the law protects us, too. No one can be judged and convicted without a burden of proof against them. Which is why domestic violence and rape are so difficult to get convictions on. But still, that's the way it should be. Our laws were designed to protect the innocent."

Ashley snorted with disgust, "All this goody-goody crap is about to make me puke. The truth is, what it usually comes down to is one person's word against another's—a *man's* against a woman's or child's. Who do you think is going to come out on top?"

Melanie looked at her youngest sister in disbelief. "You don't really believe that, do you?"

"Two peas in a pod," Ashley said sarcastically, moving her gaze from Melanie to Veronica. "Maybe you two should have been the twins."

Melanie stiffened. "How would you expect us to think, Ash? We're both in law enforcement. And what you're talking about here is vigilantism. You and Mia are saying it's okay to take the law into your own hands."

"That's precisely what I'm saying," Ashley murmured, tone fierce. "Some people don't deserve to live. Our father didn't deserve to live."

Ashley looked at Mia, then back at Melanie. "Don't you ever wonder what our lives would have been like without him? Or even better, with a real father instead of an abusive pig? Don't you ever look at your life, track it back and see exactly where it went wrong? *Who* made it go wrong?"

Melanie held out a hand. "Don't do this, Ash. Please."

Ashley ignored her sister's outstretched hand. "He should have been locked up. He should have gone to jail for what he did to us. For what he did to...Mia. But he didn't. He walked the streets, a shining example to all of a good man and model father. The prick."

"Hate will eat you alive," Veronica murmured. "You can't go back, only forward. I know from experience, Ashley. I—"

"What do you know about me!" Ashley turned on Veronica, trembling with fury. "You're not inside my skin! You're *not* one of my sisters, no matter what Mia says! You're nothing to me, do you understand? Nothing! So don't presume, never presume, to tell me what's best for me!"

"But she's right, Ash." Melanie held out a hand to her sister once more, aching for her. "The only person all that hatred is hurting is you."

Ashley stared at her outstretched hand, expression anguished, then lifted her gaze from it to Melanie's. "Have I lost you?" she asked, her tone small and devastated. "Have I lost you both? To *her?*"

Melanie shook her head. "Of course not. You're our sister. No one could ever take your place. We love—"

"That's bullshit!" she cried, snatching her purse off the counter. She bolted to the back door, stopping and turning to look at the other women when she reached it. "It's all just bullshit."

24

Melanie liked Pamela Barrett, the attorney Veronica had recommended, right off. She had a broad smile, a firm handshake and an air of uncomplicated honesty and unshakable self-confidence about her.

"Melanie," she said. "I'm so glad to meet you." She released her hand. "Come in."

Pamela told her secretary to hold her calls, then closed the office door behind them. She motioned toward the couch and love seat. "Why don't we sit over here?"

They did, Melanie choosing the love seat, Pamela the couch, facing her. "Veronica spoke of you in glowing terms. She also said you were desperate."

Melanie winced at the way that sounded, but acknowledged it was true. "I appreciate you seeing me on such short notice. I'm afraid Veronica was right, I didn't know where to turn for help."

She smiled sympathetically. "I understand. And let me assure you, you've turned to the right person."

The attorney quickly detailed her history with family law, her successful record and that she, too, was a divorced mother who'd had to fight off an ex-husband's custody bid.

"So you can see, I'm on your side in this and

I'll do whatever I can to ensure you don't lose custody of your son. Now, Veronica filled me in on a few of the details of your situation. Why don't you tell me the rest? Begin wherever you think it's appropriate.''

Melanie told her why she had left Stan, how he had constantly interfered in her life since and how she had always feared he would attempt to take custody of Casey from her. She shared the details of the conversations she'd had with Stan since he had initiated his custody bid and also her negative meeting with John Peoples.

Pamela nodded, jotting down notes as Melanie spoke.

When Melanie paused, the lawyer reviewed what she had written, then met Melanie's eyes. ''Tell me what a typical week is like for you and Casey.''

When Melanie had, the attorney asked about Stan's schedule, his new wife and their marriage, the kind of father he was. His life-style. She asked, too, about both her and Stan's extended family and their relationship with Casey.

Finally, the woman set her notebook aside. Melanie held her breath. Pamela was on her side; Melanie believed that. So, if the attorney was even halfway as pessimistic of her chances as the previous lawyer had been, Melanie didn't know what she would do.

''First off,'' the woman began, ''let me tell you that I've had dealings with John Peoples. Just between you and me, I found him to be an underinformed, misogynist windbag. Discount everything he said. However, I have also dealt with your husband's attorney. He's smart and savvy. The ultimate professional.''

"The best money can buy," Melanie said bitterly, her spirits sinking.

Pamela Barrett leaned forward, an eagerness in her eyes—to do battle, to face a worthy opponent and win. "He's good but he's not better than me."

She paused to let that sink in, then continued. "From what you've told me, I see no reason a judge would award Stan custody. In fact, from what you've told me, you're a more hands-on parent than your husband. Forget your ex-husband's argument about the advantages of his more lavish life-style. That's his value system talking, not the judge's."

"What about my job? Peoples said—"

"I told you, discount everything he said. *Everything,* Melanie." She shifted in her seat, crossing her legs. "The judge will interview you, Stan, his wife, a couple other family members from both sides. We'll rehearse, but up front I'll tell you, I want your love for Casey to come shining through. Your natural warmth. Your devotion to your family. The closeness you share with your sisters and they with Casey."

She smiled. "We're going to blow your controlling, materialistic ex-husband out of the water. Mark my words."

Melanie nearly cried out with relief. "Thank you. Thank you so much."

"You're welcome." Pamela stood, signaling that the meeting had ended. "I'll contact your husband's attorney and we'll get this thing going. Expect to hear from me in a couple of days."

Melanie thanked her again, and they walked to the door. When they reached it, Pamela held out her hand. "Don't worry about a thing, Melanie. You're in good hands."

"I believe I am." Melanie started out the door, then stopped. "Your own custody case, it was successful?"

"As a matter of fact, yes."

"And that was the end of it?"

Pamela made a sound of sympathy, seeing, Melanie had no doubt, the fear behind her question. That it would never end, that even if the judge ruled in her favor, Stan would try again. And again.

The attorney answered and Melanie saw that she had been correct. "I understand your concern, Melanie. But let me reassure you, unless there's abuse or neglect involved, it's not easy to have a judge's ruling overturned. This is your ex-husband's best shot. And I believe he's going to lose."

"And in your case? Did your ex-husband accept the judge's ruling and fade gracefully into the night?"

"In a manner of speaking. My ex moved away shortly after the ruling. It was really hard on the kids and I regretted that. I hated them growing up without their father close by."

But she hadn't personally regretted his leaving, Melanie thought, saying goodbye again. She recalled her and her sisters' argument of the other night. Yes, she would hate for Casey not to be able to see his father. But to be honest, she would feel little but relief if Stan disappeared off the face of the planet tomorrow.

25

Melanie left the attorney's, all but walking on air. For the first time since Stan informed her of his intention to sue for custody, she felt as though everything was going to be okay. No, she felt better than that. She felt unbeatable.

Halfway back to Charlotte, her beeper went off. Headquarters. Using her cell phone, she called in. Bobby answered.

"Hey, partner," she said. "You rang?"

"Where are you?"

"Twenty, twenty-five minutes outside Charlotte. What's up?"

"They're putting Jenkins in a lineup. The chief wants us there."

"When?"

"Four o'clock."

She checked her watch. *Damn.* "I'll meet you there."

The lineup was under way when Melanie arrived. She sidled over to Bobby's side. "What have I missed?" she asked, her voice low.

"Not much. The photo lineup they did this morning proved inconclusive, so here we are. They just got started."

She quickly scanned the room. Besides the

CMPD guys and Bobby, she saw the ADA who would be handling the case—the same one who'd attended Jenkins's interrogation—and another suit she guessed was the suspect's lawyer. Connor Parks was not present. She acknowledged disappointment—irritating though he was, Parks kept her on her toes and made her think.

She turned her attention to the scene in progress. Pete Harrison was calling for each man to step forward, turn to the right, then left. Melanie recognized Jenkins—number three in the lineup—from his interrogation the other day. Pale, forehead shiny with sweat, he looked a hairbreadth from throwing up.

"Okay, Gayle," Harrison said to the witness, "take a good look. Do you recognize the man you saw approach Joli Andersen in the parking lot the night of her murder?"

The woman made a small sound of distress. "I'm not…sure. I—"

"Take your time," the ADA said. "We want you to be absolutely certain."

The woman nodded, took a deep breath and leaned slightly forward. "It was dark, but…he was built like number three. And he had hair kinda like his…sort of dark…and curlyish."

"Sort of?" the suspect's lawyer said. "Kind of? Was the man's hair like his, or not?"

She glanced nervously at Harrison, then back at the viewing window. "I…yes, it was."

"Is number three the man you saw?"

The ADA cleared her throat in warning. The witness wrung her hands. "I wouldn't want to be wrong."

"Absolutely not."

She bit her lip. "Could you have number three step forward again?"

Harrison did, and she studied him a moment. "That might be him."

The investigators exchanged glances. "Might?" Harrison prodded.

"It could be." Her voice rose. "Like I said, it was dark. And I was hurrying to my car."

"Of course you were," Jenkins's lawyer interjected smoothly, his tone conciliatory. "After all, it was very late."

"Yes." She looked relieved. "Very."

"And you'd been drinking."

She darted a glance at the police. "A little."

Melanie's heart sank. There'd be no charge forthcoming from this witness's testimony.

"Thanks for coming in, Gayle," the ADA said. "We really appreciate it."

"That's it?" The ADA nodded, and the woman stood. "I'm...sorry I wasn't more help."

"You were a great help. I'll walk you out."

"I told you you had the wrong man," Jenkins's lawyer said as soon as the door shut behind them, his expression smug.

"What makes you think we have the wrong man?" Stemmons shot back. "An eyewitness just confirmed that your client has the same build and coloring as the man last seen with Joli Andersen."

The attorney snorted with amusement. "Yeah, right. Kind of, sort of. You don't have one piece of physical evidence linking my client to the crime scene, not even a fingerprint. You've got nothing.'' He walked to the door, glancing back at them when he reached it. ''Back off or I'll hit you with a harassment suit so fast your heads will spin.''

When the door snapped shut behind the man, Pete swore. ''The weasel's guilty as sin.''

Melanie frowned, unconvinced. ''With all the evidence left at the scene, we have nothing that links Jenkins to it. No print match. No hair or fiber. That doesn't bother you?''

''It bothers the shit out of me. I got a feeling in my gut about that little fuck.''

''He sure looked guilty,'' Bobby murmured. ''I'm surprised she didn't finger him on the volume of his sweat alone.''

''But don't you think that undermines her testimony even more?'' Melanie murmured. ''He looked *that* guilty and she still couldn't ID him. What's going to happen if we're able to charge and he shows up in court, cool as a cucumber? Her uncertainty's going to double.''

''Or treble,'' Pete Harrison muttered, then swore. ''This really sucks. There's something off about that guy. Something bad off.''

Melanie didn't disagree with that assessment of Jenkins's character. But it didn't bring her any closer to believing he was their guy. She kept coming back to Connor Parks's profile. And Ted Jenkins didn't fit it.

She told them so.

''Screw Parks,'' Roger Stemmons said, speaking up for the first time since the lawyer's exit. ''You didn't see him here today, did you? The man's a major pain in my ass.''

"He also gets results." Melanie moved her gaze between the men. "He was one of the Bureau's top profilers, how stupid would we be if we didn't take advantage of that experience?''

To Melanie's surprise, Pete agreed with her. "But I also say we keep the pressure on this guy. Harassment, my ass, we've got just cause."

The four agreed and filed out of the room and into the hall. They fell into step, making their way to the elevators. A car was waiting; they stepped inside. Melanie stood beside Pete and she glanced at him. "Weren't you one of the investigators on the Jim McMillian case?'' she asked, working to sound casual.

"Yeah, what about it?''

"You saw that he died.''

The man smiled. "Score one for the good guys.''

"No joke." She felt Bobby's warning gaze on her and deliberately avoided it. She had to do this. "His death, odd circumstances, I thought.''

"In what way?''

She shrugged, wanting to appear nonchalant, choosing to feel the CMPD guys out before she laid her suspicions on the table. "That essentially he was poisoned by the very substance he was taking to stay healthy. After all, the digitalis brought on the heart attack.''

"So?'' The car stopped; the elevator doors slid open and the four stepped off. "It's rare but it happens, right?''

"Right. But another batterer, a suspect of mine, died recently, also under odd circumstances."

The man looked at her, his gaze sharp. "And you think the two are related?"

"I didn't say that. I just found it a bit of a coincidence. That's all." She glanced at her watch, as if only half-interested in the conversation. "You aware of any other guys like McMillian dying unexpectedly?"

"Oh sure." The man's mouth twisted into an amused smirk. "They're dropping like flies."

"Come on, Mel," Bobby said, nudging her. "The chief wanted us to report in, ASAP."

She ignored him. "Actually, Pete, I have uncovered a third victim. His name was Samson Gold. He died snorting what he thought was coke. It turned out to be a mixture of coke and pure heroin."

"That *is* rare," Roger murmured, chuckling. "A junkie who dies of an overdose. Quick, call the FBI."

Pete patted her on the back. "You're chasing crimes that don't exist, May."

Melanie stiffened. She didn't deserve their amusement; she didn't deserve their condescension. But because she was a Whistlestop cop, everything she said was a big joke.

"And you're certain of that?" she asked. "Just like you're so certain Connor Parks's profile is wrong and Jenkins is Joli Andersen's killer? But if you're so smart, how come you haven't been able to bring him in?"

Two spots of hot color stained the investigator's

cheeks. "Instead of running after imaginary killers, May, maybe you should pay a little more attention to what's going on in your own backyard."

"And what's that supposed to mean?"

"Ask your brother-in-law."

Harrison started to walk away, but she caught his arm, stopping him. "No, you to tell me, because I don't have a clue what you're talking about."

He stared at her a moment, his expression hard. "You know what, May? It'll be my pleasure. Your brother-in-law was in a few weeks ago, said you threatened him. Said he had witnesses."

Even as a denial sprang to her lips, she remembered. *The hospital. Her telling him that if he hurt her sister again, she wouldn't be held accountable for her actions.* Melanie felt herself pale and she cursed her temper.

"It was nothing," she said. "A family misunderstanding."

"Not according to Dr. Donaldson." Pete looked at Bobby. "You might think about getting yourself another partner. This one's a loose cannon. She's going to get somebody hurt."

The men walked away, and she turned back to Bobby, furious at her treatment. "He's wrong," she said. "I am *not* chasing killers that don't exist. If his head wasn't so far up his—"

"Give it a rest, Mel. I don't want to hear it."

She saw then that the terminally easygoing Bobby was angry. That her confrontation with the investigator had embarrassed him.

She made a sound of regret. "I saw the opportunity and took it. I thought that maybe Harrison would—''

"What?" he interrupted, keeping his voice low. "Fall at your feet in appreciation of your awesome detecting skills? That he would not only validate you, but beg you to let him join you in the hunt for Charlotte's newest serial killer?"

Bobby looked away, then back at her. "Next time you want to present some far-fetched theories to the CMPD guys—or anyone else—do it alone. I don't need the humiliation."

She took a step back, surprised by her partner's sarcasm. By the depth of his anger. Obviously, this had been brewing for some time. "I didn't know you felt that way about working with me, Bobby," she said stiffly. "But I do now. I won't *humiliate* you again."

He muttered an oath. "Look, Melanie. I like you. I like working with you, you're a good cop. But you...you've got a chip on your shoulder. A big one. And it's getting in the way."

It took a moment for his words to sink in. "In the way?" she repeated. "Of what? Our relationship? Or my work?"

"Either, both. You name it." He looked away, then back, his expression tight. "Working the Whistlestop force is never going to be high-profile. The cases are never going to be sexy. And that's okay with me. Maybe it's time for you to ask yourself if it's okay with you."

26

Unable to sleep, Melanie stared at the ceiling. A week had passed since she and Bobby had fallen out, a week since she had humiliated him—and herself—in front of the CMPD guys.

In those seven days, the things her partner and the other detectives had said to her had worked at her like a splinter, a constant irritation, chafing at the very edge of her thoughts, drawing her attention away from other, less troublesome things.

Which was precisely why she was awake at 4:00 a.m., cursing her sleeplessness. For the seventh night in a row.

Suspecting that this night would be no different than the previous ones, she climbed out of bed and headed to the kitchen to make a pot of coffee.

Careful not to disturb Casey, she got a pot brewing, then leaned against the counter and watched the brown liquid drip into the glass carafe. She yawned and the aroma of coffee filled her head, seeming to jump-start her brain.

The solution to her problem was obvious.

She needed help. The support of someone with more credentials than a cop with a force no bigger than the average spit on a hot, dry day. She was alone in this. Bobby had made his position crystal clear, as had the CMPD. She didn't dare go to her chief—if she did and he told her to drop it, she would be forced to or risk her career.

So, the question was, how did she get someone to come on board with her?

She needed more proof. Something to link the victims. Something conclusive. Or too coincidental to be ignored.

She needed another dead batterer.

She straightened, suddenly fully awake. Of course. How could she have been so thick? There could be many more victims. This killer could have been operating for years.

She began to pace, coffee forgotten. She had found the three victims so easily, by chance really. But now she knew what to look for. A history of abuse against women. Deaths involving bizarre accidents.

How hard could it be?

Melanie found out just how hard. In the weeks that followed she spent every available waking moment working to locate the proof she needed. She went without sleep; she neglected Casey, depending on television and videos to entertain him; she had seen neither of her sisters in two weeks and had only had a couple of hurried conversations with them in all that time; at work, she was only doing the minimum, allowing Bobby to pick up the slack. She was a woman obsessed, totally focused on proving she was right.

The library became her best friend. The weekends Casey was with his dad, she arrived as they opened their doors and left when they closed them, spending that time searching the microfilm back issues of the *Charlotte Observer*'s obituaries.

She began with issues dated a year and a half ago, her intention to look for men who had died as the result of bizarre accidents. She'd realized quickly that depending on the information provided in the obituary, almost anything could be suspect. She ruled out murders, deaths of very young men and the very old; she also ruled out anyone who'd died after a "long illness." She made note of any victims of heart attacks.

Melanie had thought it would be easy. Instead, it was like looking for a needle in a haystack, tedious, slow going. Near-impossible. With each questionable death, she recorded the victim's name, their municipality, the names of family members left behind, if services had been held and where.

Her list grew. Her enthusiasm waned. But not her determination. She was like a dog with a bone between its teeth and she was not about to let go.

At night, she studied up on serial killers. Ted Bundy. Son of Sam. The Atlanta child killer. The Green River killer. She read accounts from the FBI's serial-crime unit, running across Connor Parks's name on several occasions.

From her research, she learned that serial killers were almost always men. She learned that they rarely killed across racial lines and that they typically operated in one place or region for a long period of time. Their killings followed a pattern, or ritual. That ritual could evolve, but it didn't vary. This pattern created a recognizable signature for the criminal investigator to read. It allowed him or her a glimpse inside the killer's mind. And offered law enforcement its most effective means of catching them.

Connor Parks was the one she would go to. When she had her proof.

The words on the page before her blurred. Melanie rubbed the bridge of her nose, acknowledging fatigue. The stirrings of despair. Standing and stretching, Melanie gave in to the first and fought off the second.

It was no wonder she was feeling depressed. The research was grisly. Disturbing. It left her wondering what could twist the human psyche to the point that such heinous acts of man against man were possible. What could contort it to the point that even murder was not enough to satisfy, that pleasure could only be attained from another's screams of agony. Who made these monsters? Where did they come from?

And how could the world be rid of them?

Melanie shuddered, then glanced toward Casey's bedroom, fear settling over her like a cold, wet shroud. Stealing her peace of mind, chilling her to her core.

Her heart began to pound; her breath grew short, her palms damp. She hurried to his bedroom door; she eased it open and peeked inside the dark room.

He was there in his bed, safe and asleep.

The breath shuddered past her lips, and Melanie stood in his doorway for long moments, letting the sound of his soft snores comfort her. He slept soundly, covers wadded at his feet. He lay on his stomach, one arm looped over his favorite stuffed bunny, the other around a plush dinosaur.

He was growing up so fast, she thought. Before long he would want her to pack away his stuffed lovies—about the same time, she suspected, that he stopped letting her kiss him in front of his friends.

She crossed to the bed. His hair stuck out in every direction; his cheeks were flushed with sleep, his mouth slightly open. Melanie lifted the sheet and blanket and drew them back over him, tucking them in at the sides.

"I love you," she whispered, bending and ever so lightly brushing her mouth against his cheek. "Sleep well."

Melanie backed carefully out of the room, loath to take her eyes off him, spirits buoyed. She had started this thing; she would finish it. Even if that finish yielded nothing but disappointment.

With one last glance at her son, she headed for her own bedroom. There, she slipped out of her leggings and big shirt and into her pajamas. Tomorrow she would begin the next step in her investigation, following up on the information she had collected from the obituaries.

For practical reasons, she had decided to begin with the most recent deaths and work back in time. She padded into the bathroom to brush her teeth. She figured the more recent the obit, the more likely the family of the departed was to still be at the same location. She would run each name through the department's computer, checking for priors. After that, she would call the family of the departed, on what pretense she hadn't decided yet.

Melanie rinsed her mouth, spit, then repeated the process. Tomorrow, she thought, yawning again as she flipped off the bathroom light, would be soon enough to decide that.

Tomorrow came in the blink of an eye. And in what seemed like two blinks she had bathed and dressed—first herself, then Casey—fed them both breakfast, dropped him off at preschool and reported for work.

There, between checking the previous night's logs and the tips that had come in on the hot line, going to the five-and-dime to photograph some vandalism that had occurred there the night before and taking complaints about the homeless in the municipal park, Melanie made her calls.

She used a different story each time, ones sometimes fashioned from information gleaned from the obituary, sometimes spun from thin air. She was an old friend from college, a sweepstakes' representative, a long lost family member.

By about the dozenth call, Melanie had to admit she was becoming adept at improvising. She had never thought of herself as a particularly slick liar—she saw now that she had been underestimating herself. Perhaps, she decided, she had never been as motivated.

Along about lunchtime, Bobby, who had been unusually quiet, asked her what she was doing.

She looked up, phone propped between her shoulder and ear, poised to dial a new number. "A bit of homework," she said.

He arched an eyebrow, and she shook her head.

"Don't ask me. You don't want to know, not officially."

Unofficially, he already knew what she was doing. She saw it in his expression. But if she remained silent, he could play dumb. If not, he would have to report her activities to the chief. Or, by his silence involve himself. And she didn't want him to do that, either. This was her baby, and if it blew up in her face, she didn't want anyone else injured by flying shrapnel.

Bobby glanced over his shoulder at the chief's closed door, then back at her. "You can't leave it alone, can you, Melanie? You just have to be right."

It hurt to hear him say that. She pushed the emotion away. "No, I can't leave it alone. But it's not about wanting to be right. It's about *knowing* I'm right. Somebody's murdering these guys, Bobby. I'm not going to let him get away with it. I can't."

"Are you sure you know what you're doing? This could blow up in your face."

His words mirrored her thought of a moment ago, and she inclined her head. "I know. And I don't want you involved in case that happens."

He gazed at her a moment more, then returned to his work, signaling that the subject was closed. And that he would support her with his silence.

"Bobby?" He looked up, and she smiled, grateful for his friendship. "Thanks."

27

Veronica dug the gardening shovel into the soft, black earth. The summer day was warm, the sky a cloudless blue. Almost July, it was too late to be getting her annuals in, but finding the time before now had been impossible. She'd had one trial after another; each had required considerable prep time and each had run long. She had been scrambling to keep up. So, here she was.

Veronica sat back and surveyed what she had done so far, a double row of multicolored impatiens, and she smiled. She loved gardening. Loved the smells and the colors and getting her hands good and dirty. If she hadn't felt the call of the law, she would have opened a nursery. She had already decided that if she ever tired of the prosecutor's office, she would retire to a greenhouse.

Her father would turn over in his grave. His daughter, a gardener.

Her smile broadened and she returned to her planting, sprinkling a pinch of plant food in each hole she dug, then dropping in the plant and filling the hole.

At the peal of her doorbell, Veronica glanced over her shoulder, toward the front of the house.

"I'm over here," she called, then returned to her planting. "In the side garden."

"Hi, Veronica."

She turned. Mia stood hesitantly at the garden gate, one hand to her eyes to shield them from the sun, the other curved around the handle of a basket brimming with plump, red strawberries.

Veronica smiled, surprised but pleased. "Mia, hello. What brings you here?"

"I was...in the area and thought I'd stop by. I hope that's okay."

Normally, it wouldn't have been. As much as Veronica enjoyed other people's company, she was also a solitary person. Her home was her private domain—a place to lick her wounds, plan her strategies and recharge her spirit. She didn't readily welcome others in, especially ones who dropped by unexpectedly.

But Mia was different. Veronica didn't know exactly why, but she was. "Of course it's okay. Come in."

"I brought you something." The other woman held out the basket of berries. "They're incredibly sweet. I tried one."

Veronica moved her gaze to the offering, then back to Mia's. She didn't have the heart to tell her she couldn't eat them. She was deathly allergic to the fruit. "They look beautiful," she murmured. "Thank you."

Mia's lips curved into a stunning smile, and a feeling of affection surged through Veronica, so strong and warm it took her breath.

One moment became several and Veronica

cleared her throat, embarrassed at the way she had been staring stupidly at the other woman. "I'll make us some iced tea."

She stood, peeled off her work gloves, then brushed the dirt and mulch from her knees. She motioned Mia. "This way."

Mia followed Veronica inside. As she poured them both a glass of the herbal tea, garnishing each with a lemon wedge and a sprig of fresh mint, she sensed rather than saw Mia appraising the sunny kitchen, with its navy blue tile counters, copper stove hood and cypress cabinetry. She wondered what the other woman thought of her restored Victorian bungalow.

As if reading Veronica's mind, she murmured, "It's lovely."

Unnerved, Veronica laid an antique doily on the counter in front of Mia, then set the glass of tea on it.

"I love Dilworth," Mia continued, referring to the section of town where Veronica lived, one of the oldest in Charlotte. "But Boyd insisted on new. And what Boyd wants, Boyd gets." She tasted her tea. "Delicious. What is it?"

"It's called Blue Eyes. Would you like a tour of the house?"

Mia said she would and chattered as Veronica led her from room to room. Veronica used the opportunity to study the other woman. She found it odd that although Mia and Melanie were identical twins, they were as different as night and day. Where Mia was often uncertain of what she wanted and seemed to need constant attention, Melanie seemed to need no one and always spoke her mind, no matter what. Although Veronica admired that kind of confidence and strength of will, those qualities weren't as personally appealing to her. In fact, she sometimes found herself put off by Melanie's emphatic approach to life.

They finished the tour in Veronica's light-filled bedroom. "It's so pretty!" Mia exclaimed, crossing to the antique four-poster bed. She sank onto it and ran her hand over the Victorian print coverlet.

"One of the advantages of being single," Veronica murmured, shifting her gaze, cheeks warm, "my bedroom can be as feminine as I want it to be."

Mia laughed and laid back against the pretty flowered print, gazing up at the ceiling. "I feel like a girl again, off at my best friend's house for a sleep-over."

Veronica looked at her friend, her mouth going dry, her heart beginning to race. Mia was so pretty and soft-looking. She didn't have any hard edges, no brittle, world-weary veneer.

"Did you do that?" Mia asked. "Sleep-overs with girlfriends?"

"What girl didn't?"

"Melanie was always my best friend. And Ash, too." Her smile faded, and she sat up. "Have you talked to Mel lately?"

Veronica shook her head. "No. I've called but—"

"She's been unavailable," Mia supplied, her tone hurt. "Too busy with that stupid theory of hers." She made a sound of frustration. "At first I thought it was intriguing. Kind of exciting. I wanted her to go for it. But I didn't think she'd drop everything in her life to pursue it. That's not right, do you think?''

Veronica didn't think it was. And she was angry with Melanie, angry about her obsession with the Dark Angel and that in her quest for so-called justice, she was hurting people who cared about her. The people who deserved her loyalty. Including Veronica. And Mia. "It's something she feels she has to do," she murmured, unwilling to share her real feelings with Mia. "Obviously. I can understand that. There are things in my life I feel that strongly about."

"But do you dump the people who need you? Do you forget they even exist?"

"No," Veronica murmured, realizing the extent of the other woman's hurt, her sense of abandonment by her sister.

She crossed to the bed and sat beside Mia. She touched her hand in an attempt to comfort. "Melanie hasn't dumped you. Or me, for that matter. And she could no more forget you exist then stop breathing. She's just…totally focused on this killer of hers. It'll be over soon, because she'll either find something or she won't. And if she does, it'll become an official investigation and part of her nine-to-five responsibilities."

"What do I do in the meantime?" Mia asked, voice high and young sounding. "Melanie's always been the one I turned to. Always."

"Turn to me." When Mia looked at her in surprise, Veronica flushed, embarrassed. By her offer.

And by how hopeful she was that Mia would accept it.

Veronica cleared her throat. "I mean, we're... friends and if you want, I'll be here for you."

For a moment Mia was silent, then she smiled. The curving of her lips lit up her face and eyes, as if her melancholy had magically disappeared. "As a teenager, did you ever play the game Truth or Dare?" Veronica nodded, and Mia went on. "Melanie always chose truth, Ashley dare."

Intrigued, Veronica asked. "What about you?"

"I never wanted to take either. What a wienie." She met Veronica's eyes, almost flirtatiously. "So, ADA Ford, truth or dare, if you could have anything in the world, what would it be?"

Veronica's cheeks heated, though she wasn't sure from embarrassment over the question or her physical reaction to it—racing pulse, breathlessness, sweating palms.

What was wrong with her?

"Well, Counselor," Mia teased. "What's it going to be?"

"Truth, if I must." She tilted her head. "If I could have anything? It would have to be love. Real love, not infatuation or lust. Someone I could trust with all my secrets. And who trusts me the same way. Someone to be with and take care of." Her voice thickened. "A person to take the loneliness away."

Shocked by how much she had revealed, Veronica looked away, forcing a laugh. "So much for the hard-as-nails prosecutor. I sound like one of those teenagers you just mentioned.''

Mia reached for Veronica's hand. She laced their fingers. ''Don't be embarrassed. It's what I want, too. It's what I thought I'd have when I married, but—'' Mia's eyes filled with tears, and she looked away, clearly struggling not to cry.

Veronica swallowed hard. She felt herself being pulled toward this woman, as she had never been pulled toward another. She curved her fingers tighter around Mia's. ''It's your husband, isn't it? He's the reason you're here today. He's the reason you're so unhappy.''

''Yes,'' she whispered, not meeting her eyes. ''How did you know?''

''I've gathered from things you've said that there was…trouble. I'm here if you want to talk about it.''

''Thanks, but…'' Mia shook her head. ''I'm sure the last thing you want to hear about is my problems.''

''That's not true. We're friends, right? Good enough friends to listen to each other's troubles and try to help?''

When the other woman still didn't look at her, she softly called her name. Mia lifted her gaze. ''Aren't we good enough friends?''

For long moments, Mia simply gazed at her, eyes swimming with unshed tears. Then she nodded. ''My husband, he…he's running around on me. And when I accused him, he flew into a rage and he…hit me. That wasn't the first…wasn't the only…''

Mia's words trailed off and Veronica sucked in a sharp breath, fighting against the rage stirring inside her, the rage that sometimes emerged, so strong and hot it all but blinded her. She tamped it back, though not without considerable effort. "You don't have to put up with that, Mia. And you shouldn't."

"That's what Melanie says." She laughed self-consciously and wiped her eyes with the heels of her hands. "Ash tells me to get a grip."

In Veronica's opinion, Ashley was the last person who should tell anybody to get a grip, but she kept that to herself.

"There's nothing wrong with you. *Nothing.*" Veronica caught Mia's hands and squeezed them for emphasis. "You haven't left him, because you're scared. Of him. Of leaving him. Because he's made you think you need him. Because he's made you think you're not smart enough or strong enough to make it without him. That's what men like your husband do."

Mia shook her head, expression anguished. "You don't understand. You couldn't. Look at you, an assistant district attorney, smart and successful. What have I done since I got married? Shopped? Lunched?"

"Stop it, Mia. Right now." Veronica caught her hands again. "What you're saying, it's what he wants you to think. How he's programmed you to think. He gets off on controlling you, on knowing he's turned you into a timid little mouse, afraid of her own shadow. It's part of his sickness. And it's not true."

"You don't know! How could you?"

"How?" Veronica repeated. "Because I was you. A long time ago, I was married to the same kind of man you are. He belittled and criticized me. To break me down. To undermine my belief in myself and my abilities. It got to the point I was afraid to make any decision without consulting him. I asked him what I should eat, wear, how I should have my hair styled. And the more I needed him, the more he belittled me."

Her voice shook; she steadied it. "I gave him everything. Even my self-respect. And he cheated on me with another woman. He laughed at me when I confronted him, then taunted me with his affair."

She had Mia's full attention now. The other woman was staring at her, eyes wide with disbelief. "What happened?" she asked, voice shaking. "How did you find the courage to leave him?"

"I didn't. He died in an accident." Veronica looked at her and Mia's joined hands, noticing how soft and white Mia's were, how flawless her skin. She swallowed hard and dragged her gaze away. "So you see, I wasn't strong. And it's only with hindsight that I can see what was happening to me. What he had done to me. That's why I know what your husband's doing to you."

She took a deep breath and looked Mia straight in the eye. "You don't need him, Mia. You'll see, I promise you will. Because I'll help you."

28

Melanie reviewed her list of possible victims. In the past week she had spoken to thirty next of kin. None of those deaths had jumped out at her as being suspicious. Next up was Joshua Reynolds. Burned to death in his bed back in January. After reading the obit, she had contacted the fire department. The autopsy showed the man's blood alcohol level had been sky-high. Apparently, he lit up a smoke, then passed out. The guy had a history of smoking in bed and had started fires that way before.

This time luck had not been with him. His cigarette had dropped into a filled wastebasket. The entire place had gone up, Reynolds with it.

He had been survived by a wife and two kids. Luckily, when the accident occurred, they had been staying the weekend at Mrs. Reynolds's mother's in Asheville.

A trip into the department's computer provided the wife's current address and phone number—Melanie punched it in. After four rings, a woman answered. "Good morning," Melanie said cheerfully. "Is this the residence of Mrs. Joshua Reynolds?"

The woman hesitated. "It is," she said finally. "May I help you?"

"Is this Rita Reynolds?"

"Who's calling, please?" Her tone had gone from marginally warm to positively frigid.

Melanie crossed her fingers. As Bobby had pointed out earlier that day, if the chief got wind of what she was doing, of how she was misrepresenting herself, he would have her badge. "The America Sweepstakes Award Center, ma'am. Is this Mrs. Joshua Reynolds?"

"Yes," she said. "If you're selling something, I'm not—"

"I'm glad I was able to locate you," Melanie plowed on. "Your husband is one of our grand-prize win—"

"Who is this?"

"I told you, I'm with—"

"Who are you really with? The insurance company again?"

Her voice rose. Melanie heard children in the background. And a dog barking. She glanced at her watch. The Reynolds' kids, arriving home from school.

"I told you," the woman said. "I had nothing to do with his death. Though I can't say I mourn his passing. Good day."

The line went dead. Excited, Melanie quickly dialed again. When the woman picked up, Melanie said, "I'm a police officer, Mrs. Reynolds. My name's Officer May and I'm looking into the possibility that your husband was murdered."

"I talked to you people already!" the woman

cried. "I answered a million of your questions. I took a lie detector test, and I've still got no house because the insurance won't pay off."

"Mrs. Reynolds—"

"I didn't kill him, all right? Now, leave me alone!"

"Wait! Please, don't hang up! I'm not accusing you of anything. And if what I'm investigating turns out to be true, your insurance will pay off."

When the woman didn't slam down the phone, Melanie said a silent thank-you. She suspected she didn't have much time and got right to the point. "Was your husband...did he abuse you?"

The woman sucked in a sharp breath. "What kind of question... Why do you want to know that? Can't you people just leave me alone?"

"Please, Mrs. Reynolds, I know this must be difficult for you, but if you could just answer the question."

For a long moment the line was dead between them. Then Melanie heard a soft, snuffling noise and realized the woman was crying. "You want to know what difficult is?" she asked, voice cracking. "Not your question, not by a long shot. Living with Joshua, now *that* was difficult. Living with his drinking. With his rages and his cruelty. Difficult was—" A sob swallowed her words.

Melanie waited for the woman to compose herself, working to suppress her jubilation. "Mrs. Reynolds," she asked softly, "did your husband hit you?"

"Yes," she answered. "Okay? Why so interested now that he's dead? When he was alive, nobody gave a damn.''

That's where she was wrong. When he was alive, somebody had cared. Cared enough to commit murder.

She had her fourth.

''I'm investigating the possibility that your husband's death may be linked to the deaths of several other men like him.''

''Linked? I don't understand.''

The children's squeals grew louder; it sounded as if the dog was going nuts. ''I'm sorry,'' Melanie said, ''but I can't tell you any more right now. Rest assured, however, if your husband was murdered, we'll see that justice is done.''

The woman laughed, the sound sharp, bitter. ''Justice was done, Officer May. My children laugh now. I can go to sleep without wondering if I'm going to wake up in the morning. The world's better off without him, and so am I.''

''Mrs. Reynolds—''

''No. I thank God every day that he's gone. And if he was murdered, I guess it's not God who I need to be thanking. My children are home now and I need to be with them. Good day, Officer.''

For the second time, the woman hung up on her. Only this time, Melanie didn't phone her back. She sat, receiver still to her ear, the woman's words ringing in her head.

''I thank God every day that he's gone...my children laugh now...I can go to sleep without wondering if I'm going to wake up in the morning.''

Melanie dropped the phone into its cradle, her

thoughts racing jackrabbit-like, from bits and
snatches of conversations she'd had during the
course of her investigation to memories of her own
childhood. How many times had she and her sisters
prayed for God to swoop down from heaven and
take their father while he slept? How many times
must the mates of Thomas Weiss, Samson Gold,
Jim McMillian and Joshua Reynolds have prayed
for the same thing?

*And their prayers had been answered. Their lives
were better now.*

On impulse, Melanie jumped up and crossed to
her files. She yanked open the bottom drawer and
began thumbing through them, stopping when she
came to *Weiss, Thomas.* Mr. Bee Sting, the one who
had, in a way, set her on this course.

She pulled the folder and went back to her desk.
She retrieved the phone number and dialed. It rang
a half a dozen times with no answer. Melanie
drummed her fingers against the desktop, a sense
of urgency pressing at her. She remembered that
Donna had worked nights, tending bar at Weiss's
Blue Bayou restaurant. She should be home.

*Pick up, Donna. I have to talk to you. Pick up,
dammit.*

She did then, sounding out of breath.

"Donna," Melanie said, "I've gotten you at a
bad time. I'm sorry."

"Not at all. I was running and just got back.
Who's this?"

"Melanie May, Whistlestop police. I was calling
to see how you were doing."

"Can you hold a second?" Melanie said she

could and heard a rustling on the other end, then the sound of a door being opened and slamming shut. A moment later Donna returned to the phone. "Sorry about that, I had to get a bottle of water. I was dying here."

"Better now?"

"Much. You were saying?"

"I haven't talked to you since Thomas's funeral, and I wondered how you were doing?"

"That's so sweet of you." She laughed. "Actually, I'm doing great. I'm back in school, finally pursuing my dream of being a veterinarian. And I'm in therapy."

"You are? In therapy?"

"I'm never going to make a mistake like Thomas again. I'm in therapy to make sure I don't. Whatever loose screw caused me to hitch up with that creep is being tightened."

Melanie laughed with her. She had liked Donna Wells right off, even bruised and scared silly. She liked her even more now. "I'm glad to hear that, Donna. I'm happy for you."

The woman lowered her voice to a reverent whisper. "I look at it this way, Melanie, God reached down from heaven to personally help me. He offered me a miracle in the form of those bees."

Her words took Melanie aback. Their sentiment was so close to the one expressed by Joshua Reynolds's wife, Rita. "And you believe that?"

"I do, with all my heart. So how could I *not* be profoundly changed after that? How could I not give thanks by turning my life around?"

Melanie agreed that she couldn't. Before she

rang off, Donna thanked her again for all she had tried to do for her. "I know that your hands were tied by the system," she said. "It wasn't your fault."

Then whose fault was it? Melanie wondered hours later for what seemed like the thousandth time. She was a part of the law enforcement system, the same system that was supposed to protect the weak and uphold the law. Sometimes, however, it seemed to her that the two ran at cross-purposes and that in upholding the one, the other was left exposed rather than protected.

Melanie pulled into a parking place in front of Casey's preschool and cut her engine. In the time that had passed since her conversation with Donna, she had vacillated between elation at having accomplished her mission and doubt about whether she was doing the right thing.

Men were dead. But the women and children they had left behind were better off. Happier and healthier. Children like Casey. Children like she and her sisters had been. Women like her sister Mia. Their lives made good by the illegal action of another. Or, as some of them believed, by God's just hand.

Melanie threw open the car door and climbed out. She saw Casey in the playground, climbing on the jungle gym with a couple of his friends. She crossed to the gate and stood watching her son play.

Casey spotted her and waved. She waved back, and he started across the playground, running full-tilt toward her. She could leave well enough alone.

And men would continue to die. And the world would be a safer place.

Or would it? The law kept order. It protected her. And Casey. It protected the poorest citizen to the richest. Sure, the system was flawed. But the world was more so.

No one had the right to take the law into their own hands. No one had the right to play God.

She hooked her fingers around the chain-link fence, smiling as her son neared her, feeling at peace for the first time in hours. She knew what she had to do.

29

Melanie decided that nothing would do but a face-to-face visit with Connor Parks. She had accessed his address through the Department of Motor Vehicles, easy to do with his name and the make of his vehicle, and sought him out. She armed herself with a file detailing her theory, supported by the data she had accumulated so far. Melanie hoped he would listen to her. Worst-case scenario, she would leave the file—whether he wanted it or not.

She found him home, bent under the hood of an old Corvette. It was red with white dimples and a white leather interior. From the looks of it, he had rescued it from somebody's shed or barn, where it had been left to deteriorate.

He'd gone shirtless, exposing a muscular back marred by a series of brutal-looking scars. Though the day was overcast, his skin was damp and shiny with sweat. She let her gaze follow the line of moisture that ran down his spine, disappearing under the waistband of his jeans.

"Parks," she said.

He didn't emerge from under the hood. "Sweetpants. You finally decided you couldn't live without me."

She arched an eyebrow, refusing to be amused.

"In classic dream interpretation, the car is a symbol of the self. Do you see yourself as a broken-down hot rod, Parks? A once-cherry speedster in need of rehabilitation?"

He held out a hand. "Hand me the torque wrench, will you?"

"I would if I knew what that was."

"Funny-looking thing. Long shaft, little head."

"You talking about one of the tools in the box, Parks? Or the one in your pants?"

He nearly choked on his laughter. But it did the trick—he emerged from under the hood. "You're a pithy little thing, aren't you?"

"And you're an irritating cowboy."

He smiled at her words, as if he considered them high praise. "If you're not here for my bod, you must want something else from me."

"I need your help with a case."

"The Andersen case?"

"Nope."

He selected the tool from the box at his feet and disappeared under the hood once more. "How's that going?" he asked.

"It's not. No leads since the witness couldn't positively ID Jenkins."

He made a sound of disgust. "Have they done anything with my profile?"

"Questioned hookers weeks ago. Came up with nothing."

"Probably rounded them up like cattle, put them in interrogation rooms under hot lights and expected them to share. Assholes."

"Basically." She cocked her head, studying the

curve of his backside, deciding that as male backsides went, his was damn nice. She smiled. "Could I actually talk to your face? Not that this view's unpleasant."

He grunted, though she suspected he'd enjoyed the compliment. "You'll have to wait. There's a pitcher of cold water in the fridge. Help yourself."

She glanced at the house, a small clapboard, painted white with dark green shutters. It looked homey, she thought. Comfortable.

"All right," she murmured, though she went more out of curiosity than thirst.

She strolled up the walk and let herself in through the side door. It dumped her into his bright but very basic kitchen.

As promised, she found a pitcher of water in the refrigerator. She took a glass from the drying rack by the sink, filled it, then returned the water to the fridge.

His house was neat and completely without frills. No framed family photos adorned the walls or windowsills, no vases of flowers graced the tabletops or children's art the refrigerator door.

She wandered to the door that led to the living room and peeked through. She found that room as orderly—and as spartan—as the kitchen. With two exceptions—the first being a grouping of framed photos on the end table, the second a large bulletin board hung on the windowless wall across from the couch.

She set her water on the counter and went in for a closer look. The board was crowded with newspaper clippings, notes that he'd apparently scribbled to himself and crime-scene photos. She scanned the items, noting the dates, realizing with a sense of shock that some of them were over five years old.

"You couldn't help yourself, could you?"

Melanie spun around, embarrassed. He stood in the door, wiping the grease from his hands with an old towel. "Was this a test?"

He didn't answer and, uncomfortable under his intent gaze, she turned back to the bulletin board. "What's this all about?"

"An unsolved crime. There's one in the bathroom and the bedroom, too."

"Different crimes?"

"No, the same one."

His answer surprised her and she turned and looked at him. He shifted his gaze. "You came to talk to me about a case?"

"Yes." She closed the distance between them and handed him the file. "I believe there's a serial killer operating in the Charlotte/Mecklenburg area. He's targeting batterers and abusers, men who have for one reason or another gone unpunished."

While she talked, Connor scanned the file's contents. "I discovered his existence when I read about Jim McMillian's death in the *Observer*. Just a couple of weeks before, a man I brought in for beating up his girlfriend died suddenly. The circumstances were freakish and…it seemed too much of a coincidence for me to ignore. So I did some digging."

"I see that," he murmured. "Is the CMPD involved?"

"No. No one is."

He looked up. "No one?"

"Just me."

"And that's why you're here? You figure if you can get Connor Parks, world-famous profiler, to hitch up to your wagon, you'll have it made? Respect, cooperation and then some?"

"Something like that."

"You haven't heard? I'm on forced leave, I can't help you." He held the file out. "I'm the last person you want tagging along, May. I'm a walking disaster."

Instead of taking the file, she slipped her hands into her pockets. "I don't believe that. I believe you're better than just about anybody out there. And if you see the pattern, I'll have a case."

"Sweetpants, you're letting your imagination run away with you."

"Are you referring to my belief in your abilities or my theory?"

He didn't smile. "Take the file, I can't help you."

"Keep it. They're copies." She started toward the kitchen. "I know I'm right about this. And I'm going to find someone who thinks so, too."

He followed her to the kitchen and the door. "Trust me, May, there are plenty of real killers out there. You don't have to dig them up, they hit you in the face with their handiwork."

"Not this one," she countered. "This one's cunning. Smarter than the rest. Patient." She met his gaze evenly. "This one thinks he's doing God's work."

30

The McDonald's at the corner of First Street and Lake Drive in Whistlestop boasted a deluxe Playland, complete with a slide, tower and ball pit. It also happened to be the only McDonald's in town, which made it a very popular place at mealtimes. Especially for families with young children.

Connor took the last available parking spot in the lot, earning a frustrated honk from the Ford Taurus behind him. He sent the frazzled-looking driver a sympathetic glance in his rearview mirror, cut his engine and climbed out.

He crossed to the restaurant and stepped inside. There, organized pandemonium reigned. It looked to Connor as if every working parent in the tiny community had decided on McDonald's for supper that night. He could understand the logic—feed the kids and tire them out all at the same time. Neat trick. And relatively easy on the wallet—if not the nerves.

Even though every register was open, the line at the counter stretched back to the Playland doors. Connor took his place in one of the lines, using the time to scan the restaurant's patrons, looking for Melanie May.

He didn't find her and frowned. Taggerty had

assured him she would be here. So, where was she? He wanted to talk to her. Now. Tonight. Never mind that he had let the information she'd left him languish on his kitchen counter for two and a half days; he was not a patient man. He did not believe in sitting still. When he made a decision, he took action. Simple as that.

And he had decided to speak to Melanie tonight.

Connor reached the front of the line and ordered a cup of coffee. He glanced over his shoulder at the Playland doors. He would bet she was there, watching her son play while the boy's meal grew cold on the table in front of her.

"Your coffee, sir."

He turned back to the girl behind the counter, smiling automatically. "Thanks."

Cup in hand, Connor crossed to the play area. The excited-sounding squeals of children greeted him as he opened the door. He stopped, memories of Jamey swamping him, bittersweet and still raw after all the time that had passed.

He heard Melanie before he spotted her, calling out to her child, cheering at something he had done. Connor turned in the direction of her voice. She was sitting at one of the tables surrounding the play gym, the remnants of a kids' meal spread out before her. While he watched, she snitched a fry.

Smiling to himself, he picked his way across to her, sidestepping discarded shoes and dodging a couple of wayward toddlers.

"May," he said when he reached her table.

She looked up. Her immediate surprise, he saw,

was quickly replaced by an expression of satisfaction.

"How did you find me?" she asked.

"Taggerty."

She nodded, a small smile tugging at her mouth. "I told him to tell you how to find me, if you came around."

"I almost didn't."

"Almost doesn't matter except in horseshoes and hand grenades."

"Clever." He sat on one of the brightly colored stools, feeling a bit like a mountain balancing on a molehill. He looked toward the gym structure. "Which one's yours?"

She turned, her gaze seeming to go directly to her child. "That one." She pointed. "The blond mop top in the bright blue T-shirt. Casey."

"Cute kid."

"The cutest. Smartest. Most lovable." She smiled self-consciously. "I'm not too biased, am I?"

"It would be pretty sad if you weren't."

She brought her drink to her lips and sipped. "You have kids?"

He hesitated. "No."

She arched an eyebrow and he silently swore. Although his hesitation had been no more than a split second, she had picked up on it. Melanie May didn't miss much.

"My ex-wife had a son. He was about Casey's age when we married."

"I see," she murmured, and he sensed that she did. That she saw right through him.

He cleared his throat. "I read your report."

She leaned forward, openly eager. Hopeful. He remembered a time when he'd been so open and eager. It seemed long ago. "And?"

"And I think you're dead on. I believe we're dealing with a serial here."

The breath rushed audibly past her lips. She brought a hand to her chest. "I can't... Hot damn, I was right."

"In my opinion. I've worked up a preliminary profile on our killer. You want to hear it?"

"Of course I want to hear it. Just give me a moment to get my bearings, I'm still back at the 'dead on' part."

"Mommy! Look!"

They both swung in the direction of the call. Casey stood at the side of the ball pit, poised to jump in. She gave him a thumbs-up and he launched himself into the sea of balls. A moment later he popped up, eager to see his mother's reaction.

Of course, she responded enthusiastically and with much fanfare. And, of course, once was not enough. After repeating his Olympic jump three times, he became distracted by the antics of a couple of other little boys and joined their play, mother's attention momentarily forgotten.

Melanie turned back to Connor, her expression apologetic. "Sorry about that."

"You have nothing to be sorry for," he said, his tone more brusque than he had intended. "This is your time with your son. I intruded on it, so I should be the one apologizing. If you're ready?"

She nodded and he began. "First off, we're dealing with a woman here."

"A woman?" Melanie repeated. She drew her eyebrows together. "It makes sense, but serial killers are rarely women."

"True. But rarely doesn't mean never. And when women kill, they typically choose a clean means. Like poison. Or suffocation. They *are* the gentler sex, after all."

She grimaced at his twisted attempt at humor, and he continued, "I place this UNSUB at thirty-two to forty-five years old. She's white, educated and financially comfortable. She's highly organized and extremely intelligent, she plans her crimes carefully down to the last detail."

"One of the reasons she has gone undetected until now."

"Until you," he corrected. "She knows her victims. That's obvious from her personalized killing methods. She is almost certainly a victim of domestic abuse herself. She is punishing each victim in lieu of punishing her father or brother or whoever abused her. These are not her first murders."

Melanie shook her head, obviously unconvinced. "Why couldn't this killer be a man? A man who watched his mother be battered? Or his sister? Over the years his feelings of helplessness became ones of rage, the rage built until it demanded an outlet. That outlet was murder."

Connor narrowed his eyes, his respect for Melanie May growing. She had done her research, thought it through. He admired that.

But he wasn't wrong about this; maybe some

other aspect he had attributed to the killer's character, but not her sex.

He told her so.

At her frustrated expression, he leaned forward. "Look, if these killings were the actions of a man, he would take his rage out in more aggressive ways, shooting, stabbing, dismembering. He would overkill his victims. We're not seeing that. We're seeing deaths so quiet they go unnoticed. We see a killer using a man's own weaknesses against him." He met her gaze. "Are you with me, Melanie?"

"I'm with you."

"Good. In her day-to-day life, our UNSUB's the picture of confidence and normalcy, though the strain may be beginning to tell on her, and her mask is beginning to crack.

"She knows something about the law, is a police buff or is personally connected to the police. She stays in touch with her victims, either by visiting their graves or their surviving kin. I also believe she follows the newspaper and other media carefully for any mention of her victims. She is delighted in the amount of press Jim McMillian's death garnered. I believe that on a certain level she'll be pleased when this story breaks. She's been waiting for it to happen. After all, what fun is it playing God if nobody notices?"

Silence fell between them, broken after several moments by Casey's shout for his mom to "Look!" Melanie did, then as if suddenly realizing how late it had become, glanced at her watch. Most of the other parents were collecting their children and making an exodus from the play area, though not without the requisite begging, pleading and occasional tantrum from their charges. "One more time down the slide, Casey," she called. "It's time to go home."

She turned back to Connor, her expression sheepish. "I hate to have to cut this short, but it's a school night."

"Actually, we're done here." He stood and she followed him to his feet. "I've made a 10:00 a.m. appointment for you and me to meet with Steve Rice, the Special Agent in Charge of the Charlotte field office. Clear it with your superior."

She agreed, then went about collecting her son. Connor had no good reason not to leave then, but he stayed anyway, even as he told himself to say good-night and walk away.

"Casey," she said, "this is Mr. Parks. He and I are working together."

The child looked up at him assessingly. Like his mother, Connor suspected the kid missed little. "Catching bad guys?" he asked.

Connor smiled. "You bet. The baddest."

The boy seemed to like that answer, because he grinned and plopped onto the ground to tug on his sneakers. Connor watched as Melanie squatted down and tied the laces for him without being asked.

Routine, he thought. Nice. Comfortable. He missed that.

Actually, he acknowledged as they made their way out of the play area and through the restaurant, he missed a lot about being a parent. The fun and spontaneous play, the warmth and the way life could go from total bedlam to quiet perfection—and back—in the blink of an eye.

Jamey had taken him outside of himself, Connor acknowledged. He had made him forget—Suzi, the grim realities of the job. All kids did that, he supposed, glancing at Melanie and Casey from the corners of his eyes. And that could be a very good thing.

They reached her Jeep. Melanie got Casey buckled into his seat, then turned to Connor. "I need to ask you a question. You were going to blow me off. Why didn't you?"

"Couple of reasons. First, you promised you were going to get someone to believe you, I supposed it might as well be me. I had nothing to lose by being associated with a crackpot. Besides, I figured this thing would turn out one of two ways—either you'd prove to be smarter than everybody else or just delusional. Either way, it'd be a good time."

"Thanks for the vote of confidence."

He inclined his head, lips tilting up. "You're welcome."

"And the other reason?"

His smile died. "What you said, about this killer believing she was doing God's work. I've seen that before. And I know it won't end until someone stops her."

31

At nine-fifty the next morning Melanie and Connor simultaneously arrived at the Wachovia Bank building's parking garage; they followed each other up the ramp, choosing side-by-side parking spots. A thirty-story high-rise located in uptown Charlotte, the FBI occupied the eight, ninth and tenth floors.

Connor alighted his vehicle first and crossed to hers, holding the Jeep's door open as she climbed out.

He smiled. "Ready?"

"Are you kidding?"

"Let's go then."

They fell into step together. Though not even ten o'clock yet, Melanie found it uncomfortably warm inside the garage, the exhaust-scented air heavy.

"I take it you brought your chief up to speed?" Connor said.

"Oh, yeah, and lived to tell the tale, too. He was so pissed, I thought he was going to pop. Told me if I *ever* compromised the department by launching my own private investigation again, he'd yank my shield so fast my head would spin."

They reached the elevators, stepped on and pressed the button for the ground floor. As the car began its descent, she looked up at Connor, a smile tugging at the corners of her mouth. "But the whole time he was chewing me out, he had this twinkle in his eyes. Like he was secretly tickled pink that it had been one of his officers who had uncovered this thing. He was all but gloating."

Connor chuckled, but didn't comment. They reached the first level, left that car only to make their way to one inside the building. They didn't speak again until they had reached the ninth floor.

The doors slid open, they stepped off and crossed to the double glass doors, printed with the FBI's blue and white seal.

"Nervous?" Connor asked.

"Excited." She sucked in a deep breath. "He doesn't bite, does he?"

"Only when provoked." Connor opened the door, allowing her to enter first. The reception area was smallish, with video cameras mounted discreetly in corners and a walk-through metal detector to screen visitors for hidden weapons. They crossed to the receptionist, seated behind Plexiglass. She greeted Connor and told them to go on back.

Steve Rice was waiting. Connor made the introductions; Melanie and the other man shook hands, acknowledging that they had met before, then they all took their seats.

"So, what've you got?" Rice asked, getting right down to business.

Connor looked at Melanie. "Why don't you fill Steve in on what led you to suspect the deaths in question were the work of a serial killer, then fill him in on the research you've done so far."

Melanie began, outlining her journey, step by

step. She handed the man a file folder containing the information she had amassed so far. Without comment, he began leafing through the material, in no apparent rush. Obviously, he was unaware that she was about to die of anticipation. Her heart was pounding so hard and fast she was surprised the agents couldn't see its beat.

She plowed on. "In terms of unearthing probable victims, the territory I was able to cover on my own was minimal. My goal was to find one more, to add weight to my theory. I stopped searching as soon as I did that, but who knows how many more there might be? As it is, we have four in less than twelve months, a rather alarming number."

Connor stepped in. "That's when I came on board. Officer May approached me with her theory. I was skeptical at first, but after I'd studied her documentation, I saw the pattern. This one's damn clever, Steve. I worked up a profile."

He handed a file to the other man, who began to read it. After a moment, he looked up. "You think this UNSUB's a woman? The true female serial is rare."

"But not nonexistent. This one's the exception to the rule."

The SAC drew his eyebrows together, his expression thoughtful. He obviously placed great trust in Connor, but also in statistics. "Could she be working with a male partner? A lover? Or brother?"

Connor shook his head. "These aren't simple killings. Our UNSUB's taken great pains to plan every step, to make the murders look like simple accidents. In the process, she's left a distinctive signature. Those clues point to a white female, working alone.''

Connor's superior leveled him with a measured stare. ''We have no room for error here. You're one hundred percent certain this killer's a woman? You're absolutely certain the boys in BSU will agree?''

Connor didn't waver. He knew the guys in the Behavioral Science Unit; he had been one of them. ''To both questions, yes.''

The man shifted his gaze to Melanie's. ''Are you as certain? After all, you've done all the legwork, this is your baby.''

Her baby. Her case. A feeling akin to wonder bloomed inside her. ''I'm with Parks on this. One hundred percent.''

''All right, then.'' Rice closed the folder and dropped it on the desk in front of him. He looked at her. ''What do you want from the FBI?''

His question surprised her. ''I don't follow.''

''As a representative of the WPD, are you soliciting the Bureau's involvement?''

She could hardly breathe, let alone speak. A part of her couldn't believe this was happening. ''Yes,'' she managed to say.

''I need your superior officer's confirmation of these facts. I'll expect to hear from your chief within the hour.''

When she nodded he turned back to Connor. ''What about you, Agent Parks? You on or off this case?''

''Meaning?''

"Meaning, there's the matter of your suspension. On or off, Agent Parks?"

The two men locked gazes; after a moment, Connor muttered an oath. "On. I'm where you want me to be, okay? Or as close as I'm going to get in this lifetime. And if that's not good enough, you can kiss my ass."

As if satisfied, the SAC nodded. "Good. You'll need to contact your old buddies at Quantico. Send them what you have so far, get their opinion."

"In the works already."

Rice inclined his head. "The next call's yours. What's it going to be?"

Connor looked at her; she indicated he should take the ball. "The way I see it, our next move's twofold. We search for possible victims while simultaneously hunting for the link between the men. That's the key to finding her. She doesn't grab these guys out of thin air. Something brings her to them."

Melanie agreed. "Because I became aware of the first three victims through official channels, I thought the link might be a police record or some sort of documented history of violence."

"And?"

"It didn't pan out. Joshua Reynolds was clean. Not so much as a complaint registered."

"Have you tried the simplest link?" Rice asked, glancing up from the folder. "Geographical proximity?"

Connor took that one. "I didn't see a pattern. Each victim lived and worked in a different area of Charlotte, no crossovers. But that doesn't mean one won't appear as we uncover more victims."

"We should check the neighborhoods they grew up in," Melanie said. "The high schools and colleges they graduated from."

"Men's organizations," Steve offered. "Gyms, athletic organizations."

"But that doesn't work because she's a woman. We need a place where a woman can meet a—" Connor straightened. He swung to face Melanie. "Maybe she dates these guys?"

A tingle raced up Melanie's spine. "It could be," she murmured. "She gets close, learns their secrets, their weaknesses, then she nails them. She could even be dating several simultaneously. That could explain the frequency of the murders."

Connor nodded, expression thoughtful. "But it still doesn't answer the question of where she finds them."

"True." Melanie glanced at Rice, then back at Connor. "But it offers more possibilities to cross-reference. Bars. Clubs. Places men and women meet."

"Sounds like you two are off to a good start. Contact the Charlotte/Mecklenburg force, ASAP. Also the other local PDs and the State Bureau of Investigation. You'll need their cooperation."

The SAC stood; Melanie and Connor followed him to his feet. He met Melanie's eyes. "Fine work, Officer May. Damn fine work."

Melanie knew she was beaming, but couldn't help herself. "Thank you, Agent Rice."

They started for the door. There, Steve stopped. "Keep me abreast of progress."

"I will."

"And, Con?" Connor met the SAC's gaze. "You got a name for this one?"

"Yeah." Connor looked at Melanie. "I thought we'd call her the Dark Angel."

32

From that moment on, Melanie's life changed dramatically. Suddenly she was at the center of one the biggest and certainly the most controversial cases to ever hit the Charlotte area.

In the first two weeks of the official investigation, four more probable victims were found, all from the Charleston area. That brought the potential body count to eight, a substantial and alarming number. Until Melanie, the Dark Angel had enjoyed free rein, acting with impunity, without the pressure of law enforcement nipping at her heels.

And Melanie was the one being lauded for having uncovered the connection between the killings. She had been interviewed by every major news organization in the Southeast; when the media wanted an update, they came to her first.

The press had had a field day with the Dark Angel, speculating daily in the news about the killer's background and motive for the murders. They sparked a lively debate among Charlottonians by calling for individual opinions—and opinions they got, citizens from every walk of life and religious affiliation spoke up, ones from the political right, left and everything in between. Even the local chapter of the National Organization for Women chimed in.

Everywhere Melanie went, the Dark Angel killings were the topic of conversation. Some argued that the killings were biblical-style justice in a world gone mad, others that society had become such that vigilantism was an acceptable, even necessary, means to an end. And still others, Melanie included, contended that taking a life outside the law, other than in self-defense, was murder. The killer's motives didn't matter, neither did the victim's crimes—no one had the right to take the law into their own hands.

Most satisfying to Melanie, however, was the chance to participate in an investigation the size and complexity of this one. Though the hours were long, she never tired; even the parts of the process that progressed at a snail's pace she found fascinating.

To her surprise, Melanie had enjoyed working with Connor. She'd found she liked him. He was smart. Honest and honorable but outspoken. A cowboy who always did what he believed was right, even when not politically correct—qualities that should have made him less than desirable partner material, but didn't.

Connor had a big ego, though he never let it get in the way of their relationship. In fact, every step of the way, he had made it clear it had been Melanie who'd uncovered the Angel, Melanie who had done the preliminary legwork, and Melanie who should head the investigation because of it.

She appreciated that. He could have benefited

professionally from accepting some of the glory, such as it was. And it would have been easy for him, with his impressive credentials, to have grabbed it.

He wasn't a glory seeker or an ass kisser. In fact, the last thing he seemed to want was attention. At times he acted as if he didn't want to be publicly associated with the case at all.

Melanie found him interesting, a complex mixture of character traits that shouldn't quite fit together, but did. However, it was the aura of sadness about him, the way his smile never quite reached his eyes, that intrigued her most. She wondered if the atrocities of the job had stolen his ability to smile—or if something closer to his heart had been the culprit.

The phone on Melanie's desk rang, and she picked it up. "May here."

"How could you?" a woman whispered, voice muffled. "How could you do it?"

Melanie frowned. "This is Officer Melanie May, Whistlestop Police Department. Who is this, please?"

"I know who you are," the woman said, her softly spoken words taking on a bitter edge. "I thought you, of all people, would be on our side. I thought you cared. Traitor."

"I do care," Melanie replied automatically. "If you would tell me who this—"

The line went dead. Quickly, Melanie punched in *69. When that yielded only an "unknown," she returned the receiver to its cradle. She hadn't recognized the voice, yet she had found something familiar about it. Something about it had struck a chord of recognition in her.

The woman had to have been referring to the Dark Angel case. But what had she meant when she said *"our side"*?

"Heads up, Mel," Bobby murmured from his desk, located behind hers. "Incoming."

She lifted her gaze and her heart sank. Her ex-husband was striding across the station, his expression thunderous.

She stood, intent at least on meeting him on his level. She was not about to allow him to stand over her, growling like some sort of human attack dog.

"Stan," she said as he stopped before her. "What brings you all the way to Whistlestop?"

"This case. I want you off it."

Behind her, Bobby cleared his throat—she imagined her partner ducking for cover. "Excuse me?"

"You heard me, Melanie. I want you off the Dark Angel case."

She met his gaze calmly. "You're no longer my husband, Stan. You have no right to tell me what to do. And furthermore, this is my workplace. I don't appreciate you showing up here and making a scene."

"As Casey's father, I have every right—"

"No, you don't." She tipped up her chin, staring him down. "If you have a concern about our son, of course I'll make myself available to you. But you will not come into my place of employment and order me about. Is that clear?"

By his expression, she could see that she had

surprised him. In truth, she wasn't sure who she had surprised more—him or herself.

Stan drew back slightly, she could see him scrambling to regain his equilibrium, the advantage he was accustomed to having when it came to his dealings with her. After a moment, he cleared his throat, then addressed her in a more reasonable tone. "Your involvement with the Dark Angel case is upsetting Casey."

"That's nonsense. He's fine."

"He's having nightmares."

"Nightmares?" she repeated, drawing her eyebrows together. "He's awakened a few times in the night, but when I asked—"

"He hasn't wanted to tell you." Stan hesitated, then went on. "He's afraid you're going to be killed."

She made a sound of disbelief. "Killed? Where would he get such a crazy idea? I haven't even mentioned that I'm working on anything out of the ordinary. Why would I? He's only four years old."

"Try the TV, Melanie. His friends at school. His teachers. It's what everybody's talking about and whenever they are, your name's mentioned."

Casey had been quiet lately, Melanie realized. Subdued. He had begun crying when she dropped him off at preschool, clinging to her neck and begging her not to go. Something he hadn't done in a couple of years. She had put it down to her not spending as much time with him lately, to her having been preoccupied.

Boy, had she been wrong.

"I didn't know," she whispered, a lump in her throat. "I had no idea."

"But you didn't ask, did you?" Stan leaned toward her, all righteous indignation. "This was why I didn't want you to become a cop."

"But I'm not in any kind of danger, Stan. This is simply a case of—"

"Of a mother spending more time thinking about her work than her family," he supplied. "*I* have our son's best interests at heart. Can you say the same?"

That afternoon, Melanie punched out early, anxious to pick up Casey and to reassure him that she was in absolutely no danger of being killed. She had spent the time after Stan left vacillating between being certain her ex-husband had been exaggerating and knowing that he had not.

It was the last that had torn her apart. How could she have been so oblivious to her son's feelings? What kind of mother was she?

When Casey caught sight of her, he let out a whoop of joy and tore across the playground toward her.

"Mommy!" he cried and threw his arms around her legs. "You're here."

She swung him up in her arms, guilt gnawing at her. "Of course I'm here, tiger. Just a little early."

He wrapped his tiny legs around her waist, clinging to her like a monkey. "Missed you, Mommy."

She gave him a big kiss. "I missed you, too, baby. Let's go home."

Although anxious to talk to him about his feelings, Melanie held off, waiting for the right moment. She thought it best for him to be relaxed and happy when she broached the subject of her job and his fears.

As a treat, they made a homemade pizza for dinner. Melanie stood back, allowing him to spread the canned dough onto the pizza pan, not caring that it was thick in places with holes in others. While their creation baked, they played two games of Candy Land—Casey beating her soundly both times. They ate picnic-style in the living room, on an old quilt Melanie spread out on the floor.

Dinner finished, Casey helped her load the dishwasher, chattering the entire time about his friends from school, the giant bug they had found on the playground and how Sarah had puked up her peanut butter and jelly sandwich after lunch. Melanie smiled to herself, just letting him talk, comforted by his nonstop monologue.

Dishes done, they curled up on the couch, Casey nestled up beside her, his favorite bedtime books on her lap. Now, she decided, was the time. "Honey," she said, "did you know that Mommy is working on a big, important case at work?"

He darted a glance up at her, his expression stricken.

Her heart sank. "Is that a yes, Casey?"

He nodded, but didn't look at her.

Stan had been right. She hadn't been paying close enough attention to their son. She took a deep, steadying breath. "Where did you hear about it?"

"The TV," he whispered, hanging his head as if ashamed. "They said your name."

She snuggled him a little closer, struggling to maintain a totally relaxed demeanor. "When you heard my name on TV, how did that make you feel?"

He shrugged. "Okay. But I told Timmy about it an' he said...he said..."

He looked helplessly up at her, and his chin began to quiver, his eyes to tear. She set the books aside, scooped him up and brought him to her lap. He twisted around and pressed his face to her chest.

"What did Timmy say, sweetheart?" she coaxed. "You can tell me. I won't be upset. I promise."

He pressed his face tighter to her chest. When he spoke, she had to struggle to make out his muffled words. "Timmy said...he said that you're chasing a really bad guy. A cereal-bowl killer. He said that...that you could..."

Her son started to cry and Melanie had a pretty good idea what Timmy had told Casey could happen to her. That she could get killed, too. Helpless anger filled her—at Casey's friend, at the media, but mostly at herself for not being more aware of what was happening with her son.

"Honey," she said softly but firmly, "did Timmy tell you that the bad person might hurt Mommy?"

He nodded, his small body shaking with the force of his tears. She rocked him, heart breaking. "Remember when we talked about what a police officer does? About how he, or she, keeps people safe by getting the bad guys?"

He whimpered a "yes," peeking up at her.

"That's what I do, I keep people safe. And I get the bad guys." She smiled gently. "They don't get me, Casey. They run from me."

He studied her silently for a moment, as if trying to decide if he believed her. "Really?"

"Really." She crossed her heart, then held up two fingers. "I promise."

She bent and rubbed her nose against his. "Now, you have to make me a promise. From now on, whenever you get an idea in your head that scares you, you have to tell me about it. 'Cause it might be a wrong idea. Like you had this time. Can you make me that promise, Casey?"

He said he could, solemnly crossing his heart. Afterward, she read him all his favorite bedtime stories, beginning with *Good Night Moon* and ending with *I'll Love You Forever.*

Next had come pj's and prayers and then before long, Melanie had been able to tiptoe out of the room. Taking one last glance at her sleeping child, she went to the phone and dialed her ex-husband's number. He answered right away.

"Stan," she said, "it's Melanie." She didn't give him time to respond, just forged ahead. "I just...I wanted to thank you for today. For coming to me about Casey. He and I talked and—" she drew in a deep breath "—you were right. A friend from school put a wrong idea into his head and he was terrified. Everything's all right now, but I just wanted... Thank you," she finished. "I appreciate what you did."

For a moment, he was silent. Melanie suspected

she had stunned him. And she could certainly understand why. She couldn't even remember the last time they had spoken to each other without open animosity, let alone when she had thanked him for anything.

"You're welcome," he said finally, his voice sounding unnaturally thick.

A moment later, Melanie hung up the phone, smiling to herself. For the first time in a long time she felt as if she and Stan were playing on the same team. And it felt good, really good.

33

A smoky haze hung above the crowded dance floor. Boyd slipped around and past the gyrating dancers, most pressed so tightly together it was difficult in the dim light to determine where one body began and the other ended.

He skimmed his gaze from one face to the next, searching, hungry. Sweat beaded his upper lip. He had awakened this morning angry. On edge. Nothing had changed from the day before, yet a blackness had settled over him, one that colored every step he took, his every thought, word and action.

It had been weeks since his last encounter. Weeks since he had allowed himself to indulge in his weakness. He had staved off the hunger chewing at his insides by reliving the last time. By closing his eyes, taking himself in his hand and remembering.

He had prayed these memories would hold him longer than the last.

They hadn't. They were useless now. Dead to him.

Boyd breathed deeply through his nose, feeling light-headed. Queasy with desperation. He reached the perimeter of the dance floor and began circling again, moving his gaze from one face, one pair of eyes, to another, each leaving him cold.

These women were like the last. Weak. Without the inner strength to satisfy him. Pain was the thing. Total domination. Humiliation.

He had to stop. Each encounter, each new woman, played a game of Russian roulette with his life. He would run out of luck; one day he would pull the trigger and find the chamber loaded.

He was running out of time. He felt the certainty of that growing in the pit of his gut.

Before him, the crush of bodies parted, as the sea had for Moses. And he saw *her.* She was moving across the dance floor, heading for the bar. She was dressed entirely in black—spike-heeled boots, skin-tight leather pants and a lace-up vest that squeezed at her breasts, pushing them up and out. Her long blond hair looked coarse and was the color of corn silk, obviously a wig but sexy as hell against the black leather.

As if she sensed his scrutiny, she stopped. And turned. Their gazes met. Her lips were painted a deep wine color; her heavily made-up eyes outlined in kohl. She smiled. As if she knew *him*—his needs, his desperation. The things that would make him happy.

The music faded—the blood rushed to his head, screaming in his ear. She motioned him closer. He started forward, mouth dry, heart fast. Completely aroused. He stopped in front of her. She motioned him closer yet, indicating he should bend his head close to hers, to put his ear close to her mouth.

He did. Their bodies brushed and they swayed to

the earthy music, in sync already. She slipped a hand between them, found his erection, straining against the front of his pants. She caught the zipper and lowered it. He choked back a sound, of pleasure. Of shock.

"I'll make you beg," she whispered, her voice thick and rough, like sandpaper. "It'll be so good, you'll wish you were dead."

As the words reached his brain, she stuck her tongue in his ear and closed her hand around his penis, squeezing hard.

He exploded in her hand. But still she held him tightly, using his own release against him, the jerk of his own muscles to milk him dry. With a throaty laugh, she zipped him up, turned and walked away.

Boyd watched her go, already fantasizing about their next encounter.

34

Veronica glanced at her watch, anxious for the team meeting to conclude. Anxious to check her messages. Mia had promised to call the minute Boyd left for the hospital that morning. Veronica hadn't heard from her even though she had held off joining the Person's Team meeting until the last possible moment.

She peeked at her watch again, the other lawyers' conversations swirling around her. *Almost eleven. Surely Mia had called by now.*

In the month that had passed since Mia's unexpected visit that Saturday, they had become the best of friends. Inseparable. They shopped together. Did lunch. Movies. An occasional dinner or drinks. They spoke on the phone first thing every morning and the last thing at night.

Veronica crossed her legs. She thought about Mia all the time. She worried about her, longed to protect and care for her. The hours they were apart seemed never-ending, the ones they were together, unbearably short.

She'd had many female friends over the years, women she had cared deeply for—loved as friends, or sisters, even. But she had never felt about another woman they way she felt about Mia.

Truth or dare?

Truth. She was falling in love with Mia Donaldson.

The thought ran through her head, bringing with it a flush. White-hot, breath-stealing. Bringing with it denial.

It wasn't possible. She wasn't that way, had never had those kind of feelings for another woman. *Until now. Until Mia.*

And with each passing day, she was finding it more and more difficult to deny those feelings.

"Veronica, do you have anything to add?"

She looked up, not having a clue what had just been presented or by whom. She met her team leader's eyes. "Not a thing, Rick."

He hesitated a moment, then nodded. "All right. Then, if there's nothing else, let's get to work."

Veronica sprang to her feet, quickly collecting her things. Before she could bolt for the door, Rick was at her elbow. "Veronica, could I have a moment?"

She curbed the impulse to check her watch again and smiled at the other lawyer. "Sure. What's up?"

"That's what I'd like to know."

"I don't follow."

"Is something wrong? Is there something going on in your life that I should know about?"

What could she say? I think I'm falling in love with another woman and it's really freaking me out?

She forced a casual smile. "Not a thing, Rick. Why do you ask?"

"That should be obvious, Veronica. In the past

few weeks you've transformed from my most aggressive, vocal and opinionated lawyer into the one sitting at the table today.''

She looked blankly at him, and he shook his head. "Veronica, you didn't comment on one case. Not one."

She felt her cheeks flame. He was right. She had spent the entire meeting mooning over Mia. Like a teenager, for God's sake.

Her job was the most important thing in her life, she couldn't afford to be daydreaming during team meetings. "I'm sorry, Rick, it's just that I...I've been fighting this bug and...it's left me without much energy. I'm not sleeping well and...I guess, I'm just not feeling myself.''

That part was certainly true. She hadn't felt herself in some time now.

She cleared her throat. "I haven't wanted to take the time to see a doctor, but now...I think I'd better.''

He smiled sympathetically, looking as if he bought her story. "Get some antibiotics, that bug'll be history in no time. Then I'll have my pit bull back.''

"A pit bull?'' she murmured. "Is that the way you think of me?''

His smile faded. "I didn't mean that in a negative way, Veronica. You gave this group a real shot in the arm, I just don't want us to lose that.''

"Don't worry, Rick,'' she murmured with a reassuring smile. "This dog hasn't lost her bite. Of that I can assure you.''

They chatted a moment more, then parted. Veronica went to her office by way of the message desk. She collected the stack of message slips, sifting through them the moment she closed her office door behind her.

None were from Mia.

Why hadn't she called?

Veronica flipped through them again, just to be certain she hadn't somehow missed it.

She hadn't and, frowning, Veronica dropped the stack of messages on her desk, then sank into her chair. Now she was really worried. Last night, Mia had been upset. No, more than upset. She had been shaken. Afraid.

Veronica brought a hand to her right temple and rubbed. Mia's mood had had something to do with Boyd, something he had done, though she had refused to reveal what, no matter how Veronica had coaxed. They'd ended their conversation abruptly, because Boyd had returned home. Before Mia hung up, Veronica had made her promise to call in the morning, the minute Boyd left for the hospital.

So Veronica would know she was all right.

But Mia hadn't called.

Something was wrong.

Heart in her throat, Veronica picked up the phone and dialed Mia's number. The machine answered and Veronica left a message. She repeated the process ten minutes later, then ten minutes after that, her panic growing.

She got to her feet, all manner of horrifying scenarios racing through her head. From what Mia had told her, her husband was capable of anything. He could have locked her up somewhere, in a closet or the attic. She could be hurt. Or worse.

In a final, desperate attempt to reason away why she hadn't heard from her friend, Veronica wondered if perhaps Boyd hadn't gone into the hospital today. Perhaps he was ill, or had taken a personal day—easy enough to confirm.

Moments later Veronica hung up the phone. Boyd had, indeed, gone into work this morning. At present, he was in surgery.

Light-headed with fear, Veronica buzzed Jen, informed her that she would be out of the office for a while, then grabbed her purse and ran.

She made it to Mia's in record time, pushing the upper edge of the speed limit and sliding through yellow lights, praying she didn't get pulled over. She wheeled into the other woman's driveway, slammed out of the car and raced up the walk to the front door.

She rang the bell, then pounded, calling out to her friend. Moments passed—they seemed an eternity. Veronica rang and called out again, leaning toward the door, listening for signs of life.

Finally, she heard a stirring on the other side of the wood panel, then the key turning in the lock. The door opened, Mia stood on the other side. Though her eyes were red and puffy and face blotchy, she was very much alive and unharmed.

"Mia!" Veronica exclaimed, relief rushing over her. "Thank God! You were supposed to call. When you didn't, I was sick with worry."

Mia simply stared at her, her eyes flooding with

tears. Without a word, she turned and hurried back into the house.

Veronica stared after her, confused. Concerned. She had been right—something was wrong. Terribly wrong. She stepped into the house, shutting the door behind her.

Mia stood at the far end of the foyer, her back to Veronica, head bowed. Veronica saw by the way her shoulders shook that she was crying.

Her heart breaking for her friend, she went to stand behind her. "Mia?" she whispered. "What's happened? Are you all right?"

She touched Mia's silky, blond hair. It was almost unbearably soft. "I was so...scared. After everything you told me about Boyd, I thought...I imagined the worst."

Unable to stop herself, she touched Mia's hair again, stroking. This time Mia moved slightly into the caress, almost like a cat rubbing itself against its master's hand.

Veronica drew in a shuddering breath and closed her eyes. "I was so scared. Don't do that to me again, Mia. I beg you."

Mia made a sound, small and lost. "I wanted to call you. You were all I...all I could think about. But I was so...ashamed. I couldn't face you, even over the phone."

"Ashamed?" Veronica repeated, dropping her hands to Mia's shoulders. "Of what, Mia? I don't understand."

"How could you? You'd never—" She bit the words back and shook her head, as if unable to continue.

"You'd be surprised what I can understand." Veronica turned her friend so she could look into her eyes. "What is it, Mia? You can tell me anything. I promise you can."

"I don't deserve your friendship. I don't—" Her eyes welled with tears once more, swamping her words when she spoke. She fought them off. "When I allow him to...to hurt me the way he did last night, I don't deserve—"

"He hurt you?" Veronica pulled in a steadying breath. "Where? What did he—"

"I don't want to talk about it."

She attempted to pull away, but Veronica tightened her hold. "Don't shut me out, Mia. Please."

"I told you, I don't want to talk about it!" With a sob, she jerked free and ran down the hall.

Veronica went after her. She found her in the master bedroom, sitting on the edge of her unmade bed. Slumped over in defeat. Veronica stopped in the doorway. "Mia?" she whispered.

"It was...awful."

Veronica felt her friend's words like a blow, like a personal cut to her own heart. "Tell me," she said softly. "And I'll help you."

She crossed to Mia and knelt in front of her, taking her hands, cradling them against her cheek. They were wet with tears. "How could I not understand? Your pain is my pain, your hopes, dreams, your disappointments. All are mine, too. I love you, Mia."

As she uttered the words, it was as if she opened up inside, fully alive, brilliant with light and promise. "I would do anything for you. *Anything*. Don't you know that?"

Mia lifted her gaze to Veronica's. Veronica brought their joined hands to her mouth. "It's true, I would."

A tear slipped down Mia's cheek, splashing on their joined hands. "He...forced me to have sex with him," she whispered so softly Veronica had to strain to hear. "I told him no, I struggled, but he—" She drew in a broken breath. "He held me down. He hurt me."

Veronica closed her eyes against the image, against the rage the image wrought. The thought of him forcing Mia, her gentle, sweet Mia...it was too horrible to contemplate. "Where?" Veronica managed to say. "Where did he—"

Mia stood. She unfastened her slacks and slipped them over her hips and down. She was trim, her body almost boyishly thin. She wore plain white cotton bikini briefs. Veronica's gaze was drawn to the dark triangle of her bush, visible through the thin cotton.

Her mouth went dry. The blood began to thunder in her head. She felt dizzy. Aware and achingly self-conscious.

Then she saw the bruises. The first, on Mia's left, inner thigh was large, at least three inches in diameter and an ugly purple-black color. The others, on her other thigh, were small and roundish—like fingerprints.

Veronica made a sound of disbelief. And outrage. She brought her hand to the large bruise and with trembling fingers, touched it tenderly, lovingly.

A breath, a sound, almost like a sigh, whispered past Mia's lips. Veronica lifted her gaze. Mia's eyes were shut, the expression on her face one of intent expectation. Veronica moved her fingers ever so slightly higher, then higher still, until they brushed against warm, white fabric.

This time there was no mistaking the sound that slipped past Mia's lips. Emboldened, the breath shuddering past her own lips, Veronica moved her hand more, cupping Mia's sex.

Veronica stroked, softly at first, kneading with her fingertips, exploring a woman for the first time.

"I'm frightened," Mia whispered, beginning to tremble. "This...can't be...happening."

Veronica quieted her without words. Gently, she coaxed. And wooed. She loved.

With a small cry, Mia dropped her hands to Veronica's shoulders for support. "Don't...leave me, Veronica. Please...never—"

"I won't, love. I couldn't."

"Then don't...stop. Yes...there—"

Suddenly, Mia stiffened, her thighs closing tightly around Veronica's hand, trapping it. She arched her back, crying out in orgasm.

At the sound, at the reality of what had happened, what she had just done, Veronica exploded, too, spontaneously.

Weeping, Mia sank to the floor, into Veronica's arms. Veronica held her, tears slipping down her own cheeks.

After a time, their tears abated. Still, neither spoke. Nor moved. Veronica was afraid to loosen her hold on Mia—afraid of what Mia might say, of

how she might look at her. She was afraid and embarrassed and so hopeful it hurt. Nothing in her life
had ever felt so right as these last minutes with Mia.

If the other woman didn't feel the same, she
feared she would die.

Finally, aware of time passing, Veronica found
her courage. She looked at Mia. In the other
woman's eyes she saw her own wonder mirrored
back at her. Her own hope and hesitation.

Veronica wept with joy again. She cupped Mia's
face in her hands and kissed her, not as a friend but
as a lover.

When the kiss ended, Mia touched Veronica's
face with trembling fingers. "What am I going to
do about Boyd?" she asked. "I'm afraid."

"You don't need to be afraid. I won't allow him
to hurt you again, Mia. I won't allow him to touch
you. *We* can't allow it."

"No," Mia agreed, "we can't."

35

Melanie rushed into the dojang dressing room. As she had known she would be, Veronica was already there. She was sitting on the bench with her open gym bag between her feet, but she hadn't dressed out yet. They had continued to meet every Friday night to spar and if one of them couldn't make it they always called.

Since the official launch of the Dark Angel investigation in mid-July, it seemed to Melanie that she was always rushing. Always apologizing to someone for being late. Tonight that person was Veronica.

"Sorry," Melanie said, dropping her bag on the bench beside Veronica. "I was on my way out the door when a reporter from the *Charlotte Observer* called for an update. I couldn't get her off the phone."

The attorney looked up, her expression tight. "The Dark Angel. *Big* surprise."

Melanie's mouth dropped at her friend's words and their sarcastic tone. "Excuse me?"

"Everything with you lately has been that damn case. I swear, you're obsessed with it."

Melanie stiffened, as hurt as she was offended. "It's a big case, Veronica. An important one. And

I'm in charge. I would have thought you, of all people, would understand.''

"Maybe I understand, but what about the other people who love you? What about them?'' Melanie opened her mouth to respond, but Veronica cut her off. ''You know, Melanie, you can't lose your life in a case. Take it from me, there's always going to be another one around the corner, one that's bigger, more important.''

Melanie wasn't quite sure what to say. She was surprised by her friend's speech, embarrassed because the other woman was right. And also resentful of the way Veronica had dressed her down.

They changed in awkward silence. As Veronica tossed her gym bag into a locker, she looked at Melanie, her expression almost apologetic. ''How *is* the case going?''

"We're up to eight probable victims.''

"Eight? Your Angel's been a busy man.''

"Woman,'' Melanie corrected automatically.

"Right. Any leads?''

Melanie shook her head as she shoved her gym bag into a locker, then snapped the door shut. ''We have a string of victims and no concrete evidence. Because of the nature of the murders and the amount of time that's passed in some of the cases, we have no crime scenes and no physical evidence to link them.''

"That's tough. I suppose it's pretty much a waiting game now.''

"Pretty much,'' Melanie agreed, although she hated the thought of them all sitting around waiting for fresh blood, as they called a new murder. But fresh blood meant new leads and evidence, both of which they needed desperately right now.

They headed out to the training room. "It'll be a juicy case to try," Veronica murmured. "Almost makes me wish I was on the homicide team. Of course, considering my history with batterers, I imagine it would feel a bit like being on the other side of the law."

Melanie murmured that it would, though she didn't really feel that way. For her, she didn't think about who the Dark Angel had killed, only that she had killed. For her, she didn't see the shades of gray in the Angel's acts—only right and wrong.

They stretched and moved through their poomses in silence, then readied themselves to spar. Over the weeks they had fallen into the practice of freestyle sparring with light contact. After the first few weeks, with Mr. Browne's permission, they had decided not to wear body armor. Tae kwon do blows were delivered with an incredible amount of force; one slip could do serious damage. However, both women were experienced enough in pulling their punches and kicks to avoid injury without forgoing the feel of real competition.

Plus, they had developed a high level of trust with each other. Of comfort with the other's fighting style. Veronica was a charger, Melanie a bull. Melanie relied on a direct, methodical attack, Veronica indirect and unexpected. They had learned each other's way and although Melanie hadn't yet bested the other woman, she hadn't lost faith that one night she would.

Tonight, it seemed, was that night. Veronica's

timing was off, her moves neither as sharp nor focused as usual. Veronica left herself open and Melanie landed a blow to her forehead. Then when Veronica took a step back in surprise, Melanie delivered a roundhouse kick to the side of her head. In a tournament, she would have received a point for each, three points would take the match.

"Next point and the match is mine," Melanie teased, dropping back into her ready stance. "You sure you're up to this tonight? You're making it awfully easy."

"All part of my master plan," Veronica retorted, also readying herself. "Now that I've got you feeling cocky and overconfident, I move in for the kill."

Melanie laughed. "Give it your best shot, lawyer-girl."

Veronica charged. Melanie blocked her punch, Veronica her returning blow. They repeated the exercise. Then, without warning, Veronica landed a direct kick to Melanie's sternum. Pain exploded in her chest and she flew backward, landing on her back, gasping for breath, ears ringing.

She opened her eyes—her vision swam. Veronica was bent over her as was the instructor. And the other black belts. Veronica was smiling.

That couldn't be. Moaning, Melanie closed her eyes, and when she reopened them her vision had cleared.

"I'm so sorry, Mel," Veronica murmured, bending closer, expression distraught. "I don't know what happened."

Melanie stared at her, unable to speak. She ordered herself to sit up, but her body seemed unable to react to her command. She opened her mouth to ask Mr. Browne why and a whimper slipped past her lips instead.

"Don't move," the instructor ordered, laying a hand gently on her shoulder. "Don't talk. Close your eyes and breathe, slow and deep."

Melanie did as her teacher described.

"Good," he said. "Now as you breathe in, focus on the oxygen, on its healing properties. Let them fill you. That's right," he murmured. "Now as you breathe out, imagine the pain being expelled with the air. With each breath, more of the pain is being carried away."

Again she did as he instructed and gradually her head cleared and her equilibrium returned, though her chest still hurt like the devil.

"I think I can sit up now," she whispered. "I'd like to try."

Veronica and the teacher helped her. Though her chest ached, there were no sharp pains that might indicate a broken rib. Melanie brought a hand to the spot Veronica's foot had connected and gently rubbed. It was hot to the touch.

"What happened here?" Mr. Browne asked, looking at Veronica.

She paled. "I don't know, we were sparring and—"

"You lost concentration," he said, angry. "You lost focus. A blow of that force, directly to the heart, can kill. You know that. This could have been serious."

Veronica lowered her head. "Yes, Instructor."

"Body armor from now on. Both of you."

Both women agreed without a murmur of protest. Melanie wasn't sure she would ever spar without armor again.

The two helped Melanie to her feet. She swayed slightly, then righted herself. Veronica helped her to the dressing room, unlocked the locker for her, retrieved her bag.

"I'm really sorry, Melanie," she said. "I feel awful about this."

Melanie pictured Veronica leaning over her, smiling. She brought a hand to her aching chest. "Do you?"

Veronica's face flooded with color. "Are you suggesting I made contact on purpose?"

Dear God, she was. Had she lost her mind? She and Veronica were friends, why would Veronica deliberately try to hurt her?

Melanie drew in a shuddering breath, cheeks growing hot. "When I opened my eyes, I saw...I thought I saw you smile..."

Veronica drew back, expression wounded. "Smile? Thanks a lot, Melanie. I thought we were friends."

The last of Melanie's anger and suspicion evaporated, leaving her feeling small and unkind. And more than a little ridiculous. She held out a hand. "I'm sorry, Veronica. I guess, that blow...it shook me up. If it had been slightly to the right, it could have stopped my heart. I didn't mean what I said. Forgive me?"

The other woman forced a stiff-looking smile and agreed to forgive. But as Melanie watched Veronica walk away, she worried she'd permanently damaged their friendship.

36

Ashley liked visiting Dilworth Square on Saturday nights. The trendy shopping area catered to an upscale clientele and consisted of unique boutiques, several bistro-style restaurants and an outdoor café. Because the shops stayed open until 10:00 p.m. on Saturdays, there was always a nice crowd for Ashley to blend in with, conversations to eavesdrop on, people to chat with while waiting in line to pay for a purchase.

Being alone in a crowd wasn't nearly so lonely as the alternative.

Ashley slipped by a couple strolling arm in arm, averting her gaze. Lately, the quiet had been pressing in on her. Nights were the worst. More often than not these days, she awakened in the midnight hours, drenched in sweat, choking on it. On the darkness and the emptiness inside her.

Then the memories would come. And she would be lost.

She needed her sisters, Ashley knew. Their arms. Their unconditional love and understanding. She needed them to make everything okay for her. But they couldn't.

They didn't understand.

Because they didn't know. She hadn't told them.

They weren't there for her, only for each other.
Ashley closed her eyes briefly, denying the thought.
She told herself her sisters loved her, that she was
as important in their lives as they were in hers. She
hadn't seen them much lately because they'd been
busy—Melanie with her case, Mia with her marital
problems.

She was kidding herself. Something had come
between them. Someone.

Veronica Ford.

As if Ashley's thoughts had conjured the woman,
she appeared up ahead, emerging from the Godiva
Chocolate store. She was smiling, obviously in high
spirits. She carried one of the store's small gold
shopping bags, swinging it as she walked. *Not a
care in the world.*

Hatred rose inside Ashley. In the past few weeks,
every time she had driven by Mia's house, the other
woman's car had been there. Of late, the only times
she and her sisters had gotten together, Veronica
had been included.

As if she was one of them.

The hatred swelled. She wasn't one of them,
dammit. They were three. Only three, not four.

Ashley caught the curious stares of people she
passed and realized she had been muttering to herself. Embarrassed, she brought a hand to her forehead. And discovered that even though the night
was mild, she was sweating.

Dear God, what was happening to her?

She was falling apart.

Ashley shook her head in denial. No. She wasn't

falling apart. Veronica Ford was turning her sisters against her. She was trying to steal them from her.

It wasn't fair. Not after all she had done to protect them. Not after the way she had suffered. The way she continued to suffer.

Up ahead Veronica ducked into another shop. A lingerie store. Ashley followed, stopping outside the store's display window. She peered through, watching as the attorney browsed the racks, holding up this and that—a teddy, a gown, a bra-and-panty set. While she shopped, she conversed with the salesgirl, laughing and smiling.

Veronica carried a simple, champagne-colored chemise to the counter. While she paid for it, Ashley moved away from the window, blending in with a group admiring the work of one of the sidewalk artists.

When Veronica emerged from the lingerie store, Ashley followed her, staying far enough behind as to not arouse her suspicions, but close enough never to lose sight of her. Several times the lawyer glanced back, as if searching for someone, but her gaze never landed on Ashley. Only when she entered a store did Ashley close in, peering at her through the shop window.

Veronica visited a perfumer, a bookstore and a shoe shop. Everywhere she went, she purchased something. She spent carelessly, Ashley saw, as only those with unlimited funds did. She didn't look at price tags or hesitate when she found an item she liked—she simply handed the shopkeeper her credit card.

Veronica emerged again, and again Ashley fell

in step behind her. Only this time Veronica turned
down the tree-lined alley that wrapped around the
back of the square.

Ashley hesitated a moment, then stepped up her
pace, not wanting to lose sight of her. She reached
the alleyway entrance. The alley was brick, one side
lined by the back of the shops and their delivery
entrances, the other with ornamental trees laced in
tiny white lights.

The alley was empty.

Where had she gone?

Ashley frowned and started forward. Her foot-
steps made a soft slap against the brick; laughter
and the hum of conversations from the business
side of the square floated on the night air, sounding
far away, almost ghostly. Gooseflesh raced up her
arms and Ashley shuddered.

"Are you looking for me?"

Ashley gasped and swung around. Veronica
stood ten feet behind her, hands on hips, all but
bristling with anger. She must have realized she
was being followed and set a trap by hiding in one
of the recessed doorways.

"Veronica!" Ashley said, feigning surprise.
"What are you doing here?"

Obviously, she wasn't fooled. "Why are you following me?"

"Following you?" Ashley repeated, cheeks hot
with embarrassment. "Why would I waste my time
that way?"

"That's what I'd like to know." The other
woman cocked her head, studying her. "You don't
like me very much, do you?"

Ashley looked her straight in the eyes. "I don't like you at all."

"But why?" She tipped her hands palms up. "What have I ever done to you, Ashley? What, except try to be your friend?"

"Maybe I don't want you as a friend. Maybe I think you're bad news."

As she said the words, Ashley realized they were true. She didn't know why, but she found something about the woman distasteful. Snakelike. Sneaky.

Veronica snorted her disbelief. "*I'm* bad news?" She touched her chest. "Me?"

"That's what I said." She hiked up her chin. "And I'm going to prove it."

Veronica shook her head, her expression pitying. "You need some serious help, Ashley." She crossed to the doorway to her immediate left, collected her bags, then looked back at Ashley. "And I really hope you get it before you hurt the people who love you more than you already have."

She turned and started down the alley. Ashley watched her go, chest aching with unshed tears. The words had cut her to the quick. "What do you know about the people who love me?" she called out, voice shaking. "What do you know about me?"

Veronica didn't stop, she didn't look back. Ashley started after her, impotent rage clawing at her. "I want you out of my life! Out of my sisters' lives! Do you hear me, Veronica Ford! Just go away!"

The other woman stopped. She turned and put her bags on the ground. Her expression had changed, become harder, colder. "That's what this is all about, isn't it? Your sisters. You're jealous of my friendship with them."

She was jealous, Ashley acknowledged silently, but her feelings for Veronica went deeper than jealousy. They came from a place inside her she couldn't name but trusted completely.

"Go back to Charleston and leave us alone. I don't want you here. *We* don't want you here."

Veronica shook her head, expression pitying. "I feel sorry for you. I feel sorry for Mia and Melanie because they love you so much."

"Stop talking about them." The words came out choked. "This is about you."

"No, it's about you. You can't stand that they like me. You're jealous of the time they spend with me. Why don't you just admit it, it might make you feel better."

"Stop it!" Ashley fisted her fingers, feeling as if a weight was pressing against her chest, crushing her. "Sh...shut up!"

"The fact is, you're afraid they like me better than they like you. I'm sorry if that hurts you, but that's the way you feel. And you know what, you're probably right. They do."

Tears flooded her eyes; so many that her vision swam. "They're my sisters! *Mine!* And I want you to stay away from them."

"Sorry, Ashley, but that just isn't going to be possible."

The lawyer collected her bags, turned and walked away. Ashley watched her go, acknowledging that she hated Veronica Ford with every fiber of her being.

37

Connor pulled his Explorer to a stop in front of Melanie's house, but didn't cut the engine. He gazed at the modest, cottage-style dwelling, noting that it looked well maintained—the paint fresh, the lawn recently mown, the flower beds tended. A toddler swing hung from the big maple tree beside the driveway and a bike with training wheels sat half in, half out of the open garage. Melanie's Jeep was parked inside.

Connor tapped his fingers on the steering wheel, uncertain of his next move.

Stay? Or go?

He glanced at the seat beside him, at the bulging manila envelope. The reason for his visit.

The trumped-up reason.

He grimaced. The truth was, it wasn't imperative that he see her now, at home. Everything he wanted to discuss could wait or be handled via fax and phone. But the Dark Angel investigation wasn't why he had stopped by the Whistlestop PD this morning. It wasn't what had caused him to leave that same PD feeling frustrated, or what had motivated him to drive the dozen blocks to her house after he had learned she was home today with a sick child.

No, the feelings that had propelled him to her front door were anything but professional.

He and Melanie had been working together over a month now. He had found her to be a thorough cop and thoroughly professional. He liked the way her mind worked, the way she approached a problem methodically but with the kind of creativity found in only the best detectives. She was impatient, but never let her impatience cause her to become sloppy. She was hot-tempered but kind, direct, moral to a fault and funny when drawn out.

And too damn attractive for his peace of mind.

Connor pushed the thought away, though it was true, and glanced toward her house. His gaze landed on the red, white and blue flag-bedecked wreath on her front door and he smiled. Not only had the fourth of July come and gone, September loomed right around the corner. He wondered if she'd simply been so busy she had lost track of time or if her son had asked her to leave it up.

His smile became rueful. One of the many things he wondered about when it came to Melanie May and her life. For, with all that he had learned about her, she was still a mystery to him. He knew she was divorced, fiercely devoted to her child and had ambitions beyond being a Whistlestop cop.

But he wanted to know more about her than just her stats.

And he hadn't felt that way about anyone in a long time.

Reason enough to go. He reached for the shift, to drop the car back into Drive, but he found the key and cut the engine instead. Grabbing the envelope off the seat beside him, he swung out of the vehicle and started up the front walk, not giving himself a chance to change his mind.

Before he could ring the bell, she opened the door. Though it was after 10:00 a.m. she looked as if she had only recently showered and dressed—she wore ancient-looking jeans and a plain white T-shirt, her hair was damp, her feet bare. She looked more like a college coed than a police officer and divorced mother of a four-year-old.

"Connor," she said softly, obviously surprised. "What brings you here?"

"Hi." He shifted his weight from one foot to the other, feeling like a gangly teenager instead of a thirty-eight-year-old man. "Bobby told me I'd find you here. I hope my stopping by isn't a problem?"

"Of course not. Casey's sleeping." She smiled. "What's up?"

He could look a suspect dead in the eyes and lie his ass off, but not Melanie. That became immediately obvious to him. He shifted his gaze slightly and cleared his throat. "We received a couple faxes this morning, one from Asheville's PD, the other from Columbia's. Both possible Dark Angel victims. I thought I'd run them by you."

"Great." She stepped back to allow him to enter, but held a finger to her lips, expression sheepish. "We'll need to keep our voices low. Casey's a light sleeper." She motioned forward, then indicated he follow her.

When they reached her small, sunny kitchen, she closed the door behind them. "Have a seat. I'll make some coffee."

"That's not necessary." He took one of the tall stools at the breakfast counter, depositing the envelope in front of him. "I don't want you to go to any trouble on my account."

"No trouble, trust me. We had a rough night and I've only had one cup of leftover so far this morning." She made a face. "And I hate reheated coffee."

"Coffee'd be good. Thanks."

She emptied what was left of the previous day's pot in the sink, then filled the carafe with fresh water. "Bobby's kids could sleep through an explosion, but not my Casey. Of course, when he was a baby, I tiptoed around because I thought I was supposed to, I thought he would sleep better. Now I know all I was doing was training him to need absolute quiet to sleep." She shrugged. "First-time moms, we do our best."

Connor rested his chin on his fist, watching her easy movements. "How is Casey? Bobby said he was ill."

"Ear infection." She flipped on the coffeemaker. "He's been plagued with them since he was a baby. I thought he'd outgrown them, but…"

She didn't finish the thought, but didn't have to. Connor got it. She bent her face toward the coffeepot, breathing in the scent of the brewing coffee. He found something about the movement sexy in a natural, earthy sort of way. The truth was, he found everything about her sexy in the same sort of way.

"So, what do you have for me?"

He blinked. "Pardon?"

"The possible vics."

"Oh...yeah." He opened the envelope and pulled out the faxes. They were one-page summaries of a couple of dead-end investigations. "As I said, the two PDs forwarded these. Both these deaths were thought suspicious, but the detectives never found anything concrete they could hang a homicide investigation on. Though they don't really fit our Angel's M.O., both men had a history of spousal abuse. I wanted to get your opinion."

The coffeemaker sputtered its final measure of water through the filter and Melanie poured two mugs of the brew. After asking him if he needed cream and sugar she slid one of the mugs across the counter to him. "Tell me about them," she said.

"First guy was a motorcycle enthusiast. He was forced off a mountain road and plummeted to his death. No witnesses."

"How do they know he was forced off?"

"Tire marks. Damage on the remains of the bike."

"Pretty risky move. Awfully public. Also, sounds like a cut-and-dried homicide."

"Not necessarily. Those mountain roads are narrow, someone may have been trying to pass and got into trouble. It was raining and slippery." Melanie came around the counter to get a look at the report. She bent over his shoulder. As she did, her hair brushed against his cheek—it felt silky and smelled of the fruity shampoo she'd used. It took all his concentration to focus on what he was saying when what he wanted to do was reach up and capture the strands between his fingers.

"And the second?"

Connor dragged his attention back to the report in front of him. "This guy was a hunter. Spent almost every weekend during deer season at his camp, sometimes alone, sometimes with buddies. Killed in a so-called 'hunting accident.' Thing is, this was no stray bullet or misaimed shot that got him. He was nailed in the chest at close range. A couple of hunters stumbled onto him. He was already dead."

"No witnesses?"

"None. This particular weekend, all his buddies begged off."

"That would have left him alone and vulnerable, just the way our Angel likes 'em."

"Exactly, though neither accident clearly fits our Angel's pattern. Both deaths employed a more direct killing method and were riskier in terms of potential discovery. In addition, neither man was made vulnerable by his own frailty so much as by his hobby. But," he finished, "the guys were both batterers. And they're both dead as the result of inexplicable accidents."

She was quiet. Connor could almost hear her thinking, putting the facts together. "These could belong to the Angel," Melanie murmured. "In fact, I wouldn't be surprised if they did."

"Why?" he asked, tipping his face to hers. He realized his mistake immediately. The movement put her mouth within inches of his. He swallowed hard and forced his gaze to remain on hers when every fiber of his being screamed for him to look at her mouth instead. Her full, sexy, inviting mouth.

"Think about it, Connor. Sometimes she has to

take risks.'' Melanie pulled a stool closer to his and sat down. ''She hand-picks her victim. She studies him. She learns his likes, dislikes, habits. She uncovers his weaknesses.''

''The things that make him vulnerable,'' Connor supplied. ''A heart condition. A drinking problem. A severe food allergy.''

''Right.'' Melanie tucked her hair behind her ear; some of the silky strands feathered back across her cheek. Connor followed the movement with his gaze, then cursed his weakness.

She, however, continued as if she hadn't noticed his gaze. As if being near him was no more sexually disconcerting than being near her brother or father. ''But what if he has no weakness for her to exploit?'' she asked. ''What does she do?''

''She either moves on to a new victim or takes her chances.''

''If she decides to take her chances, she's got to find another way at him.'' Excited, Melanie jumped to her feet and went to a small desk tucked into the corner of the kitchen. She took a file folder off the top and carried it back to the counter. She opened it and took out the sheaf of papers she had tucked inside. On the top of each sheet was a man's name, below that how and where he had died, and her personal observations about each death.

She laid them one by one on the counter in front of him, making two rows, adding the new victims. She pointed. ''These aren't so different, Connor. She finds a way in, a place in their life where they're vulnerable. Everybody's got that place. She finds it and uses it.'' Melanie met his eyes. ''She doesn't move on. She's got too much invested in these guys, she can't.''

"Serials do move on," Connor murmured, playing devil's advocate. "If they feel they're at risk."

"But she's different," Melanie said, insistent. "If we're right, she invests a lot emotionally in these guys. She—"

"No," he corrected. "Not the guys. The women they hurt."

The words landed between them like a bomb. *That was it. The women were the connection.*

The Dark Angel didn't kill to correct some global wrong, she didn't kill for personal revenge or to punish the individual victim. Instead, she was helping a woman in trouble.

"Son-of-a-bitch." Connor got to his feet. It was so clear now. So simple. "The women are the connection, not the men." He looked at Melanie. "She befriends the women *after* she learns about their situations."

"But how?" Melanie asked, as excited as Connor. "Where does she meet them?"

"Places women go. The hairdresser's. The grocery store."

"Hold on." Melanie grabbed a piece of paper and a pen from the desk, returned to the counter and jotted those down, then lifted her gaze expectantly to his. "Women's groups. PTA meetings."

They brainstormed some more. Between the two of them they came up with a list of twenty spots, everything from Laundromats to lunch places, kids' play groups to the gym.

"We need to interview the victims' wives and

girlfriends again. Learn the places they go, the names of their friends.''

"If we get lucky, a couple of the women will frequent the same place or places. Or a woman's name will appear a couple of times.''

"More than a couple.'' Melanie brought her hands together and laughed. "A breakthrough, Connor. Hot damn, this is fun.''

Connor found her laugh irresistible—the throaty sound of it, the way her eyes lit up with amusement, the way she tilted her head back as the sound bubbled past her lips. It was nice. He told her so.

"Gee-whiz, Parks,'' she joked, "a nice laugh? Thanks. Nobody's ever said that to me before.''

"They should have. Because it is. Really nice.''

As if suddenly realizing he wasn't teasing her, she stood. "How about a warm-up?''

He followed her to her feet. "I've made you uncomfortable. I'm sorry.''

"Don't be silly.'' Her smile looked forced. "It's not like you came on to me. Or made some totally inappropriate move. It was a nice thing to say.''

"Nice?''

Instead of laughing, she swallowed hard, audibly. Their eyes met. He took a step toward her. "What would you say if I did do something totally... inappropriate?''

She looked away, then back, the expression in her gaze naked with longing. He wondered if she saw the same longing in his.

"I guess that would depend.''

"Would it?'' He moved closer, heart thundering. "On what, Melanie?''

She lifted her face to his. She wet her lips. "On just what inappropriate thing you—"

The phone rang.

They both swung in its direction. After a moment's hesitation, Melanie grabbed for it like a lifeline. Connor swung away from her, disappointment spearing sharply through him. He breathed deeply through his nose, forcing aside thoughts of her mouth and body, the way both would have felt against his, the way she would taste.

What he had been contemplating would have been a mistake. He and Melanie had to work together; the last thing he needed in his already screwed-up life was the complication of an on-the-job romance. It was better this way.

Then why did he feel like killing whoever was on the other end of that call?

"An ear infection."

At Melanie's brittle tone, Connor glanced over his shoulder at her. She stood ramrod straight, her back to him. It was obvious she was anything but pleased to hear from whoever had called.

"No, he is not sick because he goes to day care. You don't *catch* ear infections." She sighed. "We've been through this before. And we both decided to pass on getting the tubes put in his ears in the hopes he would outgrow this. Remember?"

Her ex-husband, Connor realized, picking up his coffee and pretending interest in it. Calling to check on their child. And to shovel Melanie a load of crap.

"Look, Stan, I don't have time for this right now." She was silent a moment as if listening, then said, "That's *your* opinion. If you'd like, call Casey's pediatrician and discuss it with her. I have to go."

She hung up the phone and returned to the breakfast counter, her expression tight. "Sorry about that."

"It's okay." He glanced at her, then away. "Problems with your ex?"

"Always." She attempted a casual laugh, but it came out choked. She cleared her throat. "Sorry again. He does this to me. He has a gift for it."

"Is there anything I can do?"

"I wish." She sucked in a deep breath. "The thing is, my ex refuses to listen to any ideas but his own, his current being that everything I do is harmful to our son. He's in the process of suing me for custody. We go to court soon."

"I'm sorry."

"Me, too." She looked at her hands, then back up at him. "No," she amended. "Not sorry, royally pissed. That he would do this to me, but more, that he would do this to Casey. For no other reason than to punish me."

"For divorcing him?"

"That, and for having the guts to make my own life. To do what I wanted to do with it."

"He didn't want you to be a cop?"

"Are you kidding? He wanted me to *not* be a cop so much, he pulled strings that kept me out of the CMPD academy." She laughed, but this time the sound was hard, angry. "Sometimes, when I think about it, I'm so angry, I swear I could—"

As if realizing what she was about to say and to

whom, she bit the words back. "Most of the time, I can't get past wondering what I'm going to do if I lose Casey. I can't imagine living day to day without him."

"What does your lawyer say?"

"All the right things. That there's every reason to believe I'll retain custody. That Stan has zero grounds for taking Casey away. But still, I keep thinking about that worst-case scenario. It must be a mom thing." She crossed to the coffeepot. "You want that warm-up?"

He glanced at his watch. He should go. But what he wanted to do and should do were two very different things, indeed.

"Sure," he said and handed her his still half-full mug. "Why'd you marry him?"

"Stan?" She dumped the old coffee, then refilled the mug from the stainless-steel carafe. "All the wrong reasons, I know now. Not only was he incredibly handsome, but he had this aura of strength about him. When I was with him I felt safe. Protected."

She slid Connor's mug across the counter to him. "Of course, before long I realized that all that strength was nothing more than arrogance and an overbearing need to control. I also realized he didn't want to protect me so much as own me. Realizing that took a bit longer. I was young."

Safe? Protected? Connor frowned. Needing those things didn't fit with the confident, almost fiercely independent woman he knew. He told her so.

"I know." She drew her eyebrows together, as

if remembering. "I'm not the same woman now as I was then. I had a troubled childhood. My mother died when I was eleven and my father wasn't…he wasn't much of a parent. Or man, for that matter. We moved around a lot. Looking back, it makes sense that I'd have looked for security. That feeling of safety." She sent him a self-conscious smile. "That sounds an awful lot like psychobabble, doesn't it?"

"No, it doesn't. People get into relationships for all sorts of reasons."

She brought her mug to her lips, but didn't sip. "Enough about me. What about you? Why did you marry your ex?"

He grimaced, acknowledging that she had cornered him, and rather neatly at that.

"I married Trish because I thought she and her son, Jamey, could bring me back to life. I thought she could love me enough for the both of us."

"Ouch."

"Yeah, ouch. It wasn't fair to her or to her son."

"Jamey. He's the one you told me about?"

"Yes."

"You cared about him a lot, didn't you?"

"Too much. Considering the screwed-up situation."

"Kids do that to you." She began collecting the reports from the counter. "So, how do you want to divvy up the wives and girlfriends?"

He didn't answer, instead called her name softly and in question. She stopped and met his eyes. "About earlier, before the phone—"

"Forget it." She made a dismissive gesture with her right hand. "I have."

That wasn't exactly what he'd had in mind.

"Have you?" he asked. "Forgotten it?"

"Sure." She slid the papers into the envelope, then handed it to him, not meeting his eyes. He saw that her cheeks were pink.

"Not me," he murmured, dropping his gaze to her mouth, then slowly moving it back up to hers. "I haven't forgotten. I'm not sure I can."

He brought a hand to her face, cupping her cheek. Her skin was warm and soft beneath his fingers, and he trailed his thumb over her cheekbone.

A small sound of distress slipped past her lips even as she tipped her face into the caress. "Connor, I... This is a mistake. I mean, we're—"

"Colleagues," he murmured. "I know. I've been over this in my mind a hundred times already. We're working together on a big case. An important one. Getting involved with each other would make for a potentially explosive situation."

"And?"

"And here I am, wanting to kiss you anyway."

She looked helplessly up at him, and he knew she felt the same way, that she had been anticipating this as much as he had.

This was going to be complicated.

"Connor, I—"

He brought his mouth to hers. Her lips were warm. And softly parted. And almost unbearably sweet. He rubbed his lips against hers, then drew away, shocked at how the light contact affected him. Like a bottle of really fine wine. Or a strong left hook.

He swore softly. She had been right, this was a mistake. A big mistake.

He started to tell her so, but she didn't give him the chance. This time it was she who initiated a kiss, she who boldly brought her mouth to his. And God help him, he couldn't say no.

"Mommy?"

They sprang apart. Melanie swung toward the doorway, face bright with color. "Casey!"

The child stood there, cheeks flushed, his golden-colored hair sticking out in six different directions. He clutched a stuffed rabbit to his chest. "My ear hurts."

Connor watched as she crossed to the child and scooped him up. Watched as the youngster wrapped his small arms and legs around her and pressed his face into the crook of her neck.

Saved by the bell, he thought. Twice now.

It seemed to Connor that he and Melanie were being sent a message and that this time they had better heed it. Life seldom delivered two warnings, never three.

He collected the envelope he had come with, then glanced at her. She looked embarrassed. Uncertain.

"Melanie—"

"Connor—"

They'd said each other's name simultaneously.

"I'm sorry," he said. "I shouldn't have let—"

"No apologies. As I see it, I'm as much to blame as you."

A smile tugged at the corners of his mouth, he

couldn't stop it. That she was willing to accept an equal part of the blame meant she had been as attracted to him as he was to her.

Of course, that sort of thinking was in the past now. From this moment on, it would be business only between them.

She coughed. "It's better that Casey...it would have been complicated if we, you know."

It was the *you know* that would keep him up that night. "Right." He eased toward the kitchen door. "I'll see myself out. You've got your arms full."

"Okay. Thanks."

"I'll start calling the victims' spouses and girlfriends. I'll set up some interviews."

"Let me know."

"I will." He turned and walked away, wondering how in the hell he was going keep the hands-off agreement they had just made.

38

Melanie took a deep breath and rang Ashley's front doorbell. Her hands shook. She'd just gotten off the phone with Veronica. Someone claiming to be Officer Melanie May had visited the Charleston D.A.'s office yesterday. They'd had identification and had been wearing a police uniform. They'd asked all sorts of weird questions about Veronica: who her friends were, if she had been liked, if she had any strange habits.

Veronica had been furious. She believed that someone was Ashley.

It couldn't be true. If Ashley had done what Veronica had suspected, she had violated not only Veronica's privacy but Melanie's trust as well. It had been the act of someone who was both desparate and out of touch with reality.

At first Melanie thought Veronica's accusation preposterous. Why would Ashley do such a thing? Then the lawyer told her about how Ashley had followed her the Saturday before. She had shared the crazy things Ashley had said to her. Now, Melanie wasn't so sure about her sister's innocence. Now, she was deeply concerned about her sister's emotional state.

No sound came from within her sister's apartment. The blinds were closed tight, the mailbox beside the door stuffed full and sales circulars littered the mat in front of the door. Melanie shifted her gaze. The potted plants that lined the front steps were dead or dying, their once-colorful blossoms a dim memory.

Melanie drew her eyebrows together, unsettled. The place looked unlived in. Abandoned, even. Yet, her sister was home—Melanie had seen her car parked in the town house complex's lot.

She rang the bell again and waited, then knocked loudly, growing more alarmed with each passing moment. Finally, she heard a sound from within— a kind of shuffling. The dead bolt slid back and the door opened.

Her sister stood on the other side. Melanie made a sound of dismay—her vibrant, beautiful sister looked like death warmed over. Her skin had an unhealthy cast, the circles under her eyes were so dark and deep they looked like bruises.

"My God, Ash, what's happened to you?"

Ashley blinked, obviously disoriented. "I just woke up."

Melanie glanced at her watch. Admittedly, it was Saturday morning, but it was also after ten. "Big night last night?" she asked.

Ashley stepped back from the door, allowing Melanie to enter. Melanie saw that she wore shorts and a T-shirt, both of which looked slept in.

She yawned. "I couldn't sleep, so I took a pill. I don't even know what time that was. Late, I think."

Melanie frowned. *A sleeping pill? When had she*

started that practice? "Has that been happening a lot? Your not being able to sleep?"

Ashley lifted her shoulders and yawned again, then motioned Melanie forward. "I need coffee."

Melanie followed her sister, noticing that every drape or blind in the place was closed tight. The apartment was like a tomb, dark and airless.

"It's a beautiful day," she said as they reached the kitchen. "How about I open a couple windows and let in some fresh air."

"Sure. Whatever."

While Ashley started the coffee, Melanie lifted the blinds, then opened the windows. "There," she said, "isn't that better?"

Her sister didn't respond and she turned to find her slumped against the counter, staring blankly into space. Melanie dropped her gaze to the two mugs and jar of instant coffee on the counter. She arched her eyebrows. Ashley was as big a coffee snob as she was.

"Ash?" Her sister met her eyes. "Instant? Please."

"I know. But I just can't deal with the whole bean thing right now. Too much work."

Melanie shook her head and ordered her sister to sit. "I'll do it. Just point me in the right direction."

Ashley did and she busied herself making not only the coffee but some toast and juice for her sister as well. Within moments, the smell of the rich dark roast filled the kitchen. Ashley seemed to come to life.

Melanie set the toast and mug in front of her

sister, then retrieved her own and took the seat directly across from her.

Ashley sipped the coffee and sighed. "Sweet, good Melanie. The one who always took care of us. What would we do without you?"

"Hopefully, you'll never find out." She motioned with her head. "Now eat. You look like you could use some sustenance."

Apparently, Ashley's idea of eating was to tear off a piece of the bread, then crumble it between her fingers. Melanie watched her a moment, then shook her head, troubled. "What's going on with you, Ashley? What's wrong?"

She lifted a shoulder. "Nothing. I'm fine."

"I can tell. You're doing great. Super, in fact. That's why you're resorting to sleeping pills at night."

Ashley groaned. "I resorted to it last night. Don't blow this all out of proportion."

"You having trouble at work?"

"Work's fine."

"How about man trouble?"

"Get real."

"So, what is it?"

"Why are you so certain I have a problem? Give it a rest, Mel, I'm fine."

"Sure, you are. Peek in the mirror, sister-dearest. You look like a corpse."

Ashley lifted her coffee mug in a mock salute. "Gee, Mel, I love you, too."

At least her sister's sarcasm was making an appearance, Melanie thought, encouraged. "If I didn't love you, I wouldn't be here."

"Come to think of it, why are you here? After all, I haven't seen much of either of my *devoted* sisters lately."

"I can't speak for Mia, but between the Dark Angel investigation, Casey's latest ear infection and the impending custody trial, I'm keeping awfully busy."

"I can. Speak for Mia, that is."

"Oh?"

"Mmm." Ashley had destroyed one piece of the toast and moved on to the second. "She's spending a lot of time with Veronica Ford."

"And that bothers you?"

"Yeah, it does."

Melanie reached across the table. "It shouldn't, Ash. They're friends. Friends spend time together."

"So do sisters."

Melanie bit back a sigh. "That goes both ways, you know. You haven't called me in at least a couple of weeks. Not once."

"Would it have done any good? After all, you're *so* busy."

Melanie let out her breath in an exasperated huff. "What do you want me to do? Apologize? Tell you it's all my fault? Fine. Done. It's all my fault."

"Screw you." Ashley jumped to her feet and crossed to the window, squinting against the light.

"For heaven's sake, Ash! Just tell me what's wrong."

"I bet you don't even think the amount of time Mia and Veronica are spending together is unnatural."

"No, I don't think it's unnatural. They're friends."

"Do friends spend the night together? I've driven by Mia's late and seen Veronica's car. And vice versa."

Melanie looked at her sister, more concerned than ever. "Ash, hon, spying on your sister is what's unnatural."

Her face flooded with color. "I knew you'd side with her over me. I knew it!"

Melanie got to her feet. "Side with who? Mia? She's not even a part of this discussion. We're talking about you."

"No." Ash shook her head. "It's not bad enough that you and Mia closed ranks when we were kids, now you're doing it with Veronica." She brought her hands to her face and Melanie saw that they trembled. "After the way I've loved you. After all I've given you."

It was as bad as Veronica said. Worse, even.

"This isn't a competition, Ash. You're my sister and I love you." She crossed to stand before her. She caught her hands and drew them gently away from her face. She used the opportunity to look Ashley directly in the eyes. "I'm worried about you."

"And that's what brought you here today? Out of the blue? How much you love me?"

"Yes."

"And you weren't prompted by anything else?"

Melanie was silent a moment, knowing how the truth would affect her sister but unwilling to lie anyway. She never lied—it was a lesson she had learned early and had never forgotten.

"Veronica told me something about you that disturbed me." She tightened her grip on her sister's fingers. "She told me you followed her, and when she confronted you, you said crazy things."

"Crazy things?" Ashley repeated, voice trembling. "You wouldn't be referring to my comment about your good buddy being bad news? Or when I told her I wished she would go away and never come back?"

Melanie's heart sank. "Yes," she murmured, aching for her sister, "I would."

"Those aren't crazy. They're true." Ashley's voice took on a desperate edge. "She's bad news, you just don't see."

"No, I don't. Because there's nothing there to see."

Ashley pulled her hands free and backed away from Melanie. "She is bad news, Mel. There's something about her, something off. You have to believe me."

Dear God, Ashley had done it. She'd done what Veronica had said.

Melanie asked anyway, determined to give her sister every benefit of doubt. "Did you pretend to be me, Ashley? Did you go to the Charleston D.A.'s office, pretending to be a cop on official business and ask questions about Veronica's personal and professional life? Did you do that?"

"I should have known," Ashley said, voice shaking. "I should have known you weren't here because you cared about me. This is about *her,* isn't it?''

''Oh, Ash...'' Melanie fought to remain focused on her sister's needs and feelings and to keep her own emotions in check. ''Consider what you've done. You jeopardized not only Veronica's career and reputation, but mine as well. Did you think she wouldn't find out? That someone wouldn't call her? That after the things you said to her last Saturday night, she wouldn't figure out it was you? She could press charges. The only reason she's not is because she's our friend.''

Ashley brought her hands to her face. She began to cry, softly at first, then with increasing intensity. Soon her sobs so shook her body, Melanie feared she would fall.

Melanie took her sister in her arms and held her, stroking her hair, murmuring that everything was going to be all right. That she would make everything all right.

''I love you so much,'' Ashley whispered, voice broken. ''You and Mia. You have...no idea...no idea the things I've...I did for you.''

''What things?'' Melanie asked softly, urgently. ''Tell me what you've done. Tell me why you're so unhappy. I'm here for you. I'll help you, Ashley, I promise I will.''

Ashley went stone still. She eased out of Melanie's arms. ''That's bullshit. You've never been there for me. Only for Mia.''

''That's not true, Ash. You're my sister, I'd do anything for y—''

''That's bullshit!'' she said again, voice taking

on a high, hysterical edge. "I waited but you didn't...you didn't come."

"Come where? I don't know what you're talking about, Ashley." Melanie worked to stay calm. "If you'll just tell me why you're so angry—"

"I shouldn't have to tell you, Melanie. I shouldn't have—" She bit the words back and looked Melanie dead in the eyes. "Just get out. Just get out of my house and leave me alone."

"Ash, please." She held out a hand, hurting. "Let's talk about this. Please, we're sisters."

"Don't you get it? I don't want you here, Melanie. Your being here is upsetting me."

Not knowing what else to do, Melanie left.

39

Veronica drew Mia into her arms, cradling her against her breasts. They lay together on Veronica's bed, naked, damp and exhausted from their love-making. They had been lovers a couple of weeks now and Veronica had never been happier, not in her whole life.

How could she have been? She had never known life could be so abundant, a relationship so renew-ing.

She was head over heels in love with Mia.

"He was like a raging bull," Mia murmured, the sound small and choked. "Tearing my things off hangers, emptying drawers onto the floor, dumping boxes of shoes. When he was done, the bedroom was trashed, my clothes in shreds."

"Poor Mia," Veronica murmured, trembling with the force of her hatred. Despising Boyd with every fiber of her being.

"I was so frightened. So I...I struck back. I told him if he touched me again, I'd make his private life public."

Veronica propped herself on an elbow and looked down at Mia, concerned. "You didn't?"

"Yes, I did. He paled. He loves his reputation

above all else, and for a moment, I think…he was scared.''

"Dear God, Mia."

"He got back at me, though I didn't know it until later. He emptied my wallet. Canceled my credit cards. Drained our joint checking account.'' Her voice shook. ''When I confronted him with what he'd done, he laughed at me. Said that if I wanted anything, even gas for the car, I'd have to beg.''

Tears choked her. ''It was so humiliating. I wanted to die. Just go hole up someplace and cease to live.''

Veronica made a sound of fear. Her mother had felt that way, too. She had made it happen. It would be simple, too simple. One shot to the head. A handful of pills. Easy.

She eased Mia away from her so she could look into her eyes. ''Don't say that, Mia. Don't ever even think it. He's the one who should be humiliated. He's the one who should die.''

"I wish he would.'' Her eyes flooded with tears. ''I hate him so much, Veronica.''

"I know, baby. Because of you, I feel the same.'' She cupped Mia's face in her palms. ''Leave him. Forget about the money. Forget about the prenuptial agreement. I'll take care of you. I have enough money to look after both of us.''

"But it's not right. He has plenty of money and what's his is mine. Or should be.'' Mia met her eyes. ''Do you really love me, Veronica? Enough to trust me with your every secret? With your very life?''

A lump formed in Veronica's throat. She swallowed hard, uneasy. Uncertain where Mia was going with this. "I do, Mia. I promise you that."

"I love you the same way. I want you to believe that." Mia sat up. The sheet fell away from her, and the sunlight that slipped through and around the closed blinds touched her skin with gold. "I have a plan. A way to make him pay for hurting me."

Veronica's heart began to pound, her palms to sweat. "Go on."

Mia looked deeply into her eyes. "I know everything, Veronica. *Everything.* I followed him. On one of his trysts. He went to a place called The Velvet Spike."

The Velvet Spike? Veronica felt the blood drain from her face. She tried to speak but couldn't.

"Boyd's reputation means everything to him," Mia continued. "More than wealth or health or family." Her voice took on a brittle edge. "He loves to play the straight arrow, the church-attending, law-abiding, Republican surgeon. *That's* why he married me. I know that now. Not only did I fit the picture, he figured I'd never fight back. He was wrong. I now know I can get back at him. I need your help."

Veronica stared at the other woman, still processing the fact that Mia had followed Boyd. *Dear God, what had she been thinking? How could she not have considered all the possibilities?* "You didn't...go in, did you? That place's been raided so many times."

"Why does that matter?" Mia asked softly. "I'm here now. Unharmed. No one the wiser."

"Yes, but I—" She struggled to sound calm. "Boyd's a violent man, Mia. If he had seen you, recognized your car or—"

"He didn't. I'm too smart to let that happen. That morning, I took my Lexus in for servicing. They gave me a loaner for twenty-four hours." She caught Veronica's hands, lacing their fingers. "I need your help, Veronica. Boyd's into something weird. Something that would cause him great embarrassment if made public. Something that would cause him to lose his job. Something he would do anything to keep under wraps."

When Veronica didn't comment, she plunged ahead. "Don't you see? He loves his reputation too much. We can use that to get what he owes me. It's perfect. We get pictures of him engaging in whatever nasty things he's trying so desperately to hide. On a videotape. We can hire a P.I.—" She brought a hand to her mouth. "No. A P.I. could double-cross us. Besides, to really squeeze Boyd, he would need to be confident that *no one* else knew what he was involved in."

She turned to Veronica. "He doesn't know you. You could follow him, get the pictures and—"

'Mia, stop." Veronica laid her fingers gently on the other woman's mouth. "What you're talking about is blackmail. That's a crime. A federal offense. And I'm a district attorney. I would be disbarred, we could go to jail. Plans like this always fail."

"This one wouldn't. I know it wouldn't."

"Yes," Veronica said softly but firmly, "it would. Trust me, we try cases like these. And each time, the perpetrator was certain they'd get away with it."

Mia stiffened. "You said you loved me. You said you'd do anything for me."

"I do love you. And I will do anything for you, but not this." Veronica lowered her voice. "Forget this scheme, Mia. Forget about punishing Boyd. He'll get his in the end. Men like him always do."

"That's bullshit." Mia climbed out of bed. She stalked to the bathroom and grabbed Veronica's robe from the back of the door and slipped it on, though she didn't tie it. She turned her back to Veronica. "You just don't trust me enough. You don't believe in me."

"That's not true." Veronica climbed out of bed and crossed to the other woman, her heart breaking. She couldn't bear to have Mia angry at her. She couldn't bear for her to think she didn't love her. Or worse, to suddenly not love her back.

Nothing in the world could be worse than that.

She closed her arms around Mia from behind and buried her face in her sweet-smelling hair. "Don't you see?" I couldn't bear for anything bad to touch you. I can't take the chance of you being hurt."

"But I have been hurt. I continue to be hurt." Mia turned and looped her arms around Veronica's neck. "You wouldn't have to be involved in any way but taking the pictures. No one would ever know."

A knot of tension settled in the pit of Veronica's stomach. *She couldn't lose Mia. She would die without her love.* "I'll make everthing all right for you, Mia. I promise I will. Just don't leave me. Never leave me."

"Never," Mia echoed, brushing her mouth against Veronica's, softly, with promise. "How could I? You make everything okay."

40

"Mrs. Barton?" Connor held up his shield. "Connor Parks, FBI. This is Officer Melanie May, Whistlestop PD. Thanks for seeing us on such short notice. May we come in?"

The woman nodded and stepped away from the door. "I don't know how I can help you. I told the police everything I know about the night Don died."

"Yes, but sometimes something comes to light afterward, something you didn't remember before that proves important."

She led them to her living room, filled with avocado-green furniture that looked as if it had been manufactured in the early seventies. Framed photographs dotted the end tables and fireplace mantel. The three took a seat.

"How long were you and your husband married?" Melanie asked, glancing at a photograph of three young girls in summer bonnets and smocked dresses.

"Twenty years." The woman pointed. "Those are our daughters. Ellie, Sarah and Jayne."

"They're lovely."

"Thank you. They're grown now." She smiled, stood and crossed to the mantel. She selected a framed five-by-seven photograph and brought it to Melanie. "This was taken this past Christmas. They're good girls."

Melanie gazed at the photograph, then handed it back. "You must be very proud."

Connor watched as Melanie put the woman at ease. He jotted notes as they talked—the daughters' names, where they lived, their marital status.

"Were your daughters close to their father?" he asked.

The woman swung in his direction, her expression surprised, as if she had forgotten he was there. "Not particularly."

"Why not, Mrs. Barton?"

She paled. Melanie stepped in, her voice soft, soothing. "We know about Don, Mrs. Barton. We know what kind of man he was. That's why we suspect he's one of the Dark Angel's victims."

She nodded and looked at the photograph clutched in her hands. As if with great effort, she loosened her grip on it, turned and carried it back to the mantel. She returned it to the spot it had previously occupied, then looked at Melanie. "Then you also know why they weren't close to him. It's why Ellie and Sarah moved away."

"And the daughter who lives here in Charlotte?" Connor asked.

"Jayne? She's my savior. He couldn't chase her away."

They questioned her more about Jayne, then about her daily habits, the places she frequented, who her friends were and how many were aware of her husband's abuse.

"Why do you need to know about my friends?" She looked from one to the other of them, obviously uncomfortable. "You don't think—"

Connor stepped in. "We don't think anything, Mrs. Barton. We're simply looking for leads."

She wrung her hands. "Why can't you leave well enough alone? He's dead, just leave it."

Connor arched his eyebrows. "Your husband may have been murdered. Are you suggesting that letting a murderer go free is leaving well enough alone?"

Her eyes filled with tears, and she looked helplessly at Melanie. "You didn't know Don. You didn't live with him. It's just that now, I don't...I'm not...afraid."

"Mrs. Barton," Melanie murmured. "I understand how conflicted you must feel. I have personal experience with the kind of man your husband was. But taking a life outside the law is always wrong. It's murder, Mrs. Barton. And if we allow even one person to take the law into their own hands, if we okay it by looking the other way, what legacy do we have to leave our children?" She leaned toward the other woman. "Can you help us?"

In the end, the woman gave them a list of her friends' names, all she could think of. She also listed the places she visited with any kind of regularity.

None of the names jumped out as repeats from any of the lists they'd amassed so far. But that didn't mean there weren't any. They would input Mrs. Barton's list into the computer with the others, then let the computer search for duplications.

"We should talk to the daughter who lives in Charlotte," Connor said as they climbed into his Explorer. "Just to cover our bases."

"I suppose so, but in my opinion, she's a long shot."

He started the truck and pulled away from the curb. "But you never know when a long shot's going to pay off."

She sighed and turned her face toward the window. "This investigation might yield exactly nothing. And then where'll we be?"

He glanced at her, then back at the road. "It won't. The Angel didn't go undetected for this long by being careless. We'll get her."

"You're so confident."

"I've been through this before."

"But I bet 'before' had clear-cut victims, crime scenes to study, evidence to analyze. All we've got is a bunch of dead guys who liked to beat up women when they were alive."

"You'd be surprised what some of my cases didn't have, Melanie. Kid disappears. You know you've got some sort of foul play, but you've got no body, no crime scene, nothing but grieving families. Or you've got a body or body part, maybe some bones or a skeleton, but nothing else. Not even a theory." He smiled to relieve the sting of his next words. "That's why they call it detective work."

"So stop whining. I get it." She angled her body toward his. "But, with this case...don't you ever wonder—" She bit the words off and shook her head. "Never mind."

The light up ahead turned yellow, and he eased the Explorer to a stop. He looked at her. "We're partners in this. I need to know everything you're thinking."

She hesitated a moment, then continued. "Do you ever wonder if these deaths *aren't* linked? If none of them are murder? If perhaps, as some have suggested, they're acts of divine justice?" She looked away, then back at him. "Maybe I was wrong, Connor."

"You weren't wrong, Melanie. We're not." The light changed, and he started forward. "Besides, I don't believe in that concept of divine justice. I don't believe the hand of God can reach down from the heavens to single out an individual for punishment. It can't work that way, there's too much injustice in the world, too much unchecked evil."

When she didn't respond, he sent her a sympathetic glance. "Mrs. Barton, she got to you, didn't she?"

"She seemed like a real nice lady."

Which neatly avoided his question. "That man you told her about, the one who gave you personal experience with abuse, who was he?"

"My father." She looked at him, her gaze almost defiant.

He returned his own gaze to the road. "You want to talk about it?"

"Not particularly. No."

"You're sure? You're acting pretty pissy."

"Yes, dammit, I'm sure." She let out her breath in a huff. "Just drive. Okay?"

He checked the rearview mirror, then jerked the

wheel to the right, angling across two lanes of traffic to pull the vehicle to the side of the busy road. The maneuver earned a blare from several horns.

He shifted into Park, cut the engine and turned to face her. "No," he said evenly. "It's not okay."

She fisted her hands in her lap. "Don't tick me off, Parks. I'm feeling a little *pissy.*"

"Exactly my point. Mind telling me why?"

"Yes, actually, I do mind. So, could you start this heap up and let us get on our way?"

"I know what this is about." When her eyebrows shot up in question, he smiled. "It's about the other day. About us, our kiss."

She drew back, eyes wide with disbelief. "It is not!"

"Of course it is," he said, working to keep his expression absolutely deadpan. "And I understand. You've probably been thinking about it ever since, and wondering when I was going to get around to kissing you again."

Her cheeks flamed. "In your dreams, Parks!"

Well, she had gotten that right. "I'm sure it's been difficult for you to be near me. After all, I'm an incredible stud. And I know that kiss must have rocked your world."

She burst out laughing. "Stud? Rocked my world? I really hope you're kidding, Parks, because if you're not, you're in need of serious professional help."

He worked to look devastated, but couldn't quite suppress the smile that tugged at the corners of his mouth. "You don't have to laugh quite so loudly. Even we incredible studs have feelings."

She snorted her amusement. "Sorry about before, about being such a jerk. Mrs. Barton did get to me. All the women have. Everything they've said...I *recognized*. Because I'd been there, Connor."

Connor reached across the seat and covered her hands with one of his. Instead of pulling away, she curled her fingers around his.

"I didn't grieve when he died." She looked away, lost in her memories. "I was glad he was gone. Secretly, I rejoiced."

"What did he...do to you?" Connor regretted the question the moment it passed his lips. Not because it wasn't his business—which it wasn't—or because he didn't care.

He feared he cared too much.

She paused a moment, then met his gaze evenly. Something in it told him that by verbalizing the past she was facing—and conquering—her fears one more time.

"He was physically and verbally abusive to me and my sisters. Which of course is the politically correct way of saying he beat and belittled us. He was genuinely mean-spirited. Cruel to his core. Evil. I think he took pleasure in trying to destroy us. A part of me believes it was the only pleasure he eked out of life."

She sucked in a choked-sounding breath, then plunged on, though Connor could see how painful it was for her. "I got off the easiest of the three of us. In terms of direct attacks, anyway. Most of his obvious rage was directed at Mia, though I never knew why. I've wondered if he sensed she was the weakest of the three of us, therefore the most vulnerable to his attacks.''

She clenched her fists. "I wish he had singled me out instead. I hated what he did to Mia and Ashley, every slap to them was a slap to me, every barb aimed their way hit me as well.''

A tear spilled past her guard and rolled down her cheek. Connor found that single, helpless show of emotion so much more moving than a hundred tears. It was all he could do to keep from taking her into his arms and to his heart, all he could do to control the tidal wave of protectiveness rising inside him.

"I always felt so...guilty that it wasn't me.''

He tightened his fingers over hers. "Don't you see?" he murmured, his voice thick. "He knew that, Melanie. He knew that the best way to hurt you was by hurting them. He knew that a direct attack wouldn't break you, but their pain and your own guilt would.''

She stared at him, realization dawning in her eyes. A sound passed her lips, small and vulnerable. She eased her hands from his and brought one to her mouth, as if to catch the sound. "I never...I...''

She choked on the words and for several moments said nothing. When she finally spoke again, something had changed in her voice. It had taken on a hard edge, one that he was certain she wouldn't like if she heard it. "When we turned thirteen, he started...molesting Mia.''

"Dear God.''

"I fixed him, though. He woke up one night to find himself tied to the bed, a knife to his throat. I told him if he touched Mia again, I'd kill him. I meant it, too. I would have. I believe that with every fiber of my being.''

Her mouth thinned. ''So how can I condemn the actions of the Dark Angel? Who am I to hunt her down? How can I look at women like Mrs. Barton and preach law and order? I could have killed, I would have.''

''How?'' he challenged softly, understanding her internal conflict more than she could imagine. ''Easy. You were a young girl, frightened and alone. You and your sisters had nowhere to turn, no one to turn to. After all, the person whose job it was to protect you was the very one you needed protection from.

''So you stepped in. You did what you had to to take care of the people you loved. That makes you a hero, not a monster.''

''Does it? I'm not so sure.'' She lowered her gaze to her hands, eyebrows drawn together in thought. ''I got a call at the station, about the Dark Angel. It was a woman, she accused me of being a traitor. She said she 'knew' me and asked 'how could I do it?' Sometimes I wonder myself.''

He straightened. ''When did this happen?''

''Not long after we began the investigation. A week or two.''

''Why didn't you tell me?''

''I figured she was just a crank. There'd been so much in the news about the case and she never called again.'' She lifted a shoulder. ''Frankly, it didn't seem all that important.''

''Everything's important, Melanie. Every detail,

no matter how insignificant it might appear." He drummed his fingers on the steering wheel. "She said she knew you, what do you think she meant? That she knew you personally?"

"At the time I didn't think so. I didn't recognize her voice. But now that you...it was as if she knew me...spiritually. As if she knew about my past."

"Could it have been the Dark Angel?"

Melanie went stone still, then she muttered an oath under her breath. "I don't know. Anything's possible." She looked at him. "I screwed up, didn't I?"

"Don't beat yourself up over it, but if she calls again, keep her on the line. Try to get a trace."

"Done."

They fell silent. Their gazes met and held. Seconds ticked past, the interior of the vehicle suddenly seemed small to Connor. Too warm.

Stop this now, Parks. Before you do something stupid.

He cleared his throat and reached for the key, still in the ignition. "Well, I'm glad we got that cleared up. Especially the pissy part. Try not to let it happen again."

She smiled and shook her head. "You make me laugh, Connor Parks."

"That's a good thing." He glanced over his shoulder, then pulled into traffic. "Of course, I would have preferred 'Oh, Connor, you make me so hot,' but this laugh thing will do."

Groaning, she brought a hand to her eyes. "Are you ever serious?"

"I'm always serious."

"Connor?"

"Hmm?"

"About that kiss—"

"Mistake, right?"

"Right."

"Thought so. But it did rock your world?"

"Oh, yeah," she said. "Big time."

"Thank God. Now my male ego's intact." He exited onto I-85, heading west. "What do you say we go run some names through the computer?"

41

The motel room stank of cigarettes—the smell had permeated everything, even the walls. It stank of something else as well, something subtle but sour, an odor that defied contemplation.

Boyd lay on the stinking mattress, naked, wrists and ankles bound by rope to the bed's four corners. He attempted to move his limbs, but they were bound too tightly, so tightly his fingers and toes tingled from lack of circulation.

He nearly ejaculated just thinking of the restraints. Of his helplessness.

"Naughty boy," she murmured, dragging her long, pointed fingernails up the shaft of his erect penis. "You may not come. Do you understand? If you do, you will be punished." To mark her words, she brought her hand to his testicles and squeezed.

He groaned and arched his back. He didn't know which excited him more, her threat of punishment or the painful pressure she exerted on his testes.

Pain. Submission. Being dominated and punished. That's what drove him.

His lady in leather knew that. She held the key to his personal universe just as surely as she had held his testicles the moment before.

She checked his bonds, then blindfolded him. "I

have surprises for you tonight,'' she said softly. ''Good ones. Ones that will make you weak. And dizzy. And totally mine.''

He groaned again, a shudder of ecstasy rippling over him. He knew the rules. He was not allowed to speak during their time together. He could not express his likes, dislikes or expectations. He was never to attempt to lead. To disobey meant swift, severe punishment. The worst being the immediate cessation to their game.

He couldn't bear that. Not tonight.

Because tonight, he had promised himself, would be the last time with his lady. Because of Mia's threat. Because he knew that if he continued on his present course, he would be discovered. And, as had happened in Charleston, he would be quietly dismissed.

If he was as lucky as last time. Charleston General hadn't wanted to be at the center of a nasty sex scandal. The hospital hadn't wanted any of his patients to learn the kind of man who'd been entrusted to operate on them.

They had decided that discretion was the better part of valor, had provided him a glowing letter of recommendation and sent him on his way.

It had been he who had come up with the story about a wife, her sudden death, his needing a fresh start in a new city.

How many fresh starts were available to a man racing toward fifty?

''Now, for your first surprise.''

He heard a sound he recognized from years of surgery—latex surgical gloves being fitted on. He turned his head in the direction of the sound. He wanted to ask her about the gloves, her plans. He suppressed the questions, a flicker of fear igniting in the pit of his gut.

The fear excited him. Made him go hot, then cold—it made him sweat.

His arousal became nearly unbearable.

Boyd didn't recognize the next sound he heard, not until he felt the length of heavy tape being placed over his mouth. Duct tape, he thought, judging by its weight and the way it felt against his skin.

He wanted to protest, but could not. He wanted to warn her that the tape might leave a mark. A mark he could not afford.

But speaking was now impossible.

His fear took on a clammy, desperate edge. The reality of his predicament, his total helplessness, grabbed him by both the throat and balls.

He quivered with anticipation. With excitement.

"Do you remember," she whispered, bending her face close to his ear, "the night we first met? Do you remember how I told you it would be so good you would wish you were dead? Tonight you get your chance, love."

For a moment Boyd lay still, her words ricocheting through his brain. They mixed weirdly with his arousal, his growing panic, his certainty that something was about to go terribly awry with his life.

It was part of the game, he told himself, even as his heart rate accelerated. A part of his fantasy. A way to heighten their pleasure.

It wasn't real.

"I've studied the dying process," she murmured. "For you. Because you're a doctor and I thought I should know. After all, I wouldn't want to disappoint. I wanted this time...this last time, to be the best you ever had."

He drank in her words, half terrified, half exhilarated. Confused. He couldn't remember—had he told her this would be their last night together? He must have, otherwise, how could she have known?

"Do you believe in heaven, Boyd? In hell? In divine retribution for earthly sins?" She climbed onto the bed beside him. Though she didn't touch him in any way, he felt her presence, hovering over him like a bird of prey. "Or do you believe that when death comes, nothing follows. Just a rotting corpse and an ungodly smell."

She laughed lightly and trailed her latex-encased fingernails up the shaft of his penis. "All this talk of death excites you, doesn't it? Or is it the knowledge that you are completely at my mercy that excites you? The knowledge that your life is mine to do with as I please?"

She curled her fingers around his erection and stroked with increasing pressure, bringing him to the brink before she clamped her hand tightly around his testicles.

The tape silenced his gasp of pain.

She made a clucking sound with her tongue. "I must get back to the issue at hand. Your imminent demise."

She eased the pillow from under his head. "As I understand it, my love, there's a sequence of events that leads to what's called the terminal state.

This sequence can take from five to thirty minutes, depending on the cause. The sequence can vary, again depending on the cause. But it always involves loss of consciousness, cessation of the heart and lungs. And finally, brain death.

"Now, what did the book say about that?" She paused, as if to recall the words exactly. "At this phase, the brain is terminally silenced. The legal description of death. But you know that."

She leaned closer, her breath stirring against his cheek. "I'm not boring you, am I? I know this must be old hat to you, but for me it's all rather fascinating. Grisly...morbid, but fascinating nonetheless."

Fear exploded inside him. He began to tremble, to struggle against his ropes. He didn't like this fantasy anymore. He wanted her to release him. He wanted her to reassure him.

Instead, she laid the pillow over his face, holding it firmly in place, counting aloud. To ten. Twenty. Thirty.

Pinpoints of light danced behind his eyes and his lungs screamed for oxygen.

She removed the pillow and he sucked in air greedily through his nose, nearly sobbing with relief.

"The sequence I'm most interested in is yours, darling. You see, in suffocation, the heart continues beating for several minutes after the person loses consciousness due to brain anoxia—the total absence of oxygen."

She laid the pillow over his face again, held it there for a count of fifteen, then drew it away. "No wonder you became a doctor, the human machine is so incredible. I found that fact, about the heart continuing to beat, amazing. I really did.''

She sighed. ''But enough about me and my studies. We're here for you tonight. This is your special night.''

He felt her move, as if to lay the pillow over his face again and he sucked in a deep breath. Instead, she merely readjusted herself, as if to get more comfortable. Boyd let the breath out, quivering at the reprieve.

''What will it be like, I wonder?'' she mused. ''Will you feel each of your organ centers shutting down? Will you see your own death, like watching the lit numbers on an elevator panel, going down and down until there are no more floors to visit?''

His terror knew no bounds. Boyd struggled to keep his panic at bay, knowing that hyperventilating wouldn't do him any good at all. This was a game, he told himself. A staged scenario to heighten his pleasure. It would be over soon. And then, he promised, never again.

''If you could speak, what would your last words be? Ones of apology? Pleas for forgiveness?'' Her voice hardened. ''Or selfish ones begging for another chance?''

She moved then, quickly. She angled herself over his body, her leather garments cool against his fevered skin. Using her forearm, she pressed a pillow over his face, bearing down hard, with her free hand she grabbed hold of his erection and began pumping.

The sensation was incredible, dizzying. Within

seconds his lungs began to burn, the pressure in his brain matched that of his loins, building, welling, readying to explode.

She would lift the pillow. Any moment...any moment. His brain screamed for oxygen, his hips bucked up off the bed and he orgasmed violently.

Remove the pillow! Now...now, before it's too—

And then Boyd realized the reason for the tape. It was to muffle his screams for help.

He screamed anyway. The sound reverberated nowhere but inside his own head.

42

Connor's call had come in just as Melanie arrived at headquarters for the day. There had been another murder, he had told her. She needed to get to the scene, ASAP.

He had refused to say more, simply giving her the address and hanging up.

Now she knew why.

Melanie stood in the motel room's doorway, gaze fixed on the bed, on the corpse stretched out in a death bow. Her sense of déjà vu was so strong it disoriented her—she had done this exact thing, stood in a spot similar to this one a handful of months ago.

Only then she had been staring at the corpse of a woman. A victim who had been a stranger to her.

Dear God... Dear God... The words, the prayer, ran repeatedly, endlessly through her head, along with a kind of silent, unspeakable denial. These things didn't happen to people she knew. Crimes like these only touched other, less fortunate families.

Connor touched her arm. "You okay?"

She looked at him and shook her head, emotion choking her. "He was my...brother-in-law."

"I know. I recognized him from a couple of family photographs I saw at your place."

Melanie turned her back to the scene, struggling to regain her composure. She breathed deeply and slowly through her nose, concentrating on the oxygen moving in and out, until she felt her equilibrium returning.

Dear Jesus, how was she going to tell Mia? How was she going to make this okay for her?

Taking one last, deep breath, she returned to Connor's side. He was methodically examining the area around the bed. She kept her gaze trained on him.

"Feel better?" he asked.

"I'm not going to faint or puke, if that's what you mean by better. At least not at this moment."

"That's a plus."

Pete Harrison strolled over. "May, Parks tells me you can positively ID Prince Charming here."

"That's right." She curved her arms across her middle. "His name's Boyd Donaldson. Head of surgery at Queen's City Medical Center. He was my brother-in-law."

"Shit."

"Yeah," she muttered. "Shit."

He plucked a small spiral-bound notebook from his breast pocket. "You know he was into this kinky stuff?"

"No."

"How about your sister? She into—"

"No. Absolutely not."

"You know anything about their marriage?"

"It was in trouble. She confided that he was having an affair."

"She give you a name?"

"No."

"And she was upset about his infidelity?"

"He was her husband. You figure it out."

He arched his eyebrows. "No need to get testy."

"Actually," she countered, "I think there is. While you're playing Twenty Questions, I'm not only grappling with the fact that my brother-in-law's been murdered, but with how I'm going to tell my sister. Cut me some slack, okay?"

He looked sheepish. "Sorry, Melanie. Just a couple more questions. Do you think she knew he was into bondage?"

"You'll have to ask her."

"When did you last speak to your sister?"

Melanie thought a moment. "About a week, week and a half ago."

"You normally go so long without talking?"

"No. Typically we speak every day or two." Before he could ask, she added, "The Dark Angel investigation's been keeping me busy."

The words sounded lame to her, even though the investigator muttered something about having been there and done that. Why hadn't they spoken more? she wondered. How had they gone from inseparable to distant in a matter of a few short weeks?

Feeling unsettled, she refocused on the investigator. "I'm sorry, Pete. What did you say?"

"We'll need to talk to her. The sooner the better."

"Of course." Melanie glanced at Connor. He sat

on his haunches beside the bed, staring into space, his expression pensive. She frowned. She had worked with him long enough now to recognize the look—that incredible brain of his was chewing on some observations, trying to make sense of something that didn't add up.

She wondered what it was.

Melanie returned her attention to the CMPD investigator. "I'd like to be the one to tell my sister. Considering the circumstances, it seems appropriate."

"Agreed." He indicated his partner, who was across the room working with the evidence-collection team. "Roger and I will come along."

Hearing his name, the other man ambled over. He glanced down at Connor, smirking. "Hell of a breakthrough, wouldn't you say, Parks? We needed something to revive this case. Now we've got it. Big time."

"This case," Melanie knew, referred to Joli Andersen's murder, which had reached a stone-cold dead end.

Connor stood. "Looks can be deceiving. I wouldn't notify the press or Cleve Andersen just yet."

The man flushed. "You know what, Parks, I've had it up to here—" he motioned the top of his head, "—with your hocus-pocus bullshit. None of it has moved this investigation any closer to an arrest. This scene is an exact replica of the Andersen scene, down to the bottle of champagne."

"Exactly," Connor murmured. "A replica."

Melanie looked at Connor, surprised. "You're thinking copycat?"

The investigator ignored her and ticked off the similarities. "Both victims were tied spread-eagle to the bed, bound by wrists and ankles to the corners. Both were suffocated with a pillow, their mouths sealed with duct tape. Both were subjected to artificial penetration, postmortem."

"You assume."

"I think it's goddamned obvious, but until the medical examiner does his thing, yes, I'm assuming."

"You have more?" Connor asked. "Because so far, I'm underwhelmed."

"You bet your ass I have more. Both murders occurred in cut-rate motels around the midnight hour. Then there's the matter of the duct tape and champagne, both details held from the media."

"And the blindfold?" Connor asked. "I don't recall Joli Andersen being blindfolded."

Roger Stemmons's face went from merely flushed to positively florid and Pete laid a hand on his arm, as if to restrain him. "His ritual is evolving," he said. "They do. You of all people should know that."

A uniform came up to Pete. "I spoke with the desk clerk on last night's shift," he said. "Said he rented the room to Dr. Donaldson at 11:35 p.m. Saw a car exit the lot around 1:00 a.m. A blond woman at the wheel. Didn't get a plate number, but thinks the car was a midsize sedan, dark color."

The man glanced down at his notes. "Not a beater but not new either. His words."

Pete turned to Melanie. "Your sister a blonde like you?"

She bristled at the implication. "Exactly like me."

"Let's go have a chat with her, then."

43

Her sister was home. A part of Melanie had prayed she wouldn't be, so she could avoid the inevitable a little longer.

"Melanie?" The smile that had automatically brightened Mia's face at the sight of her twin faded. She moved her gaze between Melanie, Connor and the two investigators. "What's wrong?"

Melanie held a hand out. "Mia, honey, can we come in?"

She shook her head, the color draining from her face. "Not until you tell me—" She brought a hand to her mouth. "Is it…Ashley? Has something—"

"It's Boyd, Mia. He's dead."

She stared blankly at Melanie, her already pale face becoming pasty. "Dead?" she repeated, swaying slightly. "But how…that can't…I don't understand."

"Mia, he—" Melanie took a deep breath. "He was murdered last night."

A small sound escaped her sister, high and breathless. She brought a hand to her mouth, swaying again. Connor stepped forward, taking her arm to steady her.

"I'm all right," she whispered. "I… Come in."

She led them to the living room, motioning them

to take a seat, then, as if her legs couldn't support her another moment, she sank onto the white couch. Melanie took the seat beside her. The two investigators also sat, but Connor remained standing.

"How?" she asked, looking at Melanie. "Who…"

Melanie reached across and covered her sister's clasped hands with one of her own. They were cold as ice. "We don't know who," she answered, choosing to ignore the how part of her sister's question for now. "The detectives have some questions they need you to answer. You feel like you're up to it right now?"

When her sister nodded, Melanie introduced her to Connor and the two CMPD investigators.

The minute she did, Pete took over.

"Mrs. Donaldson," he began, "I'm sorry to have to disturb you at a time like this, but in a murder case every moment is precious."

"I understand." She curled her fingers tighter around Melanie's. "How can I help you?"

The man plucked his spiral notebook from his left breast pocket. "When did you last see your husband, Mrs. Donaldson?"

"Yesterday morning, before he left for work."

"And not since?"

"No." She cleared her throat. "But I didn't expect to. He had a National Heart Surgeons' Association meeting to attend last night. It was being held in Columbia, and since the meetings often go late, he had planned to spend the night there."

"I see."

"I talked to him during the day, however."

"And what time was that?"

She drew her eyebrows together in thought. "About four in the afternoon. He called to remind me he would be out."

The investigator made a notation in his book, then met her eyes once more. "Did your husband have meetings like this often? Ones that kept him away from home at night?"

Mia glanced at Melanie, then back at the investigator. "Yes."

"Away all night?"

"Not overnight, no. Just until very late."

"Would you categorize your marriage as a happy one, Mrs. Donaldson?"

Melanie stiffened slightly, knowing that Pete was testing Mia, trying to catch her in a lie. Although standard interrogation practice, this was her sister, not a real suspect, not a criminal.

Mia lowered her head. "No," she whispered.

"No what?"

She lifted her gaze. Melanie saw that her eyes were bright with tears. "No, it wasn't a happy marriage. He was...I think he was having an affair."

The two CMPD investigators exchanged glances, as if they had just learned some important piece of information. Melanie knew it was a tactic, a way to try to unsettle a witness by making her feel she had said something more incriminating than she had.

It worked. Mia squirmed in her seat, looking suddenly guilty. Melanie sucked in a quick, deep breath, biting back the nasty comment that flew to her lips. She darted a look at Connor and found him moving absently around the room, seemingly paying no attention to the questioning.

"You don't know for sure?" Pete asked.

"He never...admitted it, but I...a wife *knows,* Detective."

"I see." The investigator coughed, clearing his throat. "When you say that he never admitted having an affair, does that mean that you confronted him with your suspicions?"

"Yes."

"And how did he respond?"

She looked at Melanie in question. Melanie nodded slightly and Mia continued. "He flew into a rage and he...he struck me."

Connor, standing at the baby grand piano, studying the framed photographs that decorated its top, stopped and looked over his shoulder at Mia. The two CMPD investigators exchanged knowing glances. Melanie shifted in her seat, uncomfortable for her sister. Humiliated for her.

"He hit you? Was this something he did often?"

"I...no, he..." She began to tremble. "My husband's been murdered!" she cried. "Why are you asking me this? How can it matter?"

"We feel it's pertinent, Mrs. Donaldson." The investigator smiled in an attempt to win her cooperation. "Just a few more questions. Do you know who your husband was seeing? Do you have a suspicion?"

"No."

"Where were you last night?"

"Me?" She looked surprised. "Home."

"Alone?"

"Yes."

Melanie knew the drill. Mia would be a prime suspect because statistics proved that the majority of murders were committed by people close to the victim—family, friends, business associates.

"Did you know your husband was into kinky sex?"

The blood drained from her face. "I'm sorry, what did you—"

"Kinky sex. S&M, bondage, that kind of thing?"

"No." She shook her head. "No."

"You two didn't—"

She looked horrified. "God, no."

"Is there anyone who can account for your whereabouts last night?"

"I told you, I was alone." Mia's voice took on a high, hysterical edge. She turned to Melanie. "You believe me, don't you?"

"Of course I do." She shot the investigator an angry glance, then turned back to her sister. Depending on her next answer, Melanie was going to suggest an end to this session until Mia consulted an attorney. "Think, Mia. Did you talk to anyone on the phone? Did anyone stop by or—"

"I did." Mia brought a hand to her mouth. "I talked to a girlfriend. Veronica Ford. Twice."

"Do you remember what time?" Melanie asked the question, knowing that Pete would and that it would be better coming from her.

She thought a moment. "She called me about ten. Then again at...I don't know, twelve-thirty or so."

"Twelve-thirty? On a weeknight?" Roger, pre- viously silent, piped in. "Isn't that a little odd?"

"Odd?" She looked confused. Disoriented. "Ve- ronica knew I'd be up because…because I was up- set. She was worried about me."

"Why was that?"

She stared blankly at him a moment, then shook her head. "My husband was having an affair…he was gone for the night…I just figured, you know."

"That he was spending the night with his mis- tress?" She nodded. "But you didn't check up on him?"

She sank back against the cushions, as if sud- denly, completely drained. "No," she whispered, closing her eyes. "It wouldn't have made any dif- ference."

Melanie's heart broke for her sister. She squeezed her fingers reassuringly. "I think my sis- ter's had enough for now. Why don't we call it quits?"

Pete scanned his notes. "I can live with that. Let me just make sure I have all this down. So, you talked to your friend—"

"ADA Veronica Ford," Melanie inserted, know- ing the association would be an asset for her sister.

He stopped. "Excuse me?"

"For your records. Assistant District Attorney Veronica Ford."

"I see." He cleared his throat and Roger shifted in his chair. Connor caught her eye and grinned. "You see or talk to anyone else?"

"No, I—" Mia bit the words back, straightening. "Wait, yes. I saw my neighbor, Mrs. Whitman.

About twelve-fifteen. She was calling her cat when I was out on the deck, smoking a cigarette.''

Thank God for habits, Melanie thought. Between the calls and Mrs. Whitman and her cat, Mia had an alibi.

"One last question, Mrs. Donaldson. Did you love your husband?''

"For heaven's sake!'' Melanie shot to her feet. This had gone far beyond a simple inquiry. And she'd had enough. "What kind of question is—''

"It's okay, Mel,'' Mia murmured, cutting her off. She looked the man straight in the eye. "Yes, Detective, I loved my husband very much.''

Pete shut the spiral and tucked it back into his pocket. He stood and Roger followed him to his feet. "Thank you for your help, Mrs. Donaldson. We'll be in touch.''

"Wait!'' Mia cried, standing. "How did he... you never said...how he—''

"Died?''

"Yes.''

Mia clasped her hands tightly together. So tightly, Melanie saw, that her knuckles turned white. Melanie laid a hand on her shoulder for support.

"He was smothered, Mrs. Donaldson. His tastes got him into a situation he couldn't get out of.''

44

By the time Melanie turned onto her street later that day, it was after seven o'clock and growing dark. She had stayed with Mia until late that afternoon, when Veronica had been able to get away and take over. Any hesitation she had felt about leaving Mia in Veronica's care had slipped away when she saw her sister's response to the other woman—it had been obvious that she wanted her there, that she found her presence a comfort.

With a promise to check on her later—which she had done several times already—Melanie had left Mia's and headed straight for CMPD headquarters for an update on the investigation. After a surprisingly agreeable Harrison and Stemmons had filled her in, she'd made her way to the WPD. Her chief had taken one look at her and told her to get the hell home. When she had tried to argue, he'd said he didn't want to see her face for thirty-six hours. Period.

Even Stan had been conciliatory. He had heard about Boyd's murder and called, offering to pick Casey up from school and keep him the night, the week—or for as long as she needed.

Figuring his motive might be anything but self-less, she had accepted his offer to take Casey for the night, then reassured him she was doing just fine.

Yeah, right. She was a hairbreadth from falling apart.

A long hot soak in the tub, she thought. A glass of wine and a sandwich. She would be as good as new in no time at all.

Melanie curled her fingers tighter around the steering wheel. Sure she would be. As long as she never closed her eyes again. Because every time she did, she saw Boyd, laid out in a perverted X, his skin pasty gray in death.

The truth was, she would never be as good as new again.

Melanie thought of Connor, of the things he must have seen in his years with the Bureau, the offenses against nature, to women and children. To families. She used to think she was tough—that she could handle it. She didn't anymore. Not after today.

How, she wondered, nearing her house, did Connor handle the atrocities he had seen? How was he able to sleep at night? Had he found a way to store them in a box in his brain, lid shut and sealed tight? She needed him to teach her that trick.

As if her thoughts had conjured him, he was there. Sitting on her front steps, a pizza box and a bottle of wine beside him. When she turned into her driveway, he stood. And smiled.

A wave of pure, sweet pleasure washed over her, dispelling for that one moment all the ugliness of the day. And in that single moment she realized she had never been happier to see anyone than she was to see him.

The truth of that surprised her, but only briefly. Sometime over the past weeks, she acknowledged, Connor Parks had ceased being a colleague and had become a friend.

He ambled across the lawn to her Jeep. "Hi," he said, opening the door for her. "Figured you'd be hungry but too tired to fix anything but a peanut butter sandwich."

Melanie swung out of the Jeep. She grinned. "You figured right. Except that I'm starving and we're out of peanut butter, so it was going to be a jelly sandwich. Grape jelly."

He made a face. They fell into step together. "It's a good thing I happened along, then."

"A lifesaver, really."

While she unlocked the front door, he retrieved the pizza boxes—she saw now that he had two, one large and one small—and the wine.

"Casey's with his dad?"

It was dim inside the house, and she flipped on a light. "Considering the day, I thought it would be best."

"I brought him a plain cheese, just in case. I know how kids can sometimes be about food. Purists."

"That's my Casey." Melanie smiled, touched by Connor's thoughtfulness.

"As for us," he continued, "I brought the biggest, nastiest everything pizza they had. They call it the Kitchen Sink."

"Just the way I like 'em." Melanie held out her hands for the boxes and bottle. "You have a seat and I'll get everything ready."

"Absolutely not." He pointed at the couch. "You, sit. Feet up. I'll gather together whatever we need."

"But—"

"No buts, that was an order." He grabbed a magazine from the rack by the couch, laid it on the coffee table, then set the pizza on it. She watched him, arms folded across her middle. At her look, he arched his eyebrows. "I thought we'd eat in here. That okay?"

"Get real. I have a four-year-old."

"So, sit. And stop giving me the evil eye. I'm sure I can muddle through this."

She gave up and sank onto the sofa. "I didn't know you FBI guys were so bossy."

"Oh, yeah." He stopped in the kitchen doorway and grinned back at her. "We take a course in it. After all, we have to be bossy if we're going to push you local yokels around."

She tossed a throw pillow at him, missing because he ducked into the other room.

She leaned her head back against the overstuffed cushion and closed her eyes. As she did, Boyd's image filled her head, and she snapped them back open. *So much for rest and relaxation.*

Connor appeared at the kitchen doorway. "You have a corkscrew?"

"Drawer under the phone."

He nodded, then disappeared into the kitchen once more. A few moments later he reappeared with a wineglass and the open bottle of wine. He poured her a glass of the merlot and set it in front of her.

She frowned. "I wish you'd let me help you."

"Can't do it." He indicated the wine. "Taste, please. If it's not good, I'll have the salesman's head. He promised you'd love it."

She did as he'd requested, then made a sound of pleasure. "Delicious."

"Good. I would have hated hurting that guy. Be right back."

He returned in moments with plates, napkins, eating utensils and a glass of Coke for himself. He served them both a piece of the pie, which was, indeed, the biggest, nastiest everything pizza she had ever seen. Never a wimp about eating, she dug in.

They ate in comfortable silence a few minutes, the food and wine almost instantly reviving her. Melanie felt herself coming back to life, her energy returning, the blanket of disbelief and despair lifting.

She finished her slice of pizza and sat back, cradling the bowl of her wineglass between her palms. "Thank you," she said. "I needed that more than I even realized."

He helped himself to another piece of the pie. "Figured as much."

"Been there, done that?"

"Too many times to count."

They fell silent again. Melanie leaned her head back, content to sip her wine and watch him eat.

"How's Mia?" he asked finally, wiping his mouth with the paper napkin.

"As well as can be expected. Veronica offered to stay with her. I stayed until she got there. The doctor prescribed sleeping pills, just in case." Melanie plucked a piece of sausage from the debris left on her plate. "You were quiet today. Particularly at my sister's."

"Yes."

"Why?"

"It's my way. I like to absorb my surroundings. What's being said. People's body language."

She stiffened. "Mia didn't have anything to do with Boyd's murder." She met his eyes defiantly, challenging him to disagree.

He didn't. "Nor was Boyd's murder related to Joli's. We're dealing with two different killers. I don't have a doubt about that."

"You're still thinking this was a copycat?"

"A very skilled one." He pushed his plate away. "Think about it, Melanie. This type of crime is almost always gender specific and sexually motivated. Bundy killed college coeds. Dahmer, young gay men. The list goes on and on. In terms of motivation, why would this killer suddenly change the sex of his victim?"

Melanie couldn't argue with Connor's logic. The thought had crossed her mind back at the motel but had been forced out by other concerns. "What about the duct tape and champagne?"

"The champagne label was different. Joli's killer would have chosen the same kind. In this type of murder, the killer's ritual is very specific." Connor fell silent a moment, then continued. "This scene was completely staged. Joli Andersen's killer was disorganized. The scene was littered with all kinds of evidence, biological, trace, you name it. On the other hand, Boyd's killer was extremely organized. The scene was as clean as a hospital room. My bet is they find nothing.''

''And the postmortem penetration of the body?''

''Halfhearted, as if for appearance only. I haven't a doubt the medical examiner will confirm my opinion.''

Melanie mulled over what he'd said. Add in the blindfold and suddenly the inconsistencies began to outweigh the similarities. ''But why copy Joli Andersen's murder?'' Melanie brought her glass of wine to her lips. ''And why my brother-in-law?''

''I didn't know why at first, either. I didn't know who. Not until we were at your sister's house.''

She looked at him in disbelief. ''You know who?''

''Think about it, Mel.'' He leaned toward her. ''You know, too.''

She opened her mouth to tell him she didn't. To tell him her powers of observation weren't as keen as his.

She shut it without speaking, because in that moment, she did know. It came upon her like a thunderclap. ''Oh my God,'' she whispered. ''Of course. The Dark Angel.''

''Bull's-eye. Boyd was a batterer. And he died just as the others have—a victim of his own weaknesses.''

''I can't believe I didn't see it right off.'' She set her wineglass on the table, then clasped her shaking hands in her lap. ''I should have.''

''Give yourself a break, Melanie. You had a little more to deal with today than just being a cop.''

She sat back, going over the events of the day, the facts associated with the murder, the evidence they had amassed so far. She brought a hand to her mouth. "You don't think...could Boyd have been targeted because of me? I'm one of the lead investigators on the case and my name's been in the media a lot. How weird is it that she would strike in my family?"

"I considered that, too. But I don't think so. Because of the way she works, the time she needs to get her victim into place, our Angel had probably already targeted Boyd when you broke the case."

He leaned forward. "Do the math. First, she had to zero in on him, then pinpoint his particular weakness and insinuate herself into his life. She had to earn his trust. After all, this guy's a surgeon at a prominent medical center, he'd become adept at keeping his other life a secret, he wasn't about to play whip me–beat me with just anybody. I suspect he was extremely careful. And so was she. We've been at this six weeks. She needed more time than that in Boyd's particular case."

Melanie took it all in, weighing what she knew to be true against Connor's opinion, fitting the pieces together. She brought a hand to her mouth. "Oh my God, I just realized...if we're right about the Angel's motivation—"

"Then Mia knows the killer."

An involuntary shudder moved up her spine. "The CMPD guys aren't going to buy any of this."

"Not at first. They won't want to. But the differences between this case and the Andersen case are going to become too obvious to ignore as they process the scene. They'll be forced on board with us.''

Melanie let out a long breath. "We have another victim. Fresh blood.''

"I'm sorry.''

She lifted her gaze to Connor's. "I never liked him. I thought there was something *off* about him, you know? Something dishonest. But he was Mia's choice, not mine.''

She looked away. It felt wrong to be talking about Boyd this way. The man had been murdered. But it was the way she felt and she needed to say the words, to say them to Connor. "He hurt my sister. I hated him for that. A couple times, I was so angry, I thought I could have…hurt him myself. Even with all that…to die as he did—'' Her voice broke. "It was…horrible.''

Connor took her into his arms. She looped hers around his middle and laid her head against his chest, comforted. She didn't cry, though a part of her longed to.

"I wish I could make it better for you,'' he murmured after a time.

"I know. Thank you.'' Melanie tilted her head back to meet his gaze. "How do you handle it?'' she asked softly. "How do you see the things you do and manage to…keep it all in perspective?'' Her throat closed over the words, and she cleared it. "How do you shut your eyes without seeing…them. All the victims?''

"It gets easier,'' he murmured. "You get numb. And if you're lucky, when you sleep, you don't dream.''

He pushed her hair back from her face, his fingers dragging against her scalp, massaging. It felt wonderful.

Connor made her feel wonderful.

"I admire you," she said, speaking from her heart. "What you do. The way you—"

He cut her off with a bitter laugh. "Don't admire me, Melanie. Most days, I just manage to hang on. To not embarrass the Bureau, to not take a drink, to not sink into a pit of cynicism and self-pity. I'm not handling it, it's handling me."

It wasn't true. He was a strong man. A good man. One who felt deeply, too deeply, perhaps. Melanie reached up and cupped his face in her palms. She searched his gaze, seeing the shadows behind the eyes, the longing. For companionship. For a connection between two people, a spark that would ignite—and maybe, just maybe, chase the cold away.

She wanted to be with him that way. Tonight. She wanted to make love with him.

That truth filled her with a sense of wonder. Disbelief. Delight. It had been so long since she had wanted a man, so long since she had wanted to connect with another human being in that most intimate of ways.

She had wondered if she ever would again.

Melanie trailed her hands across his shoulders and down his arms. She caught his hands with her own—she laced their fingers and stood, drawing him to his feet. Without question, explanation or doubt, she led him to her bedroom, to her bed.

There, he held back. "Are you sure?" he asked. "I want you to be—"

She laid her fingers against his mouth, stopping him. "Yes," she answered. "I've never been more sure of anything."

They made love then. They sank to the mattress, holding one another, kissing, exploring. They didn't speak. He undressed her, she him. Each helped the other with stubborn undergarments and uncooperative fasteners, though there was none of that awkwardness of first-time lovers, none of that almost painful uncertainty.

Melanie thought of nothing but the pleasure of his hands and mouth, the ecstasy of his body over hers. Inside hers.

It was perfect. He was perfect.

Afterward, they lay on their sides, cupped like spoons, hearts beating fast. Melanie yawned and she felt Connor smile against her hair.

"I should go," he murmured.

"No." She snuggled closer into the curve of his body. "Stay."

"Are you sure?"

This time it was she who smiled. "You asked me that earlier tonight. My answer hasn't changed."

"Good." He pressed his face to the curve of her neck; he breathed deeply. "Go to sleep. I'll stand guard."

"Stand guard?" She twisted slightly to meet his gaze. "Against what?"

"The nightmares."

Emotion choked her. She couldn't speak. So she simply laid her head against the pillow. And when she closed her eyes, the nightmare images stayed away.

45

Melanie's eyes snapped open. Though instantly awake, she lay still, listening to the silence, heart pounding. She became aware of several things at once—that it was still hours before dawn, that the temperature had dipped dramatically during the night and that she was alone.

She turned her head to the pillow beside hers. It still bore the imprint of Connor's head. She reached a hand out, but the bed where he had lain was cold.

Melanie closed her eyes against the hurt that coursed through her. The betrayal. He had said he would stay, that he would stand guard for her. Instead, he had slinked off while she slept.

She tipped her face to the ceiling. Is that what had awakened her? she wondered. The click of the front door shutting? Or the sudden realization that she was alone?

Or something else? Something dark and frightening?

Her thoughts turned to the events of the previous day. They flashed behind her eyes in slide-projection fashion—Boyd stretched out on the bed, Mia's shock, Connor's tenderness. Ashley's absence.

Ashley. Melanie frowned. They hadn't spoken

since their argument the Saturday before. Melanie had called every day, and every day she had left an apology on her sister's machine. And a plea for Ashley to return the call so they could talk.

She hadn't.

Yesterday, Melanie had called again. She had left her sister a message—on both her home answering machine and with her cellular message service. And again, Ashley hadn't returned the call.

But she must have heard about Boyd's death, Melanie thought. It would have been the top news story no matter where in the state Ashley was working. Even considering how crazy her sister had been acting, how angry and jealous as she had been over Veronica's intrusion in their lives, she should have called when she heard. Her sister's husband was dead—he had been murdered.

Something was wrong. Ashley was in trouble.

Moaning, Melanie rolled onto her side and dragged Connor's pillow to her chest, hugging it to her. The pillow smelled of him, filling her senses even as Boyd's image—blindfolded and silenced, grotesque in death—once again filled her head.

Melanie forced the image out, turning her thoughts to Mia. She glanced at the bedside clock, wondering if her sister had been able to sleep. She had meant to call and check on her again before going to sleep, but had forgotten.

She'd had other things on her mind.

Connor.

She glanced at the bedside clock again, aching, feeling shallow and foolish. Some sister she was. Her twin's hour of greatest need and she had been off banging a man who didn't care enough about her to say "So long, baby."

Even as guilt gnawed at her, Melanie reminded herself that Mia was in good hands—Veronica had promised to stay, all day and all night. She had vowed not to leave Mia's side.

Melanie drew her eyebrows together, recalling the way the two women had clung to each other. Not so much with shock and grief, but with something else, something odd and out of place.

For Pete's sake! Melanie sat up and tossed Connor's pillow off the bed. She was imagining things. First about Ashley, now Mia and Veronica. She was tired and heartsick and feeling more than a little bit ridiculous over her behavior with Connor.

Shit and double-damn. How was she going to face him?

Distraught, she climbed out of bed. She grabbed her old chenille wraparound robe from the post at the end of the bed, slipped into it and cinched the belt. A cup of chamomile tea, she thought. And the mystery novel she had been inching through, the one with about as many surprises as a child's game of hide-and-seek.

She went to retrieve the book, stopping and making a small sound of surprise when she reached the family room. Connor stood motionless at the window, his back to her. The moonlight fell over his only partially clad form, creating both highlights and shadows. He looked more like a statue than a flesh-and-blood man.

He heard her softly expelled breath and turned.

In the moonlight that spilled through the glass and over his face, she saw that he was crying.

He had offered to keep her nightmares at bay.

He had his own to fight as well.

Her heart rose to her throat. He hadn't wanted her to see him this way—she saw it in the way he stiffened, in the way something about him seemed to pull in on itself. Away from her. From them.

"I woke you," he murmured stiffly. "I'm sorry."

"No." She lifted a hand, then dropped it to her side. "I thought you'd gone."

"I wouldn't do that. Not without saying good-bye."

He turned back to the window, away from her and she wondered if this was that goodbye.

He looked over his shoulder at her. "That story you told me about your father and Mia and what you did to protect her, I can't stop thinking about it. I wish to God I could."

He returned his gaze to the night. One second stretched into many. The silence shouted.

"What's wrong, Connor?" she asked finally, voice thick. "With the things you've seen, my story—"

"It's you, Melanie. You'd do anything to keep your family safe. And I didn't do enough."

She didn't reply though it hurt not to. She didn't make a move for him or reach out. She sensed that he wouldn't want her to, that he needed to stand alone.

"I had a sister." A ghost of a smile touched his mouth. "Suzi. My only sibling." His voice gentled.

Warmed. "She was a sweet kid. A good person, the kind who was always bringing home strays or helping somebody in a jam.

"I was twelve years her senior, I raised her after our parents died in an accident. In most ways, I was more her father than brother. And then she grew up. And I wanted a life."

He settled into silence and Melanie suspected that he was using the moments not to prepare his thoughts but to chasten himself for his choices, to hate himself for them. "I let her down. I was busy at Quantico. Full of myself and the *important* work I was doing. She called, she was frightened. She needed me to come home." His voice thickened. "I told her to grow up.

"And then she was dead. Murdered." He sucked in a quick breath. "If I had gone home...if I hadn't been so consumed with my own importance..." He let that thought trail off and picked up another. "Her body was never recovered. That makes it worse, it...I fantasize sometimes that she's alive. That the blow to her head, that it...that she has amnesia and can't find..."

Her heart broke for him. "Oh, Connor."

He glanced away, eyes bright. "She was embroiled in an affair with a married man. An abusive man. He'd threatened her. I believe he killed her."

"But you never found him?"

"No. I reviewed the facts, the scene, the profile a thousand times in the past five years. Probably more. It's always a dead end."

The shadows she had seen in his eyes. The sadness.

The bulletin boards in his house. The unsolved crime. Of course.

"I'm sorry."

He met her eyes and Melanie saw in them the tortures of hell. "A part of me doesn't want to catch the Dark Angel. A part of me hates those men as much as she must. I wonder sometimes, if we don't catch her, maybe she'll find him for me? I pray she does. So you see, Melanie, I'm a fraud."

Melanie held a hand out to him. She shook her head. "Come back to bed. Now. With me."

He hesitated, then took her hand. For the second time that night, she led him to her bed. And they made love, fueled by both passion and shared secrets.

Only this time, afterward, as sleep pulled at them, Melanie silently promised to stand guard for Connor.

Tonight, she vowed, the nightmares would not have him. Tonight, he was hers.

46

The medical examiner released Boyd's body for burial twenty-four hours after the murder. His funeral was held twenty-four hours after that, on a Thursday. It had drizzled on and off all morning, but the sun made a brief appearance just as the mourners began to arrive at the graveside.

To Melanie's surprise, Stan attended. He stood on Casey's left, she on Casey's right. Each held one of the child's small hands in their own—to an uninformed onlooker, they must have appeared the perfect family.

Melanie was grateful for Stan's presence. Casey needed him there. The last couple of days had been difficult ones for them all, including Casey. The child was distraught over his uncle's passing and by the bits and snatches of conversations he had overheard, the whispers and speculation. It hadn't helped, Melanie was certain, that she had been tense and impatient, his typically adoring aunts distracted and uncommunicative. He had responded by misbehaving, then bursting into tears at his mother's sharp reprimand.

None of them were handling this very well, Melanie thought. She glanced at her sisters, standing just to her right, huddled together, Veronica with them.

When she had finally connected with Ashley the morning after the murder, her sister had sounded almost hysterical. Her emotions had been all over the map, one moment angry, another despairing. Still another, deeply frightened.

Mia, on the other hand, had been emotionless. She had been moving through her days and duties like a sleepwalker, seeming to be able to access neither highs nor lows, just a disturbing, unnatural neutral.

Thank goodness for Veronica, Melanie thought, moving her gaze to the third woman. She didn't know how Mia would have gotten through this without her. The attorney had never left Mia's side, even staying with her at night. She had helped Mia make the funeral arrangements, had accompanied her to Boyd's lawyer's office for a reading of the will and to a meeting with Boyd's accountant to make certain he had left his affairs in order.

He had. He had also left her sister a very wealthy woman.

As for herself, Melanie didn't know how she would have managed without Connor. Not that he had stepped in and taken over her life, the way Stan would have insisted on doing. Simply knowing he was there for her had given her strength.

She darted a glance over her shoulder. Connor stood toward the back of the group, with a cluster of her colleagues that included Bobby and her chief. Their gazes met, and although he didn't smile, she felt warmed to her bones.

They hadn't been alone together since the night they'd become lovers. There hadn't been time or opportunity. But he'd never been far from her thoughts. She had held the memory—and her burgeoning feelings for him—close to her.

The service ended. The mourners began to depart, some stopping to pay their respects to Mia, others simply heading to their cars, heads bent low.

Stan turned to her. "Can we talk privately?" he asked.

She hesitated. "This isn't a great time, Stan. Mia's—"

"It'll only take a moment. I promise."

She wavered a second more, then nodded. "Casey," she murmured, stooping to look him in the eyes, "go by Aunt Ashley for a minute, okay?"

For a moment, she thought he was going to refuse, then he smiled. "'Kay, Mommy."

He trotted over to his aunt and tugged on her hand. She bent her head closer to his, looked over at Melanie and gave her the thumbs-up sign. Melanie mouthed "Thank you," then returned her attention to Stan.

He was watching Casey, expression naked with longing. A shiver of fear moved up her spine. She could imagine a man who looked like that doing whatever was necessary to get what he wanted.

"He's a great kid, isn't he?" Stan murmured.

Melanie frowned. "You're just discovering that?"

"No, I— Yes, in a way I am. I don't have the privilege of spending as much time with him as you do."

Here we go. She folded her arms across her middle. "It's been a hell of a few days, Stan. I don't think—"

"I'm sorry," he said quickly, cutting her off. "I didn't mean that the way it sounded. It's just that sometimes I think of everything I've missed and…"

He let the thought trail off and cleared his throat. "The hearing's next week."

"Yes, I know."

"I've enrolled him in the kindergarten in my district. In case the judge…rules in my favor."

She inched her chin up a notch. "So have I. He's excited, making plans with his friends."

He shifted uncomfortably. "My lawyer says yours is good. Top-notch."

"You sound surprised. Who did you expect me to hire?"

"Not Pamela Barrett, that's for sure. You could have knocked me over with a feather."

"A friend recommended Pamela. I'll have to thank her."

"I just wanted you to know that," he said.

He looked uneasy, she realized. Uncertain. Was the ever-confident Stan May worried he might lose the case? That Pamela would follow through on her threat to see that he had less visitation with Casey than he had now?

Was she sensing a reluctance in him concerning the suit?

Melanie hid her surprise—and the hope that sprang to life inside her. If he was worried, she really did have a chance of winning.

Or of changing his mind.

He began to turn away, but she touched his arm, stopping him. "Do you have to do this?" she asked. "Is it really so important that you punish me? Now, after all the time that's passed? I'm a good mother, you know I am. A change of custody will break Casey's heart."

"How do you know that coming to live with me will break Casey's heart?" He met her eyes. "And how can you be so certain my motivation isn't simply that I love my son?"

"Stan, please. Give my powers of observation a little credit. You've never shown that much interest in being a parent."

He flushed and shifted his gaze to Casey, playing peekaboo with his aunt. His expression softened. "I'm not the father I was when we were married." He returned his gaze to hers. "I'm not the man I was. You don't know, you're not with us when we're together. We do things, we play...I spend time *with* him, Melanie. Not just around him."

Melanie gazed at her ex-husband, weighing his words, her gut reaction to them. Casey no longer cried when he had to go to his dad's for the weekend, he didn't complain or pout. She wasn't sure exactly when that had changed, only that it had. She had assumed that Casey had simply become accustomed to his schedule and accepted it.

Now she wondered if the reason he didn't cry or complain was that he was happy to go.

When Melanie didn't comment, Stan went on. "I love Casey. I miss him when he's with you." His voice thickened slightly, as with emotion. "This isn't about punishing you. It's about me and my son, about wanting us to be together all the time."

Just like she wanted to be with him. A lump formed in her throat. She had misjudged her ex-husband. He *had* changed. It was time for her to change, too.

The fact of the matter was, one of them would lose primary custody of Casey. It could as easily be him as her.

Unless something changed.

"We both love Casey," she murmured. "We both want what's best for him. Can't we find a compromise? Can't we at least try?"

He looked at her a moment, waffling. It wasn't in Stan May's nature to compromise. It was one of the things that made him a powerhouse of a lawyer. But this wasn't about a client, this was about his son—a son she had just realized he loved very much.

She used that knowledge. "Let's put Casey first," she urged. "Let's not fight over him. I'll bend if you will."

"All right," he said finally, slowly. "I'd like that. For Casey, I'd like to try."

47

Connor strode across the central lobby of CMPD Headquarters heading for the elevators. He stepped into the waiting car, punched the button for the second floor, then stood back, aggravated at the time it took the door to close.

As he had predicted they would, the CMPD investigators had finally acknowledged that Boyd Donaldson's and Joli Andersen's murders were not related. Between the differences in the crime scenes and the lack of corroborating evidence, they had been forced to that decision.

However, they had been less willing to embrace his opinion that Donaldson had been a victim of the Dark Angel. Connor understood. The minute they did, they handed the case to him and Melanie. They weren't ready to do that.

Connor hadn't felt the need to force the issue. Until now.

He had called Melanie on his way back from a series of interviews in the Myrtle Beach area, but she had been on her way out the door. Pete, she'd told him, had called and requested that she come down to headquarters. Apparently they wanted to question her in relation to her brother-in-law's death.

She had been unconcerned. Questioning her was a formality, she'd assured him. A fishing expedition on the CMPD's part.

He had wanted her to stall them until he got there anyway.

He wasn't as certain as Melanie that Harrison and Stemmons were simply fishing. Mia's alibi had checked out. Without any other concrete leads, the two detectives were casting their nets in the direction of anyone close to the victim—and anyone who might wish him ill.

The car reached his floor. Connor stepped out, nearly colliding with the two investigators.

"Parks, glad you're here." Pete smiled, though the curving of his lips lacked warmth. "Roger and I are about to question a suspect in the Donaldson case. Maybe you want to listen in?"

Roger smirked at him. "Or maybe you already heard? After all, you and your little Whistlestop pal seem to have gotten awfully tight."

Connor decided that pounding that smirk off Stemmons's face would be infinitely pleasurable, but told himself to play it cool. The last thing Melanie needed was to deal with speculation about their relationship. "Yeah, I heard. And it sounds like a bullshit stretch to me. But hey, it's your day to waste."

"We'll see about that. I think you might be surprised." They stopped in front of one of the interrogation rooms. Pete indicated the next door down on the right. "See you on the flip side."

Connor entered the room, crossing to stand directly in front of the video monitor. Melanie was seated at a table in the next room, her face in profile; she looked irritated at what Pete was saying, something about being sorry for keeping her waiting.

Connor grinned. No wonder she was irritated—she knew as well as he did that the apology was total bullshit. It was standard operating procedure to let a suspect cool his or her heels sometime during questioning, as a way to heighten the suspected perp's unease.

Melanie glanced at her watch. "I've got a full schedule today, so if you guys don't mind, I'd like to get started."

"Sure thing." Pete leaned back in his chair and folded his hands over his gut. "I thought we might begin by talking a bit about your relationship with Boyd Donaldson."

Melanie inclined her head in agreement and for the next several moments, the detective asked questions concerning the length of time she had known the doctor, what she thought of his character and so forth. Finally, he got to the point.

"Did you like your brother-in-law?"

Melanie didn't hesitate. "No, I did not."

"You never liked him, did you?"

"No, never."

"In fact, you urged your sister not to marry him. Is that correct?"

"It is."

"And why was that?"

She lifted her shoulders slightly. "I know my sister better than anyone else on this planet. I thought he was wrong for her. I thought he was dishonest. Off somehow. In retrospect, I see that my feelings were right on.''

As if on cue, the two investigators exchanged speculative glances. Melanie ignored them, not so much as batting an eyelash. Connor gave her a thumbs-up, proud of her demeanor.

Roger jumped in. ''Could it have been that you were jealous? After all, she'd snagged a rich, handsome doctor.''

Melanie smiled. ''Absolutely not.''

''You say you love your sister. Would it be accurate to say you'd do anything to protect her from harm?''

She didn't even blink at the question. Again Connor applauded her cool. ''Within the law, yes.''

''Within the law,'' Pete repeated. ''Is that how you would categorize pulling a knife on your father and threatening to kill him?''

In her first show of uncertainty, she hesitated and glanced directly at the video camera.

She knew he was watching. Did she think he had told them about that?

''I was a child. I did the only thing I could think of to do.''

''To protect your sister.''

She shifted in her seat. ''Yes.''

''And that was within the law?''

She narrowed her eyes, cheeks pink. ''My father was molesting my sister. We were thirteen. What would you have had me do?''

''So, you feel your actions were justifiable?''

She lifted her chin ever so slightly. ''In that situation, yes.''

"And what would you have done if he had continued to molest your sister? Would you have followed through on your threat?"

"I thank God every day that I never had to make that decision."

"But if you had had to face it, what would that decision have been?"

"I refuse to speculate on a what-if scenario." She moved her gaze between the two men. "Period."

"What about your brother-in-law?"

"What about him?"

Roger crossed to stand before her. "He was knocking your sister around, Melanie. You were furious. Scared for her. You wanted him to stop."

"So, you threatened his life," Pete chimed in. "Old habits, it would seem, die hard."

"That's ridiculous."

"But you did threaten him." Pete flipped open the folder on the table in front of him. "According to the security guard at the medical center where Donaldson practiced, you said, and I quote, 'If you hurt my sister again, I won't be held accountable for my actions.' Does that sound familiar?"

"That was nothing. Just talk."

"Just talk?" Pete raised his eyebrows, his expression incredulous. "Your brother-in-law was frightened enough to come in and report it. The security guard thought it was serious enough to include in a report. Does that sound like 'nothing' to you?"

"Well, it was. I was angry, I shot off my mouth."

"Do you get angry a lot?"

"Occasionally."

"Would you categorize yourself as a hothead?"

She looked weary suddenly, as if the questions and the strain of answering them were getting to her. "Once upon a time," she murmured. "But not anymore, no."

As certain as Connor was of her innocence and as much as he disliked Harrison and Stemmons personally, he couldn't fault them for their reasoning in bringing Melanie in. She hated her brother-in-law—she had threatened him. The man was physically abusing her sister and she had vowed—past and present—that she would do anything necessary to protect her. He found Melanie's loyalty and bravery commendable, but he could see where they would find it damning.

Still, he wished they would back off.

"Where were you the night Boyd Donaldson was murdered?"

"Home."

"Alone?"

"No. With my four-year-old son."

"Between the hours of 11:00 a.m. and 1:00 a.m., was he asleep?"

"Yes, Detective, he was asleep. He's four years old."

"But you could have left the house without him knowing."

"I would never leave my child home alone. Never. No matter what."

She delivered the last while leveling first one detective, then the other, with an icy stare. The two investigators were doing their best to unnerve and intimidate her—except for that one moment when they'd brought up her father, she had seemed totally unaffected. She hadn't fidgeted in her seat and she had kept her answers succinct—her tone measured and firm, her manner confident.

If he didn't know her so well, he would have thought her totally unaffected by their questioning. But she was affected, shaken—he would bet on it. Because what she had assumed would be routine hadn't been. Not at all.

She glanced at her watch. Connor saw that her hand trembled slightly. "Gentlemen, if there's nothing else, I'm sure my chief would like to see my face again before the end of the day."

"Sure, Melanie. We appreciate you coming down and answering all these questions."

Pete smiled and stood. She followed him to his feet and together they walked to the door, Roger trailing behind.

"Wait, I almost forgot. I had one last question. About your father."

She turned to him. "Shoot."

"How did he die?"

"Heart attack."

"Anything unusual about that heart attack?"

She paused for a heartbeat, paling slightly. "Yes. It was brought on by elevated levels of digitalis in the blood."

48

Melanie spent what was left of her day pretending to have been unaffected by Harrison and Stemmons's interrogation. After she returned to work, she had informed her chief of both the direction and content of the CMPD interview, then had thrown herself into her duties. At five, she had picked up Casey, immersing herself in their nightly routine and her role of mother. Thirty minutes ago, she had tucked him into bed, kissing him the way she always did, as if she didn't have a worry in the world.

Nothing could be further from the truth. She wasn't unaffected. She felt vulnerable, exposed and bruised. By the interrogation. And by Connor's reaction to it—complete silence.

She had expected to see him when she left CMPD headquarters—she had expected him to find her. She had been wrong on both counts. Finally, just before signing out for the day, she had swallowed her pride and called him. She'd been told he was unavailable and she had left a message requesting that he call her.

He hadn't.

So, here she was, standing at his front door at eight-thirty at night, heart in her throat. Mrs. Saunders—the widow who lived next door—had been only too happy to come and sit with Casey while he slept. The woman had assumed Melanie had been called into work and Melanie hadn't corrected her.

Taking a deep, fortifying breath, Melanie rang the bell. Connor was home, she knew because his Explorer was parked in the driveway and light shone from nearly every window in the house.

He opened the door. He didn't look surprised to see her. "Hello, Melanie."

"Can we talk?"

Wordlessly, he swung the door wider. She walked through and then followed him as he led her to the kitchen. A glass of milk and plate containing a half-eaten tuna sandwich sat on the table; the sports section of the *Charlotte Observer* lay open beside his meal.

"I've interrupted your dinner."

"No big deal. It wasn't much of one." He motioned for her to take a seat at the table. "Mind if I finish?"

"Not at all." She sat, feeling awkward and more than a little bit foolish. "Were you there today?"

"Yes."

She laced her fingers together. "I thought you'd… You didn't call."

He took a bite of his sandwich and washed it down with a swallow of milk before answering. Melanie suspected he was using the time to formulate his answer. She wished she had ignored her instincts and stayed home. This was agony.

"I needed to think," he said finally. "To sort through everything and see where I stood."

"Sort through…everything?" she repeated, feeling the blood drain from her face. "You can't possibly…you don't think I…killed my brother-in-law?"

Instead of answering, he looked her dead in the eyes. "Why didn't you tell me how your father died?"

She wasn't a woman given to tears, but at this moment, if she let herself, she could bawl like a baby. She laced her fingers together. "You didn't ask."

"That's crap, Melanie." He pushed his empty plate away. "Considering the similarities between McMillian's death and your father's, you should have told me. It should have come up a dozen times. More, even. Why didn't you?"

"I don't know."

When he made a sound of disgust and disbelief, she held out a hand in supplication. "It's true. The coincidence between the two deaths was what originally caught my attention and led me to investigate McMillian's death. Then I realized what was nagging at me wasn't the similarity between my father's and Jim McMillian's deaths but the fact that two known batterers had died from bizarre accidents so close together. I guess I didn't say anything about my father because he didn't have anything to do with the Dark Angel. It was just back story."

He frowned. "Back story?"

"Yes." She tilted up her chin. "What are you trying to say, Connor? That you think I'm guilty?"

"Are you?"

"No." She got to her feet, hurt beyond words.

Angry. She crossed to his sink, then turned and looked him straight in the eyes, though hers burned with tears she would never shed. "No," she repeated.

"I had to ask," he said softly, following her to her feet. He crossed to stand before her. "I believe you."

"Lucky me."

She turned to go, but he caught her elbow, stopping her. He drew her into his arms, against his chest. Beneath her cheek his heart beat strong and steady. Melanie told herself to pull away, to reject his offer of comfort—she leaned into him instead.

He pressed his lips to her hair. "I don't think you killed Boyd Donaldson. I never did. But I had to ask. Because it's my job. And because it's who I am. I turn over every stone, Melanie. I always will. Can you live with that?"

She tipped her face up to his. "I knew you were there. When you didn't call...I thought...I was afraid—" She took a deep breath. "Turn all the stones you want, Connor Parks, but don't leave me wondering like that again. *That* I can't live with."

"I'm sorry." He cupped her face in his palms. "I should have called. I'm not used to being responsible to anyone's feelings but my own." He bent and kissed her, then drew away. "Are you okay?"

"Fine." She smiled. "Now that I know you believe in me."

He dragged his thumb across her bottom lip. "You were so cool. I was impressed."

"I have nothing to hide."

"I didn't tell them. About your dad and the knife."

"I wondered."

"I saw." He kissed her again. And again. She looped her arms around his neck and melted against him. "How long?" he asked against her mouth. "How long before you have to be home?"

"An hour," she answered. "Tops."

He caught her mouth and sliding his hands down to her fanny, he lifted her. He didn't ask permission—she didn't expect him to. She hooked her legs around his middle as he carried her to his bedroom. To his unmade bed.

They fell onto it, laughing. She shimmied out of her jeans, he out of his—the job made near impossible by their unwillingness to stop touching one another.

Finally, naked, breathless, Melanie climbed onto him. She loved the way he felt inside her, the sound of her name on his lips in that last moment before he orgasmed. She loved the way he made her feel—beautiful and sexy, adored—loved the way he urged her slowly toward her own release, until she thought she would orgasm or die, the pleasure was so intense.

Afterward, they lay in each other's arms, silent but comfortably so. Melanie sighed, aware of time passing. "I have to go."

He tightened his arms. "Stay."

"I can't." She trailed her fingers across his chest, enjoying the feel of his skin beneath her fingertips. "I told Mrs. Saunders I'd be gone no more than two hours."

He released her and rolled onto his side, facing her. She climbed out of bed. As she did, her foot landed on a book. She bent to retrieve the slim paperback.

The Pharmacist's Guide to Allergens and Toxins.

Melanie reread the title, recalling what Connor had said about his sister's death, that he hated batterers, that he sometimes wished the Dark Angel wouldn't be caught. She remembered the way he had insisted the Dark Angel was a woman.

Not a man.

"What's so interesting down there?"

She started, surprised. He peered over her shoulder and she held the book up. "A hobby of yours?"

"A little research." He reached over her shoulder and plucked it from her fingers. "I wanted to see how accessible the Dark Angel's knowledge is. To give you an idea, I bought that at the drugstore around the corner. It describes in detail what happens during a severe allergic reaction, how quickly death can occur, and lists some of the most common allergens. Bee venom being one of them."

He handed the book back and grinned. "Entertaining reading. Also proves our Angel didn't need to go to school to learn this stuff."

Cheeks hot, Melanie laughed and set the book on the nightstand. She couldn't believe she'd thought, even for a moment, that Connor might be a killer.

She stepped into her jeans, then snatched up her shirt from the floor. "I'll have to borrow it sometime. Next time I need to poison someone."

"In light of the day's events, I don't think I'd go around making jokes like that."

He was serious. She stopped buttoning her shirt and met his eyes. "Connor?"

"I have to ask you a question." She nodded, and he went on. "Have you considered that your father may have been one of the Dark Angel's victims?"

Her father? One of the Angel's victims? Melanie stared at Connor, her mouth dry, a rushing sound in her ears. She slowly shook her head. *She hadn't considered that. Not once.*

"And if he was," Connor murmured, "and Boyd was..."

He let the thought trail off—he didn't have to finish it. She understood what he was getting at. That would be two Dark Angel victims in one family.

Dear God. In her family.

49

Though it wasn't that late—just shy of 11:00 p.m.—the streets were quiet, the traffic light. Melanie drove toward home on a kind of autopilot, her thoughts whirling with the events of the day and Connor's parting words.

Her father, a Dark Angel victim? Why hadn't she considered it before? He could have been. He died in the same manner as Jim McMillian, and as all the others for that matter—a victim of his own frailty. He was a batterer, one who had lived his life without paying for his sins.

She should have seen it before. But she hadn't. *Why?*

Melanie flexed her fingers on the steering wheel. As hard as it was for her to admit, two Dark Angel deaths in her family couldn't be a coincidence. If both her father and Boyd were the Angel's victims, there was no way the killer could have randomly selected them, years apart.

What would the odds of that happening be? Too great to bet on, that was for sure.

The Dark Angel was close to her family. She knew them, their secrets.

Dear God. Ashley.

Melanie caught her breath at the thought. Her

third sister fit Connor's profile to a T—her age, the abuse in her background, her history of broken relationships with men, the way she seemed to be unraveling, that she had family in law enforcement. Ashley had been outspoken in her belief that the Angel's victims had deserved their fate. Thinking back, Melanie realized it was then, when she first presented her Dark Angel theory, that Ashley's behavior had seemed to spiral out of control. It was then that Ashley had begun alluding to the "things" she had done for her sisters. Ones they couldn't even begin to imagine.

Had she meant her sisters, Melanie and Mia? Or all her sisters, women everywhere?

Melanie pressed her lips together, hating her thoughts, but unable to stop them. As a pharmaceutical rep, Ashley knew about drugs, about poisons and allergic reactions. She talked to doctors day in and day out, she could easily obtain the kind of information she needed by asking a seemingly innocent question here and there. She traveled the Carolinas and was gone for days, sometimes a week at a time. It would have been easy for her to select a victim in Charleston or Myrtle Beach or Columbia.

Dear God, could it be true? Could Ashley be the Dark Angel?

No. Melanie curled her fingers more tightly around the wheel. No. Ashley was troubled, but she wasn't a killer. Melanie would prove that.

But how? The only surefire way she knew of to prove Ashley's innocence was to find the real Dark Angel killer.

Her beeper went off and she jumped. Thinking

first of Casey, she checked the beeper's display and saw that it hadn't been Mrs. Saunders who had called, but headquarters.

Using her cell phone, she dialed in. Loretta, the night dispatch, answered. "Loretta, it's Melanie. What's up?"

"Hey, Melanie. I hate to disturb you, but I thought I'd better."

The traffic light up ahead turned red and Melanie drew to a stop. "It's okay. Shoot."

"Call just came in for you. A woman. She sounded really upset. Scared to death. Wouldn't talk to anybody but you."

"A woman?" Melanie repeated. "Who?"

"She wouldn't give her name. Just said that *he'd* contacted her. The one you'd wanted to know about. Said you'd know who."

"That I'd know who?" Melanie frowned. "She leave a number?"

"Nope, hung up when I pressed her for more."

Melanie searched her memory, reviewing what the caller had said—that *he'd* contacted her, the one she had wanted to know about.

Joli Andersen's killer. Sugar. Of course.

Ten minutes later, Melanie drew to a stop at the west side corner where Sugar had been picked up. The west side of Charlotte boasted a disproportionate percentage of the city's crime. It was there one would be most likely to score sex or drugs, it was also the most likely place to be raped, mugged or shot in the head.

Melanie scanned the sidewalk. Sugar wouldn't

have gone home, Melanie was certain. If she had been afraid a killer was after her, she wouldn't have led him there, to her son. Nor would she be out on the street, a sitting duck.

In her rearview mirror, Melanie saw Connor's white Explorer turn the corner behind her. After making arrangements with Mrs. Saunders for Casey, she had called Connor. Protocol had dictated she contact Harrison and Stemmons—after all, the Andersen murder was their investigation.

But Sugar was her witness, so Melanie had figured to hell with protocol.

Connor pulled to a stop behind her, climbed out of his vehicle and came to her window.

"You have any ideas?" he asked.

"Yeah, she's holed up somewhere public. Lots of people. Where she feels safe."

"She going to be okay with me?"

"I'll make it okay." Melanie opened her door, then slid across the seat. "You drive, I'll scout."

They cruised within a ten-block radius of Sugar's corner, checking out anyplace there were people— several clubs, restaurants and an all-night minimarket. At each stop, Melanie went in while Connor waited in the Jeep.

Melanie found the woman on their eighth stop, at a diner called Mike's, a place that catered to people like Sugar, to the night people. She sat alone in a booth at the rear of the restaurant, her back to the wall, her gaze fixed on the door.

She looked terrified.

Melanie made her way to the other woman.

"Hello, Sugar," she said, stopping beside the table. "I hear you were looking for me."

She nodded.

"He found you tonight, didn't he? The guy I was asking you about?"

She nodded again. Melanie saw that she trembled. "On the...street. I...gave him the slip."

"How?"

"I told him I had to...pee. The bathroom...window. I...cut myself." She held up her hand. A vicious-looking gash ran diagonally across her palm.

"Come on," Melanie murmured. "Let's get out of here."

Within moments they were out of the diner and at the Jeep. Sugar saw Connor and stopped short. "Who's he?"

"A friend." Melanie glanced at him, then back at the woman. "He's okay, Sugar."

"Maybe this wasn't such a good—"

"He's the one who created the profile of the guy we're looking for, the profile of the man who killed Joli Andersen. He, better than anyone, will know if the man who approached you tonight is a killer."

She took a step backward. "I don't know. I think this was a mistake, I think—"

"You called me because you're scared, Sugar. Because you recognized the john I described, because you'd been with him. And now he's found you again."

The hooker paled and Melanie pressed harder. "He'll kill you this time, Sugar. Because he won't be able to help himself. And because you're the only one who can finger him.'' Melanie opened the vehicle's rear door. ''What are you going to do? Help me or wait for him to find you?''

The woman hesitated a fraction of a second more, then climbed in.

Melanie followed her. She made the introductions, then instructed Connor to drive. She turned to Sugar. ''Is your son okay?'' she asked. ''Right now, is he being taken care of?''

''He's with a neighbor. She baby-sits him.''

''Good. Tell me what happened.''

She began, words halting, voice low. ''You were…right, I recognized that guy you were asking me about. I'd been with him a few times. At first it wasn't so bad. He liked to play the big seduction scene, you know. He even brought wine, sometimes chocolate—''

''Champagne?'' Melanie asked.

''Yeah, the stuff with the bubbles.''

''Go on.''

''He never fucked me, never wanted me to blow him or anything like that. It was kind of nice. Like taking a couple hours off.''

''If he didn't want sex,'' Melanie murmured, ''what did he want?''

''He'd tie me up and just touch me. Real nice like. And talk to me.''

''Did you talk to him?''

''Not much. He wanted me to just…lie there.'' She was quiet a moment. ''It was as if he was…playing. Exploring. Like I was a doll. Yeah,'' she nodded, ''that's it, like I was a doll.''

Melanie glanced toward Connor. He met her eyes

in the rearview mirror, then returned his attention to the road. "Something changed then, didn't it, Sugar? You got scared."

She shuddered and rubbed her arms, as if chilled. "He started puttin' things…in me, you know, to fuck me with. Things that…hurt. Some of 'em hurt real bad. When I told him to quit, he—" She stopped, seeming to choke on the words.

"What?" Melanie urged. "What did he do?"

"He…had this…tape. He put it over my mouth so I…so I couldn't…'cause of the ropes, I couldn't do nothin'…I was…"

Her words shuddered to a halt. But they landed between them as surely and loudly as if she had shouted it. *Helpless. She had been helpless.*

Melanie leaned toward the prostitute; she covered her hand. "What did you do, Sugar?"

She met Melanie's eyes, hers filled with remembered horror. "I laid real still. Just the way he liked it. And even when he hurt me bad, I didn't make a sound. I wanted to live, Officer May. I wanted to live to see my boy again."

50

Unfortunately but not unexpectedly, Sugar didn't know the john's name. But she could describe him and Melanie convinced her to agree to do so for a police artist.

They took her to the Whistlestop PD. There, after notifying her chief of the night's events in progress and arranging for the artist, Melanie contacted Harrison and Stemmons.

The two investigators were none too happy with the situation. They became even more unhappy when they arrived and learned that not only had Sugar already given her statement to Melanie, but that Connor had been in on it.

Melanie had reminded them that without her, they would have no witness at all, then suggested they get over it and down to business.

It seemed clear that Sugar's john and Joli Andersen's killer were one and the same man. It also seemed clear, once the artist's rendering was complete, that Ted Jenkins was not that man. They arranged a photo lineup anyway—Jenkins passed with flying colors.

After Jenkins and his lawyer left, Harrison and Stemmons turned to Connor. "Any suggestions as to how we flush our man out?"

Connor nodded. "Our UNSUB's hungry, he's starting to hunt. But he's afraid. So he went back to a place where he felt safe before. Where he'd gotten relief before."

"Sugar," Melanie offered. "But she slipped out of his grasp. He's not dumb, he's got to figure she's made him."

"I agree. It's my opinion that he hasn't acted again until now because he's been afraid. The amount of press Joli's murder spawned, though exciting, frightened him. He's been afraid to cruise the bars, afraid he'd be recognized. Now he's even more frightened."

Pete swore. "The sick bastard's going to skip town."

"I don't think so. This is a professional guy, not a laborer. That's not so easy to walk away from. The time's right to stake out Joli's grave."

"We tried that, we got zilch."

"That was then, this is now. He's hungry, he's desperate and he's scared. He's going to pay Joli a visit."

Harrison drew his bushy eyebrows together. "What are you thinking?"

"Audio, video, infrared. Undercover officers around the perimeter. Three days. After that, he's cold. What've you got to lose?"

Harrison thought a moment, then nodded. "I'll call in."

He returned a few minutes later, mouth set in a grim line. "Got the okay. But I've been warned, I come up empty on this, the cost of the operation comes out of my hide.'' Pete looked at her. ''You and Taggerty want in? We could use the help.''

Twenty minutes later, Melanie walked Connor out to his Explorer—which he'd had a uniform drive over the night before. Harrison and Stemmons had left only moments before, after powwowing with her and Bobby about the coming night's undercover assignment.

Melanie glanced up at the noon sky, a brilliant, unrelieved blue. ''I should be tired, but I'm not. I'm jazzed.''

Connor smiled, understanding. ''There's nothing like a break in a case to get the adrenaline going. Sometimes it stays with me for days.''

''It's like I know this guy now.'' She looked at him. ''Like I'm so close I can almost slip the cuffs on him. And I want that, so bad I can taste it.''

''Funny, but my thoughts are running in a slightly different direction.''

''Oh?''

His lips curved into a wicked smile. ''Something along the lines of you and me and getting naked.''

She laughed. ''You're incorrigible, Agent Parks.''

''I try, Officer May.'' They reached the Explorer and he unlocked the driver's door. ''Ever do it in a cemetery?''

''Hardly.'' She arched an eyebrow. ''And if you have, I don't want to hear about it.''

His smile faded. ''Tonight, be careful.''

''I will.''

He reached out a hand, as if to touch her, then

dropped it. "Never forget, not even for a moment, that this guy's a killer. Promise me that, Melanie."

"I promise," she murmured, thinking of Sugar's statement, the ordeal she had lived through, picturing Joli's lifeless face. A shudder rippled over her. "I've got too much to live for not to."

A moment later, he climbed into his vehicle and drove off. Melanie watched him go, then headed back inside, her thoughts returning to all that had transpired the previous evening. Sugar's story had affected her deeply. Because she had understood, because she had been able to relate to the other woman's fear—to her willingness to do whatever was necessary to live another day.

What would she endure, Melanie wondered, in the hopes of seeing Casey again? In an effort to hold on to life?

Ashley. The Dark Angel.

She hadn't thought about her sister or her fears concerning her since Sugar's call had come in the evening before. Now they came crashing back to the fore of her consciousness with a vengeance.

As much as she longed to, Melanie acknowledged, she couldn't share her fears with Connor. Or anyone even remotely associated with the case. She couldn't betray her sister that way. But she could talk to Mia, feel her out on Ashley's stability, query her as to her memory of Ashley's reaction to their father's death, ask her what she knew of their sister's whereabouts of late. Then she would call Ashley herself.

While Bobby was in the rest room, she dialed Mia's number, silently cursing when she got the answering machine. "Mia," she said, "it's Melanie. We have to talk. It's about Ashley. I'm afraid—"

"Hello? Mel?" Her sister sounded winded. "Sorry, I was in the middle of my workout." She sucked in a deep breath. "What's wrong?"

"We need to talk...about Ash. But not on the phone. Can I come over?"

"Now?"

"Yes. It's urgent."

Mia was silent a moment. "Now's not good. Give me...an hour. Will that work for you?"

Melanie said it would and an hour later, she was facing her sister across her kitchen table.

"Now," Mia said, pouring herself a glass of orange juice from a cut-crystal pitcher, "what's all this about Ashley?"

"Have you talked to her since the funeral?"

Mia shook her head and took a sip of her juice. "But it's only been a couple of days."

"How about before Boyd's death, had you talked to her much?"

"Almost not at all. Why?"

Melanie stood, too anxious to sit still. "I think there's something going on with her, Mia. Something bad."

"You're just figuring that out?" Melanie looked at her sister, surprised by her harsh tone. "Veronica told me about the stunt she pulled at the Charleston D.A.'s office. I mean, *really*. Pretending to be you to try to dig something up on Veronica. How bizarre was that? Veronica thinks Ashley needs professional help and I'm forced to agree."

"This is worse than that, Mia. It's...I think she's—" Melanie couldn't say it. Not yet, not even to her sister.

She tried another tack. "At Father's funeral and...after, how was Ashley? How did she...react to his death? Even though I was there, I can't remember."

Mia thought a moment. "I don't know, the same as us, I guess. Relieved. Guilty."

Melanie jumped on the last. "Guilty? What do you mean?"

"For being happy he was dead," she said flatly. "We all were, let's face it."

That was true. A part of her had cheered when she'd learned the news. But that didn't make her a killer. It didn't make either of her sisters one.

She leaned forward. "What about nuances? Did you find anything strange about her behavior? Do you remember anything striking you as odd?"

"About *Ashley's* behavior?" Mia arched an eyebrow. "Get real, Mel."

"I'm serious. Besides, it wasn't until recently that Ashley's become strange."

Mia gazed at her a moment, her expression speculative. "What are you not saying, Melanie? What's going on?"

"I don't know for sure. But I have this suspicion that—"

"Hi, Melanie."

Startled, she turned. Veronica stood in the kitchen doorway, dressed in an ecru linen suit, briefcase dangling from her right hand. She smiled at Melanie, though the curving of her lips looked stiff. Even though they had made up, things had never been the same between them since their altercation at the dojang, a fact Melanie felt bad about.

Veronica turned her attention to Mia. "I'm back to work. Call me later, okay?"

Melanie moved her gaze between the two women, unsettled. What was Veronica doing here at noon, on a workday? And why hadn't Mia told her the woman was there? She had thought they were alone in the house.

"Thanks for everything, Vee." Mia blew her a kiss. "You're a sweetheart."

"Bye, Melanie."

"Bye," she murmured, watching her go, a strange sensation in the pit of her stomach. A moment later, she heard the rumble of the garage door going up, then the roar of an engine coming to life.

Melanie turned to her sister. "Is Veronica still staying with you?"

Mia drained her juice glass and set it on the table in front of her. "She has been, but she's moving back home tonight. She stopped back to get the rest of her stuff. I'll sure miss her. I swear, this whole thing has been such a nightmare. I don't know what I would have done without her."

Melanie experienced twin pinches of guilt and envy. Once upon a time, she would have been the one Mia turned to. The one who would have been there for her—sister, best friend and confidante.

What had happened to them?

Melanie swallowed past the lump in her throat, past the feeling that somehow, something important in her life had changed without her even knowing it.

"What's happened to us, Mia?" she asked, a slight tremor in her voice. "You, me and Ashley? We used to be best friends."

"I don't know. I guess we've grown apart."

"Grown apart?" Melanie repeated. "How can you say that so casually? You and Ashley have always come first in my life, I thought you felt the same way."

Mia looked at her. She drew her eyebrows together. "Me? First in your life? Please. The way I see it, you kept me around because I did what you wanted. Because I was your little cheering section."

Melanie recoiled, hurt. "That's not true. We've always been partners. Equal partners."

"Right," Mia said sarcastically. "You played leader, me follower. You were the strong one, I the weak."

She leaned toward Melanie, lips twisted into a bitter smile. "You never wanted me to be strong, did you? You liked being the capable, confident one, the one everyone looked up to. After all, if you'd been the wimpy little victim, then you would have been the one Dad targeted, not me."

Melanie's mouth dropped at her sister's words. At the anger and bitterness behind them. She shook her head. "If I could have, I would have taken your place when Dad singled you out."

Mia stood and Melanie saw that she trembled, as if with great emotion. "I think you might even believe that, Melanie. It's so heroic. So brave and self-less. And believing it makes the past a whole lot easier to live with, I'll bet."

Melanie followed her sister to her feet, heart hurting so badly she could hardly breathe. "Where's this coming from?" she asked. "When did you start hating me? When did you start think-ing—"

Melanie brought a hand to her mouth. "It's Veronica, isn't it? She's the one who's turning you against me and Ashley. She's the one who's...changing you. The one who's making you...bitter."

"It's always someone else who's the problem, right, Melanie? It's never you. Veronica's my friend. She understands me. She wants me to be happy."

Melanie struggled to right her reeling world. First Ashley. Now Mia. *What was happening to them? To her?* "I've never wished anything but the best for you. I've never wanted you to be anything but completely, deliriously happy."

"Well, then you've gotten your wish," Mia snapped. "Because I've never been happier."

51

Within an hour of the order, the CMPD technical team had moved in. Three cameras and their accompanying video and audio transmitters had been mounted in trees near Joli Andersen's grave. From the command post, located in an unoccupied storefront several miles away, Harrison and Stemmons were able not only to view the scene, but to pan the area with individual cameras and zoom in on any subject who came into range. Infrared spots had been mounted with the cameras. IR, invisible to the human eye, would illuminate the scene at night—the most likely time for the UNSUB to make an appearance.

Once the tech work had been completed, the stakeout commenced. Undercover officers, in vehicles and on foot, were stationed at various points around the cemetery's perimeter, including the two entrances. Each officer had been fitted with an earpiece and mike to stay in constant contact with the command post. In a lucky break, the cemetery, which was one of the oldest in the city and located on a parcel of land in historic Dilworth, was bounded by three moderately populated streets. Joggers, couples strolling or an unfamiliar vehicle or two wouldn't arouse suspicion.

Melanie and Bobby were assigned footwork—Bobby posing as the snoozing night guard inside the cemetery walls and Melanie as a runner, circling the perimeter. After two nights of running and nothing to show for it but the beginnings of a blister on her right heel, Melanie decided that Bobby had gotten the better of the assignments.

As the west entrance came into view, she slowed her pace to a walk, pretending to check her pulse. She wore jogging shorts, a sleeveless T-shirt and a fanny pack strapped around her waist. In the pouch, she carried all her undercover essentials—weapon, cuffs and shield.

She scanned the cemetery entrance. Other than a woman walking two white poodles, the area was deserted. No vehicles had arrived or departed since her last check, twenty minutes ago.

"West entrance, all clear," she murmured, frustrated and antsy for action. Aware of the clock ticking. Connor had felt strongly that considering the circumstances, the first few nights of the stakeout would be the ones most likely to yield results. She agreed. The UNSUB had experienced a recent failure—he was hungry, growing desperate and was scared. If that didn't immediately propel him to Joli's gravesite, little else would.

In truth, Melanie feared too much time had passed already, that they had somehow missed him. Or worse, that he had zeroed in on a new victim.

Suddenly, Harrison spoke. "All units, we have activity. A lone, male figure moving into view, approaching the site. Hold your positions."

Harrison fell silent a moment, then continued.

"UNSUB's wearing dark slacks and a dark T-shirt. Running shoes. Dark hair.

"He's holding back, keeping his distance. Something's spooked him. He keeps stopping to look over his shoulder."

Melanie heard the excitement in Harrison's voice—that the adrenaline had begun to pump. Hers, too. She tensed, excitement growing.

"Come on," the detective coaxed the suspect, his tone low and seductive. "You're all alone and she's right there. Go up to her...that's right, she's all yours. Yes! He's there. Hold tight, everybody, if this is our guy, we need to get as much on tape as we can."

Seconds ticked past and Melanie began to sweat. A car eased by, its headlights momentarily pinning her, then moving on. Somewhere nearby, a cat screamed, a car door slammed shut. The sound carried on the damp night air, disembodied, unnatural.

Suddenly, Harrison swore. Melanie jumped. "Parks was right. The sick bastard's on his knees in front of her marker. He's got his dick in his han— Wait...zooming. That's right," Harrison cooed, "do it nice for the jury. Give us the money shot. That's right, you sick fuck... Go for it."

Melanie clenched her jaw, focusing on her job, not allowing herself to dwell on the act in progress only yards away. Once the suspect finished reliving his fantasy, his fear would take over and he would be out of there.

Finally, Harrison gave the word. "All units, he's on the move. Heading toward the east entrance, I repeat, the east entrance.'' Harrison began issuing orders for the various units, with each announcing their position. Bobby, on foot, was the lone officer inside the cemetery.

''May, where are you?''

''Outside the west entrance.''

''Good. Cut through the cemetery to cover the rear and assist Bobby.''

''Done.'' She broke into a light run, blister screaming in protest. She bypassed the walking paths that followed the perimeter of the graveyard in favor of darting directly across.

''Anybody have a visual yet?'' Harrison asked. ''Bobby?''

''That's a negative,'' he answered. ''I'm at the east entrance, all's clear.''

Harrison swore. ''I don't like this. What's taking him so long?''

Up ahead Melanie caught a flicker of movement. A figure, she realized, moving toward the north end of the cemetery. She changed her own course, acknowledging what had happened—the suspect had taken a sharp right and was now heading north. Since there was no entrance on that side of the cemetery, she figured he planned to go over the wall.

''Shit,'' she muttered. ''Have visual of suspect,'' Melanie said softly. ''He is not, I repeat *not,* heading for the east entrance. I believe he's going to scale the north wall, have a unit ready. Am in pursuit.''

Her murmured words carried on the night air and the man stopped and looked back, spotting her. He broke into a run—she followed suit, retrieving her pistol from the pouch at her waist. "Halt! Police!"

"On my way, Mel," Bobby shouted. "No heroics."

Harrison echoed Bobby's warning, then added, "Detain him without gunfire, May. I repeat, unless shot at, do not fire. We want this guy alive."

Harrison's words ringing in her ears, she pushed harder, leaping over and dodging greenery, her breath coming hard and sharp. The suspect reached the wall and lunged. Agile for a big man, he began pulling himself over. Melanie moved into range and leaped. She caught hold of the waistband of his pants, hauling him backward, losing her pistol in the process. He lost his grip and they fell backward. He landed on top of her, knocking the wind out of her. He was up like a shot, scrambling once more for the wall.

From behind her she heard Bobby's feet pounding against the ground as he ran, heard his shout that he had spotted her. She couldn't wait for his assistance; she tackled the suspect again, sending them both sprawling.

This time it was he who was stunned, and Melanie jumped to her feet, moving automatically into her fighting stance. As he began to pull himself up, she got a good look at him—he was so handsome he took her breath away. For one muddled moment she paused, thinking she had made a mistake. This man couldn't be a murderer. He couldn't be the one who had bound, gagged and permanently silenced Joli Andersen.

But he was. He had taken Joli's breath away, too. Literally.

Melanie nailed him with a double kick, the first to his right shoulder, the second to the side of his head. He went down hard, face first. She was on top of him in a flash, his arms pinned behind him.

All hell broke loose. Bobby arrived, gun drawn. From the other side of the wall came the scream of sirens, the squeal of brakes and car doors slamming. The police beacons sent flashes of red light through the branches above her head.

Melanie snapped cuffs on the suspect, read him his rights and stood, swaying slightly. Her head ached from where it had bashed against the ground, her left knee was bleeding, and her damned heel was on fire.

Bobby frowned at her. "You okay, partner?"

"Are you kidding?" She grinned. "I've never been better, Bobby."

52

The following Saturday morning, Casey awakened Melanie by leaping on top of her. "Mommy! Time to get up!"

Melanie groaned and rolled from her side to her back, causing him to topple off her. "Watch cartoons," she mumbled, pulling the pillow over her head. Already exhausted from two nights' undercover work, she'd hardly slept, tormented by concerns about Ashley and her disintegrating relationship with Mia. "Get me up later."

He responded by doing what looked and sounded like a war dance on the bed. "The zoo!" he shrieked. "The zoo!"

She tossed the pillow on the floor and struggled into a sitting position, not an easy feat with a whooping, dancing child on the bed. "I live in the zoo," she complained, though with a smile. "A little excited, are we?"

She had to admit that now that she was actually waking up, she was a bit excited, too. Connor was taking them both to the zoo today. Although Casey had spent an hour here or there around Connor, this was the first excursion planned specifically for the three of them.

She smiled at her son and held out her arms.

"Come give me a big hug and kiss to get me going."

He did, then tumbled off the bed and bolted out of the room. Before she had even cleared the sheets he was back, eyes sparkling with excitement. "Hurry up, Mom. He'll be here *soon*."

Two and a half hours later, picnic lunch made, showers taken, faces and hair made presentable, Melanie greeted Connor at the front door.

"Ready?" he asked.

"You bet!" Casey hopped excitedly from one foot to the other. "Come on, Mom!"

Melanie laughed. "Ready. Let me grab the picnic basket."

"I'll get it." Connor searched her gaze, a question in his, then turned to Casey. "Car's open, sport. There's a surprise for you on the back seat. You can go get it now if you want."

With a whoop, Casey tore off. Melanie watched him go. "A surprise?"

"An FBI insignia cap." He shrugged. "He seemed awfully interested when I told him about the Bureau."

"Interested? Try over-the-moon. Only four years old and already playing cops 'n' robbers." She glanced back at Connor. "Speaking of which, did you hear the latest on the Andersen suspect?" He shook his head and she filled him in. "Turns out he fits your profile to a T. Guy was on suspension from Queen's City Medical Center, where he was a second-year resident. Still lived with his mother, with whom he apparently has a love-hate relationship. He drove a three-year-old BMW in perfect condition and lived way beyond his means. The list goes on.''

"Com'on, you guys!'' Casey's wail was part exasperated adult, part frustrated child.

They put him out of his misery, and began to make their way out to the Explorer. Connor glanced at her from the corners of his eyes. "You okay?''

"Sure. Why?''

"You look like you've had a sleepless night or two.''

Melanie opened her mouth to tell him about it all—Ashley and Mia. Her suspicions. She shut it again, acknowledging that now was not the time.

"Still catching up from cemetery detail,'' she murmured instead. "That's all.''

He stopped and looked at her. Heat crept up her cheeks. He saw clean through her, she realized. How did he do that? How did he know her well enough already to know what she was feeling and when she was holding back?

"I'm here if you want to talk about it.''

"Thanks.''

They reached the Explorer. Connor stowed the basket in back, then they both climbed in. Melanie noticed Casey had taken off his Panthers' cap and put on the one Connor had given him. She saw that Connor had noticed, too, and was pleased.

Connor fastened his seat belt, started the car and glanced back at Casey. "Okay, sport, you ready to have a really great day?''

The day was better than great. It was perfect. Magical. Casey was crazy about Connor and the feeling was obviously mutual. The two had a ball together. She wouldn't have believed a crackerjack FBI profiler could act so silly, down to pretending to be an elephant while Casey rode on his shoulders.

The day ended too soon, even though they prolonged it by going to Crazy Bill's Play Place for games and a dinner of hot dogs, French fries and watered-down milk shakes.

When they arrived home, Casey tugged on Connor's hand, all but dragging him toward the front door. He begged Melanie to allow him to stay up long enough to show Connor his room and action-figure collection.

Melanie capitulated, amused. She unlocked the door. "But be warned, young man, after the action figures, it's bed for you."

While Casey showed Connor his treasures, Melanie checked the mail, then the answering machine. The message light was blinking and she pressed play and waited, leafing through catalogs while she did. Suddenly, Ashley's voice filled the room. She was crying, her disembodied voice thick and broken. Gooseflesh raced up Melanie's arms.

"Mel...Mellie, it's me. You've got to...got to...I'm so sorry. So sorry."

Her youngest sister dragged in a shuddering breath. "You can't imagine what I've done for... You've never understood, never been there for me... I've always loved you anyway, Mel. I've always..."

The machine cut her off.

Melanie stared at the box, barely breathing, heart in her throat. According to the machine's automated date and time, Ashley had left the message the night before. Casey had been out with his dad, who hadn't been able to see him today because of a conference; she had been at tae kwon do. Distracted and upset, Melanie had forgotten to check her machine when she returned home.

Melanie hit rewind, listened to the message again, trying to make sense of Ashley's words, their meaning. Her concern became icy-cold terror.

Melanie rubbed her arms. *Why was Ashley sorry? What had she done?*

Melanie picked up the phone and dialed Ashley's town house. Her machine picked up and Melanie left a message begging her to call. She then dialed her sister's cell number, left another message, then tried her beeper.

"What's up?"

Melanie spun around, hand flying to her throat.

"Connor! I didn't hear you."

He motioned the phone, still clutched in her right hand. "Something wrong?"

"No." She dropped the receiver into the cradle. She would have to tell him, but not now. "My sister Ashley called, that's all. She's having some… personal problems." She pasted on a nonchalant smile. "Where's Casey?"

"Setting up a supercommando-force team. He sent me to get you."

She laughed, the sound false even to her own ears. "Wouldn't want to miss the big battle."

"Definitely not," he murmured, his gaze full of questions. "After you."

The battle ensued, complete with death, destruction and the little boy's specialty—sound effects.

After two world wars, Melanie called a cease-fire so that the general could get some well-deserved shut-eye. Though he protested through his yawns, he agreed with a minimum of fuss—as long as Connor read him a bedtime story. She opened her mouth to get Connor gently off the hook, but he agreed before she could utter a word.

One story became three. Melanie sat back, listened and watched, a strange, discomfiting sensation stealing over her. That Connor was enjoying himself was obvious. That Casey had found a new best friend was also obvious.

That it was too much, too soon, was abundantly, painfully clear. To her.

She was falling in love with Connor.

He was falling in love with her son.

Emotion choked her and she looked away. She remembered what Connor had told her of his marriage—of the reasons it had ended, of his love for his stepson. Of how much he missed him.

And she thought of today, of how Connor had come to life around Casey, of how the shadows had fallen away from him, leaving him years younger and carefree.

She felt as if her heart was breaking.

"One more story. *Please.*"

"Absolutely not," she said, standing and crossing to the bed.

After the mandatory minute of begging, Casey settled down. Prayers said, kisses delivered and blanket tucked snugly around him, Melanie and

Connor tiptoed out of the room—though Melanie knew the child would be asleep the moment he closed his eyes.

"Can I get you a drink?" she asked when they reached the living room. "A glass of wine or a beer?"

"Thanks, but I'm on the wagon." He drew her into his arms. "I had a really good day."

She smiled and looped her arms around his neck. "Me, too."

"That's a great little guy you've got."

"Thank you. I think so, too."

"And smart." Connor shook his head. "He'd keep me on my toes, that's for sure."

Her smile slipped and she disentangled herself from his arms. "How about some coffee?"

"Sure. Can I help?"

"Just make yourself comfortable."

He followed her into the kitchen and leaned against the counter, watching as she filled the carafe with water, then ground the beans.

"You forget," he said after a moment, his expression pensive. "When you're not around kids, you forget how they can light up a room. How they can turn night into day."

She murmured something noncommittal, her head beginning to pound. Talk about us, she silently urged. Talk about the case, the Bureau, the weather, for heaven's sake. Talk about anything but how much you enjoy being with my son.

"Jamey was like that," Connor continued. "I could come home with the weight of the world pressing in on me and fifteen minutes later be as carefree as a man can be. I've missed that. More than I even realized before to—''

''Stop, okay?'' She turned and met his eyes. ''Just stop.''

Connor frowned. ''Did I do something wrong?''

She wanted to shout, ''Yes! You've fallen in love with my kid but not with me.'' Instead, calmly, she murmured, ''We need to…I think we need to be clear on what's going on here. With us.''

He waited and she pulled in a deep breath, hoping it would bring her courage. She needed to do this, had to do it. But the truth was, she wanted nothing more than to take whatever Connor was willing to give her—even if it was only misplaced affection.

''Casey isn't the stepson you lost, Connor,'' she said. ''I'm not your ex-wife and *we* are not a means for you to come back to life.''

She paused, hoping he would jump in with a denial, a protest of innocence. Instead, he simply looked at her, his expression unreadable.

She swallowed past disappointment, so bitter it burned her throat. ''I can't allow you to use us, to use Casey, as a way to feel better about yourself. It won't work, you know it and so do I. We also know that Casey will end up hurt.''

''I see.'' He straightened. ''You're giving me my walking papers.''

''I don't want to, Connor. I want you to stay. I want us to make love. But what I want isn't important. Casey is.''

''Are you asking for a commitment from me?''

''That's not what this is about.'' She glanced

away, then back. "Look me in the eyes, Connor. Look me in the eyes and tell me you're not doing with us what you did with your ex-wife. Tell me you're interested in *me,* not just the package. That's what I want, Connor."

He was silent a moment, then he shook his head. "I can't do that. I'm sorry."

A sound of pain slipped past her lips. She crossed to the back door, opened it and turned to look at him. "I think you'd better go."

He crossed to the door but didn't move through it. He cupped her cheek. She realized with a sense of horror that her eyes had filled with tears, that one had slipped past her guard and rolled down her cheek.

"I can't say," he murmured, "because I don't know. Today was good. Really good. It brought back memories that are so…sweet. And in the last few years there have been damn few of those kinds of days. And even fewer of those kinds of memories to recall."

He dragged his thumbs across her cheekbones, catching her tears. "I can't say, Melanie, because I don't want to make a mistake. Because I don't want to hurt you. Either of you."

The phone rang. He dropped his hand and stepped through the door. She reached out to stop him, to call him back. The plea died on her lips. He was already gone.

The phone jangled again and Melanie snatched it up, certain it was her sister. "Ashley?"

"No, Stan."

"Stan?" She glanced at the clock, suddenly disoriented. "I thought you were out of town—"

He cut her off. "I've had enough of your little campaign of terror, Melanie. I want you to stop it."

She blinked, confused. "Stop what? Stan—"

"Cut the crap, Melanie. I know what you're trying to do, and it won't work. Did you really think you could *scare* me out of wanting custody of Casey? Did you really think you could scare Shelley enough that she could convince me?"

"Scare Shelley?" A flutter of panic settled in the pit of her stomach. "I promise you, I don't know what you're talking about! I haven't—"

"I didn't believe Shelley until I saw you with my own eyes. If you come around again, if I see you lurking about again, I'm calling the cops. Got that?"

"Stan, please. We had an understanding, why would I jeopardize—"

"*Had* an understanding. No more. You blew it, Melanie."

53

The next morning, the doorbell awakened Melanie. She climbed out of bed, careful not to disturb Casey, who had crawled in with her sometime during the night.

The bell pealed again and scowling, Melanie slipped into her robe and hurried to answer it.

To her surprise, Pete Harrison and Roger Stemmons stood on her front porch. In their dark glasses and matching suits they looked like characters out of a bad TV show. She stared at them, blinking in confusion. "Pete? Roger? What are you doing here?"

"Melanie, we need you down at headquarters for questioning."

"Questioning?" She shook her head in an effort to clear it. "What time is it?"

Roger glance at his watch. "Eight-ten."

A.M.? On a Sunday? She moved her gaze between the two. "You need me now?"

"Afraid so," Pete murmured. "There's been an attempt on your ex-husband's life."

That woke her up. "Stan? Someone tried to kill—"

"Tried to poison him."

"Luckily, they botched the job."

"Mommy?"

She swung around. Casey stood in the doorway, clutching his stuffed rabbit to his chest, eyes wide and frightened. She crossed to him and scooped him up. "It's okay, sweetie. Mommy has to go to work." She glanced back at the detectives. "Come on in. It's going to take a couple minutes, I have to get dressed and call the sitter."

It wasn't until twenty minutes later, when she was sitting in the back of the cruiser, the noncommunicative Harrison and Stemmons in the front seat, that Melanie realized what was happening— they wanted to question *her* in connection with the attempt on Stan's life.

It seemed impossible to her. A ridiculous mistake. A nightmarish joke played by someone with a sick sense of humor.

Melanie told them so as soon as they would listen. "You're barking up the wrong tree if you think I had anything to do with this."

"Your ex-husband was suing you for custody of your son," Pete murmured. "Seems like a motive to me."

They sat in the same interrogation room they had only days before, facing each other across the same bare table, the video recorder trained on her face. Who was watching her performance, judging her every word and movement? she wondered. Connor? Her chief? A representative from the D.A.'s office? Just how serious was this?

"No." She leaned forward, desperate for the investigators to believe her. "We'd come to an understanding. We'd agreed to a compromise, for the good of Casey.''

"Not according to your ex-husband," Pete countered.

"He tells us you've been stalking him," Roger chimed in. "He's seen you from his office window, hanging around outside, in the building's parking garage. A neighbor of his saw you lurking outside his home one night, the security guard at the neighborhood's front gate logged you in."

"That's nonsense!"

"What does your ex-husband eat every morning for breakfast?"

Pete asked the question, and she shifted her attention to him, momentarily off balance by the change of subject. "He makes his own whole-grain granola cereal."

"When you were married, how did you refer to this mixture?"

"I called it his leaves and twigs." She made a sound of frustration and glanced at her watch, thinking of Casey. "Stan's a health nut. He runs six miles every morning and follows a low-fat, high-fiber regime. He has for years."

"Does anyone else eat this cereal?"

"No one else could stomach it. Trust me, I tried."

The investigators exchanged glances. Pete cleared his throat and continued. "At what time does your ex-husband arise every morning?"

"At 4:00 a.m. To run. Unless that's changed since we were married."

"Would you describe him as a man driven by habit?"

"Yes."

"As a man whose routine you could set your watch by?"

"Yes."

Pete stood. He circled behind Melanie, forcing her to twist her neck to look at him. "At 4:00 a.m. this morning, as is his custom, your ex-husband arose, dressed for his workout and poured himself a bowl of his granola. He thought the mix looked a bit different than usual, the texture and color subtly altered, but shrugged off the observation. Until he began to feel ill during his run."

Melanie brought a hand to her mouth, afraid of what was coming next, knowing where this story was leading.

"He circled back," Pete murmured, "vomiting three times along the way, sweating profusely, becoming more disoriented with each passing moment. He thought he had the flu, then remembered his observation about the granola. He went to the pantry and sure enough, the mixture contained ingredients he didn't recognize. Ironically enough, bits of roots and leaves, finely chopped.

"Oh my God," she murmured, a clammy sensation stealing over her. "What—"

"Oleander. Highly toxic. A favorite in fiction and movies." He reached for his coffee.

"How is he?" she asked.

"Lucky. Wife drove him to the hospital, he had his stomach pumped. Good thing he's observant. If he had put off his symptoms to the flu—"

"He'd be dead now," Roger added. "Stone cold."

Pete folded his hands on the table in front of him. "You have several oleander shrubs in your yard, don't you, Melanie?"

She worked to control the fear that shot through her. "So do about fifty percent of the home owners in the Charlotte area. Probably in the entire Southeast. We're not talking about a rare plant."

"But fifty percent of the home owners in the Charlotte area don't have a compelling reason to want Stan May dead. You do."

She made a sound of shock. "This is crazy." She moved her gaze between the two. "You don't seriously believe I tried to kill my ex-husband?"

"Why wouldn't we? You know the stats, Melanie. In fifty-seven percent of all murders, the victim was acquainted with his killer. In seventeen percent of those, the victim and killer were related. That's a big percentage for a small pool of suspects."

A queasy sensation settled in the pit of her gut, the kind she used to get at the carnival when she was a kid. "How about the fact that I'm a police officer? That I took an oath to uphold the law, not break it. Or how about the fact that you're talking about my son's father here? Why would I deprive him of one of the two most important people in his life?"

"Why don't you tell us?"

"Do I need a lawyer?"

"It's your right under the law, of course."

She studied them, considering her options, then shook her head. "Go on. For the moment."

"Speaking of facts," Pete murmured, "here's one I think you'll find interesting. Did you know that the body's reaction to oleander poisoning mirrors that of digitalis poisoning? Or that the treatments for both are very similar?"

She frowned. "I don't understand what you're saying."

"Don't you find that an odd coincidence, Melanie? After all, your father died of digitalis poisoning. So did the first Dark Angel victim you brought to our attention."

The detective's words, their meaning and implications, plowed into her. She reeled from them, from the truth she could no longer deny.

Her father. The Dark Angel. Boyd. Now Stan. Ashley.

"Melanie?" he prodded, leaning earnestly toward her. "Don't you find that a little too strange a coincidence?"

She met his gaze. She hated to do this, it felt like the ultimate betrayal of a person she loved and had always tried to protect. But she had no other choice. Ashley needed help. She had to be stopped.

"Yes, I do."

Roger expelled his breath in a soft whoosh and Pete sent him a warning glance. "Go on, Melanie. Tell us everything."

She took a deep breath and began. "These things have only just come to my attention. I haven't said anything to anyone, not even Connor Parks, even though we've been working together on the Dark Angel case. I couldn't say anything, not until I knew for sure."

She looked down at her hands, clenched tightly in her lap, then back up at Pete. "My sister Ashley's been acting strangely for some time. I've been concerned, naturally, but I wasn't frightened over it until recently."

Voice shaking, she detailed the conversations they'd had, the things her sister had said about the Dark Angel and justice, how Ashley had alluded to having helped her sisters, about the message she'd left two evenings before. And, finally, the conclusion she had been forced to come to after considering all of the above.

When she had finished, Pete leaned back, expression disbelieving. "You're fingering your sister as the Dark Angel?"

A lump formed in her throat. "I don't want to. I love my sister. But if she's done these things, she has to be stopped."

Roger snorted with disgust. "Trying to shift the blame away from yourself and onto your own sister? That's the most pathetic thing I've ever heard."

Pete agreed. "Just tell us the truth."

"I am! That is the truth." She tipped her face toward the ceiling a moment, collecting her thoughts. "She fits the profile perfectly. Her background, age, education level. Her rapidly deteriorating ability to maintain an aura of normalcy in her life. Additionally, as a drug rep, she has access to information on drug interactions, toxicities and treatments. Her territory's the Carolinas, giving her ample opportunity to meet the women she sees herself as helping. It all adds up."

Pete didn't blink. "It all adds up with you, too,

Melanie. You fit the profile—your age, profession, education, the abuse in your background. Your history with men. You had motive and opportunity.''

She did fit the profile. Why hadn't she considered that before?

"Your ex-husband saw you, Melanie. He recognized *you*. Explain that."

"Ashley and I look alike, so much so that we're often taken for one another. We're not identical twins…but from the circumstances you described, he could have easily mistaken her for me."

"You were wearing your uniform."

She drew back, stunned. "My uniform?"

"Your Whistlestop PD uniform. Which is probably how you convinced the guard to let you into your ex's neighborhood. Want to take a stab at explaining that?"

She shook her head, thoughts a confusing jumble. Ashley had wanted to set her up, but why?

"Want to change your story?" Roger asked. "There's no way out now, you did it and we know it."

Melanie looked directly at the video camera. Connor was behind that glass, she knew that now. Judging her every word and gesture. Was he in on this? He knew her so well, did he honestly think she could do this? That she could possibly be the Dark Angel?

It hurt almost too much to bear.

She met the investigator's gaze evenly, vowing not to show how shaken—how frightened—she was. "Are you prepared to charge me with a crime?"

"Not yet," Pete admitted.

"Then I'm leaving." She stood. "If you have any further questions, you'll need to contact my lawyer."

54

Connor stood in front of the monitor, gazing at an image of the now-empty room. Behind him, Harrison and Stemmons held court with the room's other occupants—a representative from the D.A.'s office, Melanie's chief and the CMPD head homicide investigator, a lieutenant.

"I've worked with Melanie for three years now," her chief was saying. "She's a good officer and a fine person. It's going to take a lot more than this to get me to believe she's a killer."

The ADA agreed. "You're going to need a lot more than the speculative and circumstantial evidence you've got now before I'll agree to move forward."

"We'll get it," Pete responded. "We'll have a search warrant within the hour."

"She held up well under questioning," the CMPD lieutenant said. "In fact, Pete, you may have gone too far. She could skip town."

"She's not going anywhere." Roger glanced at Pete. "Her kid's here. Her sisters. Besides, she's cocky. She thinks she's going to get away with this."

Connor turned. "What about her sister? Her story sounded plausible to me."

"Both have alibis for the night of Donaldson's murder," Pete informed her. "Plus, there's the matter of the uniform."

Connor arched his eyebrows. "Yes, why don't we talk about the uniform. Why would she wear such an identifiable garment when the situation called for anonymity? She's not stupid."

"He's got a point," the ADA said.

"She's cocky. She doesn't think she's going to be caught. She figures the uniform gives her access to places street clothes wouldn't."

"Like her ex's gated neighborhood," the lieutenant interjected.

"Right." Roger nodded. "Plus, nobody's going to think twice about seeing a cop hanging around. Regular citizens like seeing the police, makes them feel protected."

Connor frowned, admitting silently that their points were valid. "I could give you the names of a half-dozen costume shops that rent authentic-looking police uniforms. And there's nothing that stands out about Whistlestop's that would make it uniquely recognizable."

Connor wasn't sure which investigator looked more irritated, Harrison or Stemmons. Pete, as usual, spoke first. "Fact is, we've got a still-breathing witness who claims Melanie was stalking him. She publicly threatened Boyd Donaldson's life. And she has no alibi for either night."

"There's not enough to charge her," the ADA said, moving her gaze between the room's occupants. "But I think it's a convincing start."

Connor shook his head. "I don't buy any of this. Melanie May is no murderer."

"Hear, hear," her chief echoed.

"Look at your profile, Parks. It was custom-made for her, down to her having been abused by her father and having a working knowledge of law enforcement."

"Wait a minute," Connor said. "Are you really implying that Melanie is the Dark Angel? She brought us the Angel. If she had killed all those men, why would she do that? It makes no sense."

"It makes perfect sense." Roger leaned toward him, expression jubilant. "There is no Dark Angel, Parks. Not really. Melanie created her as an elaborate smoke screen, a 'known' killer on whom to blame the deaths of both her ex-husband and brother-in-law.

"Think about it, she wants to be rid of her ex-husband who's giving her grief. She wants to help her sister, whose husband is knocking her around. She gets an idea, and does a little research, digs up some more 'victims.' Maybe she even builds the body count a bit, for credibility's sake. Thomas Weiss comes along. Somehow, by some accident, she learns about his allergy to bee venom. Jim McMillian has a heart condition, just like dear old dad. What's the difference? she thinks. They're nothing but abusive sons of bitches, just like her father was. Then, once she got everything in place, she went looking for someone who would believe her."

"Enter you, Connor. She meets you at the Andersen crime scene. You're a profiler, you'd worked the BSU at Quantico, this is your area of expertise. If she can convince you, she'll have it made.

Harrison paused; the room was so quiet Connor heard the movement of the second hand on the wall clock. He wanted to debunk the investigator's theory, but he couldn't. It was not only possible, it was ingenious.

"She only made one mistake," Pete continued. "She staged the whole thing to point right at herself. She came to you, Parks. You created a profile of her."

Melanie's chief muttered an oath under his breath. The ADA snapped her briefcase shut and stood. "Get the warrant," she said.

"In the works already." Pete shifted his gaze to Connor. "I'm sorry. I know you've grown close."

"I'm still not convinced."

"We'll know soon enough. If the search turns up something, we'll move forward. If not, we look elsewhere. Simple as that."

55

Melanie made it home, though she couldn't say how. She was shaking so badly she could hardly stand, let alone maneuver through traffic. The police would move quickly, she knew. They would have a search warrant within the hour and would arrive in force.

Melanie climbed out of her Jeep, slamming the door behind her. Dear God, how could this be happening to her? Why? How could Ashley—

Tears swamped her. She fought them off, afraid that once she started to cry, she wouldn't be able to stop. She entered the house through the garage door, though she didn't call out. She hoped to avoid seeing Casey until she felt less frightened, more in control. The last thing she wanted to do was scare him.

She found Mrs. Saunders in the living room, counting aloud. She and Casey were playing hide-and-seek and the baby-sitter was "It."

Melanie struggled for an expression of normalcy. "I'm home."

Her neighbor took one look at her and her face fell. "What's wrong?"

"Is it that obvious?" The woman nodded, and Melanie's shoulders slumped. "Something…terrible's happened. Could you stay a bit longer? I'm going to call my sister Mia and see if she can take Casey for the day.''

The woman agreed to stay and Melanie went to her bedroom to call her sister in private. The other woman answered right away and Melanie said a silent prayer of thanks.

''Mia, it's me.''

''Melanie! I'm so glad you called. I feel awful about the other day. The things I said...I'm so sorry. I don't know what came over—''

Melanie interrupted, feeling the moments slipping quickly away from her. She didn't have much time. ''Something's happened,'' she said. ''Something bad. I...I need you to...Casey—'' She bit the words off, fighting to keep from falling completely apart. ''I'm in trouble, Mia. Can you come?''

''I'll be right there,'' she promised and hung up.

True to her word, Mia was at Melanie's front door in a matter of minutes.

Melanie fell into her sisters arms. ''Thank you,'' she said. ''If you hadn't come... I don't know what I'm going to do, Mia. Someone tried to kill Stan last night and they think...they think it was me!''

''Oh my God.'' Mia held her an arm's length away. ''Calm down and tell me exactly what's happened.''

Melanie did, voice cracking as she fought the urge to dissolve into tears. ''They think I killed Boyd and tried to kill Stan,'' she finished. ''They think I'm the Dark Angel.''

''That's preposterous!''

''Tell *them* that.'' She drew in a shuddering

breath. "I expect them to arrive with a search warrant within the hour. Normally I'd be happy for them to do it...to prove my innocence. But if I'm being framed...who knows what they might—"

Her voice broke and she took a moment to compose herself. "I don't want Casey here when it...when it happens. Can you take him for the day?"

"Of course, Mellie. I'll help you in any way I can."

"There's another thing I need you to do, Mia. It's important." She caught her twin's hands. "You've got to help me find Ashley. She's involved in this."

Her sister's face puckered with confusion. "I don't understand. How's Ashley—"

As quickly as she could, Melanie filled her in. She told Mia about Connor's profile and how their third sister fit it. "And think about it, she pretended to be me, on official business, in Charleston. What would prevent her from doing it again?"

"Yeah but, Mel...I've pretended to be you a million times, but that doesn't mean—"

"That was kid stuff. Charleston wasn't. She had the uniform, the false ID. But that's not all, think about it. As a drug rep, she has access to the kind of information the Dark Angel would have needed. She traveled the Carolinas, which offered the time and opportunity to scout for new victims. Not only am I a cop, but she dated a cop for a while. And in the past weeks it's like she's emotionally unraveling. All of which are characteristics of the profile. She called the night before last, the same night

Stan's granola would have been poisoned. She was talking crazy. Apologizing and begging my forgiveness. For something she had done or was about to do."

Mia brought a hand to her mouth, looking stunned. "My God. Ashley? The Dark Angel. I can't believe it."

"I don't want to. But I don't know what else to think. It all adds up—the knowledge she's privy to, her resemblance to me and her bizarre behavior of late."

"I'll find her," Mia murmured. "Veronica will help me."

"No." Melanie gripped her sister's hands tighter. "She can't, Mia. She's with the district attorney's office. Her loyalty will lie with them."

Mia shook her head. "I know Veronica. She'll help us. She'll help *me*. We're—"

"Aunt Mia!"

Melanie dropped her twin's hands and Mia swung to face Casey. "Hey, tiger!" She opened her arms. "Come give your aunt Mia a big hug."

He raced across the room and threw himself into his aunt's arms. "Did you come to play with us?"

"Even better, buddy. We're going to my house and we're going to spend the whole day together. Just you and me."

His face fell. "Not Mommy?"

It was all Melanie could do not to cry. "I'm sorry, baby. Mommy has to work."

His chin began to quiver, but before he could cry, Mia jumped in. "It's an awfully hot day so I was thinking…would you mind it a whole bunch if we went swimming?''

The tears that had threatened only a second ago vanished and Casey gave a whoop of delight, then looked at Melanie. When she smiled and nodded her approval, he wriggled out of Mia's arms and tore off in search of his swim goggles and flippers. Melanie watched him go, then turned to Mrs. Saunders who was hovering near the door, uncertain of what she should do. Melanie thanked her and walked her out. After waving goodbye to the woman, Melanie returned to her sister. ''I'll pack Casey a bag.''

''Pack enough for overnight, just in case.'' She motioned toward the kitchen. ''Mind if I grab a Diet Coke for the road?''

Melanie told her to help herself, then went after Casey. Together they packed the bag—making sure he had all his favorite toys. That done, they walked to the front door where Mia was waiting.

Melanie bent and hugged him tight. ''I love you,'' she whispered, voice thick. ''Have fun and be a good boy. Listen to Aunt Mia.''

'''Course.'' He hugged her back. ''Love you, too—'' he stepped away and held his chubby arms out wide ''—so much.''

No doubt seeing that Melanie was about to burst into tears, Mia handed the small duffel bag to Casey. ''Better run this out to the car, tiger. Your bathing suit's in there and we wouldn't want to forget that, would we?''

He agreed that they wouldn't and skipped to the car. Melanie watched him go, then turned to Mia, giving in, dissolving into tears, sobbing as she hadn't since her mother's funeral. "This can't be happening."

Mia hugged her, her grip fierce, protective. "We'll get to the bottom of this, sis. We will, I promise."

"Don't let Casey hear anything—"

"I won't."

"The TV. Something might—"

"I know. I'll leave it off."

Melanie rested her forehead against her sister's, her tears abating, comforted beyond words by her twin's very presence. "We have to find Ashley. She's involved, Mia. I know she is."

"I'll work on it. I'll find her, Mel. I promise."

Melanie glanced over at Mia's Lexus. Casey had climbed in and was fastening his seat belt. She started to tremble. "I still can't believe this is happening, Mia. How could Ashley...do this to me?" Her voice broke. "Why would she do it?"

"They're here," Mia whispered. "The police."

Melanie straightened, quickly wiping her eyes. Two cruisers and a nondescript Ford had pulled up in front of her house. Harrison and Stemmons got out of the Ford.

"Go," she said to Mia. "Take Casey now."

Her sister searched her expression a moment, then nodded. "I believe in you, Melanie. It's going to be all right."

She started for the car, nodding to the investigators as she passed them. Melanie waved to Casey, not stopping until Mia had backed out of the driveway and disappeared. Then, and only then, she turned to Pete and Roger.

"You knew we were coming," Pete said, laying the search warrant in her hand.

"Yes." She glanced in the direction Mia had driven, then swept her gaze over the six men assembled at her door. "I didn't want my son here for this."

"I understand."

Melanie opened the door wider. "You're not going to find anything, guys," she said, mustering false bravado, laughable in light of her red nose and tear-streaked cheeks. "What do you say we get this over with so we can all get back to our lives?"

56

As Melanie had feared they would, the police found plenty, all items she had never seen before: a roll of duct tape consistent with the type used to gag Boyd was found under the driver's seat of her Jeep; books on allergies, poisons and autopsy techniques were on her bookshelves; and several pairs of surgical gloves were stuffed under paperwork in her desk drawer.

While the investigators and two members of the forensic team were in her house, the other two combed her vehicle for hair and fiber evidence. According to her lawyer—a top defense attorney her chief had recommended—they found what appeared to be a pubic hair in the same location as the duct tape. It had been sent to the CMPD crime lab for analysis.

Everything they had so far was circumstantial, the attorney told her, not enough to charge her with a crime. However, he added, she needed to prepare herself—if the analysis of the hair came back with a DNA match to Boyd's, he hadn't a doubt they would charge her.

Melanie was stunned. Panicked. On the verge of hysteria. She couldn't believe this was happening to her. Everywhere she turned over the next two days, she was met with suspicion and accusation. People avoided her. They refused her calls. Her chief put her on immediate leave and before the day was over, Stan had secured a temporary custody decree, one that disallowed her to see or speak to Casey. She couldn't even tell him goodbye.

That was the worst. It broke her heart. She couldn't stop worrying about him, what he thought, if he was frightened. It was almost too much to bear.

It would have been if not for Mia. Mia stood beside her, her staunch supporter. Mia paid the attorney's exorbitant retainer and she searched for Ashley, though without luck.

Ashley was missing. Mia had discovered that their third sister hadn't been home in what appeared to be some time—her mailbox was overflowing and a half-dozen newspapers dotted her front porch. When Mia had let herself in to the apartment, she'd found Ashley's answering machine full, her refrigerator nearly empty and the entire home sour-smelling from disuse. Alarmed, Mia had called Ashley's employer, only to learn that she had been fired a week before Boyd's murder.

Learning that, Melanie was even more convinced that Ashley was the one who had set her up. She had to find her—if she didn't, she would be charged with her brother-in-law's murder. She had learned her lesson with the search—she hadn't a doubt that the lab analysis would incriminate her.

The clock was ticking.

Connor.

Other than Mia, he was the only one who might

care enough to try to help her. Connor had the skill and the resources—if anyone could find Ashley, Connor could.

Without pausing to consider the lateness of the hour, Melanie retrieved the tape that contained Ashley's crazy message from the drawer she had stowed it in for safe keeping, then snatched up her purse and car keys and raced out to her Jeep. She needed Connor to believe her. To believe in her.

And, she admitted as she climbed into the car, she needed his arms around her, his reassurance that everything would be all right. Whispering a prayer, she started the engine.

Her prayer went unanswered. He stood before her, his expression and stance unyielding, closed to her. She drank him in anyway, the way a starving person might food or drink. He looked tired. Troubled. The lines around his eyes and mouth appeared more deeply cut than before.

"You shouldn't be here," he said. "Not without your lawyer."

As he began to close the door, she put her hand out, stopping him. "Please, Connor, I didn't do this. You have to believe me."

"It doesn't matter what I believe. We're on opposite sides of this thing."

"It does matter!" she cried. "To me, it matters a lot." She took a step closer to him. "You have to help me, Connor. I have nowhere else to turn."

He looked at her outstretched hand, his expression anguished. "I'm sorry, Melanie. Please try to understand, I can't. The police are mounting a case against you, there's nothing I can—"

"I brought the tape from my answering machine...the one with Ashley's call on it. I saved it. Just listen, please."

"Melanie—"

Her eyes flooded with tears. She began to tremble. "We can't find her. Mia and I... You could help."

Connor said nothing, simply gazed unblinkingly at her. Thinking, she knew. Considering what she had said, judging. One second became many. Still Melanie waited, heart pounding so heavily in her chest she could hardly breathe.

Finally, he shook his head. "I'm sorry, I can't."

A cry of despair ripped past her lips. She caught his free hand with her own, not above begging. "They've taken Casey away from me! Why would I do this, Connor, and chance losing him? I know about the law, I knew after Pete and Roger questioned me that they would get a search warrant, why would I just leave evidence lying around that way? Just listen to the message, that's all I ask. Please, Connor...you know me, I'm not a killer. You know I'm not."

The words landed painfully between them. He hesitated a moment, then with a heavy sigh, stepped away from the door, allowing her to enter. She handed him the tape, then followed him to the kitchen. He removed the tape from his machine and dropped hers in. He pressed play.

Silence greeted them.

The tape had been erased.

57

Melanie watched dawn break over the horizon. Fatigue pulled at her. As did hopelessness. She couldn't shake the strange sense that Stan had finally won. That her father, at long last and from the grave, had beaten her.

She was being punished for a crime she'd had no part in.

Connor hadn't believed her. She had sensed that he wanted to, that he was torn. The blank tape had clinched it for him. After that, what could she say to him? How could she have explained? Who could she have pointed a finger at? The police?

Instead of pointing fingers, she had turned and walked away. Humiliated. Despairing.

Now Melanie frowned, confused. She had plucked the tape cartridge from the machine after the police search. Perhaps Mrs. Saunders had inadvertently hit reset, perhaps she herself had and simply couldn't remember doing it? She had been upset that afternoon, distracted.

Melanie pressed the heels of her hands to her eyes. If she had been honest with Connor from the start, if she had shared her suspicions about Ashley, let him hear the call that night, she wouldn't be in this mess.

The tape had been so convincing. She had nothing now.

Melanie dropped her head into her hands, acknowledging defeat. How much it hurt.

The phone rang. Hoping, praying, that it was Connor, she made a grab for it. "Hello?"

"Is this the home of Melanie May?"

Melanie stiffened. Word had leaked out that she was being investigated in connection with the Dark Angel killings and she'd had to field a lot of calls from reporters. She had learned fast that most of them wouldn't take no for an answer. "Yes, it is."

"My name's Vickie Hanson, I'm with the Rosemont Mental Health Facility in Columbia."

Melanie frowned, confused. "How can I help you?"

"Do you have a sister named Ashley Lane?"

Melanie tightened her grip on the receiver. "Yes, I do."

"Thank goodness!" The woman made a sound of relief. "I'm your sister's psychiatric caseworker and—"

"Excuse me, her what?"

"Her psychiatric caseworker, here at the facility. Let me explain. Friday night your sister attempted suicide. Fortunately, a driver passing on the other side of the bridge stopped and dived in after her. The police brought her here."

"Oh my God." Melanie crossed to a chair and sank onto it. *Ashley? Suicide?* "Is she okay?"

"Physically, she's fine. Emotionally, she's… struggling."

"Why's it taken so long for you to call?"

"When she was admitted she claimed she had no next of kin." The woman paused, Melanie heard what sounded like the snap of a cigarette lighter, then the hiss of flame catching on tobacco. "But last night she began crying out for you. She had to see you, she said. You were in some sort of danger. She became so agitated, we had to sedate her."

Melanie scrambled to put it all together. Something wasn't adding up. "I'm sorry," she said. "When did you say Ashley was committed to your facility?"

"Four days ago. In the middle of the night."

"And she hasn't left the hospital since?"

"Absolutely not."

Melanie processed this new bit of information, stunned by what it meant. Stan ate his granola every morning without fail, even taking containers of it with him on trips. That meant his cereal had been poisoned sometime between Saturday morning and Sunday dawn. During that time, Ashley had been safely ensconced in a psychiatric hospital.

Ashley couldn't have tried to kill Stan. She wasn't the one who had set her up.

Then who was?

"Hello? Mrs. May? Are you still there?"

"It's Ms.," Melanie corrected automatically. "And yes, I'm still here. How can I help?"

"Like I said, she was desperate to see you."

"I'm leaving now."

58

Long after Melanie left, Connor had stood at his front door, hand on the knob, her name poised on his lips. He had wanted to call her back, wanted to so badly that now, hours later, the sense of urgency still pulled at him.

He had let her go anyway, ruled by the mounting weight of evidence against her. Instead of by what he felt in his gut—that she couldn't have done what Harrison and Stemmons said she had, that she wasn't that person.

Everything she had said to him rang true—none of "the evidence" added up, not to him anyway. She was a smart woman and if she had done this thing, there was no way she would jeopardize her life by leaving incriminating evidence just lying around.

Murderers made mistakes all the time. They got cocky, they took chances. They buried victims in their own backyards. They kept souvenirs of their crimes in their homes. They bragged to friends.

Not Melanie. Not smart, courageous, moral Melanie.

He brought the heels of his hands to his eyes, fatigue, self-doubt and despair pulling at him. He recalled the anguish in her voice when she'd told him Stan had taken Casey, relived her cry of disbelief and grief when the answering tape proved blank.

The last time a woman had begged him for help, he had ignored her. He had let his head overrule his gut instinct and she had died.

He had never forgiven himself.

Connor dropped his hands. Murderers would use anyone and anything in an attempt to prove their innocence. Psychopaths were some of the most convincing people on earth. Both he knew from experience, too much experience.

But no matter how much experience he recalled, no matter how many times he reminded himself of the facts, of the weight of evidence against her, Connor still believed Melanie was innocent.

He had fallen in love with her.

The truth of that blindsided him. He took a step backward, as if he had actually been struck. She had sneaked up on him—her integrity, her honesty and fire. The single-minded determination with which she tackled her job, the fierce way she loved her son, the way she made him feel.

Happy to be alive. Grateful for every moment.

He had to tell her. How he felt. That he believed in her. He crossed to the phone, punched in her number and waited. The machine picked up on the fourth ring.

"Melanie, it's me. If you're there, pick up." He waited several seconds, then swore under his breath. "Call me. It's important."

The phone rang before he had a chance to take

his hand off the receiver. He snatched it back up. "Melanie?"

"Connor Parks?"

He stiffened, recognizing an official call by the man's tone. "This is Parks."

"Agent Addison, Charleston satellite office. We've found your sister's remains."

59

Veronica sat bolt upright in bed, a silent scream on her lips. She looked wildly around her, expecting to see the ghouls bearing down on her, their clawlike hands reaching out for her. She saw Mia's familiar bedroom instead, bathed in early morning's soft light.

Veronica brought her trembling hands to her face. It was damp with perspiration. She wiped at the sweat, then brought her hands to her chest, to her pounding heart. It beat so heavily she feared it would burst free of her chest cavity and fly away, like an image she had once seen in a cartoon.

It didn't and she breathed deeply and slowly through her nose, working to calm herself.

She'd had this dream many times before and of late, frequently. A nightmare populated by the undead, their flesh rotting, home to maggots and disease. The stench sickening. In it her father and husband called for her, as did the woman—all laughing when Veronica ran.

There was no escape.

Beside her, Mia stirred, then muttered Veronica's name. Veronica's chest tightened, love seeming to balloon her heart to quadruple its size.

"It's okay," she whispered, bending and brushing her lips against the other woman's temple. "Everything's going to be okay."

As quietly as she could, Veronica climbed out of bed and headed on wobbly legs to the bathroom. She emptied her bladder, then went for her cosmetics case and the bottle of Prozac her doctor had prescribed for her. To help her relax. To reduce the anxiety that held her in its strangling grip. Her dependence on the pills had grown. Of late, she doubted she would have been able to function without them. Even so, she couldn't sleep through the night, she had no appetite for food or drink, no interest in her work. She had lost her last two cases and, she knew, people had begun to talk.

Veronica shook one of the small tablets onto her palm, then recapped the bottle. She took the medication, then washed it down with a glass of water. She started back to bed, stopping in the doorway. Mia lay half uncovered, blond hair fanned across the pillow, cheeks flushed with sleep. Her pink satin nightshirt gaped open at the neck, revealing the milky white curve of one breast.

Emotion exploded inside her and for a moment, Veronica couldn't breathe. Falling in love with Mia had been so easy. Trusting her had been more difficult. Trusting had required Veronica to make a giant leap of faith. Even so, bit by bit, she had allowed the other woman fully into her head and heart. Mia knew all her secrets now. As she knew Mia's.

Veronica found her breath, crossed to the bed and gazed down at her lover. She would give Mia all she possessed, would do all that she asked. Anything to make her happy. Anything to ensure they stayed together.

Anything at all.

60

Just over two hours later, Melanie pulled into the parking lot of the Rosemont Mental Health Facility. The caseworker had given Melanie excellent directions—she had only gotten lost once and that had been the fault of her own inattention.

Melanie pulled the car into a spot, shut off the engine and grabbed her cell phone, making sure it was still on before she dropped it into her purse. Shortly after getting on the road, she had called Mia and left a message, one that detailed the call from the caseworker and Ashley's location.

The Rosemont facility was a rather grim affair, although considering it was a state institution, it could have been much worse. She crossed the lobby to the information desk, introduced herself and asked for Vickie Hanson.

The caseworker appeared almost immediately. A pretty brunette, she smiled and held out a hand. ''Ms. May, the resemblance to your sister is remarkable. She told me she was a third twin, but I wasn't certain if it was—''

''True? That's everyone's reaction.'' Melanie clasped the woman's hand. ''I want to thank you for calling me.''

Vickie's smile faded. ''Your sister is a very troubled young woman. I hope you can help me help her.''

''I hope so, too. I love her very much. Is she awake?''

''Yes.'' The caseworker motioned to the elevators up ahead and they moved toward them. ''I told her you were coming. She said she needed a moment.''

A lump in her throat, Melanie said she understood, but she didn't. Regret and guilt tugged at her. Regret that her sister had come to this, guilt that she hadn't been there for her. Guilt at the fact that while her sister had been drowning in hopelessness, she had been calling her a murderer.

They stepped onto the elevator. The woman pushed the button for the third floor. ''Do you have any idea the root of her problems?''

''I have an idea. What's she told you?''

''Not much. She's extremely depressed and I sense in her a great hostility toward men. Can you tell me a little about the Ashley you know?''

Melanie thought a moment, then a smile touched her mouth. ''Ashley's really smart. And observant about people. She has this biting sense of humor and a willingness to say things nobody else will. Never mean-spirited, though. Not cruel toward others. Just...funny in a caustic kind of way. She's always made us laugh.''

The car reached the third floor and the doors slid open. They stepped off and started down the hall. Melanie continued. ''Ashley's the most intense of the three of us. The moodiest. The most emotionally volatile. Something would upset her and she would erupt. Then it'd be over. Because of that, it wasn't until recently that I realized...until I saw..."

"That she was in trouble?" the caseworker supplied.

"Yes." Melanie stopped and looked at the woman. "I feel awful about this. That I didn't help her. That when I saw the way she was falling apart, I didn't do something. Anything."

"Don't beat yourself up, Melanie. Things like this creep up on family members. Suddenly you're hip deep in a situation you didn't even see coming."

A situation? Was that what this was? Was that what her and her sisters' lives had become? Melanie swallowed hard. "She's a special person, Ms. Hanson."

"I know." The woman indicated the door just ahead on their left. "Why don't you tell her that yourself."

"Maybe we could talk again later?"

"That would be good."

Melanie watched the caseworker walk away, then took a deep breath and eased Ashley's door open a crack. "Ashley," she murmured, peeking into the room. "It's me."

Her sister stood at the window, her back to the door. She held herself rigidly, arms curved tightly around her middle, as if protecting herself against assault. Assault by whom? Her own sister?

"Ash," she said again, stepping into the room. "It's me, Mel."

She turned then. Melanie bit back a cry of dismay at her ravaged appearance. She was thin and pale, her face gaunt, eyes hollow and shadowed.

"Oh, Ash," she whispered, "I didn't know."

Her sister's eyes flooded with tears. "I'm sorry...so...sorry."

Melanie went to Ashley and folded her in her arms. "It's me who's sorry. I didn't know how much you needed me."

Ashley began to cry then, great wracking sobs of despair. Sobs that sounded as if they were drawn from the very bottom of her soul.

Heart heavy, Melanie held her while she cried. She felt so fragile in her arms, small and vulnerable, not the tough-talking, independent and acerbic sister she knew and loved so well.

How could she have seen the beginnings of this devastation and not done something to stop it?

When Ashley's tears abated, Melanie led her to the bed. They sat together in the way they had as children—cross-legged, heads bent, foreheads touching.

Melanie folded her sister's hands in her own. They were as cold as death and she rubbed them between hers. She didn't rush her sister, didn't question her or press for explanation. If Ashley wanted to talk, she would.

And she did, after many minutes had passed. She kept her voice low and she spoke in the way of someone recalling a near-forgotten and unimportant incident from the past.

"Remember when Dad began...molesting Mia?"

Melanie tightened her hands over Ashley's. Even

after all these years, it hurt to hear those words spoken. "I remember."

"You were so brave. The way you pulled that knife on him, I was always in awe of you, Mel. But especially then."

Ashley fell silent, but for only a moment. "He came to me after, though I don't remember how long." Her voice lowered to less than a whisper. Even with their heads pressed together Melanie had to strain to hear. "He said what you'd done...that you'd broken the law. That the police would come, because of the knife. That they could...take you away. Then it would just be me and Mia, he said."

The things she had done for her sisters.

Melanie squeezed her eyes shut, horror dawning. *Dear God, no. Not that. Please, not that.*

"He said if I...if I told you or anyone else what he...that he would do it. Call the police. Have you taken away."

She tightened her grip on Melanie's fingers. Even so, they were damp, clammy. "I kept waiting for you to save me, Mel. The way you saved Mia." Her voice broke. "You never did."

The root of it. The truth.

She had let Ashley down in a way she hadn't even imagined.

"I didn't know," Melanie whispered, tears spilling over. "If only I had known...I would have killed him to save you, Ashley. I would have, I promise."

They held each other, held *on to* each other—the way family was meant to—loving, protecting and above all, cherishing.

"Why? Melanie asked after a long time. "Why didn't you tell me?"

"At first, I was terrified. I believed him, what he'd said. And after, when I realized...I was too ashamed. Because I wasn't strong like you. Because I didn't say...no."

It was the last, perhaps, that hurt the most. In that moment Melanie hated their father as she had never hated before. With a heat and ferocity that frightened her. If he were alive, she would kill him now, she would take her service revolver and blow his head off.

And in that moment, too, she applauded the Dark Angel. She knew the feeling wouldn't last, that reason would win out over primitive emotions, but now, this second, she was glad those men were dead. They had gotten what they deserved.

Suddenly, inappropriately, Ashley giggled. The sound was girlish and carefree, gleeful even. Melanie leaned back and looked at her sister in concern.

Ashley motioned her closer—she bent close to her ear. "I took care of him. For all of us."

Melanie drew away. She searched her sister's expression, heart thundering.

"I killed him, Mel. For us. For you, me and Mia."

The breath seemed to leave Melanie's body—the ability to reason, to speak, fled with it.

"It was so easy," she continued. "You see, I knew what would happen if he took too much of his medication. And I knew how much would raise suspicions...and how much wouldn't. I paid him a visit, I slipped his own prescription into his food."

She smiled, the curving of her lips childlike. "It was easy, Melanie."

Easy. Painless. The world minus one child-molesting son of a bitch.

Melanie took a deep breath. She had to ask. She had to hear the words from Ashley's own lips.

She met her sister's gaze evenly, though it was one of the hardest things she'd ever done. "You have to tell me, Ash. Are you...are you the Dark Angel?"

Ashley looked surprised by the question, then angry. "No. Not me. But I know who is."

61

Connor gazed at the skeletal remains of what had been his sister. A scuba-diving class had discovered her. Discovered them, he corrected. Whoever had killed her had also murdered a man, bound them together in a plastic drop cloth, weighted them with York weights and dumped them into the deepest part of Lake Alexander. Included in the gruesome package was the fireplace poker missing from Suzi's house.

"We wouldn't have been able to identify her so quickly if not for the poker," the young agent standing beside Connor said. "Ben Miller remembered about your sister and put two and two together."

Connor couldn't find his voice. All the years of searching, of wondering, were over. Now he knew.

"Most likely," the rookie agent continued, "she never even knew what hit her."

So the forensic pathologist had told Connor. Judging by Suzi's fractured skull, the size and location of the single large fissure, he had determined that a single blow to the back of her head had killed her. It had been his opinion that she'd been dead before she went in the water.

Thank God for that, Connor thought, shifting his

gaze from his sister's remains to those of her partner. He'd always known he had been overlooking something important in his investigation of her murder. Something obvious. He realized now that he had been blinded by emotion. Blinded by prejudice against her lover, by his own certainty that he *knew* what had happened.

In the process, he had ignored a scenario as old as time.

The jilted wife kills her cheating man. And his lover. The pieces all fit now; it all made sense. The lingerie drawer, the sensible stuff the UNSUB had chosen to pack, the way the scene had been scrubbed.

A wave of sadness moved over him, one of regret. That he couldn't help Suzi, that he couldn't change the past. That the bright light that had been his sister was forever extinguished. She had been too good a person, filled with too much promise, to end up the way she had.

"This UNSUB knew what he was doing." The agent indicated the weights. "We estimated the two weighed around three hundred pounds. The killer used three hundred and thirty pounds of counterweight. The fact that our guy here was drilled in the chest didn't hurt, either."

Connor nodded. To keep a body submerged in water for a long period of time, the counterweight needed to be at least ten percent more than the total body weight since, during decomposition, gases formed that would lift the body to the surface. A puncture in the chest cavity aided submersion as it provided a release for some of the gases—a technique perfected by the Mafia.

He swung toward the rookie. "Do we know who he is yet?"

"Just got a match on the dental records an hour ago. Daniel Ford. A prominent area attorney. Crazy thing is, he was presumed dead in that Jet-Air flight that blew en route to Chicago."

"I remember it." Connor narrowed his eyes, feeling the adrenaline begin to pump through him. The excitement. Finally, after all this time, he would have justice for his sister. "Insurance company pay off?"

"Yup. Check went to the wife. One Veronica Ford."

The hair on the back of Connor's neck stood up. "Veronica Ford," he repeated. *Melanie's friend. The assistant D.A.*

"We don't know much about her yet. She's a Markham. Her old man was a wheel in Charleston, a big local benefactor. He gave to nearly every cause in town."

"Was?" Connor repeated, looking at the other agent, knowing the answer to his next question before asking it. "He's dead?"

"Yeah, a few years back. It was in all the papers. Died in a freak—"

"Accident," Connor supplied. "Son of a bitch." He flipped open his cell phone and punched the Charlotte field office number, all the while snapping orders to the rookie. "I need the coroner's report on Markham and a chopper. ASAP." He switched his attention to his call. "Steve, Connor.

I'm in Charleston. I need a warrant for the arrest of Assistant District Attorney Veronica Ford. For the murders of Daniel Ford, Suzi Parks and a yet unknown number of victims. She's our Dark Angel, Steve. We got her.'' His voice thickened. "I got her.''

62

Melanie rang Mia's bell, then pounded on the door with her fist, urgency pulling at her.

Veronica was the Dark Angel killer. Veronica was the one who had been setting her up.

Ashley had seen it, though sideways, through her distorted sense of reality. She had become obsessed with Veronica, an obsession spawned from jealousy over the woman's relationship with her sisters. She had become convinced that something was off about the other woman, that she was not what she seemed.

Through tricks like the one she pulled at the Charleston D.A.'s, Ashley had discovered that Veronica had been friends with a couple of women whose spouses had died suddenly and in freakish circumstances. A fact she had noted, but one that hadn't registered as being more than odd.

She'd uncovered another oddity while following Veronica. The woman kept unusual hours and visited unlikely places—interstate truck stops, all-night diners and swingers' clubs. And although Ashley had often waited hours, her gaze trained on the lawyer's car, Veronica hadn't reappeared on several occasions.

Other people had come and gone—one of whom

Ashley remembered seeing several times—a hard-looking blonde outfitted totally in black leather. Until Ashley had seen a news clip about Melanie being investigated for both Boyd's and the Dark Angel murders, she hadn't put it all together.

The pieces fit so neatly, Melanie acknowledged. She and Veronica were the same size, general build and coloring. Since Boyd's death, Veronica had been staying with Mia. Through Mia, Veronica had access to Melanie's schedule, the keys to her house, her spare car keys—she could even have learned about Stan's homemade granola. And Mia often picked up her sister's dry cleaning, which included her Whistlestop PD uniforms.

And who better to set up to take a fall for Boyd's murder than Melanie? Veronica had deduced, correctly, that since the other deaths were all speculative, the police might conclude that the Dark Angel was a hoax perpetrated by Melanie to cover up the murders of her ex-husband and brother-in-law. Melanie had motive and opportunity—she fit Connor's profile.

But so did Veronica—her age, educational level, knowledge of the law and her background of abuse. Her mother's suicide, the way Veronica had seemed to change in the past few months, her friendship with Mia and Boyd's subsequent death.

It all fit.

Melanie pounded on Mia's door again. She had left her sister several messages from the car and she'd been certain she would be home by now. Mia would be able to place more of the puzzle, she would be able to confirm things Melanie could only guess about.

The sidelight drape fluttered and Mia peeked out, then opened the door.

"Mia, thank God!" Melanie said as she stumbled across the threshold. "Where have you been?"

"Running. I just got your messages, what in heaven's name—"

"You've got to listen...I know who's been setting me up. It's not Ashley...I talked to Ash, she helped me see... Mia, I know who the Dark Angel is!"

Her sister caught her hands. "Melanie, slow down. You're talking crazy."

"It's not crazy. I need your help. We need to put our heads together and—"

"First, we sit." Mia closed and locked the door, then led her to the living room. Mia took a seat on the couch. Melanie remained standing, too agitated to be calm or still.

"Okay, Melanie," Mia said, folding her hands in her lap. "Start at the beginning, tell me everything."

"Yes, Melanie," Veronica said from behind her. "Tell us everything."

Melanie turned slowly, gooseflesh crawling up her arms. The lawyer stood in the doorway between the kitchen and living room. She was dressed identically to Mia—running shorts and shoes, a T-shirt.

She moved farther into the room. "And please do start at the beginning. The point where you decided to kill your ex-husband."

Melanie thought of Casey, of Connor and everything she had been through in the past days and was so angry she shook. "That's what you wanted the world to believe, wasn't it, Veronica? But it's all over now. I know about you. And soon, everyone else will, too."

"You should have been a writer," Veronica said, smiling coldly. "Fiction, of course." She went to the coffee table, opened the decorative box at its center. When she turned, Melanie saw that she had a gun. "You're a killer, Melanie May. You killed your sister's husband, you attempted to kill your own ex-husband. The police have proof."

"Evidence you planted!"

"How many men's lives have you taken?" Veronica asked, moving closer. "How many bastards who deserved to die? How many cruel, little men who'd slipped through the fingers of justice?"

"Is that why you killed all of those men?" Melanie longed to look over her shoulder at Mia, but was afraid to take her eyes from Veronica. She prayed that when the time came, her sister would be capable of doing what needed to be done. "Because they deserved to die? Because you were a helpless victim once? Is that why you became the Dark Angel?"

"The Dark Angel?" She repeated the words on a sneer. "That's your name for her. It's not right and she doesn't like it. She's an angel of mercy. Of justice."

"Really? And how many men are dead because of her mercy?" Melanie arched her eyebrows in exaggerated disbelief. "Six? Ten? Twenty?"

"Is she supposed to feel bad about that? Get a

clue, Melanie. The world's a much better place without those twelve pieces of human refuse. You know it, you're just too afraid to admit it's true."

Twelve. There had been twelve victims so far. "Maybe you're right. Maybe I am scared. Too scared to step in and help. That's what she does, right? Help women in trouble?"

Veronica's lips curved in a self-satisfied smile. "Men like that, they never change. No matter how much you love them, no matter how hard you try to please them. You give and give until you've got nothing more to offer. And still, they hurt you. They betray you. All men like that know is cruelty."

"The Angel understands that," Melanie offered. "But the women didn't, they needed guidance."

"Exactly. If she helped them, they would see, too. If she helped them, they'd have another chance. A fresh start."

She and Connor had been right. The women were the link, not the men. "So, what did she do?" Melanie asked, inching closer. "Befriend the woman, then get close to the man? Learn his strengths? His weaknesses?"

"Everybody has a weakness," Veronica agreed. "A place where they're especially vulnerable to attack. The trick is finding that place." She laughed to herself, as if remembering, and shook her head. "Sometimes you don't even need a trick, just the guts to go for it. Like with your Thomas Weiss. She learned about his allergy to bee venom without ever talking to him. She learned everything she needed to know sitting at the Blue Bayou bar, sipping wine and listening.''

The pride in Veronica's voice turned Melanie's stomach. "And let me guess, the first woman she helped was herself.''

"There are no accidents, Melanie, only surprise visits from angels of mercy. But only to the very lucky. She was one of those.''

Veronica went on, telling both women about the Angel's childhood, about her cold, critical father and how she had always tried to measure up in his eyes. She told them about her mother, how, despondent over her husband's inattention, she took a gun, put it in her mouth and pulled the trigger.

"But still, the Angel longed for love," Veronica murmured. "She prayed for a man who would adore her. Finally, she thought she had found him. His name was Daniel. He was everything she'd dreamed of, handsome, charming, successful. He swept her off her feet.

"But he was like the rest—small and cruel. She lived in fear of making even the simplest decision, for if she chose wrong she would face swift retribution. She never knew when the violence would erupt...never.''

Melanie swallowed hard, familiar with the scenario, discomfited by it. She dared a glance over her shoulder at Mia, frozen on the couch. She saw the recognition in Mia's expression, too.

Veronica's expression softened with sympathy. "She picked you, Melanie, because she could relate to your situation. Like your ex-husband, hers controlled her by keeping her down, down low.

"He bought her a gun, supposedly so she could protect herself when he was out of town. Instead, he taunted her with it. Taunted her with her mother's suicide. When would she do it? When would she blow her brains out?"

Veronica paused a moment, as if to reorganize her thoughts. "She began to suspect he was having an affair. She confronted him."

"But he denied it."

"Of course. So, she followed him. She learned his lover's name, where she lived. This time when she confronted him, she was prepared. She threatened to run to her father. How long, she had demanded, would he keep Daniel on the payroll once he knew?

"He broke down and begged. Pleaded for another chance, promised the affair was over. It was so unlike him, she allowed herself to believe he really loved her. That he'd changed."

"But he hadn't changed," Melanie murmured. "Had he?"

Veronica's mouth thinned. "He had a rich wife—that was what he loved. A wife whose father had made him a millionaire overnight." She glanced down at the gun, then back up at Melanie. "Several days later, she drove him to the airport. He was scheduled for a meeting in Chicago, he would be gone only until late that night. As was their custom, she walked him to the gate, kissed him goodbye, watched him board with the other first-class passengers, then she walked away. The plane exploded midflight. There were no survivors."

"But her husband wasn't on that flight, was he?" Melanie murmured.

"She didn't know that, not for hours. Not until late that night, when he walked through their front door. Very much alive, not a wrinkle in his Italian suit.

"At first she was overjoyed. Then confused. He was alive. He, obviously, knew nothing of the air disaster. Then she realized why. He hadn't been on that flight. He'd been with his lover. He had tricked her, had her drive him to the airport and walk him to the gate so she wouldn't be suspicious. So she wouldn't have cause to doubt him and go running to her father.

"She flew into a rage, accusing him of walking off the flight as soon as she'd left the gate area, of spending the day with *her.*"

Veronica shook her head, remembering. "He laughed at her fury. He taunted her. What would she do if it were true? Would she kill herself, the way her mother had? He urged her to do it. He went to her nightstand, he got out the gun and tossed it onto the bed. Do it, he urged her. Just like her pathetic mother. Get it over with.

"I heard the shower," Veronica said, slipping into first person, not seeming to even notice she had done it. "I stared at the gun, a part of me wanting to do it. To pick it up, bring it to my mouth and pull the trigger. It'd be so easy, so quick. I wouldn't hurt, never again.

"I reached for it. But as I did, something came over me. Something clear and strong, something freeing. I was filled with a sensation of pure power. Of purpose.

"I got the gun. I cocked it. But instead of turning it on myself, I walked into the bathroom, pulled aside the shower curtain and blew a hole in him."

"My God," Melanie murmured.

Veronica went on as if she hadn't spoken. "He was naked, the shower washed away the blood. I went out to the garage in search of a plastic drop cloth I'd used recently. I rolled him onto it, then tied the package with some nylon rope I also found in the garage. I figured I'd attach some of the weights from Daniel's home gym to the bundle and drop him in the lake."

"Lake?" Melanie repeated.

"We had a weekend house on Lake Alexander, about two and a half hours north. It, like everybody else's, was closed up for the winter. There'd be nobody around to see what I was doing."

Veronica laughed. "I felt so good, so powerful. Invincible. I was free of him. And nobody would know."

"Because he was already dead," Mia supplied, voice high and strange-sounding. "It was the perfect crime."

"Except the lover," Melanie corrected. "But you knew her name and address."

"In the end, I added her to Daniel's bundle, finding poetic justice in the fact that they would be together forever."

"And no one came looking for him," Mia murmured. "Not ever."

"Not ever." She smiled, the curving of her lips

as self-satisfied as a cat's. "My life was changed after that. It was good. *I* was good. I finished law school. I promised myself I'd never be a victim again. And I've never looked back. Never had to."

Her smile disappeared. "Until now, Melanie. Everything was going great until you came along. You had to go and be supercop and ruin it all. Why couldn't you have just kept your nose out of my business? Why couldn't you have taken no for an answer?"

"Don't blame me for your mistakes. You got sloppy. I brought you Thomas Weiss, for God's sake. Didn't you think I'd note the strangeness of his death? Didn't you think I'd read about Jim McMillian's death and put two and two together?"

"No one else did." Angry color flew into her cheeks. "*You* were my mistake, Melanie. I picked you. At Starbucks, I overheard you and your sisters talking. I heard about your troubles with Stan. About Mia's with Boyd. I liked you both immediately, I felt for you. I wanted to help."

At Melanie's disbelieving expression, she rolled her eyes. "Do you really think it was an accident we ended up at the same dojang? That we became such fast friends so quickly? Of course not. I *chose* you. And Mia. To make your lives better. And now look what you've done."

Melanie felt ill. It had been so easy for the other woman to come into her life and destroy it. Into her sisters' lives. She had made it so easy for her.

Melanie swallowed her own feelings and focused instead on Veronica. "Is that what you're doing now?" she asked, intensely aware of the gun, though purposefully keeping her gaze from it. "Helping me? By ruining my life? By making me out to be a killer? With friends like you, Veronica, I don't need enemies."

"This is your fault!" Veronica's voice rose. "Not mine. Everything that's happened to you—"

"You're a murderer. A common criminal. One of the scumbags you supposedly dedicated your life to putting behind bars."

"No." Veronica shook her head. "The women I helped deserved happiness. They deserved a life without fear. I gave them that."

"Easy to justify that way, isn't it?" Melanie inched slightly forward. If she could get close enough, catch Veronica by surprise, she might be able to wrestle the weapon away from her. "But aren't we each responsible for taking charge of our own lives?"

"It doesn't work like that. Not for a woman trapped in a cycle of abuse. Not for a woman who—"

"Other than God, only a court and jury of peers can decide who lives and who dies." She took a step closer, finally within striking distance. "Only the system can mete out punishment."

"That's bullshit!" Veronica gestured with the weapon, looking rattled. "The system falls down. They all fall down!"

Melanie made her move. With a roundhouse kick, she knocked the gun out of Veronica's hand. It sailed across the room.

She shouted for Mia to get it, even as she followed the kick with a two-punch combination, placing both perfectly.

Veronica stumbled backward. From the corners of her eyes, she saw Mia scramble for the gun.

The moment of inattention cost her. Veronica was on her feet and ready. With a cry so fierce it sent a shiver up Melanie's spine, Veronica attacked. She landed her kick dead in Melanie's chest. Pain exploded inside her—she saw stars.

With a triumphant shout, Veronica advanced. Melanie struggled to her feet, managing to block the woman's next blows. Her chest was on fire, her muscles screamed with the effort.

Veronica placed another kick and Melanie lost her footing and with it her ability to adequately block the other woman's attack.

"You can't beat me, Melanie," the attorney said, looming closer. "You never have, because I'm better than you."

Veronica moved in for the kill. Melanie threw herself sideways, out of harm's way, rolled, then was on her feet in the ready position. The move caught Veronica by surprise and it cost her her balance. Not about to give the other woman a chance to recover, Melanie attacked.

She placed her kick fully to the side of Veronica's head. The woman went down. In a flash, Melanie pinned her, fist raised for the final, disabling blow.

"Look who's on top now?" Melanie said, panting. "Look who's beaten who?"

Veronica smiled. Her teeth were bloody. "I wouldn't be so certain of that."

"Let her up, Mellie." From behind her came the distinctive click of a gun being cocked. "Now."

63

The chopper propelled its way toward Charlotte, estimated time of arrival twelve and a half minutes. Not soon enough, as far as Connor was concerned. He told the pilot so, then radioed CMPD headquarters. Rice had followed through on Connor's request—he contacted Chief Lyons, a warrant had been issued for Veronica Ford's arrest, a team had been sent to her home and to the D.A.'s office to retrieve her.

"Where's Officer May?" he asked. "I've been trying to reach her for several hours with no luck."

"She's been a busy lady this morning. Our tail followed her to Rosemont, a community just this side of Columbia. She visited a psychiatric facility there."

Connor frowned. "Did your man find out why?"

"Negative. He didn't want to blow his cover."

"Where is she now?"

"At her sister Mia's house. She's been there approximately thirty minutes. Our guys are parked out front."

Connor swore under his breath. He should be relieved, but he wasn't. His gut told him something was not right about the situation.

The truth was, he wasn't going to feel comfortable, or relieved, until Melanie was safe in his arms.

"I need that address," Connor barked. "And the coordinates of the heliport closest to it. Have a car there, waiting for me. Can you handle that?"

"Hold, please."

A moment later the radio crackled and a man came on the line. "Parks, Roger Stemmons here. Got your car. Officer White will be there waiting with the keys."

"Thanks, Stemmons."

"More good news in the Andersen case, we've got positive fingerprint and blood-type matches. DNA and trace results won't be back for a while, but we've already got enough for a conviction. Thought you'd want to know."

Connor smiled. *Score one for the good guys.*

"We all appreciate your help on that one, Parks," the investigator said. "Not that you still don't bug the shit out of me."

"My pleasure, on both counts." Connor checked his watch. "Do me a favor, Stemmons, keep that tail on Melanie until I get there. I've got a bad feeling about this."

"You've got it. Though I expect Ford to be brought in at any moment. Melanie can rest easy now, it's over for her."

64

Melanie glanced over her shoulder. Her sister held the gun with both hands, her grip rock steady, face set.

Problem was, she had the weapon trained on Melanie, not Veronica.

"Mia, what are you—"

"I said, let her up." She motioned with the gun. "Now."

Melanie backed off the other woman, who scrambled to her feet. She sent Melanie a triumphant glance, then limped over to stand beside Mia.

"Are you okay?" Mia asked the attorney, not taking her eyes from her sister.

"Fine." Veronica wiped her mouth with the back of her hand. "Nice moves, Melanie. I confess, I didn't think you had it in you."

"I don't understand." Melanie looked from one woman to the other. "Mia...didn't you hear what she said? She's a murderer. A serial killer. She—"

"It's you who doesn't understand, sister-dear." She looked at Veronica. "Come here, baby. Let Mia make it all better."

Veronica sidled up to Mia, wrapping her arms around her from behind.

Melanie took an involuntary step backward, a sound of shock slipping past her lips.

Veronica laughed. "That's right, Officer May, we fell in love. We're lovers." She nuzzled Mia's neck. "I'd do anything for her and she'd do anything for me."

Melanie shook her head. *This couldn't be happening. It couldn't.* She looked pleadingly at her sister. "Think this through, Mia. Veronica's a killer. If you side with her you're an accomplice after the fact. It's not only wrong, it's—"

"What?" Mia demanded. "Stupid? Is that what you were about to say? That poor, pathetic Mia is making yet another mistake?"

"No!" She held a hand out to her sister, pleading. "Please, just take a moment, consider the consequences of your actions. If you do this you're no better than she is."

"Think it through?" she repeated, anger seeming to explode from her. "Consider the consequences? Like I'm a child. Or an idiot."

"I didn't mean that. I just know—"

"Shut up! Just shut the hell up! I'm sick to death of your lectures. Of your oh-so-sage advice. Melanie knows best," she mocked. "Melanie's so strong and smart. Melanie's the good one. The one who deserves love. Not Mia."

"That's not true!" Melanie cried. "I've never felt that way. Never!"

"Bullshit, Melanie. You did. And so did everyone else, because they took their cues from you, little Miss Perfect. Nice being looked up to, isn't it? Nice always being the one who's right. There wasn't room for anyone else there at the top, now, was there?''

Melanie brought a hand to her stomach, her sister's verbal attack hurting more than Veronica's blows had. ''I don't understand why you're so...angry,'' she said, voice shaking. ''I tried to protect you. I only wanted you to be safe and happy. That's all.''

''Get off it, Melanie.'' Mia narrowed her eyes. ''We both know the truth. You like being the strong sister. The big hero, charging in to save the day.''

''No.'' She shook her head. ''No.''

''I wouldn't have needed saving if not for you. *You're* the reason Dad targeted me. Two's too many, Melanie. It's always been too many.''

''But we're not two, Mia. We're three. Ashley's one of us.''

Mia made a sound of pity. Of disgust. ''She's not a part of us. She came after. Separately. She's the outsider. A mistake.''

Outsider? Mistake? Melanie couldn't believe this was her beloved Mia standing before her with a gun, such vitriol spilling from her lips. Such hatred.

Melanie thought of her conversation with Ashley earlier that day, thought of the secret Ashley had revealed and tears burned her eyes. Would it have made a difference if Mia knew the offense their other sister had endured for them?

Not hardly, Melanie realized. The sister she'd thought she knew, the person she had loved and trusted, didn't exist. Mia didn't care about anyone but herself and her own skewed view of life. She couldn't be reasoned with, nor could her humanity be appealed to. She had neither. She was a twisted shell. And what there was of her was ugly.

"Did you always resent me?" Melanie asked, voice quivering. "Every time I championed you, every time I stepped between you and Dad, what was I doing? Poking at a festering wound? Would it have better if I'd done nothing?"

"You're feeling sorry for yourself now." Mia cocked her head, the curving of her lips bloodless. "I rather like you this way, Mellie. Pathetic and groveling. Perhaps we should have had this little tête-à-tête years ago. Of course, it's only now that I've been able to bring all the pieces together."

Years ago. Bring all the pieces together. Realization dawned. With it fresh betrayal, so strong and sharp it ripped her wide open. "You knew," she said, voice broken. "Before today, about Veronica...that she killed Boyd...the others?" Melanie brought a hand to her mouth. "Oh, my God...Stan. You knew about him, too. You knew Veronica...you knew she was setting me up to take the fall for Boyd's murder."

For a moment, Mia said nothing. Then she laughed, the sound so cold, Melanie shuddered. "How blind and stupid can you be? Veronica didn't set you up, I did. I poisoned Stan's cereal. I planted the evidence in your house and car. *Me,* Melanie. Pathetic, weak-willed Mia."

Melanie struggled to come to grips with her sister's words, with what she had done. She struggled to right her reeling world. "You erased the tape of Ashley's call. Before the search, when you came to get Casey."

"Bingo." She grinned. "Diet Coke, anyone?"

"And my uniform? You picked it up at the cleaners, no questions asked."

"It fit like a glove." She took a step closer, and Melanie instinctively backed up, repulsed. "It was so easy to play you, ridiculously easy, just like when we were kids. I'll miss that when you're gone, Mellie. Really I will."

"Don't do this, Mia," Melanie said, curving her arms around her middle. "Casey needs me. He needs his mother."

"He'll have his loving aunt to temper his father's rigidity. And to help him through his grief."

Melanie thought of this sick, twisted woman having anything to do with raising Casey, and a cry of denial rushed to her lips.

Mia looked at Veronica. "Who would have thought Melanie would try to kill her own sister?"

"Yes." Veronica clucked her tongue. "Who would have thought it? It's a good thing you had a gun to protect yourself."

Mia aimed the gun directly at Melanie's chest. "Here's to never being second best again."

"Wait! That doesn't make sense! I'm unarmed. How could I have tried to kill you?"

The women exchanged glances. Veronica spoke first. "You knew your sister had a gun."

"That's right," Mia chimed in. "I bought it to protect myself against Boyd. I was frightened for my life."

"You told Melanie about it. You showed her the hiding place."

"But why would I try to kill you?" Melanie said

quickly, heart hammering. "Don't you think the police will wonder? When police wonder, they start snooping around." She heard the desperation in her own voice and tried to quell it. "They ask questions."

Mia's grip on the gun slipped slightly. She glanced at Veronica, showing the first bit of hesitation.

"They won't this time," Veronica said. "You were the lead suspect in both a murder and an attempted murder. They had you dead to rights."

Mia chimed in. "You came here to enlist my help in leaving the country. But Veronica was here, she tried to talk you into giving yourself up. Into doing the right thing."

"You went crazy," Veronica supplied. "You attacked me…I have the bruises to prove it. It makes all the sense in the world. I know the way the system works, they'll be happy another case is closed, the taxpayers' money intact."

Melanie fought to control her growing panic. Their story wasn't bad, considering the evidence against her. And Veronica was right—for simplicity's sake, the police would probably lap it up.

"Ashley knows," she said, voice high, pleading. "She won't let this pass. She won't sit back and—"

"Poor old Ashley's got herself locked up in a loony bin, so who's going to believe her over me and an assistant district attorney?" Mia shook her head, disapproving. "Nobody, that's who. Besides, I'm afraid a tragic accident may befall our beloved sister."

"No! Please, Mia, leave Ashley be."

"Still playing the hero, I see." Her mouth thinned. "Give it a rest, Melanie. It's such a bore."

Melanie fought hopelessness. She couldn't die now. She couldn't die with everyone believing her a killer. Especially Casey. Dear God, especially Casey. Tears swamped her. She wanted her son, to hold him in her arms, to watch him grow.

And she wanted to tell Connor she loved him. She wanted that chance. At love. At a family and a forever.

Mia took steady aim, her lips once again curving into a glacial smile. "Goodbye, Melanie."

65

When he got no answer after ringing the bell, Connor pounded on Melanie's sister's front door. "Mia Donaldson!" he called. "Connor Parks, FBI. I need to speak with you about your sister Melanie. It's urgent."

Just as he was about to pound again, the door cracked open. He held up his ID. "Mia Donaldson?" he asked.

"Yes? Can I help you?"

She opened the door several inches wider, and as he had the first time he had come face-to-face with Melanie's twin, Connor experienced a moment of disorientation. The woman peering around the edge of the door was a mirror image of Melanie—but not quite. It was as if her face had undergone the subtlest of distortions, though he couldn't put his finger on exactly the difference between the two women.

"We met the other day. I'm an associate of your sister's. I need to speak with her. It's urgent." When she hesitated, he said, "I know she's here, her car's in your driveway." He laid his hand on the door, prepared to push his way in if necessary. "Tell her it's official business."

She glanced over her shoulder, then back at him. "Of course, come in."

He stepped inside. She motioned him forward, toward the living room located dead ahead. "Have a seat. I'll get her."

She left him, circling around the foyer to the left and disappearing through an opening that led to another room. He did as she requested, moving forward into the living room, though he didn't sit.

As he had the last time he was here, Connor studied the room. The furniture and artwork, the expensive details. But what interested him most were the photographs, the majority of them of three girls, at various ages, who looked so much alike it was disconcerting.

Yet, in each he picked out Melanie. Her bold smile, even as a youngster, was unmistakable.

Connor became aware of the time passing. Of the absolute, unnatural quiet. He checked his watch, noting that at least five minutes had passed. The hairs on the back of his neck prickled.

Something wasn't right here.

He brought his hand to his shoulder holster, to his Beretta. As was the practice of many of the agents, he carried the 9mm semiautomatic cocked and locked—a round already loaded in the chamber. He unsheathed it and released the safety.

"Welcome, Agent Parks. Mia will relieve you of that."

Connor turned slowly. Melanie stood in the doorway to what he saw was the kitchen. Veronica Ford was behind her, anchoring Melanie to her with an arm around her waist. She held the barrel of a small revolver to Melanie's head.

Mia ducked around them and crossed to where he stood. She held out a hand. "Your gun."

He didn't hesitate. He handed it to her and she motioned with it toward the kitchen. "After you."

He looked at Melanie and she met his eyes. The regret in hers broke his heart. "I didn't know we were having a party," he said. "I would have dressed up."

Mia nudged him between his shoulder blades with the gun. "No talking."

He ignored her and looked directly at Veronica. "You don't really think you're going to get away with this, do you?"

"Quite the contrary, we're *certain* we're getting away with it."

"That's awfully arrogant, especially considering that the police know—"

Mia jabbed the gun into his back, hard enough to make him wince. "I said, shut up."

Veronica backed herself and Melanie into the kitchen, allowing him full access to the doorway. His heart sank when he saw what awaited them there—two ladder-back chairs had been pulled from around the kitchen table and set up, back to back in the middle of the large room. The two chairs were secured to each other with duct tape.

"Come on, stud," Mia said. "One of those seats has your name on it."

He glanced at Melanie. Though obviously terrified, she wore a look of intense concentration. She was doing the same as he—desperately trying to come up with a way out of this predicament.

He took the seat. "The way I see it," he said as Mia quickly began securing his arms and legs to the chair with the tape, "your tying us up is either a way to buy some time or you're planning to shoot us where we sit. It's only fair that you clue us in on your plans. It does concern us, after all."

Neither woman responded. Mia finished with him, then motioned for Veronica to bring her Melanie.

Undaunted, he tried another tack. "I confess to being a little surprised with the scenario here. I had no idea you were one of the bad guys, Mia. Did you know, Mellie?"

He purposely used what he knew her sister's pet name for her was. Melanie shook her head. "No," she whispered. "I didn't."

"The other thing that confuses me is the chain of command here." He attempted to move his arms, then legs, testing the strength of his bonds. "It seems to me that Mia's head honcho. Would that be an adequate assessment of the situation, Veronica?" He twisted to look at her. "Have you been demoted?"

She looked at Mia, as if for approval. Mia gave her head a small shake, and he chuckled.

"See, that's just what I'm talking about. What's the deal, you two screwing each other or something? Is there some weird who's-on-top thing happening here?"

Mia bent to look him dead in the eyes. "Shut the fuck up. Or I'll do it for you. Got that?"

He returned her gaze unflinchingly. "Got it."

The two women left the room, no doubt to discuss a course of action and get their stories straight. He suspected his arrival had thrown a big-time monkey wrench in their day.

"Why, Connor?" Melanie asked, voice cracking. "Why did you have to come?"

Because I love you. He opened his mouth to tell her but said instead, "The police know about Veronica. They've issued a warrant for her arrest. They sent officers to the D.A.'s office and her home. I came to tell you it was all over."

"Thank God." She expelled her breath in a rush. "Now, Casey won't...he won't grow up thinking his mother was a murderer."

"They're not going to get away with this, Melanie. No matter what happens to us, you can count on that."

Melanie nodded and sucked in a broken-sounding breath. "She set me up, Connor. My own sister. All these years...she hated me. Everything I did for her made her resent me more. All I know...I only...I loved her."

Her voice cracked and Connor fought against his constraints, cursing them, his inability to hold her in his arms and comfort her. If given that opportunity again, he vowed, he would never let her go.

"I'm sorry," he said softly. "But not just about that. About last night. I wanted to believe you. After you left, I called to tell you."

"Forget it, Connor. That seems a lifetime ago already."

"Not to me. We might not make it. I want you

to know, I believed in your innocence. I called to tell you that together we'd work it out. That we'd figure out who was framing you. You didn't answer. I left a message. Actually, since then I've left about a half-dozen messages."

She would never get that message now. None of them.

Unless he got them out of this.

A sound escaped her, part laugh, part sob—as if she had just thought the same thing as he. "Thank you, Connor. That means everything to me."

"Listen, Melanie...we don't have much time and there's something else I have to tell you. Before it's too late.

"I love you. I've fallen in love with you. And before you ask, yes, I love Casey, too. He's a great kid. But this isn't about him. It's about you and me and the way you make me feel. Wonderful, Melanie. You make me feel...wonderful."

A sound escaped her, one that sounded part joy, part despair. "I love you, too, Connor."

He tipped his head back so it rested against hers, the only caress available to him. *He wouldn't let it—them—end this way. He wouldn't.* "I say let's figure a way out of this thing so we can live happily ever after. What do you say?"

She laughed, the sound small and strangled. "If you insist, Agent Parks."

"I do, Officer May."

From the other room came the sound of the women approaching. "Here's the plan," he said quickly, keeping his voice low. "Eventually somebody's going to remember that Veronica and Mia are big buddies and that we've been missing a while. They'll send somebody over here. The more time we can buy, the better. I say we try to rattle them, then pit them against each other. I'll begin. Agreed?''

Before Melanie could respond, the women reentered the room. Connor didn't waste a moment. ''I was just informing Melanie of the latest developments in the Dark Angel investigation. Shall I fill you in?''

Mia leveled him with a disinterested stare. ''I think we're a little beyond that, don't you?''

''Are we?'' He shifted his gaze to Veronica. Of the two, she was definitely the less composed. It wouldn't take much, he decided, to shake her up. ''A warrant's been issued for your arrest, Veronica. As well as a statewide APB.''

''Sure they have.''

''But they have. That's what happens when you kill your husband and his girlfriend. Certainly you didn't think you would get away with it forever?''

Veronica paled. Mia looked at her, frowning. ''Melanie told you that while we were out of the room,'' she said.

''Sorry, but you're not that lucky. You shot your husband in the chest, at point-blank range. His girlfriend you whacked over the head with a fireplace poker. You wrapped them up in plastic, weighted them and dumped them together into Lake Alexander.'' He smiled. ''Any of this story sound familiar?''

Veronica looked sick. Her grip on the gun seemed to slip. Connor pressed on, hating her for what she had done to his sister, enjoying every moment of her discomfort. "Of course, as we know, you didn't stop there. It felt so good, so freeing to be rid of your husband, you killed your father next."

Behind him, Melanie sucked in a quick breath—obviously the last had been a piece of information she hadn't known. "You had to find a more subtle approach, however. It's one thing to want to punish all the men in your life, it was another to actually get caught doing it. You settled on a sailing accident. He shook his head. "You used your father's passion for sailing against him, didn't you? Just as you used some your other victims' passions against them. Passions like hunting and motorcycling. Sloppy, Veronica. It linked you directly to the crimes."

He looked Veronica dead in the eyes. "I'll bet you don't have a clue who I am. Or should I say, who my sister was. Suzi Parks. Name ring a bell?" Veronica's already pale face became ashen. She brought a hand to her mouth.

A howl of fury rose up in Connor, one of grief. This woman had murdered his sister. In cold blood, without remorse, she had taken her life. "That's right," he murmured, holding in his rage. "Your husband's girlfriend was my sister. The one you murdered."

"She was screwing her husband!" Mia snapped. "She deserved what she got."

Connor balled his hands into tight fists, but didn't take his gaze from Veronica's. "She didn't know her lover was married and when she found out, she tried to break it off. He threatened her. He said he would kill her if she did." He let that sink in, then went on. "She was just like you, Veronica. His victim."

The lawyer didn't speak, though her mouth moved, as if she wanted to but no sound would come out. He pressed on. "I thought the Dark Angel was about righting wrongs, about serving justice to the unjust. Is killing an innocent girl what you call justi—"

"Shut up!"

That came from Mia. Connor ignored her. Veronica had begun to shake so badly the gun in her hands bobbled in front of her.

"Justice?" he finished, making a sound of disgust. "And now you're going to kill me and Melanie? Why? Because your *girlfriend* wants you to? Because she's so jealous of her sister she can't see strai—"

"I told you to shut the fuck up!" Mia grabbed the gun from Veronica, and turned toward him. In that instant, he realized he'd pushed too hard, that this time he'd bought it. He sucked in a sharp breath and said a quick, silent prayer for Melanie.

In the next instant, pain exploded in his head.

66

Melanie choked back a cry as Mia struck Connor on the side of the head with the butt of the pistol. In that moment, as she saw her sister swing the gun with brutal force at Connor's head, she realized, fully and irrevocably, that the Mia she had known didn't exist. She had been an illusion, a character her sister had played with stunning authenticity.

The real Mia Donaldson was cold, vengeful and cruel. She was mentally ill.

Melanie fought the urge to cry. Her sister didn't deserve her tears. Maybe later, but not now. Now, Connor needed her. He needed her to get them out of this.

Don't be dead, Connor. Please God, don't let him be dead.

She had to throw out everything about Mia that she had thought to be true. She had to start fresh. Melanie's mind spun back, to the events of the past months, to inconsistencies in stories, things she should have questioned at the time but didn't. Because she believed in her sister.

Boyd. Of course.

Her brother-in-law had gotten off being dominated and punished by women, not the other way around. That day in the hospital, Boyd had denied having hit Mia.

He had been telling the truth.

That was it!

Melanie looked at the woman she had once called sister and summoned a sound of admiration. "Boyd never hit you, did he? You manufactured that whole story."

"Bingo, sister-dear. The pathetic pervert didn't have the balls to do something so bold." Mia laughed, sounding almost giddy. "Boyd was a poor excuse for a man, but he made a lot of money. He afforded me a life-style I enjoyed quite well. I wasn't about to give it up and certainly not because I stupidly signed a prenuptial agreement."

Connor moaned and Melanie said a silent prayer of thanks, then stepped up her efforts, sensing that their time was growing short.

"I think I see now," she murmured, daring a quick peek at Veronica. By her stricken expression, Mia's true relationship with her husband was news to her. "So you came up with a plan. A story about escalating abuse. You conjured a few tears, gave yourself a few bruises for authenticity's sake. But tell me, what did you hope to gain besides a divorce?"

Mia snorted with disgust at Melanie's lack of vision. "The prenup only applied to divorce. If he died, I got everything." At Melanie's blank expression, she shook her head. "You have no imagination, Melanie. Think. Everybody knew what a bad temper my big sister had. How protective she was. How she would do anything for me, even pull a knife on her own father. I decided to use all those *fine* character traits as a way to get rid of my increasingly troublesome husband.''

Melanie pressed her lips together to keep from crying out. Her sister's tone, the way she mocked her for loving and trusting, hurt almost more than she could bear.

''It was going to be so easy,'' Mia continued. ''I would wear one of your uniforms, shoot him with your service weapon if I could get my hands on it, if not, with my own gun.'' She motioned to the pearl-handled revolver on the counter behind Veronica. ''Which, by the way, is unregistered. Afterward, I'd make sure you were seen leaving the scene. I'd get rid of both of you at once. Simple.''

She preened at her own cleverness. ''I planned to do it when I knew you were home with Casey. You'd have no alibi. Nobody would doubt you did it.''

''Then Veronica happened along,'' Melanie murmured. ''Making things even easier.''

''Exactly. Who better to have on my side than an Assistant District Attorney? And when I followed Boyd and discovered his nasty little secret, I knew I had it made. In the end, not only did she do the deed for me, she gave my alibi for that night a little extra weight.'' Mia laughed, obviously pleased with herself. ''Not that I really *needed* the help. You fell right into my plan, Melanie, going so far as to publicly threaten Boyd. Some detective. You never questioned anything I told you.''

''I fell for it, too,'' Veronica whispered, folding

her arms across her middle. "You lied to me, Mia. About Boyd...about it all. How...could you?"

Mia sent her a contemptuous glance. "Get a grip, Veronica. This is real life."

With a cry of anguish, Veronica turned on Mia. "I was willing to do anything for you... *Anything!* I loved you...and all along—" her voice broke "—all along you were *lying* to me? You were *using* me?"

"You were willing to do anything for me, a point you made abundantly clear from the start. And I appreciate that. You made my life a whole lot easier. And if it makes you feel any better, I'd planned to keep you around awhile. Unfortunately that's no longer possible. But hey, we had fun. Right? Alas, it's over."

"Over." Veronica took a step backward, eyes flooding with tears. "But we, I don't...understand."

"I can't imagine why, it's so obvious. The police and FBI know about you. But they don't know about me. And they won't." She sighed. "It's too bad the way you killed Melanie and Connor. I tried to stop you, tried to save them—" her voice quivered as she practiced her role "—but I couldn't. The truth is, I'm lucky to be alive."

She lifted the gun and aimed it at the stunned Veronica. "Goodbye, love."

Veronica released a blood-chilling howl of rage and betrayal, then in one seamless movement went from her ready position to a perfectly executed flying kick. At the same moment, Mia fired Connor's gun. The bullet stunned Veronica, but didn't stop her. Mia fired again.

Veronica went down, stumbling backward, hand to her stomach, vibrant red spreading across her white T-shirt. Without pause, Mia turned her back to the woman and aimed the weapon at Melanie. She smiled.

A shot rang out. The explosion of sound reverberated in the room; it blended with Melanie's cry and Connor's shout to throw her body to the right.

Melanie felt herself falling. Her life passed before her eyes, the good moments, the ones worth taking with her—Casey's birth, his first smile, walking on the beach with her mother, laughing with Ashley, making love with Connor.

The chair hit the floor. Pain tore through her shoulder. Her head snapped against the tile; pinpoints of lights popped behind her eyes.

It took a moment for Melanie's head to clear, for her to realize that neither she nor Connor had been hit. She craned her neck.

And saw her sister. She lay on the floor in a growing pool of red, head twisted toward Melanie. Her eyes were open. Staring. Vacant.

Melanie moved her gaze. Veronica had dragged herself up to the counter and retrieved Mia's gun. She stood there still, hanging on by sheer force of will, gun in her hand.

She met Melanie's eyes. In them Melanie saw real regret. Resignation. Apology.

A small smile curving the corners of her mouth, she brought the gun to her mouth.

And pulled the trigger.

67

Sunlight spilled over Melanie as she stepped out of CMPD headquarters. The sudden brightness stung her eyes, but she welcomed its burn. Only a few hours ago she had thought she would never see the sun again, never again bask in its brilliant heat.

She and Connor had made it. They were alive.

As Connor had predicted, one of the CMPD investigators had been tipped by Bobby to Veronica and Mia's friendship. Bobby had also pointed out that both Melanie and Connor hadn't been seen since going into Mia's home, hours before.

The cavalry had come—and found the two of them strapped to those damned chairs and lying in a pool of blood. Uncomfortable, but very much alive.

After receiving a doctor's okay and getting cleaned up, they'd given their statements to the police. Her chief had been there. Chief Lyons, Harrison and Stemmons. Steve Rice. Chief Lyons had commended her for the job she'd done on both the Dark Angel and Andersen cases. Steve Rice had suggested there might be a place for her at the Bureau. Not to be outdone, the CMPD chief had echoed a similar offer.

Funny, she had waited so long to hear just such an offer, yet all she felt was numb.

Statements complete, she and Connor had been released to their own devices. Released to face tomorrow. And every day after that.

Mia.

A small sound of pain slipped past her lips and Melanie stopped, the horror of the past hours overtaking her. She struggled for an even breath, for a way to put it behind her, for a place to put it.

Connor drew her into his arms and against his chest. "I know how much it hurts, baby. I know."

"How am I going to put it behind me?" she asked, voice breaking. She lifted her face to his. "How am I going to...forget?"

"You won't ever forget. But someday you'll wake up and it won't hurt quite so bad." He cupped her face in his palms. "I'll be there that day, Melanie. And every other day, too."

"I love you, Connor."

His lips lifted. "And I love you."

"Mom!"

Melanie turned. Casey stood down the sidewalk from them, his father beside him, a hand on his shoulder, holding him back.

"Casey!" She knelt and held her arms out. Stan let him go and Casey raced toward her, face wreathed in the most beautiful smile she had ever seen.

In a flash, he was enfolded in her arms, held tightly to her chest, to her heart. "I missed you so much, sweetheart," she whispered. "So much."

He hugged her back, tighter and harder than she would have thought him capable of.

After a moment, Melanie loosened her hold, but didn't release him. She lifted her gaze to her ex-husband. He gave her a small salute, turned and walked to his car.

She watched him go, then smiled, forcing thoughts of Mia back, along with them the ache of betrayal, of disbelief and disillusionment. She would have plenty of moments for mourning the sister she had loved with all her heart, but not this moment. This moment she dedicated to life.

Lifting Casey in her arms, she turned to Connor. "What do you say we go home, Agent Parks?"

"I like that idea, Officer May. I like it a lot."

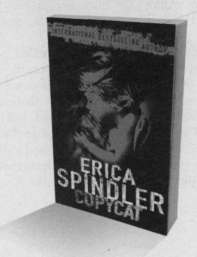

Also available by **Erica Spindler**

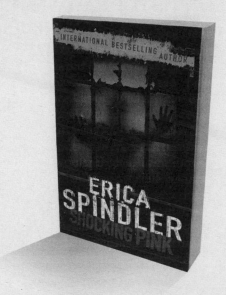

... What they saw was murder

The mysterious lovers the three girls spied on were engaged in a deadly sexual game. No one else was supposed to know. Especially not Andie and her friends. But curiosity can become obsession.

Now, years later, someone is watching Andie.

Someone who won't let her forget the unsolved murder of Mrs X.

Andie. Julie. Raven. Three very different women bound by much more than friendship.

They are about to discover that loyalty can be murder.

Also available by **Erica Spindler**

A killer is chasing the ultimate vengeance

Seventeen years ago, Jane's life was almost destroyed
when she was hit by a speed boat. After surgery
restored her face, she has everything to live for.

But her happiness is shattered when a woman with
ties to her husband Ian is found dead. Jane's convinced
that the man she's always believed hit her deliberately
has found her again – and is determined to
destroy their lives.

Digging into Ian's past, Jane finds that each new clue
points not to her husband's innocence – but to his
guilt. Meanwhile, her stalker is moving
closer, waiting for the moment when he
can at last…*See Jane Die…*

MIRA

Also available by **Erica Spindler**

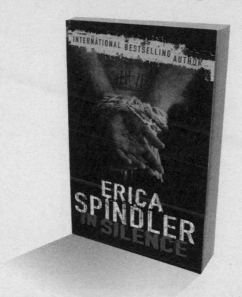

Outsiders don't last long in Cypress Springs...

When Avery Chauvin returns home after twelve years, it's as if time has stood still. Yet for her everything has changed – how could her father, a physician who dedicated himself to preserving life, have taken his own?

Soon Avery starts hearing strange rumours about a mysterious group called The Seven, and the events of the past and present take on a terrifying new meaning – a woman is found murdered, an outsider disappears and neighbours go missing in the night. Uncertain where to turn and who to trust, Avery faces the truth: that in this peaceful town a terrible evil resides, protected by the power of silence.

MIRA

Also available by *Erica Spindler*

Evil lives in paradise...

A panicked message on her answering machine is the
last time Liz Ames hears from her sister Rachel.
Determined to find her, Liz heads to Rachel's
home in Key West.

Within hours of her arrival a man jumps to his death.
Then a teenage girl is found murdered. The ritualistic
style of the killing is hauntingly similar to that used
by the notorious "New Testament" serial killer –
now on death row.

Could these deaths be related to Rachel's
disappearance? Is a copycat killer at work?
And why do the police refuse to help?

As Liz peels away the layers of deception,
she finds this island paradise harbours
an unspeakable evil...